# THE FIRST WHISPERS OF FATE

THE FIRST WHISPERS OF FATE
Copyright © 2025 by C.J. Nolen

Published by Madestein Press

All rights reserved. No part of this book may be used or reproduced in any manner whatsoever without written permission except in the case of brief quotations embodied in critical articles or reviews.

This book is a work of fiction. Names, characters, organizations, places, events and incidents either are the product of the author's imagination or are used fictitiously. Any resemblance to actual persons, living or dead, events, or locales is entirely coincidental.

For information contact:
http://www.cjnolen.com

Cover design: by J.N. Ignacio
Developmental Editor: Emily Dahl
Copy Editor: Allison Nolen

ISBN: 9789083554204

First Edition: June 2025

10 9 8 7 6 5 4 3 2 1

*For my tabletop adventurers:
Kate, Glen, Micah, Nick, and Zac.
This world wouldn't exist without you.*

*For Allison, my audience of one.*

# THE KNOWN WORLD

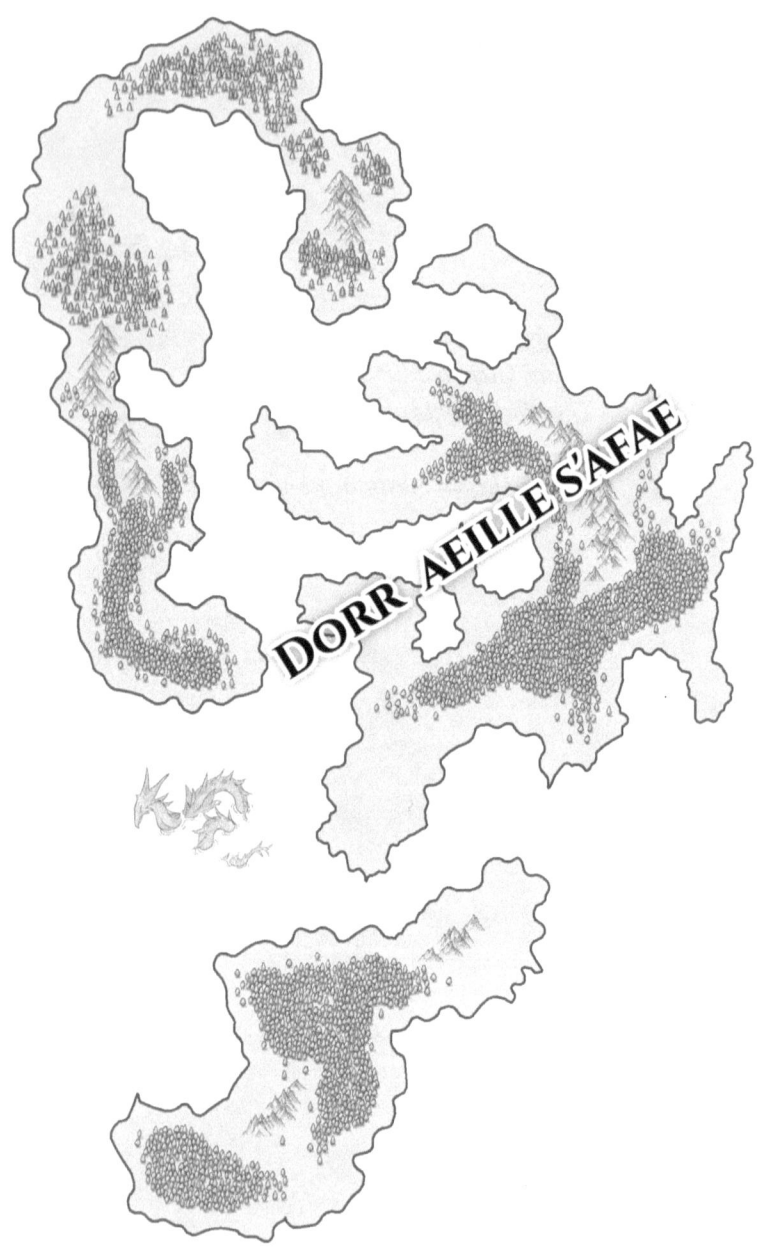

# THE UNIFICATION OF ELORA

# PART I

*No person is born a hero. Our stories tend to paint them in neat strokes, but heroes were ordinary, messy people first.*

*And so, dear reader, our story must begin with people, not heroes. To ignore the first whispers of fate is to tell only a partial truth.*

FROM THE FORGING OF THE TALAVARA IN THE SECOND AGE, BY THE SYANI LEANNA GWENHERT

# PROLOGUE
## BEATRICE

A hundred ships swayed in Sona harbor—formless, shadowy hulks creaking in the inky midnight waters. Their masts were bare, the sails packed for the coming storm, decks still and silent and empty except a few squinting sailors keeping watch. It was a moonless night, the stars strangled out by thick clouds that had rolled in over the city with low, rumbling growls. Glowlamps flickered on the city walls, their blue glass orbs a neat row upon the great limestone rampart that encircled the city. But this far out into the harbor waters, their light was just a distant decoration.

Beatrice gripped the oars tight in her hands, pausing between each stroke to listen out across the water. She was dressed in all black—black leather breeches, black shirt, a black cowl pulled down to hide any glint of light on her face. The rowboat still smelled of the greasy black stain painted on only hours ago. The seat was tacky where it hadn't quite dried, gripping at her breeches with each pull of the oars. She checked the rowlocks again, where the oars pivoted on the boat's rim, just to be sure that the canvas and cotton muffles were secure. Beatrice checked that the thick cloth wrapped around the oar looms was fastened tightly. She had to be perfectly silent. She must be a ghost tonight. She didn't know when they might get another chance like this. The twisted black markings on her arm tingled in anticipation, their power awakened and set on edge by fear.

Beatrice slid into what might have been the shadow of the ship, if there were enough light to permit such a thing. She eased up against the anchor chain, tying the boat to it with a waxed canvas pillow wedged between. No creaks. No rattles. No mistakes. Beatrice took a deep breath to steady her nerves. Her heart was already thumping in her chest, her hands sweaty and beginning to blister from the unaccustomed task of rowing. She didn't feel particularly ready. But hesitation would gain her nothing now.

She took the anchor chain in both hands, finding it slick with salt water, but each link was large enough to slip her hand inside and grant her purchase. Her feet were another matter. The best she could manage was to wrap her legs around the great chain as she hauled herself up hand over hand. Her motions were careful and deliberate as she climbed, her arms and shoulder muscles straining and her breath shallow with effort. When she was even with the ship's deck she stopped, not venturing over the railing. She hung from the chain, motionless except her eyes flicking beneath the cowl, searching for any signs of movement onboard. Anyone who remained still enough in the gloom might be impossible to see. She would have to be patient. There were the two obvious men on the ship's waist deck, playing cards beneath the sooty glow of a lantern. Both of them were armed—not as sailors with a dirk in the belt, but like guards in chain armor with proper swords. Private security, again. Beatrice searched the shadows a moment more, just to be certain.

There was a third. Nestled deep in the gloom, the barely there rising and falling of a man's chest as he breathed. He sat on a stool leaning against the wall of the ship's forecastle. Was he asleep, or merely very still? Was he alert? Beatrice couldn't be sure. His face was only vague darkness from her vantage point. Beatrice watched the slow and steady breathing, watched the guards, trying to think through her options. She could climb around the ship's edge, but that wouldn't be easy and it might make noise. The windows to the captain's cabin were most likely locked fast with the coming storm, and reaching them would be a challenge from the outside in any event. She gritted her teeth. The man on the stool was still enough, though, wasn't he? He must be asleep.

There was only one guaranteed way to her destination, and it was through the door just beside that vague shadow of a man. She would have to accept the risk. There were only three paths before her—go forward, turn back, or try something stupid. She opted for the first.

Beatrice pulled herself up over the rail as fast as she could. She dashed to put the ship's mast between herself and the guards. Her feet were shoeless, wrapped in soft leather that made little sound on the wooden deck of the ship. She pressed against the mast, listening, but heard only the continued mutterings of the two men at their game. She peered around at the man by the door and was now more certain he was asleep. His cap was tilted over his eyes, shading them from the lantern light above the card game. This did nothing to slow the drumming of her heart, but it was enough to propel her forward. She slipped quietly past him through the door that led into the officer's quarters, slinking by two snoring lumps slung in hammocks there, and finally entered into the captain's cabin.

The cabin was empty, thank the gods. Beatrice quickly set to her work. The desk was the most obvious place to search. She hurried over to where it stood in the corner, fixed to the floor to keep all steady in rough seas. She tried the drawers and to her surprise found them unlocked. She slid the largest open, hopeful. The drawer contained the usual writing implements—a few dip pens, stoppered bottles of ink, and a few small stacks of paper. But it was mostly empty. The bottom was lined in stained yellow felt, and there was the obvious indentation of where a large and heavy book usually rested. The ship's ledger was gone.

Beatrice swore under her breath. "It has to be here," she whispered to herself. She tore through the room, opening drawers and cabinets and trunks. She checked all the clever nooks worked into the limited space aboard a ship to keep the important things safe during a voyage. Her search was fruitless. There was no ledger here, no notes, no papers of any sort except those yet to be written upon.

Fine, Beatrice thought. If not here, then in the officer's quarters. The purser might have the ledger among his things. But Beatrice's stomach was already sinking, even as she rummaged through smelly laundry and personal items in the footlockers in the officer's quarters, two men asleep and swinging just above her head.

Why, she wondered? What does House Gwenhert have to hide amongst these cargo ships? Why so much caution? Why the armed guards? Why so much secrecy? And why on only some of their ships? There were secrets here, and she needed to uncover them. She needed to know if her suspicions were correct.

Beatrice stood in the doorway, caught between the open deck and the snoring officers, thinking. The captain must have taken the ledger with him. The ship had pulled into port only a few hours ago. A handful of rowboats moved some cargo to another ship in the darkness, which had then immediately departed towards the East. And now the rest of the cargo remained on board under armed guard, far out in harbor.

Taking the ledger off the ship wasn't suspicious by itself—it was likely bound for House Gwenhert's Master of Ships for inspection. But almost every week, there was a House Gwenhert ship following the same pattern. The guards. The staying back in harbor for several days without attempting to unload. Something being transferred to another ship. It positively reeked of something foul. The truth would be in that ledger, but it was nowhere to be found.

The ledger may be lost, Beatrice thought, but that didn't mean there wouldn't be clues. And the most likely place to find them would be below deck, amongst the cargo itself. Beatrice closed her eyes, trying to talk herself out of what she already knew she had to do. Now she was down to two options—turn back or do something stupid. This time, it would have to be the latter. Turning back wasn't something she was in the habit of doing. She counted down from ten, tensing herself against the task. When she opened her eyes again, her feet were already carrying her out onto the waist deck, round the corner, and down the stairs into the belly of the ship.

Beatrice skulked between and beneath a dozen sleeping sailors in their hammocks. She was no sailor, but she knew a bit of how ships like this one would be laid out. The men and galley would be here in the middeck. The bulk of the cargo would be at the bottom, and she just needed to find the way down to it. But where the hell were the stairs? Some of the sailors snored, some shifted or scratched. She froze at every movement, barely daring to breathe. Beatrice was only one lazy glance in the darkness away from being found out, and her teeth clenched so hard her head began to throb.

Once her eyes had acclimatized to the darkness, she realized the stairs had been right beside her when she first came below decks. She silently chided herself for her haste, then slunk her way back and padded down the steps.

At the bottom of the stairs, the hold was blocked by a heavy door. This was closed with a padlock. Beatrice wondered if it was normal to lock the lower hold. It seemed odd to her, more a measure for keeping out sailors than thieves given that you'd need to be a fool to try and sneak past an entire ship's crew. She cast a look back over her shoulder toward the sleeping men. A fool, indeed. Beatrice plucked a small cloth from a pocket in her shirt, unrolling it and taking out two thin pieces of metal. She inserted both into the keyway, twisting the bent one for tension and using the other to carefully test and lift the pins inside the lock. She heard voices from above her now, and she tried to work faster. Seconds ticked by as her fingers manipulated and prodded in the dark, feeling her way through the pins as they clicked, one by one, setting against the tension.

The lock shackle finally came free with a deep, metallic *clock*. Beatrice sucked in her breath, holding the lock still in her hands to keep it from jostling. The voices above seemed calm enough, but they were louder now. Closer. If she went through the door, she might be trapped there. There would be no windows below, not this far down. This door would be her only way back out. The voices grew still louder, and she could hear what sounded like footsteps on the stairs to the middeck. Beatrice swore, then slid the door open and went through it, closing it back behind her. The padlock she slipped into her pocket. She hoped nobody would notice it missing in the next few minutes.

The lower hold was completely dark, and Beatrice lit the stub of a candle from her pocket. The hold seemed to run the whole length of the ship as one continuous room. The space was filled with crates, stacked high and nearly to the ceiling in places. Most of these were draped in dark cloth. Beatrice found a crowbar and began opening crates as quickly as she dared.

Waxed canvas. Dried herbs. Silks. Wine. Lifting tarps and searching crate after crate, Beatrice found nothing but the mundane. Nothing to warrant secrecy. Barely enough to warrant a ship—none of these items were exotic enough to bother importing from Dahk Ahani, where this ship had originated. There was something else here, she thought. There had to be.

Beatrice climbed atop a stack of crates to better survey the room. The containers were not arranged in such a way that storage was maximized, she realized. Rather, they were in rows, so that items closer to the hull could still be reached. But only after walking quite a way through the winding maze made by cloth-covered barrels and crates. That caught her attention. Access, but not for casual inspection. And why the tarps? There had been nothing suspect about the crates she had opened so far. No markings, no scandalous contents. She started climbing over rows towards the outer hull.

"Oi! What's this?"

Beatrice immediately snuffed her candle, ducking down into the next row. The voices were muffled by the door, but Beatrice had no difficulty making them out.

"Eh? What d'ya mean?"

"That door's to stay locked. Captain hisself locked it just a'fore he left. And now?"

The punchline hung in the air, unspoken. Beatrice heard boots on the stairs, then saw the door to the hold creak open, the light of a lantern spilling in. The voices were low now, barely above a whisper, and she ducked behind crates to stay out of the searching rays of lantern light. There was the shush of something metal sliding across leather—a blade leaving its sheath. Beatrice crept closer to the door, her back to the row of crates and keeping her ears attentive to the footsteps of the men who had entered. She dared a peek through a gap between crates—two men, both wearing armor and with swords drawn. The guards from above? Or were these two new? In tight quarters like this, those swords would be awkward. So that was something. But it would be better to slip out behind them and avoid confrontation altogether. She would just need to work her way around until she was behind them. They couldn't look everywhere at once.

"These 'ave been opened," a voice hissed. "Come on."

Beatrice crept toward the front of the ship, hurrying around a corner. As she did, her hand touched one of the tarp-covered crates. Only, no. That wasn't quite right. Her hand didn't find the expected solid heft of a crate at all. The tarp flexed inward beneath her touch, as if it were floating. Beatrice stopped, looking around. She was far from the stairs, but also from the sweep of the lantern. She lifted the tarp and peered beneath it.

It took her a moment to understand what she saw in the gloom. The shadows played tricks on her eyes, revealing only a crisscross of shadowy lines dancing as tiny slices of light shifted between the maze of barrels and boxes. But then she realized what she was looking at. It was a cage. A simple geometry of rectangles, a door latch, a pile of dirty straw, and a bucket.

Beatrice looked down the row of tarp covered shapes. She peeked under the tarp from the next one. And the next. And the next. The whole row seemed to be cages. She tried to rationalize that. To explain how man-sized cages would be in a merchant ship flying the colors of a noble house. In Elora. Here, in the capital city of Sona, the alleged beacon of free men. She imagined that maybe the great running birds from Dahk Ahani could be fit into such cages. She imagined that the smell of urine she hadn't noticed until just then could mean nothing at all, only animals or filthy sailors. But then she saw something nestled amongst the dirty straw in one of the cages that made bile rise in her throat—the tattered remains of a little rag doll, its hair in pigtails. Beatrice winced, then had to look away.

When the two men rounded the corner, a heavy tarp flew over their heads. They both cried out, one crumbling to the floor as a heavy padlock slammed into the side of his head. It didn't buy Beatrice much time, but it was enough to get past them.

Beatrice flew up the stairs, rushing through the lines of hammocks suddenly coming to life as a bellowing sounded from the hold below. Voices, shouts, and confusion filled the midship as Beatrice stormed upwards. Half-naked men tumbled from hammocks and shouted for light. Beatrice bowled right into a sailor on the stairs, his youthful face screwed up in confusion even before her shoulder collided with his ribs from below. The wind guttered out of his belly with a wheeze, his bewildered eyes looking at her as he sank to his knees. It briefly occurred to Beatrice that, if he'd been a better man and had a blade at the ready, she would have just skewered herself on it. Beatrice barely saw the ship's deck, crossing its width in a few long strides. A second lantern sprang to life as she vaulted over the rail and dove into the waters below.

Her dive was flailing in its form, and she plummeted into the waters gracelessly. The sudden cold was shocking and the long fall from the ship had plunged her deep beneath the surface. In the murky darkness, it was impossible to see which way was up. Panic started to clutch at her heart. Her drenched clothes and tools hung heavy from her in the salty waters as she thrashed to gain her bearings. Whichever direction they were dragging her, she decided dimly, must be the wrong way. As her lungs began to burn, her hand touched something hard and slimy. She followed it up and gasped as her head surfaced next to the ship hull she was clinging to. She was dizzy, and it took her a moment to be sure she was even on the right side of the ship. But then she saw her rowboat as the light of lanterns danced overhead, angry voices shouting down at her.

Beatrice pumped the oars as fast as she could, salt water still stinging her nose and throat. Another rowboat splashed down from the side of the ship and immediately began pursuit. Her arms burned with effort. She tried to use her legs with the strokes, as she knew she was supposed to. But exhaustion and panic were making her clumsy. The other boat was steadily gaining on her. It had four men at the oars, and it sliced through the waters toward her with a menacing gait, a man standing on its prow with his sword drawn. She could not see his face, only his still silhouette. The sight made her blood run cold, and she pumped the oars harder. If any of them had crossbows or the like, she would already be dead. At the speed they were gaining, she still might be. Thunder began to rumble in the distance as the storm swelled toward the city. She did not like the omen of it.

Beatrice came near the docks only a few boat lengths in the lead. The docks jutted far out into the water, crammed with small fishing boats tied up at every available slot. She leapt from her boat onto another, falling hard as the tiny skiff rocked at her sudden intrusion. Wrenching herself back up, her shoulder and wrist now blazing with pain, she scrambled up onto the solid footing of the docks. She ran without looking back.

Beatrice heard them shouting, heard the stamp of their boots on wood decking behind her. The docks were mostly empty tonight, so nobody stood in her way. At most, a few people stopped to gawk at the dripping woman in black being pursued by armed men in the middle of the night. The docks gave way to the rutted dirt and cobblestone streets that lined the shore, and her feet pounded towards the warehouses nearby.

She was still a long way from the city proper. The city guards were unlikely to be nearby. And with no authorities to intervene, Beatrice would have to lose her pursuers here in the harbor district. She turned down familiar streets and alleys, trying to get out of sight long enough to do something unexpected. Two of her pursuers had the stamina to keep up. She wondered what House Gwenhert was paying them to inspire such tenacity. The thought of those cages, of the doll, flashed in her memory. She reached for the long knife on her belt, then thought better of it. These men were keeping pace with her even in armor, so they were clearly professionals. Beatrice was winded, panicked, and her wrist throbbed from her fall moments ago. She might be able to best them. But it was unlikely. Not without a sword of her own and time to catch her breath. She would have to do this another way.

The markings on her arm began to itch and burn, as if reminding her they were there. These looked like a tattoo to a casual observer, but they had been slowly tracing their own path on her skin for two years now like a disease. She ducked down an old familiar alleyway. One she had taken shelter in many a night as a child living on these streets.

The alley was narrow, running between two rows of warehouses and shops. Beatrice rounded a corner, eyeing where the alley came to an abrupt dead end a dozen paces ahead of her. She heard sounds of the pursuit behind her, still dangerously close. Beatrice ran for the wall at the end of the alley, too tall and sheer to climb. As she neared, she reached down inside of herself, feeling the markings flair and crackle on her skin like a fresh brand. She searched for the thing inside her she barely understood. A thing that dwelled deep down in a nameless place. A dark place. Her heart beat fast in her chest, and yet she could feel a power thrumming there as well. Beatrice seized hold of that feeling, that dreamlike sense of being elsewhere. The alley and the rooftops and the dark sky above were shrouded in inky vapor, and she swam through the twisting trails of it. Beatrice vanished from the alley.

The darkness and the sense of elsewhere receded an instant later as she materialized indoors on the other side of the alley wall. Beatrice slammed into a table, tumbling painfully over it as her momentum carried her across the room. She was inside a sailmaker's shop. Her pursuers would have to backtrack through the alley and around the block to find her now. She wasted no time looking around. She unbolted the front door and dashed out into the street, running for the gates of Sona.

# 1

# AIDEEN

Aideen twisted her feet into the dust beneath her, feeling her shoes grip in the gritty red clay. Whatever direction she needed to dart, she would be ready. She stared across at Davin, who stood poised across the red clay court at her. She eyed him in anticipation, watching his movements to see what they would give away.

"Are you ready, *piti rosandra?*" Davin called out.

Aideen sneered at him. "You're stalling, *l'ansyen*."

Davin grinned. He tossed the grey rubber ball into the air, then with a fierce overhead swing sent it flying toward her. Aideen darted to the left, bringing her racket up to send the ball sailing back to his side of the court. They dueled back and forth, the grey ball a bouncing blur between them, two figures flitting across the clay expanse. The damp morning air was cool and empty of any sound except for the *thock* of racket against rubber and the *chuff* of their shoes in the clay. The game court was surrounded by high green hedges that shielded them from the rest of the manor gardens.

Aideen moved across the court like a dancer, her movements thoughtful and fluid as though rehearsed. She was dressed in the same short cropped pants and linen tunic her father opposite was wearing. Her red hair was tied up and out of the way, leaving long stray wisps of crimson chasing after her as she dashed to intercept the ball. Her father was quick, too, despite the streaks of grey in his beard and hair. Davin lunged for the ball one last time, stumbling as his racket whiffed and cut through empty air. Not quick enough.

"Point and match!" Aideen cried, twirling on one toe and laughing. "You must be slowing down, *l'ansyen*."

"I am not," Davin said with mock indignation, hunching to rest his hands on his knees. "And I'm not an old man yet. I beat you just two days ago."

"An exception that proves the rule."

"And last week?"

"A fluke." Aideen stuck her chin out. "Besides, you have longer arms and legs. And years more experience, for that matter. You have all the advantages, by my reckoning. Perhaps it is inevitable that you might win occasionally, what with so much stacked in your favor."

Davin clapped her on the back, laughing as they walked through a gap in the hedges to a nearby fountain. Water spilled from a stone mermaid's splayed fingers down into a shallow pool trimmed in colorful tile work. They drank and splashed water on their sweaty faces and necks. Then they walked along the garden path for a while, chatting quietly and letting the morning air cool them from their exertions.

The path meandered lazily through hedges and flowerbeds and open spaces, curving about fountains and winding around the marble statues scattered throughout the gardens. The path was sometimes bordered in boxwoods and azaleas, other times it wound through bog primrose and camellia and witch hazel. There was dappled shade from the waxy leaves of stretching dogwoods and the bold fans of red emperors. Flowers bloomed in these gardens throughout the year. It was Aideen's most favorite place.

"Your stepmother would faint if she saw you dressed like this," Davin remarked as they walked.

"Like what? I'm dressed exactly as you are."

"Exactly," Davin laughed. "Sweating through a man's tunic and pants."

"Well, what exactly would your wife have me wear? I can't be expected to play in a corset. That would be yet another advantage you'd have over me."

"I think she'd rather we didn't play at all."

"Ridiculous." Aideen blew a loose strand of hair out of her eyes. "What I do while she is still in bed sleeping cannot possibly harm her. I will be proper when I am out about town. But I'll not be a slave to the opinions of others in my own home. Besides, who would you play with if not for me? I'd not deny you your daily trouncing."

"And I'd not deny you at least a weekly serving of crow."

"Fair enough, I suppose." Aideen sighed. "Tennis is not the only thing she'd rather I didn't do, you know."

Davin was silent for a long moment. "I know."

"And you continue to be ambivalent about this?"

Davin smiled as he walked. "No, I continue to allow you to make your own way. Your own decisions."

"And so I have your blessing to clash horns with my stepmother as I see fit?"

"Within reason."

"Within reason?" Aideen gave him a mischievous look.

Davin placed a hand on Aideen's shoulder, stopping her progress down the garden path. "She does not understand, but that does not mean she is incapable of it. This is new for all of us, *piti rosandra*. We are set in our own ridiculous ways. Your stepmother and new siblings are set in theirs. It has only been a few months. Be patient. It takes time for two families to become one."

Aideen patted her father's hand where it rested on her shoulder. "Alright. Within reason."

Aideen and Davin emerged from the gardens and parted ways as they returned to the house. Lindenhall was a grand house, four stories of tan limestone on the lofty edge of the Upper City with sweeping views of southeastern Sona stretching from the sails of the harbor to the trees of Salar Park. Aideen walked in through the kitchens, where two servant women were already toiling about. They welcomed her with a cheery greeting and a smile, and she returned them both as she took a hot roll from a tray just out of the oven. Aideen tossed it from hand to hand to keep it from burning her fingers as she climbed the rear staircase up to the third floor and to her chambers. A bath was very much in order.

Aideen's chambers were in the southern corner of Lindenhall, providing her with a wide and sunny view of the gardens overlooking lower Sona and the distant glittering of the harbor. A large canopy bed divided the room in two—her dressing area on one side and a sitting area on the other by the windows. The window seat and chaise were adorned with a number of discarded books. The shelf on the wall still held a line of dolls from stores in the Upper City, their smiling porcelain faces framed in curls of real hair. These were joined by the small carved wooden animals made for her by Master Lodai. It had been long since she'd done anything but look at these, but she couldn't bring herself to be rid of them just yet. Aideen undressed as she ate the roll, regretting she'd taken only one from the kitchens.

In her bathroom, the shutters were all closed. Aideen reached for the knob of the glowlamp, finding the polished stone circle after a moment of fumbling in the dark. As she turned the knob, the glass orb sprang to life. Blue light rose inside it, glittering motes drifting in the depths of the magical light like fireflies in a jar. Aideen drew a bath, the water summoned and heated by a knob similar to the one on the glowlamp. Once she was clean, the steamy room sufficiently filled with the scent of lilacs and lavender, Aideen rang for her servant, Kayla.

THE DINING ROOM walls were decorated with intricately carved panels and painted white. Paintings of landscapes hung on the walls, their vivid colors framed in gold leaf. The long table was dressed in pale blue damask and large enough for ample company, although most often it was just the five of the Bormia family. Not so long ago, it had been two. The house, it seemed, had been too large for two.

"Oh, I did so enjoy our time at Lord Brinnan's ball," Carolyn was sighing into her tea as Aideen sat down at the table. "I'm still positively exhausted from it all. And yet, I cannot wait to attend the next!" Carolyn was wearing a frilled green dress, her golden hair a tumble of curls around her cherub face. At fourteen, it was just now beginning to shed its childish shape to reveal the woman emerging from beneath.

"A fantastic evening, to be sure," Deidra chirped. "The company, the music, the food and wine. All of it splendid. One could not ask for an event comprised of more refined tastes." Deidra, Davin's wife of only half a year, was all elegance and poise. Deidra's curls were once blond like her daughter's, now a regal white.

Aideen felt herself straighten at the mere sight of her, angling her chin a little higher and lifting her shoulders out of their usual hunch. She took the empty seat next to her father, allowing a servant to help her with the chair. Davin did not look up from the morning's letters, seeming to be absorbed in their contents. He was a large man, barrel chested with thick arms that betrayed his long-ago years as a sailor, when the Bormia Trading Company was just one ship and its crew.

Riann, her new stepbrother, was telling the family something of today's business at the Bormia Trading Company, where he was studying under Davin. He had been an apprentice there even before the engagement. Riann was tall, his short blonde hair swept back with argan oil that made it look darker and less wavy. Aideen only half listened. While the business of sailing was fascinating to her, the sailing business was much less so.

Aideen took two rolls from the platter on the table and split them both open, smearing the resulting quartet with sticky sweet lemon curd. She took a bite and reached for the teapot, not waiting for the servant Pernah to come and fill her cup. She resisted the urge to shove the rest of the roll into her mouth.

Deidra had been trying these past months to instill in Aideen a proper sense of decorum and manners. Davin had done his best, and Kayla had tried some more, but Aideen had spent her first seventeen years taking a more academic approach to manners. She understood the topic well enough, but she and her father had never really observed those sorts of customs within their own home. The household had become decidedly stiffer since Deidra and her two children had taken up residence there. The meals and conversations were boring and formal now, and there was certainly no more bouncing tennis balls off the walls of the foyer on rainy days. Aideen took a dainty bite of the roll, feeling her stomach turn on itself as she did in protest. *Patience*, she thought at her belly. *We'll have our fill soon enough.*

"Don't you think, Aideen?" Deidra asked.

Aideen's eyes snapped up at the mention of her name. She glanced around, chewing, having not heard most of the conversation for being lost in her attempts to eat properly. She swallowed quickly. "I'm sorry, what?"

"Oh, she hasn't even heard the news!" Carolyn said,

bouncing in her seat. "Lord Cathal Gwenhert is hosting a ball of his own, one week hence. We just received the invitations this morning."

"Indeed," Deidra said. "Which is quite a bit of news."

"Is it?" Aideen still felt third party to the morning's conversation. She did her best to recover. "What I mean is, the social season is still in full bloom, with the Festival of Eridayah still weeks away. I'm sure we have invitations to many more balls before then."

"Lord Cathal Gwenhert has recently finished setting up residence at Oleandra," Deidra said. "And now he is hosting a ball of his own!" She smiled at Aideen, as if she expected some new understanding to be obvious now that she had explained it. Aideen blinked back at her.

"It means," Carolyn offered, "That he obviously intends to marry."

"Indeed," Deidra said, seeming satisfied that at least someone had understood her meaning. "It will be quite the talk of Sona, I'm sure. He is the second youngest heir to House Gwenhert proper, but very well respected. The Master of Ships for the house, which is why he resides in Sona instead of Lyramae. He is a brilliant man and of a most remarkable character. As a younger heir to the house, he has the fewest explicit expectations of his family. Which makes him a most eligible bachelor. He need not marry nobility if the right match can be made."

"I see," Aideen said. But what she really saw was the rolls on the platter growing cool, and her own still only half-eaten.

"Oh, come now, Aideen. Surely you must find this intriguing. You must marry sooner or later, and it would be a shame to let this season pass you by entirely. Especially with a man such as Lord Cathal entering the scene."

"Aideen will consider marriage when she is ready," Davin said from behind his letters.

"Of course, of course," Deidra said. "I only meant this is a rare thing, and I had hoped it would spark some interest."

Aideen looked over at Davin to give him an appreciative smile, but she saw a dark shadow had passed across her father's face. She leaned closer to him. *"K'isa ki mal?"*

*"It's nothing."*

*"It doesn't look like nothing."*

He smiled at her, but the shadow remained. *"You're right, my little flower. But it's something I want to put behind me. So long as it stays there, you have nothing to worry about."*

"Can we speak Elorian, please?" Deidre said, giving Davin a hard look. "Let's not have secrets at the table."

"Or you could teach us all elvish," Carolyn said. "Wouldn't that be nice? We could have our own secret language here in the house."

"No, your mother is right," Davin said, his attention returning to the stack of letters on the table beside him. "We shouldn't have secrets in the house."

Aideen watched him, studying his darkened face. And yet, you are keeping a secret now, she thought. She would let it alone for the moment. But she would have to ask him later.

"I'm sorry, Aideen," Deidra said. "I do not mean to push." Then she looked back at Davin. "Oh, but why shouldn't she be thinking of marriage? It's only natural to desire companionship, and she is already of such an age."

Aideen looked at her father to respond, but instead of addressing his wife he looked back at his daughter. "Within reason," he said with a small smile.

Aideen squinted at him in annoyance, then straightened in her chair to address her stepmother. "I do not mean to imply that I am uninterested in marriage," she said. "But there is, of course, the issue of my mixed heritage. A half elf out in Sona society? I do not think any of us here truly know what a scandal that would bring on the family. It might be prudent to let

Carolyn be married first. That, at least, is not unheard of. It is certainly the smaller scandal to be the eccentric older sister until she is wed."

"But you needn't make it a scandal at all," Deidra said. "You hide your ears well enough with your hair. You are fortunate that, while the color is rare among men, it does not mark you as an outsider. I see no reason to complicate things by coming out to all of Sona."

"And hide it from my suitors?" Aideen balked. "It is not as though I could hide it from my betrothed. Should a man propose, and then I reveal my heritage, I would be asking him to keep my secret. And if he then refuses me, that seems an even bigger scandal for the family should it be revealed in such a manner."

Deidra stiffened. "The right man, who truly loved you, would not care in the least. You would simply need to choose carefully."

"While that may be true," Aideen said, "You must allow that this is not simple for me. I do not like the idea of beginning an engagement with secrets. I might prefer to drop the secrecy altogether and then deal with whatever ramifications society forces on me." She nodded over at Carolyn. "But I would only do that if I can ensure it does not prevent my new sister from finding her own best match. Which means waiting."

"I really do not see why you shouldn't simply –"

"The choice is Aideen's," Davin interrupted, putting down his letters. He looked back and forth between his daughter and wife, his face stern but not unkind. He patted Deidra's hand, somewhat diminishing the blend of annoyance and surprise on her face. "We have been caught in this predicament since her birth, dearest. I insisted when she was young that we keep her elven blood a secret in Sona. I did so because that was the only way to leave the choice of what to do with the secret for the woman she would become. Now, she is that woman, and she has a choice to make. But she is only seventeen. She needn't be in a hurry."

"And indeed, I am not." Aideen gave her father a grateful glance, then smiled at her stepmother, hoping to diffuse the tense mood. "Father waited a very long time to remarry after my mother died, and I'm glad he did. Otherwise, I would not have the wonderful new family I have today. That I will marry is, I assume, an inevitability."

Deidra shifted almost imperceptibly in her chair, her eyes flicking between Aideen and Davin. Then she smiled, seemingly placated. "Indeed. I should assume so."

Aideen returned her attention to the lemon curd dripping down the side of one cold breakfast roll, hoping the topic of conversation concluded. Would she marry someday? Perhaps. The idea was not without its charms, but the whole affair seemed so complicated and it was not a matter she wished to explore with her stepmother. For now, the idea was best left hypothetical. It was a concern for the future. True, an unmarried woman in Elora had little freedom, not unlike the elves. But in her particular circumstances, the possible paths towards such a union were full of hazards and unknowns. If she were to live life on her own terms, she must decide what those were for herself. For now, those decisions could wait.

## 2

## HAMFAST

The morning had barely broken, the first strokes of amber and carmine having just begun to brush themselves across the heavens. Hamfast stood on the ship's deck, peering over the rail. Watching the darkness give way to the inevitable light. Watching the sun compose this morning's canvas out where the ocean rose up to meet the sky. Listening to the creaking of the ship beneath his feet, of the men tending the sails in the early morning watch, of the seabirds hovering overhead in search of their breakfast. Hamfast scanned the horizon for signs of land. The birds had shown up days ago. He knew that meant nothing, that the birds would happily fly a week out to sea if it fancied them. And he knew the lookout would inevitably spot land before he could. But he'd been watching for land every day anyhow. Hamfast was homesick.

"That don't look much like work." A man ambled up and leaned against the rail next to Hamfast.

"It isn't. Breakfast will be ready on time, though. Isn't it always?"

"Eh, I'm just poking at'cha, half-man."

Hamfast glared up at him. It was Brogan, the newest

member of the crew. Hamfast was eye level with the man's belt buckle. Hamfast was a Lindle, the small folk often called Halflings in the world of men. Halfling usually had no bite to the word, even though it wasn't the proper term. But to call one a half-man was uncouth at best, malicious at worst, and certainly an insult anywhere in between. Hamfast bit back a retort. Perhaps the newcomer didn't know any better. He would give him the benefit of the doubt for now. One did not seek quarrels with his shipmates. Weeks together in tight quarters did not lend itself well to petty bickerings. Hamfast instead took a sip from his mug and bit back his pride. "Coffee is ready if you want it."

"Aye? Think I might. You make a damn fine brew, you know that? Damn good grub all around. Can't say that about any ship I've worked before."

Poor breeding was all, then. Hamfast nodded. "The secret is a small amount of cinnamon. Not enough that you'd ever know, but enough to cut the bitterness. I take pride in my work. We all do here, I think you'll find. The Dragonfly is a damn fine ship to serve on."

"Oh, that she is. Fine ship. Fine crew. Captain is a decent fellow, too."

"He certainly is."

"Suppose it was my lucky day when you folk needed another man. There I was, down on me ass on Eagle Rock, not two coins to rub together. I'd taken ill on my last ship, y'see. And the whoresons left me on that island. Crew safety, they says. Says they'd hire me back next time they passed through, maybe." He snorted and spat out into the sea. "Maybe, they says! Fucking bastards. Being a ship's carpenter is worth shit-all on an island like Eagle Rock."

"Well, lucky you that we needed a new carpenter."

"Aye, 'twas."

"Guess you heard what happened to the old one?"

"No. I guess not. Dunn never mentioned it."

"Ah. Took ill. Had to leave him on an island somewhere. I forget exactly where now, poor bastard."

Brogan snapped his head round to look at Hamfast, his mouth agape.

Hamfast chuckled. "I'm kidding, of course. We had two—Clint and his apprentice Dunn. Clint retired in old age to a little island on the coast of Rodomata, to fish and play cards and drink away his remaining years. Dunn took his place as master carpenter, and now here you are."

The tall one blinked for a moment, and then roared with laughter. He slapped Hamfast on the back, nearly knocking him over. If there hadn't been a rail as tall as he was, he might have gone toppling overboard. "You're alright, half-man. What's your name again? Hammy?"

"Hamfast Hilltopple. And you're Brogan."

"Aye, Brogan. Just Brogan, though. From Esterly." Brogan scratched at the scruff on his chin. Then he sighed and slumped against the rail to stare out at the sea, pushing a wad of tobacco into his cheek. Hamfast waited to see if the man looked as though he might move on. He did not. So much for admiring the sunrise alone with his thoughts. Hamfast went on admiring it anyhow.

"Gotta say," Brogan mused after a while, his voice wet with tobacco spittle. "Never met one of you little folk before. Wasn't sure what to think when I first saw you. Thought you was a child, to be honest."

"Never been to Sona then, I take it?"

"Nah. First trip there." Brogan spat again. "Always sailed the Sea of Ahani, never north."

"Well, we Lindle aren't usually much for traveling. We tend to keep our own company. There aren't many of us outside of Reseda. That's the hilly country in the western parts of Celae. I grew up in the capital, though. Sona is right in the middle of the continent on the southern coast. There aren't a lot of Lindle in the city, but enough not to feel out of place."

"Even fewer on ships, then?"

"Oh, most certainly not. I suppose I am a rarity among rarities. Which is a surprise, really. For a people at least twice my size, a ship must be at least twice as cramped for you men. My kitchen is marvelously spacious, all things considered. You'd think ships would be swarming with Lindle sailors."

"Aye, maybe most of you Lindle are smart enough to stay away from the sea."

"Maybe so." Hamfast was surprised to see that adoption of the proper name just after having first learned it. Perhaps there was hope for this one after all.

Brogan spat out over the rail again. "The sea's a heartless bitch. But I love her. Tried to settle down a dozen times now, but she always calls back to me."

Hamfast studied the man for a moment, then nodded. "When I'm home, I miss the sea. And when I'm at sea, I miss Sona."

"Hah. Folk like us are never happy, are they?"

"No, I suppose not. But at least we haven't given up on the prospect."

"True enough."

They stood in silence for a while, leaning on the rail and staring out to the distant horizon, Brogan spitting tobacco into the water from time to time. The ship cut smoothly through the waters, the waves lapping half-heartedly against the hull as they glided northward. The sun crested the horizon and began its climb into the sky, painting the clouds in pinks and purples until finally revealing the first true blues. Hamfast had sought solitude, but he supposed one could have a worse companion than this Brogan fellow.

"Well, I've breakfast to attend to." Hamfast said at last. "Welcome aboard."

"Thank ya. See you in a bit."

In the lower deck, Hamfast dodged between the hammocks of the still sleeping crew, who would trade places with the watch above soon enough. Many slept naked, their clothes hung on lines between hammocks to air dry after a washing in seawater. Captain Killian insisted on a clean ship and a clean crew, in the Bormia tradition. Beyond the lower decks Hamfast slid open a wide wooden door, locked it in place, and passed through into the ship's galley.

The kitchen on board the Dragonfly was designed for a cook of human height. To accommodate this, Hamfast had long ago nailed stools to the floor in strategic places around the room and spent his days climbing up and down them and occasionally hopping from stool to stool when the waters were calm enough to allow it. An iron box stove dominated the center of the room. This he had named Bertha, and she was his constant companion. A layer of brick and sand underneath protected the floor from the heat of her belly, which Hamfast swept and tidied every morning while coffee brewed. Hamfast walked into the pantry and began assessing the stores there. This far into their journey, the pantry was a long way from brimming. He fished a few apples from the bottom of a crate that were bruised but edible. There was honey left. There were raisins. He gathered these into a basket and returned with them to the kitchen.

Hamfast climbed onto a stool and began mincing the raisins so they'd go farther. Even just a few would do for flavor. He peeled and smashed the apples, finely mincing the peels and adding them back into the mash. The raisins, apples, and honey then all went into the cut oats he'd been soaking overnight. Breakfast was the easiest meal to prepare—he needed only warm it through. The porridge seen to, he busied himself getting a head start on the midday dinner. The salt pork would need to be thoroughly soaked to pull out all the salt that kept it preserved. However, he found that the barrel of pork had a large quantity of bones in the bottom—the seller in Remah must have used them to pad the weight of the barrel. Hamfast noted this with aggravation in his ledger so he could address it next time they traveled there.

When life gives you bones, you make stock. Hamfast fished out several pounds of the bones, transferred them to a wide pan, and placed them inside Bertha to roast for later. He had a bin of vegetable scraps in the pantry he could use. Once the bones were roasted, he'd have them simmer all morning with celery tops, carrot peels, and onion peels along with peppercorn and bay leaf. He began soaking some beans as well. Stew wasn't originally the plan, but it was now on the menu for tonight's supper. If he'd known, he could have already peeled potatoes and carrots and chopped onions, gods damn it. He supposed tomorrow night's supper could be puddings and gravy with a bit of the leftover stock.

The ship's bell rang out above deck—eight brass notes that sounded throughout the ship in sharp pairs—*king-king, king-king, king-king, king-king!* It was the end of the morning watch, which meant breakfast. The first of the sailors began jostling into the galley within moments, wooden mug and plate in hand. "Hammy!" the first one through the door cried. "I'll take mah eggs runny today, please an' thank you."

"Over-easy, as you please," Hamfast answered, ladling porridge into his plate. "Coffee and biscuit on your way out."

"Ah, smells lovely. Wish it was eggs, though."

"Sorry, mate. Only a few left, and they're destined for supper tomorrow night. Puddings with onion gravy. I doubt you'll complain when you taste it."

The line had formed quickly out the door. The sailors, for all their rough edges, followed rules very well. The line formed on one side of the wide door, made a U-shaped path around the stove to be served, and back out. Hamfast had laid out coffee and water in covered pitchers on a table, along with a hard biscuit as big as a man's face for each of them.

"What's he got up there this mornin'?"

"I heard something about eggs."

"Nah, it's the usual seaweed and horse shit."

"That's some fine smelling shit up there, in that case."

"Aye, it's the finest shit yer like to find this far from shore."

"Mind your manners, Strawn," Hamfast called out. "If you don't care to actually eat shit, you'll be kind to your cook."

"Ah! There he goes, you've done insulted the Ham!"

"He's like to spit in yer cup and call it seasonin'!"

"He'll do no such thing, he's a right gentleman, that Ham is."

"Look, now Strawn's an ass-kisser. It's no wonder he's got a pock face."

"Will you whoresons shut your gobs and lets Ham answer the question? What's for breakfast?"

"Oat porridge," Hamfast shouted as he ladled into another plate. "With apples and raisins. Oh, and honey today, lads, no shit or spit I'm afraid. Spiced biscuits and marmalade at the door. And coffee, of course. That should set you on your way."

The crew made their way through the line—36 men in all. Behind the seamen came the officers. It was tradition on all vessels bearing the mark of the Bormia Trading Company for the seaman to eat first and the captain last. A tradition lost on most of the men, but observed nonetheless. Once everyone was served and eating noisily in the room beyond his galley door, Hamfast began cleaning up breakfast, washing pots, and preparing the midday dinner. For weeks at a time, this kitchen was his world. And he liked his world well tidied.

Land was spotted just before supper the next evening. When the cry went out, Hamfast checked the puddings in the oven. They'd be a few minutes more. He rushed upstairs and clamored to the side to see what could be seen. Several other seamen stood at the rail and squinted into the distance, shielding their eyes from the afternoon sun with their rough and gnarled hands. Hamfast pushed between them and looked, but could see nothing. Instead, he retreated and climbed up to the quarterdeck where he saw Levin, the second mate, peering through his spyglass. Normally Hamfast wasn't to be on the quarterdeck unless on official business, but his long history on the Dragonfly afforded him many privileges usually reserved for officers. He was careful not to abuse them very often.

"Where are we? Can you tell yet?"

Levin lowered his spyglass and was consulting some kind of chart. All these years on ships, and Hamfast still had no understanding of navigation. "That's Petry straight ahead. Damn fine sailing, if you ask me. We'll arrive in Sona by tomorrow afternoon if the wind holds."

"Wonderful!" Hamfast exclaimed. And before Levin could say anything else, he dashed back downstairs to pull the puddings out just before they started to burn. The dark corners wouldn't matter when they were smothered in gravy.

The next day was spent following the coast northeast, skimming along in sight of shore. Other ships were visible by morning, their billowing sails appearing as white flecks in the distance skimming in and out of the harbor. These specks and the seabirds soaring overhead in abundance now was the sure sign of their imminent arrival in the harbor. Mid-afternoon, the capital city of Sona rose up on the distant horizon at last. Even then, hours away, the massive rising rings of its white terraced walls were unmistakable. The city rose above the harbor like a gleaming white mesa, crowned with a twisting spire that reached toward the heavens. The sight was breathtaking, even for Hamfast who'd lived there most of his life.

At the foot of the city was a harbor teeming with ships of all sizes and hailing from across the Eastern world. Shipyards and docks and several harbor districts flowed from the ocean's edge up to the city's outer wall. In perfect concentric circles, the massive limestone terraces of Sona rose like a miles-wide ziggurat. At fifty feet tall, the outer wall formed a circle six miles in diameter. The wall was a structure in its own right, as thick as a house, with barracks and weapons of warfare inside and large enough for mounted soldiers to ride six abreast at the top. The wall separated the Outer City from the districts that constituted the city proper. Inside, in the shadow of the wall, was the Lower City, teeming with industry and merchants. A mile in from the outer gates, the first white terrace rose twice as tall as the outer wall and formed the foundations for the higher districts known as the Inner City with its artisans and guild halls. A mile further in was the second terrace, and the city rose another hundred feet higher, with the Upper City built upon this shining limestone pedestal, home to the nobility and wealth of the city. At the center of the Upper City was the Spire, the seat of all government across the continent—a glimmering obelisk three hundred feet tall surrounded by six curving structures that wrapped around the central spike like vines. These coalesced at the top, creating something that resembled a flower bud preparing to bloom in six colors.

"I've never seen anything like it," Brogan breathed as he leaned out over the railing. "I don't even understand what I'm seein', to be honest."

"It's unlike any other city in the world," Hamfast said. "Built over a thousand years ago by the sorceress Eridayah."

"It's like a mountain carved down and polished."

Hamfast nodded. "That's not a bad way of putting it. Something like that, yes. It's a city so full of magic that those who live there take it for granted, just as they do the inevitability of rain."

"You live here?"

"I do. Grew up right inside the city walls."

"The sea is a powerful mistress to pull you away from a place like this."

"That she is, mate. That she is."

**3**

# LESSONS

Aideen and Carolyn passed much of the morning in the drawing room with Deidra. Carolyn spent several hours sitting at the pianoforte. She was diligent with her musical studies, and quite talented. Aideen always remarked at what emotion her music could carry, especially her own compositions. Such weight, such depth, such complexity of feeling. And always some hint of darkness there dwelling, hiding beneath the surface, teasing to break forth but always masked by movements of strength and hope.

On the surface, Carolyn seemed to possess only a shallow sense of anything beyond frivolity and self-gratification. Some of that was to be expected at fourteen, of course. But even so, Carolyn had struck Aideen as especially silly and uninteresting at first—more interested in gossip and pretty baubles than anything of worth. It was only through her music that Aideen ever suspected the richness of the soul dwelling within. It still mystified her, and so Aideen suffered through the shallows and hoped to someday understand the depths.

While Carolyn played, Aideen stood at an easel by the window. She was painting her view of the gardens below, the vibrant greens and flecks of floral color traced in the curving pewter lines of the winding garden paths. These all ended at the terrace wall, where the Upper City dropped off to the Inner and Lower City sprawling below, the ocher and slate rooftops appearing like gravel steps down from her gardens to the sea. Aideen had painted this scene at least a dozen times out of sheer convenience. She took a calm sense of pleasure in painting, and had some small talent for it. Watching a world spring forth on canvas from nothing but some pigments and brushes was always a wonder. Her brush dotted the sea with the tiny white squares of sails, transforming the sea into a harbor.

When Aideen was a young girl, her father used to take her with him on his travels. His first ship was called the Dragonfly, a fully rigged bark a hundred feet long with over three thousand yards of sail. The ship was far from the grandest that sailed from the capital city of Sona. But Aideen thought it was the most beautiful ship in the world. She adored its golden, sweeping curves. The sighing sounds the sails made when they grabbed hold of the ocean breezes. How boldly it cut through the waves of the sea. And as a child, she had thought it had the bravest captain to ever conn a ship.

The men of the Dragonfly were always kind to her, indulging her endless questions and tolerating her games as she scampered around the deck, her long red hair a tangled, frizzy mess from the salt spray and the wind. A ship was no place for a child. Not even Davin would deny that. But the men of the Dragonfly adored Davin Bormia and would have gone to the end of the world for him. On several occasions, they had done just that. The Dragonfly had twice hazarded the Misty Sea to visit *Dorr aeille s'afae*, that distant mystery continent of elves and nymphs and fantastical creatures from the stories for children. It was there Davin had met Aideen's mother—the crimson-haired elf Saira.

When Saira returned with him to Sona, she was already pregnant with Aideen. The story of her parents' courtship was a mystery to her. Davin had always dismissed her questions and curiosity, saying simply that it was complicated and he would tell her one day, but that theirs was a story of love. The rest mattered little. When Saira died during childbirth, Davin devoted himself to his daughter and to his company. Davin had been a simple sailor, but had harnessed one lucky turn of fortune into owning the Dragonfly. He then turned one trading ship into many, and thus the Bormia Trading Company was born. It flourished over the years, and he counted himself one of the wealthiest men in Sona. As did many others. He'd long ago stopped captaining the Dragonfly to instead steer the company itself.

Aideen checked the time on the mantle clock, then hurried to put away her paints. "I'm late for my lessons," she said quietly, walking toward the door.

Deidra was sitting in her usual chair, reading a book. "Another afternoon spent swinging sticks at your tutor?" The woman sighed. "I mean, honestly, Aideen. One would think you're preparing to become a man and then a soldier. It's completely unbecoming of you to keep this up. And with a servant, no less. For all your efforts to keep your mixed heritage a secret, spending time with an elven servant so casually is highly inappropriate."

Aideen stopped in the middle of the room. Heat began to rise inside her, a sudden flare of anger that she had to fight to keep down. "It is part of my heritage."

"Yes, and Elora is the greater part of your heritage, yet you seem very resistant to much of Elorian culture and customs." Deidra stiffened in her chair. "It is one thing to learn the language and the culture of your mother. But it is quite another to engage in the basest parts of that culture. You live in Sona. You hide your ears. You are Elorian, my dear. You should act like it."

Carolyn's eyes were wide from her perch behind the

pianoforte. Her fingers continued stroking the keys, but the notes grew tense. Her eyes were fixed on her stepsister.

Aideen stared at Deidra, trying to keep the anger at bay. "I can be both Elorian and Elvish," Aideen said. "I don't ask you to understand it. But I ask you to respect it." She left the room, not trusting herself to keep her composure if she stayed there any longer.

Aideen fumed as she walked the halls to her chambers, annoyed that her soft shoes weren't louder on the carpeted floors. She wanted to stomp away. There were times when she questioned why her father had ever married Deidre. She always knew Davin must marry eventually. The Bormia Trading Company had to pass on to someone one day. He cared too much for what he had created, and so many relied on the jobs it provided. So Davin needed a male heir, one he could mold and shape in his own image to ensure the Bormia Company remained what it was. A widow with a grown son, perhaps. And Deidre, whose son just so happened to already be an apprentice to the senior accountant for the company, was a convenient choice.

Davin certainly couldn't leave the company to his daughter. Elorian customs forbade such a thing. Never mind that Aideen would never have wanted it. That little fact did not lessen the sting of the automatic injustice of it all—an injustice that seemed lost on nearly everyone else. Women couldn't be without a chaperone. Women couldn't hold property. Women couldn't do this. Women couldn't do that. Oh, but a woman could be Queen! The rules were different for the noble houses. There were so many damned rules about what a common woman couldn't do, and if Aideen thought about it too much she began to wonder what a woman could do but marry and raise children. That was another thing about elven culture, Aideen thought. They were not so hung up on what a woman could or should be.

"Why must I hide my ears?" Aideen had pouted on countless mornings as a young girl while her father helped her coil her hair up in ribbons. Her ears were not as prominent as those of a full-blooded elf, which protruded back like curved knives. Hers were half the length, only slightly larger than a human ear and curving gracefully at the tips like an olive leaf. "I think my ears are pretty."

"They are pretty," Davin said, kissing the top of her head. "They and your fiery hair are my daily reminders of the beauty your mother brought into my life. And I pray there will come a day when you will not need to hide them from the world. But there are too many people who would treat you as less than you are for no other reason than your mother was elven. Keeping this one part of you a secret means freedom to be whomever you choose to be. When you're grown, the choice will be yours."

And so Aideen hid her ears. It was as much a habit now as dressing oneself. Every morning, the servant Kayla parted Aideen's hair into sections that spilled down the back of Aideen's dressing room chair. The sides were braided, then rolled and pinned into coiled buns that covered the points of her ears. The rest was left down in back. Aideen's mixed heritage was known only to a few. The house staff knew, and were paid well to keep their silence. Her stepmother and step-siblings now knew. Beyond Lindenhall, however, Aideen had spent a lifetime concealing her ears through elaborate hairstyles. A small arsenal of hairpins served as the only armor protecting her secret, but they were enough.

In her chambers, Aideen undressed, yanking on light breeches and tunic, then donning a thin chain shirt and leather leggings. She replayed the conversation with her stepmother in her mind. This had been her home long before Deidra had come onto the scene. She wished she had pointed out that Deidra still often dressed in the fashion of women from Lyramae, despite having lived in Sona for over ten years. No woman of stature wore open-toed shoes in Sona, and yet Deidra even painted her finger and toenails in matching bright colors like they did in Trenton or Roseglade. But it was a minor hypocrisy by comparison, Aideen knew. Mentioning it would have only worsened things. She did her best to put the thing behind her. She needed to clear her mind for her lessons. She had never been overly fond of these lessons, but after the tiff with her stepmother, she felt she would be a hypocrite to not pour herself fully into them today.

It had begun to drizzle by the time Aideen reached the gardens. Master Lodai was waiting for her, his lithe form settled on a bench reading a book. He was shorter than Aideen—tall for an elf, but still a full head shorter than most men. His pale blue-tinged hair was pulled back in a knot, the almost white iridescence of seafoam. Deidra had called him her servant. That was yet another secret, known only to herself and her father. Lodai was no tutor, but her uncle. He had made the journey to Elora along with his pregnant sister, Aideen's mother Saira. And he had promised his sister in death that he would teach Aideen what it meant to have elven blood in her veins. Why this was so important was a point he seemed to have no interest in clarifying.

"Good afternoon, *jen youn*," he said.

"*Mei we i'en solye, dai onora*." Aideen bowed. The sky was darkening, and the drizzle threatened to turn into a proper rain. "Where shall we begin?"

"We start with *l'onta n'epe*."

Aideen withdrew a sword from the leather bag she had brought down from her chambers. The weapon was elven in design, although made by human hands locally in Sona. She drew it, laying its scabbard down on the bench, and turned to face Master Lodai. As she did, a blur of steel was already flying at her. She snapped up her blade with a cry, deflecting it as she dodged to the side. The elf did not wait for her to recover. He advanced calmly toward her, his sword flashing high and low as he tested her defenses, the sound of their steel singing out in rapid percussive beats. Lodai feigned twice, then lunged forward. Aideen swatted the sword aside, the blades scraping harshly against one another as she slid out of the way. The cobblestones beneath her feet were just wet enough to be slick. She could use that. So could he.

"Last Tuesday," Lodai called out as he drew a parrying dagger from its sheath in his belt. A blade now in each hand, to Aideen's one. "When you joined me here, I was reading a book. What was it?"

"The Treatise of Eridayah," Aideen responded. She dodged and parried another flurry of blows, then without pause turned the attack back on him. The sword was long and straight, well suited to both piercing blows as well as slashing. While not as quick as the lighter basket-hilt blades employed by the nobility in their sword games, it was remarkably nimble nonetheless. In the right hands, the smallest motion could send the tip of the blade flying from place to place faster than most eyes could perceive. She pressed him, varying her patterns constantly, not letting herself be predictable, trying to keep Lodai on his heels.

"What did I say about it?"

"Nothing," Aideen panted through gritted teeth.

"Incorrect. I spoke without words. What did I say about it?"

"I don't know," Aideen dodged back as Lodai blocked a strike with his sword, bringing the dagger up toward her torso. "It annoyed you."

"How do you know?"

"The way you sighed as you closed it."

"Good enough. Where was I in it?"

"In what?"

"In the book, *jen youn!* Beginning? Middle? End?"

"Just over halfway."

"Excellent. And tell me. What is the premise of her treatise?"

"Equality through merit proven."

"*Fou t'ez*. A slogan. What does it mean?"

"*N'eim pa konnen!*" She lunged and beat back at his sword.

"*Fou t'ez!*" Lodai caught her blade with his dagger, sweeping it up as he brought his sword down. He trapped her blade between the hilt of the dagger and his sword, throwing her off balance and landing a chop of his blade directly in her ribs. Aideen yelled in anger as much as in pain. The swords were blunt, and she had the protection of light mail, but a blow still smarted and could still leave bruises. "Do not give me merely the interpretation of some other. This is the mind of the founder of your nation. What does it mean?"

Aideen spat. "Philosophy. Fine."

"No, *timaoen*. Philosophy is a distraction to busy those who cannot understand the complexities of truth. This is politics, and politics is philosophy grounded in reality. Philosophy in action and backed by the power of law and sword."

"Semantics."

"Precision."

"Fine. Politics, then." Aideen blew a loose strand of damp hair out of her eyes. "Her premise is equality through merit proven. It means all men are equal. All equal in spirit. But not equal in deed."

"Which means?"

"It means it is natural for some men to be above others. To rise above others. For whole families to rise above others."

"But not because the gods will it."

"No. A man rises above his brethren only through strength, through courage, through cunning, or through virtue. Only because he deserves it." She leapt back from another strike. It was poor form, at least on the surface. But she was trying to bait him. "And should he cease deserving it he should lose it." Aideen thrust low at Lodai's forward leg. Her sword was blocked, as anticipated. She brought the tip flashing up towards his opposite shoulder, leaving her exposed. The dagger parried, and his sword leapt at the opening. Aideen spun, her sword deflecting this blow over her shoulder as she pivoted around it. Rather than the obvious move of using this momentum to swing through with her blade, she danced through to the side and swung from the hip rather than the shoulder. But Lodai's blades were there before hers could arrive. She sidestepped again, swearing to herself.

"How did I cross you just then?" Lodai asked, taking a step back and pointing his sword toward her in accusation.

"Because I attempted the rising gull."

"No. Because you gave yourself away." Lodai shook his head. "You attempted the rising gull yesterday to more success. But now your initiation is much smoother. You have been practicing it. You are like a child who just learned a new word and is overeager to use it. These are not the Songs, *timaoen*. We are not dancing. This is a fight. You must translate the movements of the Songs, transpose then, apply them without predictable rhythm. Use the proper technique against your opponent, not the newest novelty you wish to impress yourself with." Lodai sighed. "Enough. Elorian longswords now."

Aideen shoved the *l'onta n'epe* back into its sheath, gritting her teeth. She'd spent hours last night in the ballroom in her nightgown, sword in hand as she practiced the chain of feigns and attacks against the shadows. First counting out the strokes to a counter rhythm, then shifting them into a single, fluid dance. Somehow, she'd practiced too much—practiced the moves so thoroughly that it had become obvious she'd practiced them. How would she ever master the move if he could see right through it? Facing the same opponent day after day for so many years had become more like a game of chess than of swordplay.

She slid the longsword from its sheath. This was the design common in Elora. The sword was slightly shorter and wider at the base than the elven blade. Like the *l'onta n'epe*, it had a long hilt so that it could be wielded in one or two hands. It was heavier, too—which had both advantages and disadvantages.

Lessons with Lodai were always like this. Fighting give and take, dancing around one another with blades flashing. And all the while, the quizzing and questioning, seemingly at random, on topics from history to philosophy to the obscure. He was the only elf in her life all these years, and her only window into that mysterious culture that was half hers but always felt so distant from her.

"We remain on your country, this Unification of Elora." Lodai drew his longsword and took up a fighting stance.

"It is your country as well, now."

"I merely live here because I promised your mother to train you for a time."

"And I merely live here because my father's life is here. A tree does not choose where it grows, but to dismiss or hate the soil that sustains it is foolish just because more fertile ground may be found elsewhere. There is inequality. There is prejudice. There is greed. But the great majority of people here are good."

"An interesting outlook!" Lodai came at her, and the singing steel dance began again.

"You despise the human culture in Elora while making exceptions to love the virtuous that are forged by it."

"And you are blinded by your familiarity of it. You allow its virtues to overshadow its iniquities. And you do so from the most sheltered of viewpoints."

Aideen let her retort come from the sword in her hands. She let the momentum of the swing carry through from attack to attack. The blade spun as she shifted it from hand to hand, its motion a blur before her, her parries and strikes coming from all sides as she struck with one hand, then the other, then smashing hard into his defenses with the blade gripped in both hands as she drove him back.

"You are of two worlds, *timaoen*! You belong fully to

neither, and so you cannot be blind like the sheep of this fair city. You must learn to see through facades. So now I ask you—what is the purpose of the Syani?"

Aideen hesitated for a moment at the new topic, and it was enough for Lodai to turn the momentum back against her. "They... advise the Queen."

"No, that is their role. What is their purpose?"

"To also choose from among themselves who the next queen will be."

"Quit accepting like a child! Who are the Syani?"

Aideen fought to parry the onslaught of her uncle, earning another painful blow on her left arm. Gods, and always with the questions! Her answers were coming through gritted teeth now. "They are daughters of the noble houses. Raised by no family but themselves. Dedicated to the Unification from the time they can walk. They live their lives in service of all."

"And why are they in equal measure from each noble house?"

"For equality!" Aideen panted as she dodged.

"Foolish girl. Question it. Look beyond it."

"I'm trying. I cannot always think while I am fighting."

"Yes, you can. You must. The most important things happen when you are busy looking the other way."

"I don't know, gods damn it!"

"They live in a spire above their people!" Lodai cried, his strikes flashing at her like lightning as Aideen desperately fought them off. "And the six noble houses live aloft above the rest of the city, along with the wealthiest houses like this one. Equality! What is the purpose of the Syani? Equality for whom?"

Aideen was on her heels now, her parries bordering on desperate as she sought to keep him at bay. She leapt up and stood on the walls around the edge of the nearby fountain. Her legs were now exposed, but she was nimble enough. She rained blows down on him, forcing Lodai to keep his blade high. Then when he took the bait and went for her legs with the dagger, she leapt over his attack, planting a foot squarely in his shoulder with a satisfying impact. She leapt off the wall and down beside him. He spun around toward her, but she had snatched the parrying dagger from her belt and now held it to his ribs as she deflected his sword with her own. "Peace."

"What?"

"You wish me to say their purpose is to preserve the power of the ruling classes."

"And now you have it."

"And I have you." She wiggled the dull knife against his torso. She had only bested him a few times in all these years, and she grinned in triumph.

"Ah, but we are both dead," Lodai said, and Aideen felt a similar wiggling pressure against her back. "But I commend you nonetheless. Your heart is in it today, at the very least."

They parted, circling each other once more. Aideen pushed a damp lock of hair from her eyes, annoyed. "You would wish me to accept your own interpretations of Elora. Your own cynicism. The truth is deeper than that. If the ruling houses are equal, then there is peace. They are kept busy at their political games, and their squabbles remain in the Spire and not on a battlefield soaked in the blood of their citizens."

"That is inequality dressed in aspirations. It is a lie."

"Yes, but it is a beautiful lie."

**4**

# THE BALL

"Aideen!"

Carolyn burst into the bedroom without knocking. She was wearing a blue satin dress, her golden curls bouncing. Arms stretched wide, she spun as she crossed the room, an image of the child she had barely outgrown, the dress billowing out such that she became a twirling, blossoming flower of blue and gold. "How do I look? Aren't I just the prettiest thing you've ever seen?"

Aideen sat at her dressing table, her thick red hair in disarray. She might have shaken her head in amusement, but the hands of her servant Kayla were surprisingly firm and held her fast as she worked to tame Aideen's hair. "Oh, to be sure," Aideen said, watching her stepsister in the mirror. "Never before has the world beheld such a girl in such a dress. There will be tales told of this night for years to come."

Carolyn ceased her twirling and regarded Aideen with suspicious eyes. "I can't tell if you're making fun or being good-natured."

"Why can't it be both?"

Carolyn looked ready to retort, but something else caught

her attention. "Oh, by the gods!" Carolyn exclaimed. She stomped across the bedroom and snatched up Aideen's dress from where it lay on the bed. "You cannot honestly be planning on wearing this?"

"And what's wrong with that dress?"

"It's a party," Carolyn moaned. "A dance! A ball! You can't wear taupe to a ball, you shrub. Taupe is for old matrons. Here." She flung open the wardrobe door and disappeared behind it. Aideen could hear the muffled sounds of her rummaging and muttering to herself. She could also see Kayla standing behind her in the mirror's reflection, her deep lined face twisted up in amusement beneath silver hair and a bonnet.

"You're not supposed to laugh when someone calls me a shrub, you know."

"Aye, miss," Kayla said, biting back her laughter. "A thousand pardons."

"Do you think the dress is too dull?"

"It's a fine dress, miss," Kayla said. "Not a thing wrong with it."

"So you hate it, then."

"I would never have said that, miss."

"Well, I hate it," Carolyn interjected as she emerged back from the wardrobe carrying a pile of green fabric. "And even if you don't, Kayla, I need you on my side in this matter." Carolyn laid the green dress out on the bed, smoothing the fabric with a delicate touch. Then she threw the taupe dress through the open wardrobe door, where it landed in a heap. "Just think of who all might be there!"

"Don't think I'm not giddy with excitement," Aideen said. She pointed at her head, where Kayla was coiling a long crimson braid into a bun. "I'm just a bit occupied at the moment. The whole thing will be wonderful, and I'm just as excited as you are. Or nearly so. I'm afraid your potential for enthusiasm is unrivaled, sister."

"Good," Carolyn twirled again, watching herself in the mirror. She grinned. "Oh, I can barely contain myself! It's like I've gone and stepped in an ant mound!"

"Well, you'd better contain yourself, at least a little. Get as much of your silliness out now while it's safe. Your mother will be expecting us to be our most proper tonight. She wants us both married, after all."

"She's your mother too, now. And your father is now mine. Don't go being greedy with parents."

"Your mother implies our mother," Aideen said, rolling her eyes. "And I mean it. For all our sakes, don't go letting your mouth get us into trouble tonight."

"Oh, please," Carolyn swished her way back towards the door. "I'm delightful. Everyone thinks so. And you're one to talk about letting your mouth run. You've never met with an opinion you didn't either despise or feel the need to echo all the louder. Kayla, dear? Don't you dare let her walk out of here dressed in taupe. If my sister is not dressed for gaiety, I'll be quite cross with you!"

Kayla grinned back at her. "Aye, miss."

"I quite liked that other dress," Aideen muttered.

"Aye. But the green is very pretty with yer colorin' and all."

Aideen studied her reflection as Kayla's strong fingers did their work. Her coloring was usually something she avoided calling attention to. Her hair was the deep red of garnet, her skin pale no matter how much sun it saw, her almond shaped eyes a deep and dazzling green. Aideen's allure was exotic enough in Sona to fetch frequent admiration, but not so strange that it ever raised any suspicions. So long as she kept the curving, pointed tips of her elven ears hidden beneath carefully pinned hair, nobody ever had a reason to suspect a thing.

Kayla had parted Aideen's hair into five sections, braiding each and twisting them into buns that ringed the back of her head from ear to ear. She now teased out a few wisps near the temples to soften the look. Kayla had mastered a dozen such hairstyles.

"The green dress is lovely, I'll admit. But if I didn't know any better, I'd think you two were conspiring to turn me into a proper lady," Aideen said.

"Bless my soul, miss." Kayla grinned down at her. "We wouldn't dream of it. Your stepmother, on the other hand..."

"Oh, her I can contend with well enough. I just can't go having you turn against me."

As the sun began to set over the Sona harbor, the Bormia family assembled in the foyer of the manor. Carolyn preened in a mirror while listing all the great houses that might be represented tonight from across the Six Kingdoms, Lords of the Assembly, and all the young men of those houses she might dance with.

Aideen stood waiting with her stepbrother Riann. He was telling Davin of today's business, something about negotiating for port privileges in one of the Dirk Isles. Aideen only half listened to both monologues. She had nothing to add to either, but welcomed the sounds of their voices. Her life had been quiet for so many years, and the introduction of these step-siblings had brought new life into Lindenhall.

The skycoach drifted down into sight through the front window, and the Bormia family stepped out to meet it. The skycoach was fashioned in the same manner as a horse-drawn carriage—four large wheels placed around a center frame. The long wooden beams curled up at the front and rear, and between these curls a thoroughbrace of thick leather straps held the passenger compartment suspended away from bumps. It was ornate in design, as were most skycoaches, with intricate carvings in the wood and gilded highlights and the rune-carved stones that powered it. It appeared on first glance as any well-appointed horse-drawn coach, only lacking a tongue for attaching horses. The driver, his hat buckled firmly under his chin, untied the rope that kept him safely attached to his driving seat and hopped down to open the door for the five passengers with a bow.

Once all were inside, the driver remounted his perch. A moment later, the carriage lifted soundlessly up into the air. The Bormia Estate fell away beneath them as they turned east, the cool Autumn wind rumbling softly against the windows. The glowlamps that lined the streets of the Upper City below were just being lit, their gentle blue lights tracing the outlines of avenues and plazas in cool hues as the sun crept away behind them. The carriage followed the curve of the Upper City terrace. This highest ring was populated primarily with large houses like theirs, the homes of Sona's wealthy and nobility along with the boutiques and galleries that catered to them.

Oleandra was the house of Lord Cathal Gwenhert, four stories of white limestone brick that echoed the great walls and terraces of Sona itself. The skycoach traced two slow, sweeping circles through the skies around Oleandra as they descended, giving the Bormia family ample time to appreciate both the architecture and the five acres of preening gardens. It was large by Sona standards. It was nothing like those outside the city, where the hilly estates could roll on for miles. Still, such a place inside the city walls was an extravagance only possible through great generational wealth. There were perhaps only a dozen larger.

"It's smaller than Lindenhall," Carolyn remarked, with some disappointment.

"Yes, but you can be sure no expense was spared," Deidra said, looking down at it from her window. "He bought it last year from House Barthes after Lady Karena passed away, and immediately set to renovations. Lindenhall is most certainly large, and is no doubt beautiful, but I think you'll see tonight that we have much more we could do with the place."

The skycoach landed on the front drive and the driver slid down from his perch to open the door for them. The family dismounted the carriage and made their way toward the great redwood doors beneath the fluttering banner of Lyramae. Servants opened the doors with a bow, and another announced their arrival to the room. "Presenting Davin Bormia! Wife Deidre, son Riann, and daughters Aideen and Carolyn!"

Aideen could feel eyes upon them from around the room. And what a room it was, she wondered. The floors were great sheets of marble, a pale blue traced in gold. Matching marble columns held aloft a sweeping half circle mezzanine that overlooked the entrance hall. The dark hardwood panels of the walls served only as frames for intricate inlay patterns of white wood and gold leaf, all in delicate detail that seemed never to repeat and flowed across the room like water. Twin staircases curled up towards the mezzanine like ribbons, and large doors stood open on one side that led to what Aideen imagined must be some equally grand room, where the resonant thrum of bowstringed instruments could be heard.

In the entrance hall, nearly a hundred people watched the newcomers with curiosity from little circles of interrupted conversation. The women wore dresses and hairstyles from all over Elora. The flowing bright colors of Lyramae, their hair all in elegant buns. The high collars of Rodomata, with hair piled atop their heads and spilling down like snowmelt from the mountains. The intricate beadwork of Celae, hair long and curled. It struck Aideen as funny that today she looked more the part of a woman from Lyramae, just like Deidre and Carolyn, even though she had spent her whole life in the capital city of Sona.

Aideen could feel the curiosity emanating from the other guests. She could not hear the whispers, but she knew what gossip they contained. The Bormia family were commoners, but

The Bormia Trading company was the first of its kind. A whole fleet of ships owned not by one of the noble houses, but by ordinary men. Davin had taken on investors from the merchant class to build ship after ship, to fund voyage after voyage, and had built a trading empire. New trading companies had sprung up to emulate the model, but Bormia was still by far the largest in all of Elora, which had made Davin Bormia wealthier than many of the nobility here. The Bormias were of no house, and yet wealth and influence made their standing in Elorian society a novel uncertainty.

"It seems Lord Cathal invited half the city tonight," Riann whispered. "I see quite a few amongst this number that I know, but am surprised to see them at such an event."

"How so?" Carolyn asked.

"I know them from their trades, not from proper society. Merchants and artisans of the Inner City. Families of many cuts, in short."

"Lord Cathal fashions himself as a progressive thinker," Deidre said. "Some find his ideas eccentric, some as simply more open minded than most of his station."

"Some say he is simply a politician," Davin remarked. "And that he aspires to a station that would benefit some warm feelings from the ever-growing merchant class."

"Do not insult your friend so," Deidre whispered.

"He is my friend," Davin said, nodding to several groups as they walked past. "But I believe we've been invited to a bit of theater tonight."

Aideen walked behind her father towards their smiling host, who stood near the base of one staircase waiting to greet his guests as they arrived. "Oh, isn't he handsome?" Carolyn whispered to Aideen. Aideen nudged her with an elbow in response.

Lord Cathal of House Gwenhert was perhaps 10 years Aideen's senior. He was indeed handsome, with strong angular features framed in the thick, dark waves of his hair. His white frilled shirt and dark jacket were finely made, his black pants equally fine. All this finery was interrupted by a well-worn pair of riding boots. He stood looking poised and cheerful, the straightness of his back and square of his shoulders so practiced as to look natural on him. He looked the part of a noble through and through, but had the air of a man who wore it casually, as though he might discard it at any moment as easily as a pair of gloves.

"Well met, my young friend," Davin said, clasping hands with Lord Cathal.

"I'm glad you could join us," Lord Cathal said.

"We were most grateful for the invitation," Deidra said with a bow.

"Deidra, a pleasure." Lord Cathal nodded in her direction. "You look lovely as ever."

"It seems you have amassed quite the audience for your first ball," Davin remarked.

Lord Cathal smiled. "Indeed I have. Customs be damned. I think Elorian society is better served with fewer walls between us."

"How liberal of you," Davin said. "And as Eridayah intended, I should think."

"Perhaps so. Indeed, I hope so." Lord Cathal smirked, then turned his attention on the three step-siblings. "Well! Riann I've known since he was a lad. He was sharp then, and now the protégé of the incomparable Davin." He clasped hands with the young man.

"I have had the great fortune of excellent teachers," Riann said, puffing up a bit.

"Carolyn," Lord Cathal inclined his head toward the girl, some secret amusement written in his smile. "You are as pretty as a flower tonight."

"My lord," Carolyn said, bowing with a grin.

"And you must be Aideen," Lord Cathal said, his dark eyes

falling on her. "A pleasure to meet you at last. Your father has spoken much of his daughter."

"My lord," Aideen said, bowing.

He gave them all a warm smile. It seemed quite genuine, Aideen thought. Davin had referred to Lord Cathal as a politician, but Aideen did not think this the smile of the politician. It was disarming in its kind sincerity, making him immediately likable without knowing a thing about him. Then again, perhaps that was simply the mark of a skilled politician.

"You are all quite welcome in my home," he said with a sweeping gesture. "Please, enjoy your evening here. I will find you when I've finished with my hostly duties. I'm a bit new to this sort of thing, so I am not entirely sure how long I am expected to stand here awaiting the fashionably late."

"I believe it's like popping corn," Aideen offered. "You are finished when the pops come with sufficient time between them."

Lord Cathal pursed his lips and squinted at her. "Ah, but how much time is sufficient between?"

"One only learns through practice, my lord. And a few burned pans."

At this, Lord Cathal laughed. "Indeed, and such is my quandary. I shall endeavor not to burn anybody tonight."

As soon as they'd left their host, Carolyn elbowed her. "It's like popping corn? Honestly?"

"Oh, hush." Aideen took Carolyn by the hand and pulled her towards the sound of music. Carolyn let herself be led, tossing a helpless smile over her shoulder at their parents. Davin only chuckled in response, and the sisters swished away into a ballroom filled with dancers.

Aideen glided through the party on the outskirts, staying with Carolyn as they mingled and laughed with an ever-shifting cast of friends and strangers. Aideen was relieved to know many families present. The artisans and merchant class had ample representation in addition to all the nobility and great houses. The familiar faces set her at ease, and she was able to enjoy herself even more than she had anticipated. The circles of people segregated roughly along class lines, but she noted a few bold breaks in rank once the wine had been flowing for some time. Carolyn danced with the Braugh boy, whose name Aideen could not remember. His father was an importer of silks and other fineries from Dahk Ahani, and had a long relationship with Bormia. She had never seen them at such an event.

Aideen sipped on a fine red wine and clapped as she watched Carolyn and the boy join the dance. Carolyn's hopping contretemp and assemblé were exactly as flashy and practiced as Aideen expected them to be. The boy's movements were clumsy by comparison. The pair only lasted a single dance, Carolyn returning to her sister afterwards.

"Well, the poor boy did his best," Aideen remarked, watching him walk away.

"Oh, he was fine," Carolyn said. "Nobody really watches the men anyways. How did I look?"

"Like a peacock."

"A pretty one?"

"The prettiest. He left looking a bit red. You weren't cruel to him, were you?"

"Of course not!" Carolyn took Aideen's wine glass and sipped from it. "He is just unpracticed. Rwen has had an eye for me for two years now. Ever since I..." She stumbled on the thought for a moment. "Well, you know."

"Started filling out your dresses?"

"Yes, that."

"Is that red in your cheeks?" Aideen laughed. Carolyn was capable of embarrassment. Who knew? She resisted the urge to tease her. "Do you like him?"

"I haven't decided yet." Carolyn sipped the glass of wine and hid her embarrassment behind it. "Say, aren't you going to dance?"

"Only if someone asks me." Aideen sighed. "Daughter of Davin Bormia, heiress to the Bormia fortunes and all that. You'd think men wouldn't fear me so."

"I think they fear your father."

"Our father?"

"Oh, come off that. Let's dance."

Aideen acquiesced with a smile. She took up the man's place across from her sister as the next dance began, the only woman on that side of the line. It drew many looks, but she ignored them all. If it wasn't proper to dance with your new little sister at ball, well, then the world was just plain backwards.

Aideen matched her sister step for step, flourish for flourish, as they wheeled and twirled and laughed around the dance floor. Carolyn had a natural musical sensibility, her shoes clicking out the beat as precisely as a drum, and Aideen was light on her feet after so many years studying under Master Lodai. Aideen warmed as she realized the looks about them had shifted to smiles of admiration. They left the dance floor after three dances, arm in arm, Carolyn beaming with contentment and her cheeks full of color. They parted, Carolyn seeking their parents and Aideen seeking another glass of wine. Carolyn had stolen most of the last one.

"You two were lovely out there," a rich voice spoke from behind her. Aideen turned to see Lord Cathal emerging from the general throng. "I suspect it comes as quite a shock to some here that the merchant class is capable of such fine dancing."

"Indeed, my Lord?" Aideen said. "Perhaps if the nobility mingled with their neighbors more often, they would not be so surprised."

"Just so. This little event was devised to accomplish just such a thing. What do you think of it?"

Aideen pursed her lips, surveying the room. It was indeed an interesting affair to see the classes intermingled. And yet its novelty only highlighted the very issues Lodai was so quick to point out. Elora was an imperfect thing, and the very existence of the nobility was a hypocrisy to the values set forth by Eridayah. Lord Cathal himself was a manifestation of these inequities. And yet, this ball was something, wasn't it? The juxtaposition was an intriguing one. Deidre wished Aideen to consider this man. Very well, she thought. She would see just what sort of man he was.

"Well, it's lovely," Aideen remarked. "I can't help but wonder how many families of the Lower City responded to your invitation? For I only recognize a few families here, all of them wealthy enough to live above those parts of Sona."

Lord Cathal blinked at her, then smiled and shook his head. "Your point is well aimed. Fair enough. Small steps, my dear. Let me warm the noble houses one scandal at a time. If we can normalize the Upper City mingling with the Inner City, perhaps one day we can stop classifying the people of Sona by the elevation of their front doors."

"Is it your lone duty then to see to social change, my Lord? It seems as though the Assembly would shoulder such responsibility."

"It would seem so. But if the Assembly will not move Elora into a better future, then I shall do my own small part. There are many houses who did not accept my invitation once they heard who else had received one. But as you can see, many others did. Likely as a curiosity, but even so. I can take their whisperings."

It was a better answer than she expected, Aideen thought. She looked past him at the dancers twirling about the room, and at those who lingered on the edges watching. She spotted Deidra and Carolyn on the far side of the dance floor, smiling in conversation with a young man about Aideen's age. His face was the softened reflection of Lord Cathal's—his younger brother perhaps. There was a whole spectrum of attitudes on display around her, from oblivious merriment to well-meaning awkwardness to the haughtiness of those who believed themselves above this whole affair, but too curious to miss out on it. "You have certainly given the city something to gossip about for the rest of the season. Perhaps when these curious noble houses return home without skin rashes, they may tell their friends it is safe enough to be near the rabble."

Lord Cathal laughed. "Surely social class is not contagious."

"Oh, certainly not, my lord. Or else the wealthy would quickly find themselves waking up with a case of nobility."

Lord Cathal quirked an eyebrow at her. "Do you always speak so pointedly?"

"Only when I have an opinion, my Lord."

"I see. And I take it you hold many such opinions, then?"

"Oh my. A great number, I'm afraid."

"A great number? That seems a lot of opinions to hold."

"I haven't bothered to count them, my lord. But the description seems apt enough."

"I would hear them, then."

Aideen shook her head. "No, my Lord. I may be bold, but not so bold as to pontificate to my host. I've been explicitly warned against it. And anyhow, I would not be so rude as to ruin your evening with talk of politics."

"On the contrary, Aideen Bormia. Tonight is all about politics. So, I must insist on a summary at the very least. A hundred words on the matter, perhaps. My skin is thick enough, I can assure you."

There was a kind of playful confidence in him, Aideen thought. She had been testing him. Perhaps some spiteful part of her wished to elicit a rise from him, so that she might discount him after Deidre's proddings. Any other host may well have been outright offended. Yet she sensed he was testing her in some way as well. Perhaps only for his own amusement. "If you are sure you want it, my Lord. In short, we profess to believe that all are born equal. That a man can rise above his birth, and that the promise of Elora is prosperity for any who strive."

"Indeed."

"And yet, this party showcases the hypocrisy of such a belief. If this party is scandalous, how can those born of truly humble means ever aspire to gain access to such circles when simply mingling is scandal? It seems to me the game is stacked to prevent such access."

"Ah. But your father managed it."

"Yes, but he is the exception. And while I admire him greatly, I do not accept that his rise was through virtue alone. Social mobility is not easy, and it seems to take as much luck as virtue. I am lucky to be his daughter, and therefore have all the benefits of wealth. But not through any virtue of my own."

"An interesting perspective." Lord Cathal stroked his chin. "But it has merit. I, too, was born lucky. But I believe that comes with a responsibility. I believe it is the responsibility of those with wealth and power to ensure the happiness of those without it."

"A generous ideal. Yet those with wealth and power are not quick to share it. Rather, most use wealth to build wealth. They wield power to attain more. The rest of society must make do with what is left."

"What would you propose, then? What is a man such as myself to do?"

Aideen shrugged with some exaggeration. "Oh, I could not say. I am just a woman, my lord. My wealth is my fathers, and will then be my husbands. As for power, I have none except that granted me by the men in my life."

"Oh, but now you're changing the subject."

"Have I? I thought we were discussing the inequities of wealth and power in Elora. I hope you do not regret asking me my opinions."

Lord Gwenhert was studying her. There was something in

that look—what was it? "I don't believe I've ever had a conversation quite like this one. You are a most remarkable woman."

"Thank you, my lord. I am glad to know that I am remarkable for a woman."

He stared at her for a moment, then threw his head back with laughter. "By the gods, you are Davin's daughter. His tongue is sharp and his mind sharper. And here I thought it was your sister whose words rode out in front of her."

"Oh indeed?" Aideen cocked her head. "And who slanders my sister so? I should have quite a few words for him."

"I believe that would be your father."

Aideen laughed. "Then I suppose I will be very cross with him on our way home."

There was that look once more. Aideen could not quite read the expression. It was a sparkling flicker behind his dark eyes. Something hidden behind the smile. She had thrown a dozen barbs, and he had barely flinched. He had been surprised, but instead of backing away he had leaned in. There was a part of her that was wary of the look he gave her. And yet.

And yet at the same time, she felt a flush as a long moment passed between them in silence, the pair standing close enough to hear one another in the loud room, their eyes studying each other. Had she been testing him, she wondered, or was he the one doing the testing? The silence between them drew longer, and Aideen felt a heat rising in her cheeks that could not be blamed solely on the wine.

Lord Cathal broke the silence first. "Would you like to dance?"

"I thought you said you would only inflict one scandal on these people at a time?"

"What is one more? I can bear their whisperings if you can."

"I have never paid them any heed before. Why should I now?"

5

# THE FESTIVAL OF ERIDAYAH

The social season in Sona was drawing to a close. Aideen might have had her fill of balls and dances by now. But such events had a new luster beyond the finery and the music. Now there was Lord Cathal. She had danced with him again at a ball given by House Premroe. Twice, in fact. And again at the Derchand ball the next week, and then again the next.

Their dancing felt hardly limited to the foxtrot. They seemed to circle each other throughout the night, week after week, on opposite sides of the room from their respective places in society, casting veiled glances across the dance floor. Each waiting for some socially acceptable amount of time to pass between their mingling. Aideen waiting to see what he would do next. Waiting to see how he might weigh the inevitable whispers against his desire to speak with her. The whole charade thrilled her, though she told herself it was nothing more than a dalliance. Nothing would come of it. But why shouldn't she enjoy the dance in the meantime?

Autumn had blustered its way into Elora now. The glamorous balls were done, the couplings they formed now sealed with proposals and wedding vows. The excitement and spectacle of horse races around the city walls was now over. Most of the nobility would leave Sona for their respective kingdoms. The wealthy would follow suit, wintering in their estates in the countryside far from the bustle of the city. But the social season was not concluded until the Festival of Eridayah printed the final exclamation point on the year's narrative.

The festival originally marked the anniversary of the Unification of Elora—the end of the War of the Six Kingdoms so long ago. It was intended to be a celebration of these many generations of peace in Elora. But such noble ideas were lost on the people of Sona these days. It was a grand party for the whole city, filled with lights and color, and the holiday was the year's highlight for noble and commoner alike. It was an event nobody missed, and the Bormia family was no exception.

The sun was setting over Sona as the Bormia skycoach reached the eastern curves of the upper terrace. Aideen sat bundled in a woolen coat against the fresh Autumn chill. Carolyn was dressed as though she was heading out for another ball. She had waited impatiently for Riann in the foyer, twisting back and forth in a red dress, watching the hundreds of waterfall ruffles cascade over one another in little waves.

The skycoach carried the three Bormia siblings down past the hanging gardens of the Upper City houses and flew over the lower terrace, the Inner City, and then down yet again. Where the Salar River cut through the eastern side of the city on its final journey to the sea, the humble homes and street markets of the Lower City were interrupted by Salar Park. Almost a mile wide and twice that distance from north to south, the park ran along the river and was filled with carefully curated nature of all types. Its meandering paths wound through dense groves of deciduous woods, open meadows bright with wildflowers and butterflies, lush flower gardens, and neatly trimmed playing lawns for children and sport.

The crowd was already thick when their carriage arrived.

The festivities had begun at noon and a throng of people filled the Western Lawn, looking like ants swarming a dropped sugar lump at a picnic. Vendor carts dotted the lawn as well, their umbrellas serving as landmark and advertisement rather than shade in the fading light. Lanterns and glowlamps lit the scene haphazardly. Aideen saw there were jugglers and fire-breathers here and there. The city was truly alive tonight. And it was said the Wizards of Sona would be unveiling a new wonder amongst the festivities.

"Look, there it is!" Riann said, pointing out the window. The three of them crammed to one side of the carriage to see. Against the western wall rested the center of the evening's spectacle—the Skyway. It was nothing like what Aideen had imagined. It looked nothing like skycoaches or carriages at all. Great cylinders, each the length of at least ten carriages, sat in a line. Small round windows ran along the length of them. The cylinders gleamed like brass against the fiery breath of sunset. Each was rounded on the ends, and each attached to the next by heavy chains.

"Aren't they marvelous!" Carolyn exclaimed. "How fast do you think it will be?"

"I have heard it will be much faster than a horse can gallop," Aideen said. "Can you imagine? Something so large moving at such speed?"

"It will still be much slower than a skycoach," Riann said. "A skycoach takes you directly to your destination. This new Skyway only goes in circles. Imagine needing to loop around and around the city until you finally arrive only at the nearest city gate or ramp, and not at all where you want to be."

"Of course it's no skycoach, but that isn't the point," Aideen said. "Those who can afford a skycoach have no trouble at all moving freely about the city, up the terraces and all. The common folk are bound to the streets and ramps. With the

Skyway, a man would be able to traverse the city in no time, comparatively."

"Honestly, Riann," Carolyn said. "Where is your sense of wonder? There are not even skycoaches back in Lyramae. Have you already grown so spoiled here in Sona?"

Riann smiled down at his sister beside him. "You're right, Cara. It is always a wonder to see things which are impossible anywhere else in the world."

"See how they glow in the light of sunset," Carolyn said, pressing her face against the glass. "I think them quite beautiful."

"They look like a chain of great copper sausages ready to be strung up by a butcher," Aideen said.

"Oh no, you're right!" Riann laughed. "They do look like sausages."

"How unfortunate!" Aideen laughed. "Still, they will be a wonder to see at work. Taken together, they're longer than any ship I've ever seen. Imagine such a thing flying!"

The skycoach lowered itself beside a raised platform erected nearby, where some familiar faces milled about from the Upper City. Aideen, Riann, and Carolyn disembarked their carriage and pushed out onto the platform. From there, the Upper City folk were well above the general congregation below, but the din of the excitement carried up easily to them. Riann went to greet some business associate, leaving Aideen and Carolyn to mingle on their own. Aideen chatted politely with people she knew, reining Carolyn in from time to time as her mouth ran out in front of her good senses. The evening was chilly, and the harbor breezes nipped at her cheeks as a foreshadow of the winter to come.

"My, don't you two look lovely this evening," came a voice from behind them. Aideen turned around, already recognizing the voice's owner.

"Good evening, Lord Cathal." Aideen bowed, smiling at him in greeting.

"An exciting evening for the people of Sona, don't you think?"

"Aideen thinks the Skyway looks like big, flying sausages," Carolyn said. Aideen shot her a look, but Carolyn was too busy smiling up at Lord Gwenhert to notice.

"Oh?" Lord Cathal cocked his head and looked at Aideen with an expression of amusement.

"Well, they do." Aideen saw no way around the observation, so she may as well own it. "Or perhaps I'm just hungry, and I'm beginning to imagine that everything looks like food. My sister ought to be careful that I don't get after her with a fork." She redoubled her look at Carolyn, who received it welcomingly with her chin jutted out in a grin.

Lord Cathal laughed. His voice was deep and rich. Aideen remembered the quivering feeling it had given her at the Premroe ball when she'd already had three glasses of wine. "I'm happy to see your new family all getting along so well," he remarked. "When your father was intended to marry Deidre, I was curious to see how you all would fare."

"Oh, come now," Carolyn said. "You have known my family long enough to know we would get along marvelously."

"I always had high hopes, of course," Lord Cathal said.

"Lord Cathal knew my father," Carolyn told Aideen. "It was he who made the introductions for Riann to apprentice for your father's company, which brought us to Sona in the first place."

Lord Cathal nodded. "Riann is bright, and was perfectly suited for such work. It is no small thing to combine households, on the other hand. Especially when they are so full of strong personalities."

"Well it won't stay so full for long," Carolyn said. "With two beautiful daughters of marrying age, or nearly, it may well be quiet in Lindenhall before summer."

"Is there an arrangement I am not aware of?" He looked genuinely surprised, and perhaps a bit concerned, Aideen noted. She did not mind the look.

"No," Aideen said. "But I should wish my sister all the happiness in the world if someone else were in charge of keeping her out of trouble."

"Any man would count himself lucky to have such a responsibility," Carolyn said.

"To be sure," Lord Cathal agreed with a smirk. "Will your father be joining us tonight?"

"No," Aideen said. "You know how he can be. He's practically allergic to social gatherings. It's a wonder he was convinced to attend your ball."

"Ah, but the evening would not have shone so bright had the Bormia family not come."

"I think..." Aideen turned to say something to Carolyn, but found her no longer by her side. She spun around, and saw her sister disappearing into another circle of people. Aideen stared after her. That little fiend, she thought. "Well, it seems my sister has abandoned me."

"Indeed. At least she left me in good company." He smiled at her, and Aideen felt that fluttering in her stomach again. Only this time, there was no wine to blame it on. "You said you were hungry?"

"Famished, actually." And there was a new excuse, though she was all too aware that she was making them.

"I'm sure there will be a spread around here somewhere."

Aideen wondered if Carolyn leaving her alone with Lord Cathal was her own scheme, or her mother's. But it didn't really matter. She was alone with him now, and did not mind it in the least. It was just the next step in their dance, and she wondered where it might lead. She glanced around, looking for the inevitable servants carrying trays of finger foods and wine. Then, she reconsidered. "Would you lower yourself, my lord?"

"I'm sorry?"

"I mean literally." Aideen gestured down to the revelers below them. "I would like to see what treasures those vendor carts below us might hold. But of course, I would require a chaperone."

Lord Cathal smiled at this, and bowed his head slightly. "In that case, I would be obligated to join you." He offered Aideen his arm. With a moment of hesitation, she took it. "Shall we?"

Aideen and Lord Cathal took the stairs down into the general throng. They walked amongst them, no longer spectators from above, taking in the sights and sounds of the roiling party that surrounded them. Many of the people wore costumes or what finery they had, and nobody paid any mind to the two Upper City outsiders in their midst. They chatted, which amounted to yelling above the din of the musicians and ale-sloshed laughter. One group was singing a bawdy song about Eridayah, which questioned a great deal more than her virtues. Aideen recognized it from her time aboard the Dragonfly and sung along for a few lines without thinking.

"An old favorite?" Lord Cathal was watching her with an amused curiosity.

"Just a reminder of another time, my lord. We didn't always live in the Upper City, as you well know. When I was very young, I sailed with my father. The sailors were rough cut, but always kind to me."

"I knew a bit of Davin's progress from sailor to his successes today, but not that you shared in his adventures."

"Well, those trips were quite a shade less adventurous than when he ran the Dirk Isles before my birth. I would have liked some adventure, as I'm sure all children imagine they do. But it was quite safe."

"It sometimes seems you live in two worlds," Lord Cathal remarked.

If you only knew, Aideen thought. "There is only one world,

my lord," she said. She pointed up at the raised platform, now some distance above them. "But there are many views of it."

After much meandering, they sought out one of the vendor carts. Aideen bought some brown bread and sliced Rodom sausages from one of them. The man was an elf, his sharp ears protruding from under a woolen cap. Aideen touched at her hair self-consciously, where the coils of crimson were pinned to hide her own ears. There would be no elves on her raised platform, not even as servants. Except for her, and then only in secret. Aideen pushed down the bitterness of the lie, returning her attention to Lord Cathal and the sandwich now in hand.

Aideen really had been hungry, and did not bother with daintiness as they walked and ate and took in all there was to see. From down here, one had to walk and discover what lay beyond the horizon of the crowd just before you. One had to listen for the sounds of excitement, to look for people pointing. Otherwise, you might walk right by a fire eating juggler and never know what you missed simply because some drunken gaggle was standing in your path.

Lord Cathal had joined her without hesitation, which Aideen liked. It was nothing for them to be on friendly terms, but after all their dancing she knew people would ascribe more to their friendliness than perhaps was warranted. She told herself she didn't particularly care one way or the other. But she did not actually believe herself.

They chatted easily for a while, returning to the raised platform just as a bell began to ring out signifying the beginning of the ceremony. Carolyn rejoined Aideen on the platform, giving her constant and meaningful looks. These would have earned her an elbow to the shoulder, but Carolyn anticipated it and moved just out of reach.

Lord Cathal pretended not to notice. "Well. I suppose I should find my own family now that the event is underway."

"Your brother Conner is just over there by the railings, watching the festivities below," Carolyn offered.

"Is he?" Aideen asked, cutting her eyes over at the girl. Carolyn had spoken with the younger Gwenhert, Conner, at her mother's elbow on several social occasions recently. Carolyn refused to look at Aideen and pretended not to hear, but Aideen noticed the color rising in her cheeks.

Lord Cathal suppressed a smirk. "Well, then I shall be dragging him from his perch back to the rest of our house. Besides, I fear I've stolen too much of your sister's patience for one evening."

"Nonsense," Aideen said. "It has been a pleasure."

He smiled broadly—not the smile of a politician, but one reminiscent of the boy he once was. "Indeed it has been. But my uncles will hear nothing of my pleasure if I am not at their side for the ceremony. And so, I will bid you both a very good night."

Aideen and Carolyn bowed in unison. "My lord." Aideen watched him walk away for a moment, then turned her attention to the festivities. She could feel a flush on her own cheeks, and did not dare to look at Carolyn. Both remained silent.

A hundred men of the city guard had taken places all along the raised dais that ran by the line of Skyway carriages, their armor glistening in the many-colored lights of glowlamps and oil lanterns. After the bell sounded one final time, a shining brass section in the middle of one carriage slid open, and a cheer rippled through the crowd. From inside the carriage stepped the Queen, her Syani, and several wizards from the College Arcana. The wizards were always easy to spot, their colorful robes and collars signifying their school and rank. They looked foolish in their robes and floppy hats, but they commanded much respect. Their work was responsible for so many of the wonders in Sona.

Queen Aeren was something else altogether. Her features were plain, her blond hair pulled back beneath her golden crown. She wore no jewelry. She wore a simple white gown lacking any adornment. It needed none—the Queen was resplendent and glittering with her own light, the same sparkling blue that lit glowlamps with magical fire seemed to emanate from the Queen's fair skin, blond hair, and flowing fabric of her dress. There was no mistaking her for anything less than what she was. A sense of power emanated from her which was more than the crown on her head. The Syani standing in a line behind her were dressed in a similar simple fashion, twelve women ranging in age from rosy youth to grey. All stood with the poise of royalty. All exuded the power of the mysterious Shard they commanded which fueled the wonders of the city.

The last Queen had stepped down only last year to spend her final years without the burden of the crown. The choice of the Syani for a new Queen from their ranks was immediate. Queen Aeren was crowned in Spring of the Year of Eridayah's Peace 1252.

Queen Aaren addressed the crowd briefly, her voice carrying across the lawns with a wondrous magic amplification. She spoke of the Skyway. Of the need for it, of the equality it represented to all men and women of Sona. And that it would be free to use for all people of Sona—starting tonight—as a symbol of the Unification of Elora, and in remembrance of Eridayah.

Queen Aeren stepped forward and began gesturing with her hands in elegant circles. The dozen Syani behind her echoed her movements and bright blue light sprang from thirteen pairs of hands. The audience gasped in unison. For all the magic that powered the wonders of Sona, seeing the art firsthand was an incredible rarity. With a sparkling flash, a thousand blue iridescent butterflies flew from fingertips and fluttered their way up to the heavens. All eyes followed them, the creatures trailing blue and white motes of glitter with each tiny flap of their wings. The whole western lawn lay in a hush as though all were holding their breath together. As the blue lights rose higher in the sky, in a tumultuous bang they exploded into fireworks. The crowd erupted in a delighted cheer. The Queen, the Syani, and the wizards were no longer anywhere to be seen. The doors of each Skyway carriage slid open, the line of guards parted, and the crowd surged forward toward it.

"See how they push and shove to be first to ride?" Riann remarked. "I know it's exciting, but there's no reason to get hurt over it."

"Can you blame them?" Carolyn said. "Most in Sona have never ridden in a skycoach before. Most will go their whole lives without so much as seeing the inside of one."

"This is the first time any of them will ever fly," Aideen said, smiling down at the crowd below. "It is a gift."

The doors to the long, shining row of carriages all slid shut. People leapt out of the way, most of them inward rather than out as they crammed their way into the Skyway. Each of the ten carriages were filled with a hundred people when surely each was intended for half that many. Light crackled around the train of cylinders, their underbellies glowing that familiar cool blue. Then, as if they weighed nothing at all, the line of gleaming carriages lifted up into the air as one. As soon as they cleared the trees, the whole of the train glided forward, gaining speed more quickly than seemed possible for its size. It was out of sight, around the curve of the lowest terrace, in a matter of moments. The congregation below cheered, as did all the people standing on the raised platform above them.

THE FIREWORKS DISPLAY STILL OUTSHONE the stars overhead when Aideen stepped off her skycoach in front of Lindenhall late that night. The Skyway had wound around and around the city for hours, the riders coming and going and the festival slowly spreading from the park to all parts of the city as the revelers came and went from the belly of the flying metallic wonder. The flashes of fireworks were visible even from here. Aideen watched them absently as she walked toward the front door, their rainbow hues and patterns showering the city in light.

"I wonder how long until Lord Gwenhert asks to marry you," Carolyn said with a yawn.

"What?" Aideen started.

"Oh, please. You fancy him, and you know he fancies you. And don't even start with your protesting. It doesn't matter that he's a noble and we're not. You're likely the wealthiest girl in Sona."

"I'm also half elf, you'll recall," Aideen said, touching at the red spirals of hair that covered her ears. "You want to talk about a scandal? Him dancing with me at balls would be nothing compared to it coming out that a Lord has married an elf."

"Oh, I forget about your ears. So who cares? I live with you and I forget your secret, so it can't be too hard to keep."

"That's not how Sona would see it," Riann said. He placed a hand on the shoulders of his two sisters. "We love our Aideen, sister. But we must not be frivolous in this matter. We are not sworn to secrecy in this for nothing. I cannot see Elora ever truly accepting elves here, and certainly not in the lines of nobility. As we've been told, this is a delicate matter."

"I will admit I am fond of Lord Cathal," Aideen said, wishing to escape the subject. "But I am happy with my life as it is. It's lovely and quiet here, and except for suffering you two, it lacks any real strife or drama. I am free to pursue my studies and interests without worry. What do I want a husband for right now?" She chose to ignore the longwinded mutterings from Carolyn.

Aideen climbed the stairs to her room. Kayla helped her take her hair down and brushed it thoroughly, complaining all along that she should be washing it tonight instead of tomorrow morning. Complaining about Aideen getting hurt with all her swordplay with Master Lodai, that she'd seen the nicks and scrapes and bruises and she really ought to be more careful. Kayla was a servant, but she was also the only grandmotherly figure Aideen had ever known. Davin's parents had died long before her birth, and she knew nothing of Saira's parents. Aideen changed into a nightgown and walked to her father's study to tell him goodnight before she tucked into bed with a book.

The door to Davin's study was closed. Aideen knocked, and hearing no protest from within, opened the door. Davin was not sitting at his desk. The glowlamps were still lit, papers were still strewn across the desk beside his open ledger, a teacup serving as paperweight. Aideen eased the door shut again, wondering where he'd gone off to. Then something flashed inside her that made her throw the door back open. There was a low shadow coming from behind the desk that should not be there. Aideen rushed into the room, her throat clamping shut and her veins turning to ice as she ran toward what she already knew she'd find but her mind could not possibly fathom.

Davin lay behind the desk. His eyes were open and saw nothing. Aideen fell onto him, grasping desperately at his shirt and already cool skin. When Riann found her there minutes later, she was still screaming.

# 6

# THE DUSTY PEARL

If you were to wander down the cobblestone streets of Sona harbor, away from the thronging docks and the fishmonger stalls, when the salted wind blows just right, the smell of creosote will give way to that of savory roast chicken and plums. And if you followed that smell far enough, if you nose your way down the right alleys and track it right to its source, tucked away on a quiet backstreet in the shadow of the city walls you'd find The Dusty Pearl.

The Pearl is a truly ugly building. It is composed of two of the shabbiest stories ever constructed. Its cracked stuccoed walls are stained a muddy shade of brown between splintery wooden beams. The eaves sag as though they were draped on as decoration, like icing on a half-hearted cake. But inside this inelegant hovel is one of the most famous watering holes in all Elora.

The Pearl is known for its excellent food and an eccentric group of patrons. Merchants, fisher folk, smugglers, unsavories, and the occasional adventurous soul from the Inner City are all drawn there by the rich food, the nutty ale, and the cheery hearth. A Lindle by the name of Corrin Hilltopple is the third generation of Hilltopples to run the establishment. It's a decidedly wholesome spot considering its eclectic mix of clientele. The Hilltopples don't judge—just so long as you mind your manners. If you ever want to taste the herb-crusted chicken or the Lindle applejack again, you'll keep your squabbles elsewhere. And so, over the long decades, The Pearl has become a kind of unspoken neutral ground for the capital city's underbelly, where differences are left outside and rivals can come to palaver in good faith.

Growing up in this tavern, climbing stools to pour ale and ladle out pork and white bean stew, a young Hamfast Hilltopple loved listening to the stories told by the sailors and travelers that passed through his home—tales of wondrous cities, of fantastic creatures, of exotic places filled with mysterious cultures and races. These accounts may have held only a fraction of truth, but they nevertheless sparked a wanderlust in him, a need to know a life beyond the safety of the city walls. Sona was undoubtedly a wonder, but there was a great big world out there to discover.

And so, when Hamfast came of age, he convinced a young man named Davin Bormia to allow him to run the galley of the battered old ship he'd just acquired. Hamfast had spent decades there now. The seas were beautiful and dangerous, the kitchen below decks was a dominion he had mastered, and the ship often spent weeks in port unloading, undergoing repairs, and reloading. That was ample time for Hamfast to explore each new port and to get a taste for what every corner of the world had to offer. The Dragonfly had been to more ports than Hamfast could count.

Hamfast sat at a table in the middle of the tavern, sipping ale with his feet up on an empty chair and smacking his lips with satisfaction. There was a fire crackling happily in the nearby hearth, and familiar smells wafted in from the kitchen—hearty notes of roasting meat and garlic, the snap of aromatics sizzling and popping in a pan of butter, of herbs and warm rolls fresh

*The First Whispers of Fate*

from the oven. Hamfast was at home. And it certainly felt good to let someone else do the cooking.

The evening crowd would arrive soon enough, and Hamfast would be obliged to give up his table to paying patrons rather than hogging a plank table large enough for six. But for now, he relaxed with his back to the fire and let the mug of ale warm him through. The Dragonfly would be in port for several weeks, and Hamfast would inevitably end up working in the Pearl's kitchen soon enough with his father grumbling about how everything he did was wrong, with his mother scolding his father in much the same way, and with Hamfast and his sister Lavinia ignoring them both as they busied themselves with the frying and boiling and baking.

Tabitha sat behind the bar looking sleepy. She was an Elorian woman, unlike everyone else that worked at the Dusty Pearl. Her long legs made her much better at bustling around the room taking orders and refilling drinks than any Lindle could be. And those legs also had more of a draw for customers than the crusty old Corrin could muster.

"Our food speaks for itself," Corrin had insisted when the idea of hiring her was first brought to him. "Always has. That was good enough for my father and for my grandfather. It should be good enough for us. We don't need some trollop cheapening this place."

"Who said she was a trollop?" Lavinia said. "She's got experience working in a tavern in the Inner City."

"Experience? Bah!" Corrin crossed his arms. His bushy eyebrows scrunched in defiance across his wrinkled forehead. "Just what we need. An experienced woman."

"Would you listen to yerself? You sound right crass. Nobody is saying we're turning this place into a whorehouse. She's a nice lass, and you and mum aren't going to be young forever. We need the help."

"Blech." Corrin made a sour face. "Fine. We'll give her a

week." That had been over two years ago, and Corrin still often grumbled during slow nights that he would only give her one more week to turn things around.

The evening crowd started to appear around sunset, and Hamfast shifted over to a barstool at one end of the bar, where he had a good view of the room. He sipped his ale, his head feeling a bit swimmy from the afternoon spent nursing one after another. Tomorrow, he'd need to finalize the inventory on the Dragonfly's supplies. For today, he had promised himself he would do nothing. After a good dinner, he would turn in with a real feather bed and a book and read until he fell asleep. When he awoke in the morning, he'd go back to sleep until his head didn't hurt and he was bored with laying about. And that might take a while. It was a lovely plan. Hamfast called to Tabitha for another ale.

Killian Gilmeade, the captain of the Dragonfly, came in through the door. That wasn't unusual. The Pearl was popular with sailors returning to port in search of a fine meal. Noticing Hamfast, the captain came around to his side of the bar and took the stool beside him. That much was unusual. Hamfast was on fine terms with the captain, but they were hardly friends.

"Captain," Hamfast said, wondering what this was about.

"Good evening, Hamfast."

"And a good evening to you, sir. Can I buy you a drink?"

"Certainly." Tabitha brought Killian an ale, and he took it automatically. His brow was furrowed, and Hamfast watched him expectantly. After a long drink from his ale, he spoke again without looking at Hamfast. "How well do you know Davin Bormia?"

"Davin?" Hamfast asked. "I have served on the Dragonfly since it first came into his hands. It was his first ship, as I'm sure you are aware. The very beginning of the Bormia Trading Company."

"That had to be thirty years ago."

"Ah. I see your confusion," Hamfast said. "I suppose I look like I'm thirty or forty to you, but we Lindle don't age the same way as humans do. I'm seventy-two years old, and my father is one hundred and five. Lindle can live to be a hundred and fifty if they mind their health."

Killian nodded, taking another drink from his cup. "So you knew him well, then."

The phrasing struck Hamfast, and he felt something in his chest clench in response. "Knew?"

Captain Killian nodded. "Davin Bormia is dead." Hamfast drew in a sharp breath. It came back out in a stutter as the sentence sank in. The captain sighed into his drink and continued. "Levin told me you had been close to him somehow, so I thought I ought to tell you myself. I didn't know your history went that far back."

"What happened?" Hamfast breathed, hardly believing it. Davin was no old man. He would have been, what, just over fifty? And healthy last time Hamfast had seen him only a few months ago inspecting the Dragonfly—more out of nostalgia than any doubts as to its operations.

"The doctors say his heart gave out. He'd lived a wild life in his younger years, I hear."

Hamfast couldn't respond at first. He held his face in his hands, breathing heavily. Tears welled up in his eyes, and he hadn't the will to stop them. Davin had been a friend. A dear friend once, though they had drifted apart over the years. Hamfast had served as cook on the Dragonfly, back when his crew called him Madman Davin instead of Captain. Back when they sailed through pirate waters to trade with the Dirk Isles off the coast of Omaas to bring back silks worth fortunes. Back when they'd crossed the Misty Seas twice—or four times, rather, since they'd somehow returned alive both trips. Davin bringing back an elven wife in secrecy the second time after some mysterious and undoubtedly wild affair in those elven lands in the distant West.

After that, things had changed. But while Davin may have mellowed somewhat with raising a motherless child, he was still a lion of a man. He had brought his daughter on the Dragonfly several times over the years, unable to content himself back in Sona while the sea still beckoned him. "The man was fearless," Hamfast breathed at last. "Fearless but kind."

"I hardly knew him," Killian admitted. "He hired me on, but that was business. I've captained three ships for Bormia in my career now. He trusted me for my talents, but I regret that I never truly knew him. I only know people speak highly of him as a man."

"When is his funeral?"

"Already passed."

Hamfast finished his ale quickly and motioned to Tabitha for another, wiping hot tears from his cheeks. When his cup was full again, he raised it wishing there was someone here who could understand the bitterness of his sorrow. "Men do not live long enough. The best among your race pass on before they've finished making their mark upon this world."

Captain Killian touched his cup lightly to Hamfast's. "To Davin. May we know more men such as him."

"To Davin."

They drank in silence for a while. Hamfast wiped at his tears, propping his elbow on the bar and perching his red and wet face on his hands to hide his grief from the whole of the room. Captain Killian seemed uncomfortable with Hamfast's display of emotion. There was nothing for it. Hamfast had loved Davin, and now simmered in regret at how they had lost touch over the years. One always imagines a future reconnection, that one day a friendship can be pulled off the ice and thawed and found to be the same as it once was. But that day would never come now, and both parties were equally to blame for the negligence.

"Perhaps it is fitting that our next voyage is the last one Davin signed for," Killian said.

Hamfast wiped at his eyes. "How so?"

"Our cargo will hardly be typical. Only a handful of Wizards."

Hamfast cocked his head. "From the College Arcana?" His voice creaked, but his surprise and the strangeness of this comment forced the words out anyhow.

"Yes."

"Why would they want to hire a ship as large as the Dragonfly for just a few passengers?"

"Because the Dragonfly has proven itself across the Misty Seas already."

Hamfast nearly choked on his ale. "What? We're bound for the elven Lands?"

"No," Captain Killian said, his eyes sparkling as he smiled to himself. "We're going somewhere southeast of them. Some island not on any map I've seen before." He clapped Hamfast on the back. "This is no normal journey, halfling. This will be an adventure, and a fitting tribute for the Dragonfly now that it has lost its true master."

THE DRAGONFLY WAS fresh from the graving dock, where the ship had been stood on blocks in a great trench in Beacon Point near the Sona harbor lighthouse. The entire hull had been scraped of barnacles, re-tarred, and all three masts replaced for good measure. The main sails looked new as well. Hamfast could not help grinning as he boarded the ship. The decks smelled with the smoky tang of fresh pine tar, turpentine, and linseed oil. A new figurehead had been carved and painted for the ship's prow, a crimson haired woman perched at the head of the ship with dragonfly wings sprouting from her shoulders. Brogan was a more talented wood carver than he'd let on. The Dragonfly was reborn as it had not been since Hamfast had first sailed with her.

During its time in the graving dock, Hamfast had emptied the kitchen and stores of anything not nailed down. Everything had been cleaned, and now the store was restocked as it had not been in years. The voyage would take eight to ten weeks across dangerous open seas. Finding an uncharted island in uncharted waters would cost them gods knew how much time. There was no guarantee their destination even existed. It was on no maps except the one the old wizard in the blue robes had shown Levin and Captain Killian. And then, who knew if there would be any resupplying on this mysterious island? That meant twenty weeks of provisions were the absolute minimum if they were lucky, and he had better plan on several more just to be safe.

There would be 39 men to feed. Three shifts of 8 able seamen. Captain Killian and his two mates. The Boatswain and his mate. Two carpenters, a caulker, a ropemaker, a surgeon, and a clerk. Their three strange passengers. And Hamfast, the cook, who also served as the ship's purser. They could perhaps sail with fewer, but the men worked so well together the captain deemed it too risky.

The fare would be meager toward the end. Hamfast had enlisted the help of his sister in making large amounts of spiced jam from lemons and ginger and hot peppers. Those ingredients were supposed to prevent the sailor's disease, and would keep long enough to provide some desperately needed flavor to the end of the journey, which would be mostly simple biscuit and porridge and whatever they could pull from the sea at speed. Hamfast oversaw the delivery and stocking of the stores personally. No expense was being spared, and his every request was fulfilled with an almost dismissive attitude. Part of the lower hold had been converted into private quarters for the three members of the College.

As all Hamfast's final preparations were seen to, their unusual cargo began to be delivered. Painted crates covered in brightly colored symbols were brought in by grey-robed College apprentices. Hamfast watched them in amusement, the young scrawny men struggling with the manual labor in their robes and slippers that were as ill-suited for the tasks as they themselves were. But they insisted none of the crew touch these items.

The final cargo were three old men. Hamfast and several of the crew leaned over the rails and watched from the deck as they arrived in skycoaches adorned with the same brightly colored runes as their boxes. The Wizards of the College Arcana were their own bizarre culture unto itself. Those born of a certain station that showed aptitude for such study were sent to the College on their tenth birthday. But while many professions required a lifetime of dedication to a craft, the Wizards wore it worse.

The brightly colored robes, the slippers obviously meant to be worn indoors, and a general sense of obliviousness of normal life were the hallmark of a wizard if you ever met one. A lifetime spent shuffling around in the laboratories of the College debating the mysteries of the cosmos made conversation with them impossible. A wizard had once stumbled into the Dusty Pearl somehow, and Corrin Hilltopple had booted him out thinking him a drunk vagabond. His protests of this ill treatment were nearly incomprehensible.

The three men boarding the Dragonfly seemed to fit the stereotype perfectly. All three men wore their beards long. Two of them wore purple robes striped with yellow. Their faces were unremarkable, or at least difficult to distinguish behind the beards and shadows of their purple hoods. Hamfast catalogued them as the Tall Purple One and the Taller Purple One. The third, a head shorter than the others, wore pale blue robes.

"Fucking weird," Brogan muttered from beside Hamfast, chewing a mouthful of tobacco.

"That they are," Hamfast agreed.

"Think they'll get us all killed out on the edge of the world?"

"Maybe. But if not, think of the stories we'll have to tell."

# 7

# THE WILL

Aideen was ten years old when Lodai first told her of *pouv'oua*. She stood sweating in the small garden behind their Inner City home, the sword hanging heavy from her small hands as she rested from practicing the Songs. Lodai sat on a bench, having watched her latest attempt at *tanp'et* without correction or remark. She knew she had made mistakes. She had felt them. But she had weathered those mistakes without stutter, feeling the movements flow through her body. Feeling the heft of the sword not as an obstacle, but as an extension of herself. Of her mind and body. It had all fallen together somehow. In a delirious but delicious moment she had moved without thinking, as though she was watching herself from some exterior vantage. She had become enraptured by the music of the Song, the beat of her heart thrumming, the tempo of feet chuffing the gravel, the strum of her sword against the air. She stood in silence, in awe of the way it had felt. There was such a rightness to it.

"*Do you know of pouv'oua, child?*"

"*I...,*" Aideen wiped the sweat from her face with her sleeve, his question breaking her reverie. "*I do not know the word. Is it a special conjugation of the word power?* 'My power?'"

Lodai was studying her with a strange intensity. "*Yes. But it means a great deal more than that.*"

"*I am your student, teacher.*" It seemed the correct response.

"You may drop the formality, *timaoen*." He slipped into the Elorian tongue. "This lesson is important. More important than your respect." Aideen was unsure how to respond, so she simply stood there, looking at him. Lodai leaned forward, staring at her intently. "Are you good?"

Aideen blinked at him. "I..."

"Are you evil?"

"Certainly not," she said with her chin jutted out in confidence. "And I try hard to be good."

"You may not think yourself capable of evil, *timaoen*, but that is folly. All are capable of it. You are young, and you have yet to find yourself in a situation where selfishness, greed, or anger seeks to consume you. But that day will come. No matter how strong the sin, no matter how weak the virtue in you feels. You always retain the power of choice. And that choice, that power to choose, is *pouv'oua*. Do you understand?"

Aideen nodded. "I can always choose to be good."

"Yes. This is important, *timaoen*. Perhaps the most important lesson I will ever teach you. You always have a choice. Sin and virtue are Elorian words, and come with the Elorian flippancy towards their deeper meaning. Elorians mark sin as a disobedience to the gods. I do not mean religion. Sin is *pech'a* and it can mean many evil things, both great and small. Virtue is *ve'eti* and it may take many forms. You must always choose. You must practice this choosing. You must become aware of it, lest you become blind to the choice and rely on your goodness. And therein lies *pouv'oua*."

"I must always choose," she repeated.

"The obstacles in your path may often seem to contain both sin and virtue together. It may be possible to convince yourself that they are neither, or that a balance can be achieved. But then you must choose what you embrace. And that is *pouv'oua*. Sin and virtue may be actions that no soul will ever know. It may be things you only keep in your heart. And choosing what your heart embraces is *pouv'oua*. Choosing your words is *pouv'oua*. Being mindful of your actions and their effect is *pouv'oua*. All have the capacity for good and evil, great and small, in their hearts or their words or deeds. Some have greater capacity than others. And in their choosing is *pouv'oua*. It is indeed power, and one that must grow in you. This is what makes you, or unmakes you. Do you understand?"

Aideen nodded. "I do."

"You understand as a child may understand these things. I can ask no more of you now. But you will not always be so young." Lodai settled back on his bench, seeming to relax. "Something happened in your *tanp'et*, yes?"

"Yes!" Aideen was happy to move back to the previous lesson, and was excited to discuss what had happened. "I..." She searched for the words that might capture the feeling. "It was different. It was like..." Her mouth hung open stupidly for a moment, and she felt herself flush with embarrassment.

*"I am patient. What was different?"*

"It was like something changed."

"Yes. But how?"

*"It flowed like a stream without ripple,"* she said, quoting his words. "But it actually did. I finally understand what you've been trying to teach me in the Songs. I felt myself inside it. But outside. I know that doesn't make sense, but that is how it felt."

A rare smile crept across his face. Lodai nodded. "And so it shall one day be with *pouv'oua*. The instruction must come first, but the learning will only come with awareness and practice.

That will end our lesson today. We shall try again tomorrow and see how the water flows."

AIDEEN STARED at her reflection in the mirror. The young woman looking back at her seemed strange, like a poor forgery of herself. The two women studied each other with a distant, hazy curiosity. Their almond shaped eyes were too sunken, the skin underneath showing puffy and dark. Their mouths were drawn too taut, as well. Lips made for smiling, for wit and laughter, were now pulled harsh across her face like those of a bitter taskmaster. The hair was at least right, thick and burning red as ever. The ears still told their tale of mixed heritage—sharp elven ears from her mother, softened by her father's humanity. And now both of them gone. This face, this hair, these ears, were all that remained of them except memories.

Aideen's servant Kayla stood behind her, running a brush through the long red hair with a slow and practiced repetition. Kayla's aged and wrinkled face twitched, seemingly at odds with itself. She was doing her best not to appear worried for her young mistress. She was failing miserably.

"Kayla?" Aideen reached back and took the woman's strong hand holding Aideen's hair. She found it timid now, and it shuddered beneath her touch.

"Yes, miss?"

"You look positively a mess. Don't just stand there making faces."

"Faces? I meant to make no faces, miss."

"And yet there you stand, eyes twitching and swallowing continuously like a cat who just caught a cockroach."

Kayla squeezed her hand in response. Her mouth twitched into a pained smile. "It's just I know what yer goin' through, child. Losing your father like this, an' so young. I lost me father when I was a mite older than you, and it was still murder on me heart. I see you hurtin' so, and I hurts for ye. That's all."

"Then you may look hurt, as you are. Stop with the worrying and the cockroach eating."

Kayla patted her shoulder and went back to brushing her hair. "Aye, miss." When she was younger, the buns of Aideen's hair would have been coiled with ribbons and tied into place with bright bows. Today, the buns had been covered in black floral lace.

Kayla powdered Aideen's face with rice powder, then lightly blushed her cheeks with sandalwood while Aideen stared at the imitation of herself in the mirror. Kayla hesitated. "I guess no eye makeup today, Miss."

"It doesn't matter," Aideen said. She stared at the husk in the mirror that stared back at her. She had not cried a single tear since the shock of finding him. Her screaming, her madness had driven all that could feel out of herself. She was empty now. "You can paint me like a porcelain doll. You can kohl my eyes and draw out my eyelashes with elderberry and ash if you wish. I feel nothing, Kayla. I am hollow and dried out. I do not fear smeared eyes today. I can fear nothing now when I have nothing left."

"Oh, Miss." Kayla's chin trembled. "Don't speak so."

The funeral yesterday had felt like it was happening to someone else. Aideen walked through the motions like a ship gliding through grey mist. The ceremony. The symbolism. Candles lit in a circle around the cemetery vault. The people. Oh, the people. There had been a sea of them, such that city guards had been there holding back the crowds, just like at the unveiling of the Skyway. It was as if the whole city of Sona had come to bear witness to her sorrow. Davin had been well known. He had been admired. He had been loved by merchants and sailors, idealized by those who aspired to success and wealth. But this sadness belonged to those who truly knew him. The rest were simply spectators, and she hated them all for their curiosity. She wanted to scream at them. She wanted to take up a sword and chase them all away from the graveside. She wanted to snuff all the candles that ringed the shining marble tomb that would soon hold her father's remains. There should only be one candle. Grief was hers and hers alone. But she stood as one of the angelic statues that loomed over the graves nearby. All emotion was buried in some deep place inside her. She was frozen behind her black veil. Her eyes should have been black as well, she thought dimly. There was no light in the world left to see.

Aideen left her dressing room wearing a black dress. She wore the veil still, too. The elves wore veils for a year to show their sorrow at the passing of a loved one. Perhaps Aideen would as well. Her shoes knocked loudly against the floors of the halls, the echoes of her footsteps returning to her ears as if only to confirm their emptiness now. She walked down the stairs and joined the rest of her family in the drawing room.

Upon seeing Aideen, Carolyn immediately burst into tears and ran to her. Aideen patted her on the head, in the same way one might comfort a dog who was growling at the thunder. Riann stood behind the chair his mother sat in, watching Aideen enter the room with a solemn look drawn across his face. Deidre wore a veil as well. Aideen couldn't decide if she should love or hate her for it. She supposed Deidre had loved her father, too. A woman was allowed to grieve for her dead husband. But Deidre was a new accessory in her father's life. Carolyn's emotions seemed more appropriate, at least. Carolyn cried not only for Davin, but for her new big sister's grief. That much was warranted. Her new big sister had died in a way, too. Aideen felt her former self buried alongside her father, and the woman whose eyes she looked through today was a ghost flickering between bittersweet memories and the tortuous present.

Aideen sat in the chair by the window. Riann cleared his throat. "Are we ready to start?"

"Fine," Aideen said, her voice sounding flat. She looked out the window at the gardens where they used to walk.

A servant standing by the door bowed on this signal, and left the drawing room. He returned a moment later with Mr. Conmera, the Bormia Company's legal counsel. Mr. Conmera looked more like a beetle than a man, Aideen had always thought. Something about the way he hunched, the wide flabby chin, and his tiny eyes—the sum of it was grotesquely bug-like. But Davin had trusted him completely, and so Aideen bore the lawyer no ill, even on a day like today. Mr. Conmera sat down behind the small table that had been brought in for him. He opened his leather satchel and withdrew a series of papers.

"My sincere condolences for your loss," Mr. Conmera said through his perpetual head cold. "We shall keep this brief, as I'm sure there are no great surprises here. I found Davin Bormia's will in his study, bearing his seal. I have insisted that he have one and review it yearly despite his relative youth. Today, I shall read and explain the contents of his last wishes, revisited since his recent marriage. It has two primary concerns—what should be done with his estate and fortune, and what should happen to the Bormia Trading Company." He cleared the phlegm from his throat noisily and began to read. "I, Davin Bormia, being of a sound and disposing mind..."

Aideen stared out the window. Davin's life work, his passion, the fruits of all his strivings being carved up as though it were nothing more than a holiday roast. Roast and foul gravy. It all made her nauseous.

"...to my wife Deidra Bormia, I leave one-tenth of my fortune, such that..."

She looked down at the gardens and saw him walking there with her in the early mornings, sweat cooling from the exertions of their daily sport.

"...my step-daughter Carolyn, one-tenth of my fortune..."

She remembered when her father had first settled upon this

house. It'd been known as Lindenhall, named for something to do with its previous owners of House Premroe. And though it was still called Lindenhall, they had made it so very much their own. Aideen was but twelve years old when they'd moved from their modest home in the Inner City to this grand house. In some ways, she still thought of the old house as home, though. Her childhood memories were all there. And alongside them, the stories Davin told her about her mother.

Saira had died in childbirth, only living in that house for a few months. But to hear Davin speak of her there, how fierce were their hopes of a love and a life together there, that Aideen could almost feel her mother's spirit still dwelling in those oak paneled walls, hear her soft bare feet walking down hallways and singing to Aideen in the womb.

"...my step-son Riann, one-tenth of my fortune. In addition, I name him as my successor at the Bormia Trading Company, in accordance with the division of shares listed below..."

They had been happy there. Her father had doted on her, pouring his love into her upbringing. If it had not been for her uncle, Saira's brother Lodai, Aideen would have turned out completely spoiled. Lodai had been the balance against Davin's indulgence.

"...and this subset of shares to be divided amongst my investors as dividends on the trust they placed in me..."

The company had luck upon luck, and when they moved into Lindenhall, Davin had catered to Aideen's every whim. Furniture and wall hangings and draperies were debated over and the result of a child's tastes had been eclectic. The fountains had already been in the gardens. But the statues had been commissioned by their special request. They'd spent every weekend for months wandering the city seeking out artisans of all walks, from the famed to the undiscovered working in the Lower City.

"...and remaining shares to be divided between the captains

of Bormia Trading Company ships, at an even distribution for the first half, and the remainder based on seniority not to exceed..."

The playing courts, too, had been a whim. Aideen had never even played, but had seen some children once in the streets of the Lower City playing handball, and had joined in. Davin had told her there was a form of the game played in the Upper City, and for her birthday surprised her by having the courts laid out. They'd played every morning since. As Davin's life running the company had gotten busier, their mornings together had remained sacred. It was their sanctuary.

She thought of Davin's voice. Of that barely there accent when he spoke elvish, and how he'd never been able to lose it entirely. It had been their secret language over the years. Even in a room full of people, they could speak in complete privacy. Like they had their own secret world, all to themselves, whenever they wished it.

"...to my daughter Aideen, my dearest child and my blood, I leave one half of my fortune, as well as Lindenhall..."

Aideen shook her head with a grimace. She didn't want this empty house. She didn't want wealth. She didn't want the lavish lifestyle they had so easily slipped into simply because they could. How she would give it all up to have him back again. A fortune was nothing without him. They could play handball in the streets. They could wander the city and take in its wonders and artistry without ever owning the smallest piece of it. They could live together in a hovel down in Pigtown or by the docks, and wonder at the beauty of the sunset over the harbor and how it lit the fluttering sails of the ships creaking through the evening tide. They could read all the books in the great Sona library.

"...for both my daughters, their fortunes shall be held in trust until marriage to a man of stature. While this is customary in Elora, I reiterate my intentions here for the benefit of my daughter Aideen. I know you are strong-willed and independent, and I want to ensure you do not let your nature stand in the way of your long-term happiness and security. Riann will oversee the trust of both his sisters until they are married, and shall see to the household of Lindenhall until Aideen marries."

Aideen barely heard the words anymore. She and Davin were playing handball in the streets, dirty and poor and happy like so many others who lived on the edges of Sona.

# 8

# BORN OF TWO BLOODS

There was a knock at Aideen's bedchamber door. She lay in her bed, propped up on pillows and staring absently at the ceiling. She'd gone down to breakfast that morning, and then returned to her bed after only a few bites. She could not bear the chatter at the breakfast table, and thus returned to the dim and quiet solitude of her chambers.

"Come," Aideen called.

The door opened, and Master Lodai stood at the foot of her bed. His face was placid as always, and difficult to read. "You are late for your lessons, *jen youn*."

"I haven't been in much mood for lessons, Uncle," she said.

"Your lessons are not optional, child."

"I am not a child anymore."

"You are a child!" the man thundered. Aideen sat up in bed in surprise. "And you will address your teacher with respect until you prove yourself otherwise."

*"Manada pay'don, dai onora,"* Aideen said in a small voice.

"I do not come here for apologies," Lodai said. "Dress yourself and come down for your lesson. Wrench yourself from your bed, *timaoen*."

*"W'ei, dai onora."*

Aideen got out of bed as her uncle left the room, feeling shaken by his tone. She dressed in her leathers and chain shirt. She did not feel like swordplay today. She did not feel like being questioned. And yet she obeyed her uncle, taking up the bag that held her various sparring blades and walking down to the gardens.

Lodai waited for her there. Without a word, he drew his *l'onta n'epe*. Aideen drew her own and, without preamble, launched herself at him with it.

She fell into the fight like a dance. She watched his movements and his blade, the subtle variances of grip, the minute glancing of his emerald eyes, the nearly invisible twitches of muscles that forecast his next move. She watched, she assessed, and she responded. They spun around each other, two dancers moving fluidly to the rhythm of steel ringing out against steel, the muted scuffs of their shoes on the flagstones and their even breathing filling the spaces between that crazed staccato beat.

Master Lodai moved from style to style as they fought, almost predictable in his constant changing of stances and techniques. Aideen matched him style for style. There were no questions today, she mused dimly. He was speaking only with his body and blade. She preferred it. Aideen sought no advantage, merely matching his energies and exertions to maintain a kind of stalemate. She feigned, she attacked, she pressed and retreated and flitted around his sword.

Master Lodai withdrew. "You fight differently today."

"Pray tell me, what am I doing wrong now?"

"Nothing and everything, *timaoen*. You are distant. You are emotionless. You fight like an elf."

"Then you should be pleased. You've spent most of my life trying to teach me to fight like an elf."

"No," Lodai said, holding his sword before him and beginning to circle once more. "I have spent your whole life teaching you to fight better than one." He swept forward, his blade spinning in a dizzying pattern of blows. Aideen gritted her teeth and leaned into the attack, controlling the momentum of it. "Show yourself!" Lodai cried. "Your father is dead!"

Aideen did not falter her cadence, but the words shocked her. "What?"

"Your father is dead, child!" Lodai circled her, his steel pointing at her in accusation. "Show yourself!"

"I know he's dead," she spat back at him, her blade grinding coarsely against his as she shoved him back. "Do you mean to mock me? To goad me into a mistake?"

"He is dead!" Lodai cried, flying toward her. "He was a good man! A just man! A kind man! And yet you stand here dishonoring him!"

*"Fou t'ez!"* Aideen cried, staggering back, his words now putting her on her heels.

"You dishonor him, I said! Fight me! Show yourself to me!"

Aideen's mind reeled. "I don't understand you, you wretch!"

"Your father is dead, and it is not fair." Lodai punctuated his words with the strikes of his blade. "Not fair to the world. Not fair to his friends. Not fair to those who loved him. And now look how you dishonor him so!"

"Shut your fucking mouth!" Aideen cried. She flung herself at her uncle, smashing against his defenses, her sword crashing like wave after wave upon the shore, beating and grinding until stone turned to sand. "I do not dishonor my father! I love my father!" Aideen hammered and twisted until she found the gap and exploited it. She knocked his sword wide, then pivoting, cut a savage gash in his arm even with the dulled edge of the blade. Lodai faltered for a moment. Aideen screamed, smashing his face with the hand that held her sword. There was a heavy crunch, the sound of bone and cartilage popping, Lodai's nose giving way beneath her clenched fist and the weight of the blade it held. His knees buckled.

Lodai was on the ground, his sword lost somewhere on the flagstones nearby. Aideen had a knee on his chest, the edge of her sword against his throat. Blood soaked the arm of his shirt, and flowed from his twisted nose. "There now, child," he said calmly through the blood and the spittle in his mouth. "There are your tears. There is your humanity."

Aideen blinked. Her face was hot with rage, her eyes wet.

"Your tears honor him. Your anger honors him. You are human, child, and you must feel as one does. As your father did. Davin is dead, and it is an injustice that is proper to rage against. Your elven blood runs deep and cold and calm. But you cannot retreat into one half of yourself to spare the other your pain. You are of two natures, child. And you must embrace them both."

Aideen's sword fell to the ground. Aideen followed shortly after it, rolling off the broken form of her uncle and collapsing to the flagstones as sobs wracked her body. The pain came on as a flood now, bursting forth from some place deep inside her. The hurt was pure and senseless and clawed at her heart, digging at her insides horribly, tearing angry ragged wounds. Aideen could not breathe. The tears poured down her fevered cheeks and mucus ran from her nose disgracefully, mixing with her tears in her sleeve as she covered her face and hid from Lodai and the world. She wept dreadfully, curled upon the flagstones in her chain and leathers, moaning and sobbing with grief. She was oblivious even to shame.

How much time passed, she could not tell. She lay in the cocoon of her anguish and misery, her mind void of any semblance of coherent thought. Eventually, however, she began to feel drained. Her sobs slowed and her eyes dried, red and aching. The pain still clawed at her, but the seizure of it all had passed for the moment. She sat up, finding Master Lodai sitting on a bench nearby, his arm bandaged with the torn hem of his shirt but his nose still twisted.

"Welcome to your *renan'de, charr m'wen*. You are a child no longer. Do you understand my meaning now? Of what I have been trying to teach you for so long?"

Aideen looked at him, feeling spent. Her head throbbed. "Of two natures?"

"Yes. In elven, it is *ke'i gen de'san*. Literally, a child of two bloods. While it is a slur, it is an accurate one."

"I don't know *renan'de*. A tearing?"

"A rending into two things. It was inevitable, and I have been waiting for it to happen. You are elf, and you are human. The result of this mix usually manifests near adulthood. It is a second coming of age that is unique to your rare kind. I have heard it described as becoming two people, as both sides fully manifest. Two natures warring for control of the mind. You are the calm waters of your elven blood. And yet you are the flaming passions of your humanity. You must not choose. You must not favor one nature over the other. To be true to yourself is to embrace them both."

Aideen dragged herself to her feet and walked over to the fountain. She washed her face there. She felt better, somehow. Better even though she hurt, even though those ragged gashes in her heart were throbbing in her chest. She felt more herself now, and yet still different.

This had been new, she realized. For years now, Lodai had been trying to teach her to unlock those calm, cool waters. They had always seemed so distant. She simply was who she was, which seemed to be just like any human. She'd had glimmers before, those accidental moments where the world peeled back before her eyes and she saw with a kind of slow calm, a greater clarity. When she felt, but distantly by comparison, where feelings were ripples instead of tidal waves, and could be savored or ignored as the situation warranted. Usually, only when she practiced the Songs. But since that awful night in the study, she had somehow submerged herself in the placid streams and hidden from the conflagration of feeling that raged above the surface.

"I think I understand. Although I do not know how to tell you that I do. It is something hard to explain. Words do not capture it well."

"And thus it had always been that I struggled to teach you," Lodai smiled gently at her.

"I am sorry about your nose."

Lodai touched at it, flinching slightly. "Had I realized that letting you break it would bring you such insight, I would have let you do it years ago."

"I would have thought it was one of your tricks."

He smiled at Aideen. "Teaching you has not been easy. You are only the second child of mixed blood I have ever known."

Aideen sat down on the edge of the fountain, curiosity rising above the throbbing of her head and aching in her heart. "You have never told me of another."

"Indeed, I have not. I have been waiting for your *renan'de*, so that you might understand it better. You have slipped through these past days submerged in your cool waters, and only when I goaded you did your fiery half emerge. So perhaps you can grasp it." He hesitated for a moment. "Yes, yes I suppose so. Tell me, child. Why did I travel with my sister, your mother, from *Dorr aeille s'afae* to this land of Men?"

"To protect her. And to be the tutor of her child."

"True, but there is a further context. Elves do not conceive easily, as you know. Our lives are long, and so are our generations. Children of mixed blood are especially rare. The two races so rarely couple as it is, but offspring is almost unheard of. And yet, whether through chance or a trait of heritage, it has happened twice in as many generations in our family. Your grandmother bore two elven children—Saira and myself. But she also bore a *ke'i gen de'san* many years before. Her name was Kiva. And her journey to understand her two natures was… tumultuous."

"I have never before heard her name spoken," Aideen said. "I had no idea I had an aunt."

"That is because her story is sad and shameful. The same two natures that war within you warred within her. She was able to understand her two natures faster than you have, but not without difficulty. She was a brilliant student in all things. History. Swordplay. Magic. But her heart was also dark at times. Her rending did not leave her as she had been before. She was like two different people, one kind and well meaning. And the other..." he sighed and closed his eyes. "She saw injustice in the world around her," Lodai said at last. "Some correctly and some I would argue less so. And she sought to correct these injustices. She committed crimes, Aideen. She caused horrific harm to come to many in her madness. And for these crimes, she was banished from the elven lands."

Lodai paused for a long moment, his face falling with a sudden pang of sorrow. "Madness is said to be common in *ke'i gen de'san*. I knew my sister, and did not believe her truly mad. I believed that we failed her. We failed to prepare her for her Rending. We failed in trying to raise her simply as an elf, rather than what she was. And we failed because she was raised in a society that saw her as something less than others. Her life was one of isolation. That is why I came here with Saira. And why your father and I insisted you be presented to Sona as fully human, to prevent such an isolation, at least until you were grown. That is why I swore to your dying mother that I would be your teacher, to try to help you understand who you are even if I cannot fully fathom it. To do better for you than we did for your aunt."

"Why have I never been told this?"

"Would you tell a child her teacher is watching to be sure she is not growing mad?" Lodai laughed.

"I suppose that is fair."

"You are slightly mad, of course." Lodai smiled. "I think that is, perhaps, inevitable for a child of mixed blood. But your heart is kind."

"I had a good teacher."

"You had a good father," Lodai said. "But none of this is enough. Kiva was good as well. At the start. But all have capacity for evil. And she fell onto a dark path, justifying her sins in the name of a greater good. One wrong turn at a time."

Aideen nodded. "*Pouv'oua*."

"*Pouv'oua*," Lodai agreed.

## 9

## ARRANGEMENTS

Deidre was wringing her hands around a handkerchief, kneading fingers into themselves and the cloth. Aideen watched her from across the drawing room, wondering why she didn't go into the kitchens and put all that hard work to good use against some sort of bread dough. Her stepmother looked more frazzled than she'd ever seen her before. Her face was creased with worry marks, the normally mild haughtiness that marked her brow replaced with new furrows as she fretted.

Deidra seemed to have aged considerably in the past weeks since Davin's death. The veil of mourning was long gone, though. And Deidra had returned to her usual dress and adornment—the gay colors, the jeweled necklace, and the open toed shoes with brightly painted toenails that spoke of her home country in Lyramae. The cheerfulness of it all was quite the counterpoint to the shadow across her face. Aideen watched her patiently, crossing her legs in the chair opposite her and waiting to see why she had been summoned.

"I'm sorry, child. I don't exactly know how to begin," Deidre said. "This was a conversation your father was supposed to be having with you, and I'm a poor surrogate for it. Only a month ago, it wouldn't have been my place. And yet, now here we are."

Aideen merely looked at her and waited. There was nothing she could do to spare her stepmother the awkwardness of whatever this was. So, she simply sat, watching the hands at their nervous kneading.

"Well, there's no point in dallying about it, I suppose. It's about marriage, dear. Your father had been discussing the possibility of your marriage to Lord Cathal, you see…"

*"Fa'tra oute s'di?"* Aideen exclaimed.

"I'm sorry?" Deidre looked at her, seemingly shaken and confused by the sudden outburst of Elvish.

Aideen shook herself. "Do you honestly wish to speak of marriage right now? In the midst of our family's despair?"

"I know, dearest. I do not wish to be insensitive. But it has been many weeks, and at some point life must go on. I am just trying to do right by your father's wishes. He had been preparing to speak to you on the matter in his very final days, you see. Lord Cathal had come to him to ask for his blessing."

"Lord Gwenhert had made no indications of such an intent with me."

"Hadn't he?" Deidre said, smiling. "It was plain enough to the rest of us how he looked at you, fully knowing the mutterings it caused within his own family. I hear the two of you walked off alone for quite some time at the unveiling of that flying contraption. He has clearly been testing the waters, dear. Not only with you, but to see what society in Sona might think and say."

Aideen closed her eyes. "Perhaps," she admitted. "Carolyn certainly thought so, but I had dismissed it. I thought it more of a dalliance on his part than anything serious. A few dances and a few conversations is hardly a courtship. And yet…" Aideen trailed off. And yet, it was hard to deny there was not at least the first flickering of a spark between them.

"Lord Gwenhert was your father's friend, and spoke to him first about his intentions. You cannot be surprised by that much, at least."

"I suppose not, but it shocks me that father did not speak to me about it. He obviously spoke to you about it. We kept no secrets. If he had intended me to marry Lord Gwenhert, why was I not included in this discussion?"

"You were to be! Very shortly, in fact. Your father had been thinking through the situation, dear. There are many things to consider, as you well know. A noble marrying outside the lines of nobility is not without precedent, but it is unusual. And then there is the issue of your elven heritage. Davin wanted to have time to ponder it all before speaking to you. What all it might mean for you, for the family. He wanted to be able to properly advise you in this, as a good father should."

Aideen sat quietly for a while. Her stepmother was still speaking, but Aideen had ceased listening to her. Marriage had been the farthest thing from her mind only a handful of minutes ago, no matter how often Carolyn and Deidre had pressed her on the issue before. And now? She tried to search her feelings and she found them messy. But perhaps she could entertain the thought. Marriage. It was madness, wasn't it? But it would mean some new purpose in life. Children of her own, to care for as her father had cared for her. She could sing to them, as Saira had never had the chance to do for her daughter. She could love again. Open her heart again. Lord Gwenhert seemed a good man, and the idea of marrying him was certainly not without its charms. But even so, would the idea have even crossed her mind had others not been attempting to plant it there?

"... on that dreadful night of his passing, he was, in fact, up late studying elven customs on such matters, so that when he spoke to you about this he wanted to be sure that..."

"Thank you, mother," Aideen interrupted, standing up from her chair. "I understand, and I have some thinking to do. In the meantime, please send word to Lord Cathal that I would like him to come visit us at Lindenhall. He and I should speak on the matter. There should be no further mediations in between if he seeks an answer from me."

Deidra's face lit up, her hands ceasing their ridiculous kneading. "Oh, wonderful!"

Lord Cathal Gwenhert stepped into the foyer of Lindenhall with less than his usual self-assured swagger. Why, he looked nervous! Aideen thought with a little thrill. The family came forward together and presented itself with their pleasantries. "How lovely to have you here, my lord," Deidre said with a sweeping bow. "You honor us."

"Thank you," Lord Gwenhert said. His face was solemn, his back stiff. "I have not wanted to disturb your family since Davin's passing. Your family has my deepest regrets. In truth, I wondered how being here would make me feel, now that Lindenhall has such a vacancy in its heart."

"You are very kind," Deidre said graciously.

"You are certainly always welcome here," Riann said, stepping forward and clasping hands with Lord Cathal. Since the passing of Davin and the naming of Riann as his successor in the company, Lord Cathal had taken it upon himself to assist Riann in learning some of the complexities of running such a large endeavor. The assistance had been much appreciated, for the same accountants and advisors who served Davin now served Riann, and the young man appeared to them as unbelievably capable when his spare time was spent in study with a Master of Ships for a noble house.

"A pleasure, as always," Carolyn bowed with a broad smile

on her face. "Although, all pleasantries aside, we all know you're truly only here to see the one of us. And I can assure you, we all welcome you here with spirited hearts!"

"Carolyn!" Deidre said, her eyes cutting over at her daughter.

"It's quite alright," Lord Cathal said with a small smile. "I would expect nothing less than such plain honesty from Carolyn. Truth be told, I wish more people in my circles spoke plainly as to their intentions. Although it would eliminate the need for so many politicians, which my uncles and cousins might oppose. But it is as you say, my dear. I have come in hopes of having a private conversation with your sister, if you will all permit me to be so forward."

"Of course," Deidre said. "Perhaps you two can speak in the drawing room just this way, and the rest of us can join you presently?"

"Perhaps my lord would take a walk with me in the gardens?" Aideen offered. "We haven't many autumn days left to enjoy before winter robs us of all color."

"A walk sounds marvelous." He offered her his arm, and Aideen took it with an easy smile.

As soon as Aideen and Lord Cathal were out of the room, the family could be heard chattering in excited voices. The young couple looked at each other, and both laughed. "My family is rather a mess," Aideen said.

"All families are in their own way."

"You seem nervous."

"Do I?"

"It is a new look for you, my lord. Perhaps Carolyn's honesty is rubbing off on me."

"On the contrary, you have never needed much prodding in matters of honesty."

"And so?"

"And so, perhaps we walk a while. Let me see if I can leave the nervousness behind."

"Then I shall lead the way. These gardens are wonderful for forgetting yourself. Or remembering yourself, for that matter."

"Perhaps we should do one, and then the other."

"In which order, my lord?"

"I suppose we shall see."

They wandered through the gardens in silence for a while, feeling the cool afternoon breeze on their faces. The autumn wind warned them of winter, and it blew strongly today in the Upper City above the rest of Sona below. The dogwoods were a blaze of color, their final defiant cry before a winter's death reduced those reaching arms of pink and orange to empty, boney fingers. Aideen's fingers were warm where they tucked into the crook of his arm, and she walked with her shoulder lightly against him to see how it felt. The path meandered, and they meandered with it, the silence between them growing thick. She could feel him looking down at her, and she occasionally met his eyes.

They came to a fountain, and she felt him hesitate. She anticipated he would turn to her, but instead he stooped down on one knee. Well, this is dramatic, Aideen thought biting back a nervous smile.

"Is this blood?"

Aideen looked where he knelt, and then laughed. He looked at her, confusion washing across his face. Aideen laughed harder. "I'm sorry," she said, trying to control herself. "Yes, it's blood. And your confusion is understandable."

"I don't understand," he said, still kneeling over the stained flagstones.

"Everyone is fine. That blood belongs to one of my tutors."

"You say that as if it explains things."

"Swordplay," Aideen said, still giggling. "I got a little overzealous a few days ago with my training partner. He's fine, though. And the next rain will clean these flagstones if a gardener doesn't get to it first."

Lord Cathal stood, dusting the knee of his trousers. "You know, I'd heard rumors you practiced fencing."

"Not fencing," Aideen corrected. "I do not play at scoring points while confined to a lane, as I know many nobles do. No offense to that sport."

"I see!" Lord Gwenhert shook his head in surprise. "And are you any good?"

"Oh, I'm quite deadly," Aideen replied. "That is the blood of an elven swordmaster. It could be from the cut I gave his arm. Or it could be from his broken nose. It is hard to say."

Lord Cathal was still shaking his head. "Aren't you just full of surprises."

"I try not to be too predictable. One might get too comfortable with me."

He took a step closer to her, his eyes softening as he did. He took her hands. His touch made the breath catch in her chest. "I suppose I had better get on with my courage, then. It isn't as though you don't know what I'm here to ask you."

Aideen pulled away from him. "I do know, my lord. And before you ask, I owe you some more honesty."

"Oh?" The playful glint was back in his eyes.

"I mean it. I would rather give you the option of not speaking your mind than to put you in the position to take words back. It is kinder to the both of us."

The smile on his face faded to uncertainty, but Cathal nodded. He took a step back and sat down on the bench where Lodai usually waited for her. "Please, then. Speak your honesty."

Aideen drew a deep breath. She had never revealed her secret to anybody before. Her father had, out of necessity, to some of the servants. Kayla. The family's doctor. But Aideen had never had to be the one to speak of it first.

"My father, you knew well. And you know his first wife, my

mother, died many years ago, during childbirth. But it is important that you know who my mother was."

"I know that your father is the son of a tailor. That he rose quickly aboard a ship of House Premroe. That through his cunning and bravery when attacked by pirates in the Dirk Isles, he saved the lives of many aboard. And that the small wealth he was rewarded with he used to secure a loan for his first ship, underwritten by that same house. The Dragonfly, which still sails today. I am not concerned with the humble beginnings of your family. The ability of a man to exceed the station of his birth is supposed to be the dream of Elora."

"Not humble," she corrected. "But something else entirely. My mother's name was Saira. *S'aira eilia ti'fle n'an twa rivye*. They met when my father traveled to *Dorr aeille s'afae*." Aideen watched the countenance of Lord Cathal shift as he comprehended her words and their implications. "So just to be clear, that means that I am half human, my lord. And half elf."

Her words hung heavy in the air as his face went through a rapid succession of emotions before her eyes. "Truly?" he said softly, looking up at her from the bench, his forehead still furrowed in disbelief.

"Truly," Aideen said. She felt her heart pounding in her chest. The nakedness she felt at exposing her secret like this was unnerving.

Lord Gwenhert stood and walked over to her. His face was still a contortion of mixed emotions. His eyes searched hers, then she saw him studying her anew. Her face. Her hair. Her hidden ears. Aideen blushed and looked away. "I suppose I always knew there was something exotic in your beauty," he said softly. The gentle tone of his voice caused her eyes to rise once again to meet his. "You have managed to keep this secret to yourself your whole life."

"Only my family and our servants knew."

"Until just now."

"Until just now."

"It must have been lonely for you, hiding a part of yourself from the world."

Aideen felt her throat tighten at his words. "At times."

Cathal took her hands. "And now with your father..." His voice trailed off, and he shook his head. "Perhaps you needn't be alone anymore."

Her heart swelled at his words, at possibilities impossible to fathom. Her mind reeled under a torrent of emotions. She shied away from the piercing look in his eyes.

"May I see? Your ears, I mean. Is that impolite to ask? I'm afraid I am outside of the normal bounds of etiquette, my dear."

"It's alright," she said in a small voice. "I can show you."

Aideen plucked at the pins that held her hair into their usual buns. It was a dozen per side. Then, inserting her fingers under their spirals, she shook them loose. Her hair fell down between her fingers and she pushed it back, tucking it behind her ears, exposing their curving, pointed tips. Her hands were shaking. She felt more exposed than she had ever felt in her life.

Lord Gwenhert stepped forward, and Aideen struggled to meet his gaze. His hand caressed the nape of her neck, gingerly pushing back her hair, the edge of his thumb brushing against her exposed ear. Aideen shuddered beneath his touch. It was an intimacy she had not been prepared for. She felt naked before him, and her face grew hot. "And so you are," he said. "Tell me, Aideen Bormia. Are you hiding anything else? Are you still Aideen, the same spirited young woman I met only a few months past? Are you still the bold and independent woman who is unafraid to speak her mind? Are you still the Aideen who danced with me? Who looked at me in that sparkling way, oblivious while the whole room whispered?"

"I hide nothing else from you," Aideen breathed.

He took both of her hands in his once more. "Then if you

would have me, I am certain that you would make me very happy."

"Even still?"

"Even still."

"Our children would likely bear the signs of an elven heritage," Aideen said, hardly believing what she was hearing. Or what she was saying. "It is not easy to hide, I can assure you."

"Then on that day, or perhaps before even, we would have to lay that secret bare as you have to me."

"What would the ramifications of such a revelation be?"

"Scandal, I suppose. Whispering. Grumbling. Many withdrawn invitations, I'm sure." Cathal blew out a breach and cast his eyes off into the distance for a long moment. "It will be complicated. I do not mean to diminish that fact in the slightest. You have kept this secret, and it will remain yours for as long as you deem it fit. Perhaps I am being flippant and have not fully thought this through. But you would still be Lady Gwenhert, pointed ears or not, and I cannot see how whispering or complaining by others should dampen our happiness one bit."

"So it changes nothing for you?"

"No, it changes a great many things. But it does not change my heart's purpose. You have stricken me like no other woman has before, as I never imagined possible. I came here today to ask for your hand in marriage. Nothing will deter me from that course. And here I am before you, asking. Will you be my wife?"

Aideen felt the warmth in his eyes blossom in her heart. She did not hesitate in her answer.

# PART II

*The forces of magic are seen as some sort of mysticism by the uninitiated. But magic is just the movement of energies. All energy must come from somewhere. All energy must go somewhere. And so when a wizard casts a spell, he is simply transferring energies from one place in the cosmos to another. It is no different than drawing a bucket of water from the river and fetching it up a hill. This has little effect on the river. A dam on the river is quite another matter, however, and there are those who through great will or coordination may channel energies such that may plunge a world into chaos. We can only guess at what the true consequences might be.*

*Gaia exists to maintain the balance of the cosmos, offering a pathway between worlds to keep equilibrium. But the Shards cut both ways. In the wrong hands, they pose a risk to existence itself.*

FROM THE FORGING OF THE TALAVARA IN THE SECOND AGE, BY THE SYANI LEANNA GWENHERT

## 10

## THE WIZARD

The Misty Sea did not take its name lightly. For days or even weeks at a time, the skies would be shrouded in heavy fog that blanketed the waters and suffocated the ships that dared them. No sun, no stars to navigate by. A captain was left to aim his ship as best he could at the outset as he plunged into the mist, and then cling to instinct on holding it straight until a glimmer of sky could be seen once more. The waters here were a deep green, and far rougher than any in the East. The Dragonfly lurched as it pounded against the sea, the bow nodding wildly as they rattled and jounced through turbulent waters. Few ships attempting these seas were ever seen again. It was a curious thing that the Dragonfly had crossed it safely so many times. There was nothing special about the ship. But nobody had ever seen fit to question why it remained so lucky.

Hamfast had fastened a rope to the ceiling of his kitchen so he always had something to hold on to in these waters—even if it sent him swinging occasionally. Peas and barley simmered in a pot with root vegetables and herbs and the barest amount of water. He would thin it out just before serving into something more like a soup, but for now he wanted to be sure some crazed wave didn't slosh his pot all over the floor. Hamfast stood on one of his nailed-down stools, one hand holding the rope and another holding onto the huge pot lid, securing the whole apparatus in place. Just in case.

They were six weeks at sea. Three weeks since they had last seen the sky. They may still be on course, or they may be headed for the edge of the world. The officers of the Dragonfly were talented, but Hamfast could not help being nervous. When he'd made a similar journey before, they were at least aiming this ship at a continent. Now they were aiming at an island not on any maps, and no maps showed anything beyond it except the sketches of grotesque sea serpents and the vast unknown. One could not help imagining these green misty waters stretching on forever, and when they had no choice but to turn back home, having a poor idea of which way that was.

After serving the men that evening, Hamfast made his regular delivery to the lower hold, where their bizarre cargo dwelled. The wizards had only come out above decks a handful of times, and then only to vomit over the rails. Hamfast brought meals to the wizards thrice daily, after he had served all others and seen to the kitchen after. Each time, one of the purple robed men opened the door and took the tray, and Hamfast would try to peek into the dark room behind him. It was full of strange-looking devices, metal rods attached to one another at all manner of odd angles, faintly glowing crystals that looked somewhat like the glowlamps of Sona, jars filled with a range of substances that were hard to make out but were certainly not spices. Tonight, rather than the door creaking open to reveal a curiously green face beneath a purple robe, his knock was answered with a voice calling, "Ah, yes! Please, come in!"

Hamfast hesitated for a moment, then opened the door. Inside, he saw only the blue robed man. He was hunched over the table that occupied the middle of the room. The table was strewn with books and papers, the curled edges of old parchment scrolls held down by an eclectic scatter of ink wells and candleholders and small glowing crystals.

"Ah! If it isn't the diminutive bearer of sustenance!" The wizard straightened on his stool and studied Hamfast. "I had just been pondering what internal state was so askew, and lo it seems my day has fallen into chronological disarray. Of course, it would be the state of appetence! Come, come. Bring the nourishment hence." He cleared a spot on the table, causing the papers to bunch and pile up in an even greater jumble as he did so.

"I have dinner for three, but I see only one of you," Hamfast said, laying the platter down and giving the wizard a wide berth.

"Truly? I am only in the habit of sustaining a singular form. There must have been a misunderstanding."

Hamfast blinked. "There are normally three of you."

"Is that the perception? How peculiar! A strange illusion, indeed." The wizard left his stool, scratching his chin deep within his beard. "It must be the side effect of the protection enchantments. But no, such a spell should not produce such an effect. Unless it is somehow a trick of light upon the facets of the... no, no, that is impossible, the phrasing of it being a prism is merely a failure of language, the energies are neither material nor visible. So perhaps -"

"The purple wizards!" Hamfast interrupted, exasperated. "There aren't three of you in the singular. Three wizards in total."

"Ah!" The man slapped his belly with a chuckle. "Yes, well, that makes more sense. The others are above us getting some fresh air. I personally find it more pleasant here. The farther one traverses the ship in the positive vertical direction, you see, the farther you are from the center of mass, which only amplifies the motions of the ship. I cannot imagine how the man on the top of the mast manages to hold on, much less see anything."

"The waters here are too rough to send a lookout up," Hamfast agreed.

"Indeed! It is folly to try it at all. Too risky. A series of mirrors would serve you better. If mounted in a tube along the mast, the angles would provide you the vision sought. Then, you would only need to send a man up to clean off the mirror on occasion. One might even mount it in such a way that it could rotate, although such mechanical feats are beyond the scope of my study."

Hamfast stared at the wizard blankly, not understanding him in the least. "Pea and barley soup, Master. Can I get you anything else? There is yet some wine reserved, which you and your companions have not touched."

"Please, call me Whitaker. Whitaker Premroe, Master of Bedakhali, preeminent scholar on abjuration, evocation, and history of *sarada* and their respective *cakara*."

"Hamfast Hilltopple, master of the kitchen here. Is there anything else you need?" Hamfast was already walking backwards to leave.

"A Lindle!"

"I..." Hamfast blinked. "Yes, I am."

"I once read a theory that Lindle are more closely related to the elves than men. There are no records of a successful mating between humans and Lindle. While I imagine that is more a matter of geometry, one must imagine that some have at least tried. Then again, there are no records of Lindle and elves successfully mating, either. But it is curious, don't you think?"

"It could be that we Lindle simply aren't attracted to creatures that look nothing like us."

"Oh, quite the contrary. You appear much like men, only diminutive. Shrunken in many proportions, similar to a human child. But you have much longer lifespans. Meanwhile, those humans who are born deformed and small like Lindle often have dramatically shortened lifespans. I find that quite curious. What do you think?"

"I'm sorry. What do I think about what?" Hamfast had never wanted to escape a conversation more than this one.

"About where you Lindle come from?!"

Hamfast blinked. "My people are from Elora. We long predate the arrival of men on the continent, though there are few of us left outside of Reseda. Before men arrived, we were -"

"Yes, but all races must come from somewhere. Humans, elves, dwarves, goliaths, orcs, giants. All have two arms, two legs, two eyes. If I handed you a clay model of one, you'd have little trouble changing it into another. A little stretching here and there, a few pokes about the face, and you'd have it. Now, if I handed you a clay horse or fish, you'd need to be a sculptor to turn that into a man or an elf. No, they all most certainly came from somewhere. A first race. Or a common ancestor."

"Perhaps we came from clay, then. I must be getting back to my kitchen, Master Whit -"

"What? Are you mad? You cannot make a man from clay. Not even with magic. It lacks the basic component structures!"

"The dwarves tell stories that the first of their kind were carved of stone by the gods. They, too, were in Elora long before men."

"Bah! Stories. Mythologies. They tell you much, but only about the cultures that perpetrate them."

"I really must be going."

"Have you even met a dwarf?"

"Many times. I've sailed to the four continents."

"Ah, of course. A traveler! Fascinating. All four, you say?"

"Indeed."

"Well, there are more than four, but that hardly matters. I myself have never left Sona."

"What?!" Hamfast started. He looked from the wizard to the scatter of documents and maps strewn around the room. "Then how do you know this island exists?" The idea that they were following the whims of an untraveled madman now clawed at him.

"Because I've spent most of my life looking for it. Taking measurements. Studying scraps of histories before history. Chasing down rumors to find their origins! The Circle may have been lost, and the reasons may remain a mystery, but the where? Oh oh!" Whitaker wagged a finger at him. "But the where, my dear Lindle, I am certain I have discovered."

"What Circle?"

"Ah, yes. I suppose the crew would not know what we seek." He stroked his beard in musing. "Quite right. That is as it should be. The upmost secrecy, this mission must remain. Our destination even a mystery!"

"We all knew the destination." Hamfast said. "If this mission was supposed to be secret, then someone probably should have told the crew that."

"Well, it couldn't be helped. You commoners are not usually accustomed to dealing with secrets, I suppose. And this, oh this one. No, it is more than the common man can comprehend. The power of a Shard! Oh, I myself can hardly fathom it."

"A Shard? Like the one in Sona?"

"What?" Whitaker gasped.

"The... Shard?" Hamfast was now more confused than ever. "The one that the Syani keep? That powers all the magic in Sona?"

"How do you know of the Shard?!" Whitaker was now wide-eyed, backing away from him.

"Everyone knows. I mean, we don't know how it works. Or what it really is, I suppose. But we all know there's something called the Shard in the Great Spire of Sona. And that the glowlamps, the skycarriages, all those things are only possible in Sona because of it."

"Everyone knows? That is preposterous," Whitaker spat. "The Heart Shards are a closely held secret. Their mysteries are kept from all but the highest orders. Not even the Assembly or the House of Lords knows of their existence."

Hamfast pinched the bridge of his nose in frustration. "You're not listening. I don't know anything about a heart shard. I don't know a goddamn thing about how it works."

"They! How they work!"

"Right. Well, they. Apparently. All I know is that Sona runs on the magic of a Shard. You're telling me there's another like it? And that is what we're after? Another shard?"

"You confuse me, Lindle. You know too much, and yet you know so little. Are you a spy? Sent by the College to ensure our success? To gauge our aptitude for secrecy?"

"You honestly think the cook is a spy?"

"Ah! There it is!" Whitaker cried, raising a hand in triumph. "Ah, a devious trick, Master Hamfast. Was it Master Sherbert who sent you? The Queen? Was it Leanna? Ah, but I'm too clever for such games. I am on to you, sir! It was masterfully done, to be sure. Who are you, really?" Whitaker poked him in the chest, then on the top of his head and pinched his cheeks. Hamfast backed away quickly for the door. "You certainly look like a Lindle. And I can't detect a mote of magic about you. Oh, masterfully done indeed!"

A polite exit many times thwarted, Hamfast turned on his heel and ran from the room. Each night after, he left the tray at the door.

## 11

## THE TEACUP

Aideen opened the door to the study for the first time in over two months. The curtains were pulled back and the sunlight streaming through the windows caught a few glimmering motes of dust that rode on the tiny eddies of air disturbed by her opening the door. She had requested the room remained closed off and left alone by the servants after that horrible night.

She crept in cautiously, as if entering a tomb. The room felt sacred somehow, the last place her dear father had drawn breath. She hadn't dared come in here yet. The memory of finding him here, of seeing him dead and lifeless there on the floor, were too vivid. Even now, she saw flashes of that night, of the calm normalcy of the scene that held such a terrible secret when she'd first peeked inside. And then she saw his face, the flash of his cold eyes, and the memory drove ice into her heart. Aideen gasped and closed her eyes, pushing the memory down. But she didn't leave. She had to face this. It was time to lay the ghost to rest. It was time to move on with her life.

She walked slowly around the desk, half expecting to see the blank face of Davin on the floor behind it. But as she came around, there was only the continued pattern of the rug there. It should have been a relief, but Aideen saw it with a pang of sadness. She stood staring at the floor for a while, feeling silent tears roll down her cheeks. "By all the gods in the heavens," she whispered. "How I miss you. How I wish you were here with me again. I loved you so much that my heart can hardly bear it."

She sat down in the chair behind the desk. She had not seen it from this vantage point in many years. Back on Quill Street, she spent many an afternoon in his lap as he worked, surely more of a distraction than he had ever let on at the time. She would pester him with questions while he bent over ledgers or letters or receipts or maps. The desk had dominated the room in that house, unlike in this grand study. His books had overflowed the shelves and were stacked around the room in little pillars of knowledge, leather-bound stalagmites of fanciful stories and histories and bizarre volumes on subjects ranging from astronomy to Frendarian metal working.

The desk was neat now, which had never been his fashion. Several books were stacked in the corner of the desk, their bindings in a perfect line. His dip pen was cleaned and his ink bottle capped. The servants must have tidied up that night, as the whole house fretted. It must have been before Aideen told them to leave the room closed, she supposed. It all certainly had a film of dust and hadn't been disturbed since. Where did dust come from anyhow, she mused. Nobody in or out to track dirt from outside, and yet it found a way to fly about the house and settle on everything anyhow and require regular dusting. It was just like cobwebs, which never seemed to hold spiders. It was a mystery.

Aideen slipped off her shoes and sat cross-legged in her father's big leather chair, drying her cheeks with her sleeve. She ran her fingers through the dust on the desk and wondered what should become of this room now. She and Cathal had not discussed yet where they should reside. Lindenhall was the larger house of the two, but Lord Cathal's manor was grander in many other ways. Aideen was unsure of how she felt on the matter. This place had been home, but only for a while. If they lived here, she supposed this room could become a library. If not, it made sense for Riann to take this office. His mother and sister could live here with him, at least until some man agreed to marry Carolyn. The Bormia Company would certainly stay prosperous enough to continue Lindenhall's upkeep.

But what of the things here? The books Aideen would want to keep regardless. They had been her father's. Most of them had little pertinence to the business. And yet, everything was all bound together in her mind. The desk. The books. The room. How many evenings had she come in to tell him goodnight, only to see him behind this desk, in this room, reading one of these books? Occasionally with a pipe in hand, often sipping a glass of wine.

Of wine.

A glass of wine.

That was funny, she thought.

And then the thought exploded in her mind and sent her reeling.

Aideen shoved herself away from the desk in sudden horror, gasping and nearly toppling out of the chair. She found herself across the room, her shoulders wedged into the corner of the bookcases. She stared at the desk, her mouth agape.

There had been a teacup there.

Davin never drank tea in the evenings. It kept him awake, and he was an early riser. He barely drank tea in the mornings. He barely drank tea at all! Aideen took a deep breath and tried to calm herself. It was just a teacup. But the teacup in her memory from that night was perched on the desk like a bloody dagger. It meant something wasn't right in the room when Davin had died. That someone else had been there that night. A visitor? A witness? Nobody had spoken of a visitor that evening. Most of the family was out—most of the city was, in fact.

Look through your elven eyes, Lodai's voice whispered in her mind. See all without feeling, without prejudice. See all as it truly is. Your mind will catalogue every detail, whether you wish it to or not. You must only push past the humanity that clouds your sight.

Aideen walked in a wide circle around the desk, recalling back to her mind the scene of that night. The horrors of the scene rushed at her, of the cold, unseeing eyes staring up at the ceiling. Her father on the floor, a body instead of the man he'd been. She heard her own screams from that night, the anguish and horror she had felt. Aideen recoiled at the memory and everything it held. She closed her eyes and let herself feel it all, felt the tears well up in her eyes and her throat close, felt her breathing grow shallow.

And then she stepped back from her feelings, and let those waves settle into ripples. She opened her eyes, her cheeks still wet, and let the room peel back. She looked at the awful scene from a distance. She let her mind's eye step between the reality before her and the memories, comparing the dusty husk this room had become against all it had ever been.

That night the desk had a ledger open on it. There were papers there, scattered and pushed aside. A book lay open. The dip pen was sitting lazily on a piece of paper, an ink droplet from the pen marring the notes scribbled in Davin's hasty handwriting. And then there was the teacup. The papers, the book, the mess was normal. The teacup was the one thing out of place. Never before had there been a teacup on that desk. Not in all her memories.

What did it mean? Aideen began to pace around the room. Perhaps it was nothing. The teacup could have been there from earlier in the day. Although, no. That wasn't possible either, unless it had belonged to someone else. Davin had been down in

Dockside all day on business. He'd left straight from the breakfast table. Aideen walked over to the desk and stared down at where the teacup had been, seeing it as clearly as if it were there now. She saw cup and saucer, the same unremarkable ceramic as all the other teacups in the house. She saw the last inch of tea in the bottom, the tiny flecks settling there that had made it through the strainer, the faint ring around the edge of the cup that marked where the tea level had been before someone had drank it. "Who do you belong to?" Aideen wondered at the phantom cup.

Aideen left the study and walked around the manor, muttering to herself, sifting through her memories. She found various servants, and she questioned each of them as innocently as possible.

"Did Davin have any visitors on the night he died?"

"Did you bring Davin tea in his study? Ever?"

"Did you tidy up the study after Davin died? Do you remember cleaning up his desk?"

She was met with puzzled looks and the same series of answers. No, miss, no one called that night. No, Master Davin never had tea in his study that I can recall. No, we were told to leave the study as it was once the doctor came for Master Davin.

Aideen spent the day sitting in her father's chair, staring at the desk in front her, her fingers tracing patterns in the dust. Perhaps she'd read too many fantastical stories. Perhaps she was losing her mind over a gods damned teacup. But something was wrong. She could feel it in her bones. And that teacup was the key to discovering what it was.

She slept poorly that night, so when she sat down the next morning for breakfast, she had to dismiss questions from both Deidre and Carolyn regarding her health. "Your eyes are dreadfully puffy," Carolyn exclaimed. "You haven't taken up the bottle, have you? Surely engagement isn't all that stressful."

"I'm fine," Aideen insisted, taking a hot roll and trying to keep her voice even. A servant filled her teacup for her. Aideen stared down at it for a while. There was nothing special about this teacup, either. She sighed, drinking the tea to wake herself. She set her teacup down and took a bite of her buttered roll. And then she saw. There was a slight wet ring in her teacup. But it was wrong. Or rather, it was right, and the one that night had been wrong.

Aideen excused herself, ignoring the calls from her family at the breakfast table. She spent the rest of the morning shut in her father's study, deep in thought.

LODAI WAS NOT in the gardens when she arrived for her lessons. Aideen sat on his bench, her bag at her feet, and waited. She had much on her mind, and it did not occur to her for some time that she could not recall ever needing to wait for him. Had she lost track of time sitting in the study? Was she the one who was late? She took up her things and walked back to the house.

Aideen rapped on Lodai's door in the servants' quarters on the fourth floor. It was rare that she ever came to this part of the house. The male servants occupied the rooms along one hallway, the females on another. There was no answer from within. She put her ear to the door, and hearing no sounds from inside, let herself in.

The room was simply furnished. A bed, a chair, a dresser. But it was missing most of the things that made it her teacher's. There was no meditation mat beneath the window. There were only a few books left on the shelf beside the bed. A panic began to rise within her, and she ran into the room. Aideen flung open the dresser. She found it empty.

It made no sense! Aideen spun in circles, trying to take it all in, trying to make meaning of it. Trying to see something there, as she had in her father's study. Some clue. But all was a blur through tears in her eyes. Why would he leave? And why now, when she needed his counsel so desperately? The room did not peel back. There was only panic and confusion and a sense of overwhelming loneliness. She could not face this alone.

Aideen collapsed onto the bed and wept.

~

AIDEEN FOUND Deidre in the drawing room once she had composed herself. Deidre sat reading a book by the whispering crackles of the fire. Aideen cleared her throat, not so much to get her stepmother's attention as to be sure her voice would be steady.

Deidre looked up from her book. "Yes?"

"My tutor was not at lessons today." Aideen decided to keep it simple, hoping to keep the emotion from her voice.

"I know," Deidre said. "He has been dismissed."

Aideen sucked in breath. *"Fa'tra oute s'di?"*

Deidre smiled thinly. "Exactly. The family secret is not just ours now, but House Gwenhert's as well. I have never liked you cavorting around with that elf in the gardens, constantly blurting out elvish around the house, but Davin allowed it and I respected that. But now?" Deidre shook her head seriously. "Now we must tread carefully. The family will be under much scrutiny with the engagement, and keeping an elvish tutor about will do nothing but harm your attempts at secrecy. So, I did the prudent thing."

"You..." Aideen could hardly believe what she was hearing. "You had no right. This is not your household to command."

"No, it is Riann's. And he did the dismissing."

"Where did he go?"

"Where does any elf go in Sona? Who can say?" Deidre put her book down in her lap. "I knew you would be cross with me for it, but I hope you can eventually see that I did it in your best interest. He is gone now. And that is that."

She didn't know, Aideen thought. She thought him just a tutor. Just some elf we picked up for language lessons. And that the time spent in the gardens—the swordplay, the Songs, the interrogations, the prodding, the counsel—well, she knew of nothing but the language lessons and sparring. She knew nothing. And her view of it from the outside was worlds apart from the truth.

"You should have at least let me say goodbye."

"Better to have a clean break, my dear. I did not want you making a scene. And I know you won't make one now. You are an engaged woman, and your diversions should now be replaced with planning a wedding."

Aideen stared at her stepmother. Anger blossomed hot inside of her. It felt like that day in the gardens with Lodai, when rage had led her to smash his nose. There was something inside her that wanted to do the same now. Aideen entertained the thought for a long moment, her eyes fixed on Deidre as rage grew inside of her. She felt something deep in her belly begin to unfurl, like the fiery wings of a demon. She could feel the heat of those wings, could feel the dripping embers and ash falling from them. Beneath their cocoon was a beast awakening from a long slumber. Aideen peered out at Deidre through its molten eyes, and imagined...

No, Aideen thought. *Pouv'oua*. And with that thought, she merely firmed her jaw and quelled the turbulent anger that had begun to froth inside of her. Sucking in her breath, she spun around and left the room.

She would simply find him. Where do elves go in Sona, indeed?

∽

AIDEEN PULLED the hood of her cloak down over her head as she exited the skycoach. The carriage had settled on a quiet street on the north side of the Lower City. The streets here were far more crowded than any in the Upper City. People bustled about pushing carts, street vendors sold smoked meats and fresh bread, and every tiny building seemed to have two or three others stacked atop them. Where the Upper City was all broad and green and open, this was more like walking through a canyon of humanity.

Shops and houses and stables and storage warehouses were all mixed in together here, with apartment dwellings above many of them. Street sweepers were passing by her, half a dozen men forming a line that sang a cheery song as they walked, their brooms chuffing ahead of them. They paused every so often to shovel animal dung into a small cart, or push the dirt into grate-covered holes, which the rainwater would eventually wash through the sewers and into the sea. The people parted as the sweepers came. The song the sweepers sang reminded Aideen of her time on the Dragonfly, with the sailors singing as they worked. The thought gave her a pang of bittersweet nostalgia.

Guards patrolled the streets here, too, and although the denizens were cut of a rougher cloth, it never felt actually dangerous to Aideen when she'd visited the Lower City. Anything inside the walls of Sona was relatively clean and safe. Aideen set off down the street. She wanted to walk for a while before going to her actual destination, turning this way and that down narrow streets. She didn't want anybody associating her to the skycoach. She didn't want anybody to recognize her, although it was unlikely. So, she clung to her cloak against the chill and meandered through the Lower City.

She took in the sights and the smells—that earthy smell of people and horses and cooking food. It was easy to keep one's bearings in the city, even if you didn't know what street was which. The Spire rose above all, hundreds of feet above even the upper terraces, and the six curling tendrils that wrapped around it were each a different color. Where they splayed out at the top, they pointed in the general direction of each of the six kingdoms they represented, their colors derived from each kingdom's banners, providing a high-flying compass over the city.

Aideen pushed west, following the curve of the city streets that mirrored its ringed walls. As she passed an intersection of streets, there was a sudden shift in the coloring of the crowds. The heads around her were now all varying hues of red and blue and green, the colorful hair pierced by prominent elven ears. There were no elves in the Upper City, not even as servants. And in the Inner City, their numbers were limited to the most accomplished of artisans. But here in the small Fae Quarter in the shadow of the Inner City terrace, the only humans were those passing through the district. The market stalls and their patrons were all elves here, elven families shopping with their elven children and chattering in elvish. It was an unspoken rule that elves would keep to themselves if they wished to live in peace. And so they did. Those with some means had the Fae Quarter to themselves, and in Pigtown outside the city walls the less fortunate tended livestock or fished or worked the docks.

Aideen had been to this part of the Lower City before, but she usually avoided it. Her red hair and almond eyes passed as exotic in the Upper City, allegedly inherited from a Seggrit woman from distant Dahk Ahani. But here, in the midst of a crowd of elves, her elven heritage was fairly obvious. With half-elves being practically unheard of, at casual glance she would be assumed an elf, not a human. Aideen tugged at the hood covering her hair. And she felt the sting of guilt for it. These people were as much hers as the rest of the city, yet she hid this part of herself away. And for what? For acceptance by a prejudiced society? By the gods, she was such a hypocrite. But she shook the thought away. She mustn't get distracted. She had work to do.

She peppered strangers with questions. *Have you met a man named Lodai, recently come? He has white blue hair, like the people of the Sa'Fin bay.*

*Where can a newcomer find housing? A boarding house? An inn?*

A day spent wandering the streets had gained her nothing, except to tell her that her accent still marked her as outsider. The elves of Sona had their own peculiar accent, an amalgamation of the various dialects from both the west and those elves who inhabited Leander on the southern continent. Her speech was that of Lodai, of her mother's family. And she realized she had no idea what accent that was, exactly, or what it meant to the people here. She felt ignorant, and a stranger among people who should be her own.

Aideen persisted. Day after day, she stole away to the Fae Quarter, wandering the streets and asking strangers if they knew his name. Walking into inns and boarding houses and asking after him. She was beginning to give up hope. The Fae Quarter was only so large. But then one afternoon, the portly owner of a small hostel cocked her eyebrow at Aideen.

*"Lodai? W'ei, il de'o. N'an do'a."*

Aideen found him through the back door, pulling shirts down from a line strung between the buildings. She ran to him, wrapping him in an embrace before he had time to make more than a sound of surprise.

*"I found you. I found you. Thank the moon and stars, here you are!"*

Lodai patted her on the head. *"I am here, child. You received my letter, then?"*

Aideen wiped at her eyes as she pulled away from him. *"There was no letter, teacher."*

*"Ah. I had feared your family would not deliver it to you."*

*"It does not matter. I found you without it."*

Aideen's words came in a rush, as though she had been

saving them for weeks. She told him of how she discovered his absence. Of the teacup. Of her suspicions that someone had been in the room with Davin. That, perhaps, there had been something wrong with the tea. Lodai listened as they sat on the rear steps of the hostel, his brow furrowed.

*"This is dangerous information, child."*

*"Why? Do you think someone wishes ill on the rest of the family? Why should they? Why should they even wish ill on father?"*

*"I do not mean in that way,"* he said. *"I mean for you."*

Aideen blinked at him. *"I do not understand you."*

*"How goes your rending?"*

*"It is nothing. I am simply myself."*

*"That is good. But now this is thrust upon you. I had intended to keep watch on you, to counsel you. Even if I was ill-prepared for it. I have only the stories, and of what my sister Kiva revealed of her experience. And my own theories."* He closed his eyes. *"Those born of two bloods seem to experience both natures in extremes. Men and elves are different, true. But that difference is a chasm when manifest in those such as yourself. You saw your father's study through an elvish eye, but what you describe is not how I experience the world. And the way you raged at me when I drew you out was with an intensity I would have never expected from you."*

Aideen was quiet. She remembered her anger at Deidre. She considered it carefully before speaking. *"I felt something rise up inside me when Deidre told me she had dismissed you. I wanted to... to hurt her. It was like a beast awakening inside of me. It was me. And yet it wasn't."*

His face was unreadable, as it nearly always was. *"And so?"*

*"And so I chose to leave the room, and seek you out. It wasn't hard to do. The anger came on suddenly, which surprised me, but then I chose."*

Lodai nodded. *"Then I have taught you well enough."*

*"So what do I do? About the teacup."*

*"What do you wish to do?"*

*"To seek the truth."*

*"To what end? For the sake of truth? For justice? You must consider the outcomes. For justice sought is not always found. And should you fail to find it, then what? Nothing you can do will bring your father back."*

Aideen chewed her lip. She knew better than to answer him without thinking. So she thought. She chased the possibilities through the shadows of her mind. But it was hard to conceive where those roads might lead. *"I do not know. But I wish to know the truth. Even if it is to no end at all."*

*"Then you must tread carefully, and be mindful of your choices. Your inner self is changing, but it seems to me that your natures are within your control."*

*"Pouv'oua."*

*"Pouv'oua,"* he agreed.

*"I will return when I know more,"* she said. *"I will always seek your counsel. Now more than ever."*

*"I am sorry, but you will not find me here."*

*"What?!"* Aideen stood from the step, looking down at her teacher in shock.

*"I cannot live forever like this. What would you have me do? Sit in an inn and await your visits in secret? I have given you many years of my life. And I did so for duty to my sister, and for love of you. But I left a life behind me eighteen years ago. This is not my country. These are not my moon and stars. They shine dimmer for me here, so far from home. I would return to their familiar light before I am too old to see them."*

Aideen felt her stomach drop, a new surge of emotions rushing in. *"You leave me as well?"*

*"I am to leave tomorrow on a ship to Dahk Ahani, and from there seek a ship to the West. I am sorry."*

Grief rose up in Aideen, an overwhelming sense of loss that

felt like it would choke her. She wept into his shoulder beside her. *"It is selfish for me to ask you to stay. And so I am selfish. I cannot imagine life without you."*

*"I have taught you all I can, dear one. You seem to have come through your rending unscathed. Your heart is still good. It is all I could have hoped for. Now you must simply be true to yourself. You must make your choices, and follow your own path. You cannot be a pupil forever."*

## 12

## THE SUSPECTS

Once the house was asleep, Aideen went down to the kitchens in her dressing gown. The floor was cold against her bare feet. She lit the glowlamps and found the kettles. She had not spent much time in the kitchens since coming to Lindenhall. All was handled by servants here. She filled the boiling kettles with water—every one of them—and put them on the fires. The water was boiling long before she found where the tea was kept. The pantry was vast and methodically organized, assuming one knew the method behind it. Aideen assumed tea would be with the jam or butter or something breakfast-related. But it was kept with the spices. That made some sense once you knew it, both being dried leaves and all. But it had taken her nearly an hour to uncover this knowledge.

Aideen set the counter with teacups. All the teacups she could find. She arranged them in neat rows on their saucers. Then she went to work with the boiling water and the teapots. There were fourteen kinds of tea in the pantry. Aideen had no idea tea came in such varieties. She knew the tea was supposed to be different depending on what it was being served with. But honestly, who had ever given tea a second thought? Now, Aideen was giving tea a great deal of thought.

She brewed a small pot of each kind, which took a considerable amount of time. There were only four teapots in the kitchens that she could find. She considered letting tea steep in bowls, but reconsidered since she really couldn't be sure if the teapot made any difference. There was a lid for a reason, surely. To keep in the steam? It didn't matter. She could be patient. She needed to be certain.

Each pot of tea she poured into two cups, each in a row. She separated the cups according to the type of tea and waited. As soon as the tea was cool enough to drink, she began sipping from the cups. One of each type. She drank each until there was a noticeable difference in the level of tea in the cup. The rings were barely noticeable, however. It would take more time. Aideen paced the kitchens impatiently, staring at the tiny army of cups and saucers. She wondered why Lindenhall needed so many cups. They had never had half as much company as there were teacups. Perhaps they came with the house, and the former occupants had thrown exotic tea parties every weekend. Aideen shook her head. She'd drank entirely too much tea. She was grinding her teeth and her head had begun to ache. Perhaps the tea wasn't entirely to blame, but it was a contributing factor.

She returned to her work, this time armed with a small gravy ladle. She ladled tea from each cup into a pitcher, leaving just the smallest amount in the bottom. She needed that last inch of tea to remain, exactly as it had that night. Color mattered. She went down the line of teacups, hunching over each one and scooping out the cooling liquid into her pitcher.

"Are you alright, Miss?" Aideen spun around to see Kayla peering into the kitchens. "I thought I heard bustlin' 'round down 'ere. Can I help you with somethin'?"

"Oh, gods," Aideen fanned herself, holding the gravy ladle behind her back and feeling the tea dripping from it onto her heels. "Goodness! You startled me, Kayla." Aideen's mind whirred for a moment, realizing just how bizarre this whole display must look. "I'm fine, I'm fine. I'm just sampling some teas. For the wedding, you know. I realized today I have no idea what kind of tea I prefer, so I made several kinds to sample."

"Tea this late will keep you awake all night, miss."

"Oh, I know it will. I already couldn't sleep. I'm tossing and turning lately, so I thought, well, why not?"

Kayla looked back and forth at the spectacle—between Aideen and her dressing gown and bare feet and the spread of teacups amassed on the counter. "Are you sure you're alright, Miss?"

"I'm fine, Kayla." Aideen laughed. "I'm engaged, dear. Aren't I allowed to be a mess?"

Kayla smiled in response to that. "I suppose you are, Miss. Mind that you get some sleep though, yes?"

"I will, I promise."

"Alright. Goodnight, Miss."

Aideen smiled and watched as Kayla disappeared back through the door. Then she turned back to her army of teacups. None of these were right. Perhaps if she let them brew a bit longer. Or left it in the cup longer. She would have to wash everything and start over. So she set about her work.

AIDEEN PACED through the gardens wrapped in a fur-trimmed cloak. Nobody thought it strange for her to go on long walks out here. Apparently, shutting yourself in your dead father's office all day was strange and made people worry about you. She didn't think it was strange at all. Not when you've become convinced that he was murdered.

Who would benefit from such a horrible thing? Aideen wanted to scream, but she kept her emotions in check. It was not easy to do. She wanted to tell someone. But the whole world was still suspect. There was nobody she could trust. She walked over to the tennis court and took her place on one side. The red clay crunched beneath her feet, making a familiar sound she found she was now nostalgic for. Who would kill you, she wondered across the rope to where her father should be this morning. Who would benefit?

There had most definitely been something unusual in the teacup. Poison, Aideen had decided. Poison in a teacup, and Davin had been tricked into drinking it. But who could convince him to drink tea against his usual habits? That was puzzling. But one question at a time. Who would benefit from Davin's death?

Carolyn benefitted nothing. Of that much she could be certain. With Davin's death, she had inherited precisely what she likely would have received upon marrying anyhow. And she was surely incapable of such an act. Carolyn, at least, was innocent. But she also could not be trusted. Not even with a simple secret, so Aideen could not dare to speak with her little sister on this matter.

Riann stood to benefit. He had inherited the company as planned, after all, and a small fortune as well. Riann was ambitious and a bit of a fool, but ambitious enough to commit murder? Although he could never have predicted his mother would marry the owner of the company where he was an apprentice, he had wasted no time in making the most of the situation. Or could he have predicted the marriage? Influenced it in some way?

Well, in any case, his inheritance of the company was inevitable as Davin's male heir through marriage. Would he have been so impatient as to murder Davin? It seemed hard to believe. Riann was still a young man. As it was, he was leaning on the counsel of Lord Cathal and a host of advisors, and his eyes betrayed his exhaustion lately. Still, it was hard to imagine who else would have benefitted from Davin's demise.

Aideen crunched circles in the red clay court. She spun on one foot, feeling the grip of it beneath her shoes. She needed exercise. She headed back toward the house. It was cold outside anyhow. The gardens still held their charm in winter, but the portrait of death on all but the evergreens was too gloomy for her current musings.

What of Deidre? What could she possibly gain from her husband's death? She inherited nothing in death that she did not already effectively possess. Indeed, she stood to lose in the arrangement. Aideen had inherited the manor, after all. Deidre was now a guest in her own home. And Deidre had most likely known the contents of Davin's will, and so would have expected to gain nothing else.

Aideen climbed the stairs to her room and changed clothes. She took her leather bag with her down into the ballroom. It was large and devoid of any furniture except around the periphery, making it her preferred indoor practice space. There she shut the doors behind her and drew the sword of elvish design. She began working through her practice routines, feeling her muscles loosen after the first few minutes. It felt good to have a sword in her hand again.

In childhood, she had practiced against straw-stuffed dummies and spinning targets. A wooden training sword in hand, Lodai had instructed her in the elven sword Songs, the *fleri ea chante*. Aideen would rehearse a chain of movements—of body, of blade, of shuffling feet—until her muscles ached and her hands blistered. Until the whole dance was so ingrained in her that she no longer thought of the movements as individual, but simply a part of a grander whole. Each flourish had a name. Each had a purpose. Each could be interrupted or improvised on. Each could be connected, like links in a chain. The elves called it a song, but Aideen thought of it as a dance.

Then there were the drills. Some for cutting, ensuring that the edge of one's blade always remained with the arc of travel.

Some for measuring distance. Some for dodging. Some for speed. Some for accuracy. And then a whole host of exercises for improving her strength and stamina. Her life would never be dangerous, but for the elves danger was not the point. The song connected one's mind and body, and for Aideen it was a connection to the half of her heritage that was hardest to comprehend.

The Songs had always been her favorite part of her lessons. The sparring she had suffered through, always feeling inept despite years of training with Lodai. She was miles better than an untrained fighter, to be sure. But she had always approached it much as she had her lessons on the pianoforte with Miss Nedley, the surly woman who twice weekly came to the house to accuse her of skipping her daily practice. Rightfully so, but even still. It was a thing she suffered through and ceased the moment her father had allowed it.

Not so with the Songs. Each one a pattern of steps and movements, body and blade in harmony. Once she had mastered them she found a peace in returning to them daily, finding reverie in their intricacies. Settling into the trance of them, of the rhythm and music that came only from within. Fighting nothing, thinking nothing, feeling nothing but herself and the air around her. She would emerge from them sweating but invigorated.

Aideen had an adversary today and was not here with a sword seeking peace. Aideen squared off against the shadows, spinning and striking at her father's faceless killer. She felt her body fall into its old familiar rhythms. She sighed into it, into the comfort and simplicity of it. Parry, dodge, thrust. Her feet danced, transferring her weight from heel to toe and foot to foot, her core and shoulders tensed but flexible, her body serving as the foundation for her sword as it whirled and cut through the air. It helped her mind to settle.

Now, who else? The servants? Surely none of them bore their master any ill will. All were well paid and seemed happy.

She had never heard any complaints. And besides, who among them stood to benefit even in the slightest? Even if one had disliked Davin, it was hard to fathom that any of the servants should have killed him. Murder was a hard solution to any problem that amounted to simply finding a new manor in the Upper City to serve in.

Who else? Aideen drew the other sword in her left hand, wielding both swords now against her faceless foes that hid in the shadows everywhere she looked. The style of two long swords was more complicated, more likely to look impressive than actually serve any purpose in combat. A shield was much more useful in one's second hand. Or even a dagger. But she knew Songs that incorporated two blades, and she blended them into dizzying flourishes as her heart began to pound.

A competitor? Yes, beside Riann that was the one angle that made some sense. Davin may not have had any personal enemies, but the Bormia Trading Company certainly had many professional ones. It held exclusivity deals with several trading partners in Dahk Ahani. Bormia had priority at port on several islands between Elora and the southern continent as well, the work of many years of favors and politicking. It meant Bormia ships were in and out of harbor faster than any others. Aideen would need to speak with Riann, then. But could she trust him on the matter when he himself was still suspect? Should she confide in him her suspicions, or merely probe him for information? She was unsure.

Unless the poison itself could be a lead. Was there some way to find out what the poison was? Perhaps an alchemist or a botanist or a doctor may know something. But how to ask such a thing without revealing her suspicions?

"If I didn't believe you before, I most certainly do now," a familiar voice said from across the ballroom.

Aideen spun around and addressed the voice with her

swords, falling into an aggressive stance with them poised and ready to attack it. She blinked. "What are you doing here?"

Lord Cathal stepped out of the shadows of the doorway and onto the ballroom floor. "I was nearby this morning on business, and thought I'd stop in to call."

"I'm not exactly decent," Aideen said, trying to decide if she should be embarrassed. It was true. She was wearing the pants and sleeveless linen vest she wore to play tennis during the summer. And then, only with her father. It was not the same as being caught in her underwear, but it was in the neighborhood.

"I'd say you're quite a bit beyond decent," Lord Cathal said. "I saw the way you handle those blades." He stepped closer to her, reaching out and touching one of the swords she held pointed at him still, tracing the flat edge with a finger. "This design is unusual."

"It's the elven style of long sword," Aideen said, turning the blade in her hand and offering him the hilt. "It's called *l'onta n'epe*, which translates simply to longsword. But you'll note, it's longer and thinner than an Elorian longsword. About the same weight overall, and the same one or two-handed design. The guard is always angled away from the hilt, and not so in Elorian blades. The angle is better suited for the hand exchanges and spins common in the elven sword songs."

"It feels foreign in my hands," Lord Cathal said, stepping back and swinging the sword a few times. "The balance is closer to the hilt."

"My Lord is familiar with swords, then."

"I am. It is almost like a middle ground between a longsword and the—how did you put it? The playthings we nobles use in the sport of fencing."

"And I said I meant no insult to the sport, my Lord."

"I think I shall stick with the Elorian blade." He tossed the sword across to Aideen, who caught it easily. She similarly tossed him the other sword. He caught it. "Ah yes, this feels better."

"Would my Lord fancy some sparring?" Aideen flashed him a smile. "I've already been found by you here indecently dressed. I might as well make use of the opportunity."

"Shall I end up bloody as your swordmaster in the gardens?"

"Of course not," Aideen said, settling into a proper stance. "The blades are blunt. And I'll go easy on you."

A smile spread across Lord Gwenhert's face. "What a woman you are," he said. "I accept the challenge, so long as you swear not to mar my face for our wedding."

Aideen didn't give him a chance to reconsider. She leapt at him, trying his defenses in a quick succession of jabs, and then spun out of the way of his wide retort. He regained his footing after the first assault, and came at her with a rakish grin. His attacks were solid and smooth, his arm strong. He had talent and his practice was evident. But he was predictable, and he could not begin to match Aideen's speed. He came at her several times, only to have his sword knocked wide and for Aideen to have already spun around behind him, waiting patiently for him to turn again to reengage. Perhaps she was better at sparring than she thought. Years of fighting Lodai had made her accustomed to losing.

After several skirmishes, Aideen decided she would wound his pride only a little further. She parried, sliding the flat of her blade rapidly down onto his knuckles, which brought a surprised exclamation from him. At the same time, her free hand was coming up from below. His sword was in her hands now.

The tips of both swords rested lightly on his shoulders, crossed just in front of his neck. "Do you submit, my lord?" Lord Cathal's breathing was heavy. He looked down at the swords at his throat, to his wounded hand clutched in the other, and then back at Aideen. His eyes were shining. He made to step back and around the blades, but Aideen stepped with him, keeping the crossed blades at his neck, shaking her head with a smile curling on her lips. "Do you submit to me?"

He touched the edge of one blade with a fingertip, then carefully shifted the tip of the sword off his shoulder. She let him. He stepped closer, the edge of her other blade hissing along his collar. "You amaze me," he said. He stepped closer again, and Aideen's chest began to tighten at the way he was looking at her. His eyes were searching hers, and she felt as though they could see deeper into her than they should. Then the guard of her blade was the only thing that held him away from her. "I submit to you, Aideen Bormia. I am yours." Before she could fully comprehend what was happening, his lips were pressed against hers in the darkness of the ballroom.

## 13

## RIANN'S STUDY

Aideen questioned herself with every step down the hallway. It was a violation of the most basic family trust, but how else could she be sure? She needed answers, and she wouldn't find them by pacing around the gardens shivering and talking to herself. She needed to do something if she was to find her father's murderer, and Riann was first on her list of suspects.

Aideen opened the door into Riann's study. It was smaller than Davin's, originally fashioned as a nursery and left untouched by the Bormias until Riann had taken it up. It still bore the pale blue wall paint and thick cream-colored rugs. A desk faced the northern windows, strewn with papers and books, much like her father's had always been. The thought sent another pang through her heart. She eased the door closed behind her and fixed her attention on the desk.

On the desktop were ledgers and letters. Aideen glanced through the ledgers quickly, unsurprised when they bore no fruit. The letters were of little interest, all dealing with matters of interest only for the Bormia Trading Company. The books likewise were useless to her. She sat down at the desk and began attacking the drawers.

Dip pens. Ink bottles. An unopened package of blank paper, tied in twine like a present. A compass. A small carved wooden dancer, missing one foot at the end of her jagged ankle. A lone key. Notes on paper scraps in Riann's neat handwriting.

*Move to double entries at the beginning of next month. This is atrocious.*

*Write a letter of introduction for Master Hammond to Lady Charlotte Premroe.*

*Send a servant for more argan oil. Nearly out.*

*Dinner with Captain Thurgan. Possible promotion if he is the right sort of man. Need to be sure.*

*Doctor advises more sleep and exercise. Ha.*

In the back of a drawer, Aideen found a small leather-bound book. This caught her attention, as it was smaller than the sort one placed on a bookshelf. It was also well worn. On the opening page, she recognized Riann's handwriting. *January 1253.*

It was a journal. Aideen glanced at the door, feeling a pang of remorse and uncertainty at this intrusion. But had this not been exactly the sort of thing she had come looking for? She skimmed the first entry, which made mention of his mother's upcoming wedding to Davin Bormia but was otherwise a lengthy description of the beauty of some girl Aideen did not know and his unspoken feelings towards her. Aideen winced and was about to thumb on, until something prickled in her mind. She looked again.

*He.*

She had skipped right over the pronoun, her expectations inserting an extra letter where Riann had not penned it. But there was no mistake, the handwriting was too precise to think it an omission. It was not some young woman Riann was enamored with, but a young man. Riann was tinged, as people called it.

To be tinged was scandalous anywhere in Elora. It was said to be unnatural, a sin against the gods and the natural order of things. There were whispers about those in society rumored to take men as lovers. But those men took wives just the same, hiding their shameful nature in the same way Aideen covered her ears.

But was it truly shameful? Aideen had never given the idea much thought. The elves did not have a word for such people, and yet there were those in elven society who coupled with their own gender. It was uncommon, but it happened and without much consideration from their friends and neighbors. Not so in Sona. This was a secret Riann must hold as closely as she held her own. And while Aideen must only hide her ears, her stepbrother must hide his heart, his feelings. His very sense of self.

This was not the secret Aideen had come to find. And yet now it was hers to keep. And she would keep it, she decided. Even if whatever she found pointed to Riann as a murderer, one had no bearing on the other. She may not understand what it was to be tinged, but surely it was not a crime to be attracted to someone. To love someone. It occurred to Aideen that Riann must understand her secret more than she could have ever known. She wondered who carried his secret with him? To carry it alone must be a lonely existence. Who could know what burdens other people carried? She would likely never know. That was the nature of secrets, after all.

To the task at hand, Aideen told herself. She left one secret in search of another, thumbing through the pages until she found them blank. Moving backward, she searched the dates written at the beginning of the entries, trying not to read much else to keep this invasion at a minimum.

She found the one she sought. It was the day after the

Festival of Eridayah, when Davin was murdered. The entry was short.

*I have now lost two fathers, I have failed to truly know either of them.*

*I am now the only man Cara has left. How can I ever be enough?*

There were footsteps in the hallway. Aideen closed the journal and hurried to put it back where she had found it. She tidied the desk and stood stiffly beside it, staring at the door, her mind racing to think how she would explain herself. The footsteps continued on down the hallway before fading to obscurity.

Aideen felt a wave of relief wash over her. Riann was almost certainly innocent. He was a good man, and a good brother. His secret was harmless, and thinking of it only made her sad for him. The specter of her father's killer still loomed, but at least it did not reside in Lindenhall with her. She slipped out of the room. She could now move on to the next questions. And that meant returning to this room when Riann was here to invite her in.

WHAT SHOULD SHE SAY? How much should she reveal? Aideen had something of a plan, but it felt flimsy and she could not be sure how it would hold up once she started. She stood outside the doorway steadying herself. She needed to be calm. Casual. At least this time she wasn't skulking about. Aideen took a deep breath, and then another. She saw no other path than the one before her, and so she rapped lightly on the door.

"Come," came a voice from the other side.

Her step-brother's face lit warmly at the sight of her, and seeing him seated at a mirror of her father's desk gave her encouragement. She thought of his secret, and wondered at how it shaped her picture of him. All he ever talked of was business, but he was not such a simple man to know after all. Aideen smiled back at him. "I hope I'm not intruding."

"No, not at all." Riann brushed the hair out of his eyes with a sigh. "There is no end to work, and so there is not much to interrupting it. I fear eating and sleeping are even an imposition to my new duties. How are you feeling?"

"I am well."

"I am glad to hear it. Carolyn tells me you have been aloof and fretful these past days."

"A bit. My nerves have been frazzled, but no more than to be expected, all things considered." All things including that our father was murdered, she thought. She entered the room and seated herself on the edge of an armchair, looking toward the desk opposite her. There was a smoking pipe and a book on the table next to her, and she straightened them as she gathered her thoughts and courage. "If you have a few minutes, I wondered if I might ask you some questions?"

Riann shrugged. "Certainly."

"I've heard father speak of competition many times. And you as well, since your coming into the family's business."

"Well, surely. It is a risky business, but with high rewards for those who succeed in it."

"And the competing trade companies. They obviously stand to gain much should Bormia falter?"

"Of course. That is what has my nerves frazzled now. With Davin's passing, there could be seen some opportunity to take advantage of a young and inexperienced new head like myself. An attempt to muscle us out, or to convince some party that our contracts are less dependable given the change in leadership."

Aideen studied him, reading him as best she could. He was stressed, she could see that in his eyes. He hadn't been sleeping well enough. There was a tension in his jaw, that too had not been there before he'd assumed his new position. "Do you think..." Aideen hesitated, choosing her words carefully. "Do you think a competitor would have sought such a situation?"

"How do you mean?"

"Would a competitor have desired my father's death?"

Riann's brow furrowed as he looked at her, and she measured his reaction. Surprise. Worry. "To be plain about it, I think many would have welcomed it. But what are you getting at?"

"Would someone stand to gain enough at father's death to kill him?" Aideen watched his face. She watched as he processed her words, as confusion set into his brow. She didn't wait for his retort—that Davin's death had been a fluke, a natural death of a failing heart, that perhaps he'd had symptoms and had ignored them. Or hid them. The same story she'd heard from the doctor. "Look. If I tell you something, I need you to swear to me that you will keep it a secret."

He chewed on her words, his face still lined with perplexity. "What are you saying, then?"

"Do you swear to me?"

"Swear to what? I don't understand what I'm swearing to."

"Please. Just give me your word that this conversation remains between us. That you won't tell your mother or sister or anybody else." *I know you can keep a secret*, she thought. But she needed to be sure he gave it the appropriate weight.

"Now I can see why Carolyn is worried about you."

"Will you swear or not?"

He sighed. "Yes. Alright. I'll swear."

"Nobody," Aideen was emphatic.

"I give you my word," he said, somewhat exasperated. "This conversation remains in this room, between us only. Now, what are you on about?"

Aideen told him. She told him everything. About the teacup. About Davin's habits. About testing the teas in the kitchens. About him being nearly alone in the house that night while most of the city was at the festival. "Nobody stood to gain from his death except the other trading companies," she said. "Nobody else except you, perhaps. But I trust you," she added quickly, seeing he was about to interject. "I've seen how the role wears on you, and there was no reason for you to hurry into it before you were ready."

Riann's jaw clenched. "I do not appreciate the accusation that I could have killed our father."

"I'm not accusing you."

"No, you danced around it prettily enough. So I can assume that you suspected me at some point."

"Well, yes. But you have to understand that I had to suspect everyone at first. Anybody. But I'm not accusing you of anything. I've come to you for help."

"For help with what?" Riann's voice was thin with her. "You honestly expect me to entertain that Davin was murdered because there was a teacup on his desk? A teacup? And that you think, weeks later, that you remember it having a tinge of color to it?"

"Because it did. And I still do."

"Do you hear yourself? Are you aware of how mad that sounds? Of course, I'm sure you're right back to suspecting me now."

"Not at all!" Aideen protested.

"Whomever you suspect is irrelevant, I suppose. Look. Sister." He leaned forward in his chair. "I know losing your father is hard. I lost mine as a young man, and it devastated me. And I looked for meaning in it as well. I cried out to the gods and sought for any reason he should be taken from us. That is a normal thing, I think. To seek meaning in a world that is unfair. But this? This is just madness. Your father's death was seen to by the same doctor who has cared for this family for years. Who kept your secret. Who kept your mother a secret."

"Yes, but a man can be wrong. Especially if the poison is one chosen to disguise its presence."

"How much more likely that you are wrong? That the doctor, the expert in these matters, is right?"

Aideen pushed down the anger that began to rise inside her. "I'm not wrong. I know what I've seen."

Riann shook his head and settled back into his chair. "That troubles me greatly, then. Please. Do not let your grief lead you into such hysterical conclusions."

"So you won't help me, then?"

"I'm trying to help you. I'm trying to make you see how insane you sound right now. Yes, Bormia's competition was likely delighted to see the stability of the company shaken. But look at it logically. If one wanted to kill Davin, they should have done it years ago. Before he married my mother and took me as the heir to the company. Before that time, the company would have passed on to whom, exactly? To you, against all Elorian traditions? Nobody really knows what his intentions were then, but it was surely a more precarious situation than it is now. Now, the company remains in the family. So if I follow your own logic, a murder—I can't believe I'm even saying this—a murder would have been a far better plot any time over the last ten years than it is now."

"So you don't believe me?"

"Of course not. But I see that you believe it, and that is worrisome."

Aideen stood up from the chair. Her clenched hands had left deep indentations in the upholstered arms. "I see I misjudged you. I will have to find the truth for myself."

"You didn't misjudge me. Aideen, stop." She was already walking toward the door. "Please. Listen to me. I care for you, and I know your grief firsthand. Davin was like a father to me, and I wish to all the gods I could have him back. But there is no revenge to seek here. No meaning to uncover. Death is cruel, and it leaves us all with horrible scars we must carry. Please, do not continue down this path. Face your grief, and do not use this imagined plot as a shield to hide behind. No good will come of this."

Aideen paused at the door. "Remember your oath. You will speak of this to no one."

"I will keep my word. But you must -"

Aideen did not hear the rest as she slammed the door behind her. Riann did not believe her. Riann would not help her. She wished Lodai were here to advise her. He at least understood what she knew, what she saw. But she was alone now. She would have to see this through by herself.

## 14

## THE MASQUERADE

"It is done."

Beatrice sank into the sofa, relaxing for the first time in days. She had ridden from Lyramae to Sona in haste and had come here directly. The room was dark, the walls hung in thick tapestries and the floor deeply carpeted. All was a deep shade of red, the color of spilled wine. Her words seemed stifled in this room, the sounds hushed by all the thick fabric and the air thick with the bitter tang of cigarette smoke.

"All is well then?" a voice came from the darkness of the corner, the orange glow of a cigarette casting shadows across a featureless porcelain face.

"William Jameson's name is cleared of any wrongdoing, and he is returned to freedom. But he still has an enemy in the constable of Roseglade. He will need to keep his head down."

"It cannot be helped." The figure in the corner glowed in the light of a long drag on the cigarette. "You're soiling my sofa, darling."

Beatrice looked down at her clothes. Her boots were caked in mud. So were her breeches, for that matter. The splatter likely ran all the way up her back. She was in desperate need of a bath. "I'm tired."

"Get into costume. The others will be here soon. It is time we let them know what we have discovered."

Beatrice hung her filthy cloak on a peg on the wall. She took off her muddy riding boots for good measure, as she had indeed tracked filth across the carpets. She took a red silken robe from a trunk and put it on, placing a porcelain mask on her face and pulling the red hood over her hair. She reclaimed her perch on the sofa, now looking identical to her mistress in the shadows.

A bell rang outside and the door swung open. A stream of men and women entered, discernible only by shape and stature for all wore the same red hooded robes and white masks that hid their features. They found seats around the room in silence.

"Let us begin," the Queen of Masks said from her dark corner.

"The pieces begin to fall into place in Lyramae," Beatrice told the room. "We have a nearly complete picture of how slaves are imported from Dahk Ahani, despite the attempts to obfuscate the process."

"Indentured servants," a man corrected.

"Semantics, darling," The Queen of Masks said. "Since the contracts are all a farce, we shall call these slaves what they are."

Beatrice continued. "The slavers who steal them away from villages in the wilds of Leander have been well known to us. Yet the slaves for sale in Lyramae are always presented as criminals from elsewhere, bound to a contract of indentured servitude. Usually originating in the Sundrelands. We now have confirmation of the secret agreements between the Black Rose mercenary group that steals the slaves away from their homes and the judiciary in Bryarhart. Their crimes are forged there by judges, for a price, and the contracts of indentured servitude originated thus appear quite legal."

"It is hard to imagine such a mass import of slaves could go unnoticed for so long," a woman said from behind her mask.

"One need only visit the plantations of Cashmere or Cricson to see it for oneself," The Queen of Masks said. "No Elorians tend those fields. Only people in chains, under the vigilant eye of a taskmaster."

"The import is done on ships owned by House Gwenhert," Beatrice said. "The slaves are transported amongst the cargo in Gwenhert ships. There is no record of this, of course. But I have seen it for myself. I have seen the cages with my own eyes. The slaves are removed from the ships under the cover of darkness moments after arrival in the harbor, sometimes even out at sea just beyond the Sona horizon. No different than a smuggler, really. This avoids any proper unloading or customs inspections. They are transported to ships already loaded and bound out of harbor, such that their origination from Sona gives them easy passage elsewhere in Elora. They are unloaded in Granite Bay, far from any prying eyes. From there, they reach the slave markets."

"House Gwenhert is complicit in this, then?"

"To some degree, at least." The Queen of Masks mulled over her cigarette. "Lord Cathal Gwenhert is Master of Ships for the house. We have no evidence that he is aware of such systemic abuse of his enterprise. He is either directly involved or has poor oversight of his ships. Or, perhaps he turns a blind eye to what he knows is nefarious without knowing the depth of the thing."

"The ships that bear slaves from the southern continent have armed mercenaries aboard," Beatrice said. "There are too many people involved for it to be a complete secret."

"Why use House Gwenhert ships at all?"

"Control, most likely. Finding enough ships capable of crossing to Leander is no small thing. Hiring a ship here and there spreads the conspiracy. Too many untrustworthy people involved. Having it all within one house or trading company makes the enterprise predictable."

The Queen of Masks stood, stepping out from the dark corner to address the room. "The newly appointed Baron of Cashmere is sympathetic to the issue of slavery in his lands, but his hands are bound. Indentured servitude is legal in the Kingdom of Lyramae. We bring you all into this now that we have laid the groundwork. We have information, but possess no leverage toward recourse. I remind you all that we play at a long game with such matters. Keep your masks in place as you move about your places in society. Keep your eyes and ears open. It is time we do something about slavery in Lyramae. We now wait and watch for an opportunity."

Once all the cloaked figures had left the room, only Beatrice and the Queen of Masks remained. Beatrice took off her costume, grabbing her dirty cloak from its peg to leave.

"Duke Sturlis is having a party," the Queen of Masks said from behind her.

"Well, that is convenient."

"Isn't it though? Prepare yourself. You will want a partner on your arm for this bit of thievery."

"Gregory remains in Roseglade."

"Tying up loose ends?"

Beatrice rolled her eyes. "No. Just being Gregory."

"We will find you another, then."

## 15

## ASKING QUESTIONS

Aideen had found Lodai. She would find answers in the same way. She once more donned her cloak and took a skycoach into the city.

Her first stop was to see a doctor. Her questions were met with suspicion. If a man is poisoned, how can you tell? No, I'm not trying to poison anyone. I think a friend was poisoned. Why, no, I haven't gone to the authorities about it. They may think I'm crazy. Where would someone acquire such a poison? The kind that makes it look like a natural death? No, I'm not asking because I want to kill my husband! She learned nothing and handed him a coin for the trouble, which he took warily.

Aideen pressed on and asked around for another doctor, hoping a different line of questioning might bear more fruit. If someone is trying to poison me, how can I tell? I think they put something in my tea, and it made it the wrong color. No, I don't still have it. I remember the color well, though. No, I haven't spoken to the authorities about it. Is there a way to try and test poisons in tea to see if it turns the same wrong color? Where would I find such substances? No, I'm not trying to poison anybody!

The next day she journeyed into the Inner City terrace and visited a tea seller there. She asked about tea colors, and what they might tell you. She asked about making herbal teas from things in the garden or in the park, and how you might know them to be safe. Her troubles there gained her a much better knowledge of tea, but nothing of poison. She left with nothing useful beyond a purse of expensive tea, for which she was certain she had overpaid.

Aideen wandered the streets, frustrated and seething. Three doctors, a tea seller, an herbalist, and a man selling exotic plants from across the sea out of a little road-side cart. She'd spent the better part of the day in this endeavor, and had nothing to show for it except more dead ends and a purse full of random purchases to cover suspicions. Her family was asking their own questions about all her days spent out in the city alone. She kept telling them she was visiting flower sellers, bakers, and the like in preparation for the wedding. In truth, she had barely given the wedding a moment's thought.

There seemed to be no way to ask people about poison without immediately raising their suspicions. She couldn't fault them for that. It was a very suspicious thing to be asking. But what else could she do?

A breeze picked up, blowing in from the harbor. She could smell the salt in the air, the distant tang of fishiness and pine tar. She checked the Spire above her for a sense of where she was. She'd made it back around to the southern extremity of the Lower City, back to where the city walls divided the city proper from the harbor area. That made sense, now that she thought of it. There were more fish sellers here, even though most of those markets were beyond the walls in the harbor district. She must be close to the southern gate.

There was something else in the air, though. Mingling with the smells of the harbor district was the savory note of roasting meat. Aideen's stomach growled at her in protest, and she realized she was famished. She had meandered the streets of Sona for hours, and had not eaten all day. It was certainly doing nothing to help her mood. She walked on, looking for some place to buy herself something to eat. Anything would do, certainly, but she hoped to find the source of what she was smelling. It was roast chicken and herbs, she thought, with something of that smokiness that comes from cooking over apple wood. She passed by a bakery but did not stop. She had her stomach set on a roast chicken now. It was probably just a family preparing dinner, but what could it hurt to seek out for a few minutes? She walked on, the wind on her face. She had to laugh at herself. She was following the scent like some dog.

The wind died back down as she rounded a corner. The street was not much more than an alley nestled in the shade of the city walls, which must have permitted no light except at noontime. Even without the wind, there was no mistaking the smells now. Aideen saw the sign for a tavern up ahead, and she ventured towards it. The sign read The Dusty Pearl.

Aideen stood looking at the sign for a long moment. She knew this place. She had come to this very tavern once as a child with her father. It was the only tavern she had ever been in, in fact. It was the model tavern she saw in her imagination in every story she read to feature such an establishment. Taking a meal at The Dusty Pearl was a kind of tradition with the men of the Dragonfly after returning from a voyage, and the thought flooded her with memories. Aideen blinked at the unexpectedness of it all. What a strange thing to have simply stumbled upon this place. "It is almost like I was supposed to find my way here," she whispered to herself. The thought sent a chill tingling down the backs of her arms.

The outside of the tavern was quite a bit shabbier than in her memories. The whole building seemed to sag under the height of itself, its steep pitched roof smiling in the middle. The upper story must be an inn of sorts—the kind of place for travelers or drunks to pass the night. Or perhaps it was just the proprietor's home. The sun was beginning to set, and she wondered exactly how safe this sort of place really was. Coming here with her father, safety had never crossed her mind. But a sailor's watering hole? As she stood outside debating, a guard passed by her, whistling. It's fine, she assured herself. This was still Sona, after all. She pushed open the heavy wooden door.

Inside, the tavern was already vibrant and bustling, and the smell of food immediately caught her attention. Sailors and tradesmen drank at the bar, while others ate at a scatter of ramshackle tables. A few threw darts at a poorly painted series of circles on a far wall, fashioned as a kind of map of the city. The memories from this place flooded back in from all those years ago, and she smiled to herself. She found an empty table against the wall, not far from where she remembered sitting with Davin that day as a child when they'd watched while the crew ravaged themselves on food and drink after their long voyage. She looked around, wondering if the little Lindle folk she remembered were still here. Lindle were a rarity in Sona, and there had seemed to be a whole family of them here before.

Instead, a tall, pretty woman walked over to her table. "What can I gitcha, mam?"

"Oh, I'm not actually sure. Something certainly smells good. I'm afraid I don't know how this works." Places like this did not exist in the Upper City. One took their meals at home, with the cooks, or at the home of a friend. With their cooks.

"Works? We got food, we got drink. Foods bread and cheese for a penny, or roast chicken tonight if you like, an' there's fish. Corrin's a right beast in the kitchen, mam. He'll set you up right. As for drink, we have it aplenty. Just tell me what ya like."

"I'll have the chicken, then. I'm awfully hungry. And... an ale?" She looked around the room and saw mostly tankards, not wine glasses.

"Roast chicken an' ale, out in a speck." The woman bustled

off, snatching empty cups from several tables on her way and shouting something incoherent into the room behind the bar. A large mug of ale appeared before Aideen a few moments later, and Aideen sipped it while she studied the room. It was nutty and rich, almost a meal unto itself. She sighed back into her seat and contented herself with watching the room. Remembering. Picturing her father there, seemingly huge in her memories from her youth. She thought again how strange it was to simply stumble into this place.

The chicken arrived, its skin crackling and still on the bone, an entire half bird steaming on her plate along with roasted potatoes and two sauces smeared onto the plate edges. One was creamy and tart, glistening with strong browned garlic, while the other was dark and sticky sweet and smelled of plums. Aideen tore meat from the bone and alternated between the sauces, taking pleasure in the back and forth of savory and sweet flavors. The chicken was crisp and greasy, the smell of herbs rising from it strong. It was delightful, and Aideen feasted on it without worrying about decorum in a place such as this.

When the ale was done, Aideen asked for strong liquor. She was not one for drink, but her father had been. Especially in his younger years. Drinking the foul-tasting stuff in this place was an odd kind of homage to him, in a way. By the time she'd finished it, she began to understand it better. It made her feel warm and relaxed inside, and so she sought to order another.

"Careful there, love," the woman smiled at her. "That whiskey has a way of sneakin' up on ya. I take it you're not from around here?"

"No, I'm not."

"Inner City, then?"

"Upper," she admitted.

"Ah. On a minor rebellion tonight, I take it?"

"Something like that," Aideen smiled up at her.

"Well, it's none o' my business. We get all sorts in here. I'll get ye another."

Aideen looked around the room. All sorts, indeed. It wasn't just sailors. And not all the patrons were rough cut, either. There was a table across the room where well-dressed men were speaking hunched forward, as if their conversation was meant to be secret. At the bar, a man dressed in all black had sat down next to another who was dressed plainly, but whom she could tell by the shoes was more likely to know nobles than the barkeep. Aideen remembered the story her father had told her about this place. That the Dusty Pearl was a kind of neutral ground for disputes among the smugglers and thieves. It had given her a thrill at the time, imagining conspiracies and alliances being forged all around her. And that gave Aideen an idea. A stupid one, perhaps. But her day had gotten her nothing but frustration and a hot meal thus far. And there was a part of her that chose to believe that this place was exactly where she was supposed to be. If fate had somehow brought her to this tavern, then she would test fate and see if it gained her more than wandering the streets.

When the woman returned with another glass filled with strong-smelling liquor, Aideen stopped her. "I'm sorry, what was your name?"

"Tabitha, love."

"Tabitha." Aideen drew a breath. "Maybe this sounds mad, but as you said, this place brings in all sorts. Do you have any idea where I might go for information in secret?"

The woman eyed Aideen suspiciously. "What sort of information?"

"Poison," Aideen said. And then, seeing the look on her face, quickly added, "Look, I know that sounds awful. But my father died, and I think he was poisoned. I haven't a clue where to begin or whom to talk to. I've tried doctors and the like, and everyone assumes I'm aiming to hurt someone. But I'm not. I'm just trying to find the truth."

Tabitha chewed her lip. "It's a strange thing to be asking', love."

"Exactly. And it's gotten me nowhere. But I'm not sure what else to do. As you said, this place brings in all types. I know it's a cliché, but don't barkeeps hear things? Maybe you would have overheard something that could help me? Or at least point me in some direction that isn't walking around the city asking mad questions of strangers?"

Tabitha was looking Aideen up and down, taking her in and making no attempt to hide it. It felt awkward, and Aideen shrugged her shoulders, as if to say, 'This is me, for whatever that's worth.'

"Ye seems like an honest sort. There be a place ye can go, love. I canno' promise you'll find help there, but ye can try."

"Oh, thank you!" Aideen's hope rose for the first time in weeks. "You have no idea what this means to me."

"And if she can help ye, it's like to no come cheap."

"Of course. I can pay. Please."

Tabitha dipped her finger in an ale she was carrying. She drew a loose circle on the table in front of Aideen. She repeated this, until there were three rings. A very rough map of Sona. "Walls, inner terrace, upper terrace. Ye kin?"

"I understand," Aideen nodded.

Tabitha jabbed her finger at a spot in the Inner City, near the walls of the upper terrace. "Go here to the Red Dress. It's the street nearest the terrace wall. You'll know it by the red door. Go during the day, and ye ask for Beatrice. Tell 'er I sent ya. If she's no there, ye come back the next day an' the next until she is. And best not ask around town anymore. Even I'd be suspicious of ya askin' 'bout poisons, if'n ye did no' seem so damned clueless."

## 16

## THE ISLAND

After eight weeks at sea, the mist lifted and the sun shone at last. Two days later, land was spotted. A great cheer went up across the ship as men ran to strain their eyes against the horizon to see what the lookout said he saw out there. One sailor began ringing the bell wildly. Captain Killian allowed them all a few moments of lapse in duty and decorum. In truth, written across his face was the same elation and relief that had swept up the rest of the men of the ship. Nearly two months at sea without a grain of sand, not a single seabird in sight. Only endless green waters and blinding fog. They clung to their training and instincts and not a small amount of hope to hold down the fear that grew in their bellies as each day passed.

Hamfast clamored up to the quarterdeck just behind the wizard Whitaker. The wizard wheezed with exertion as he climbed the steps, clinging to the handrail as though the seas were much rougher than they were today. Levin was peering out with his spyglass. "What can you make of it?" Captain Killian asked from beside him, fighting to keep his voice steady in the midst of his emotion.

"It looks like an island. Fairly large and rocky."

"And does it..." the wizard seemed close to fainting from exertion. "Does it have two pillars of rock jutting off to the southeast? Two large crags that stick up like this?" Whitaker withdrew a tube of parchment from the sleeve of his robes and handed it to Levin.

The second mate withdrew his eye from the spyglass and looked at the character before him, blinking. His annoyance at the wizard's presence on the quarterdeck melted away quickly when he unrolled the parchment and saw it. "That's it," he breathed. "That's the island before us."

"Then we are nearly there, Captain. This is the Giant's Shoulders on the map I provided for you."

Captain Killian looked through Levin's spyglass briefly and then handed it back to him. He wore a broad smile on his face and clasped hands with Levin. "We shot an arrow into the dark, my friend. We shot an arrow in the dark and managed to hit a beetle in flight."

"That we did, sir. I can hardly believe it."

Hamfast stood quietly by, grinning but unnoticed by the tall folk. What luck he'd had all these years. There must be some magic in the Dragonfly—it had now completed its fifth voyage across the Misty Seas. It was a journey most would never dare, and those who did were often never seen again. Hamfast had now served on the Dragonfly with two of the finest captains and crews the world had ever known. Men would tell stories of this ship for generations.

THEY ARRIVED at their destination three days later. The beach was a grey-black sand. Beyond the sand, the island interior was wild and dense, rising up to a weathered peak of black rock in the middle, and the whole was covered in trees and brush of the darkest greens imaginable. The trees were tall and twisted, bearing broad leaves as large as a man that fanned out in wide, arching canopies. The dark sand, the dark foliage, and the thick shadow underneath it all was foreign and mysterious and exciting. One had the sense that anything could be in that jungle. And it probably was. Wonders. Dangers. And most importantly, something so important to the wizards of Sona that this expensive and risky voyage rendered it worthwhile. The wizards were eager to disembark, but Captain Killian insisted on caution.

The ship sailed slowly around the island, Levin marking their speed with a knotted rope that dragged in the waters and giving him a round measure to estimate the island as roughly seven miles in diameter. There were no signs of life except for the large seabirds, a kind of long beaked albatross from what anybody could tell. No smoke from fires. No boats. No docks. No signs of trees felled by tools. It was as much reconnaissance as could be managed from the ship. The Dragonfly dropped anchor in a broad, sheltered cove. Hamfast watched over the railing as two dozen sailors loaded into row boats and set to shore to scout the landing area, much to the annoyance of the wizard Whitaker, who was pacing on deck and grumbling incessantly at being coddled by scuff necks while there was important business to see to.

The men spent several hours ashore, machetes in hand as they scouted the area surrounding the cove. They reported back of having found nothing but strange plants and brightly colored birds. At last, the captain gave the go-ahead. A dozen men accompanied the three wizards, and the party set off into the jungle in search of whatever the wizards sought there. Meanwhile, others set about making a somewhat defensible camp at the landing site.

It was now Hamfast's turn to be impatient. "Please, Captain," he begged. "I won't go far, I just want to see what can be foraged. We don't know how long we'll be here, and surely there's fruit and wild roots and bulbs, herbs and mushrooms and the like. Once we set sail again we will be glad to have fresh food in our stores, even if just a little." It was a farce, however, and both Killian and Hamfast knew it. Hamfast only wanted to see this strange place firsthand. But the Captain allowed it at last, if only to shut him up. Although, he was given an escort.

"We really ought to turn back," Brogan protested. "I can 'ardly see ten feet ahead of me in this damned forest. And these fucking bloodsuckers!" There was a loud slap as the burly man swatted his arm for the hundredth time that hour.

Hamfast scampered over a fallen tree, half rotted and overflowing with termites and grubs that spilled from its entrails. "There are a few advantages to being small," he called back. "For one, I don't have to worry about tree branches smacking my ugly face."

"Are you saying my face is ugly, or yer own?"

"I didn't say." Hamfast's satchel was brimming with mushrooms. Much of the fungus was surprisingly familiar, the same types that grew in the wild islands on the coast of Dahk Ahani, and he harvested them with confidence. Brogan was carrying a satchel heavy with mangoes and bananas. Hamfast had spent most of the afternoon rubbing leaves on his arm, inspecting sap color, sniffing and tasting and scratching notes with a pencil into the back of his ledger. For everything familiar, there were a dozen surprising and new types of plants out here, and he explored as much to feed his own curiosity as to feed the bellies of the sailors. He knew how to avoid the obvious poisonous plants—the shiny leaves, the umbrella shaped flowers, anything that smelled of almonds. He wouldn't take any risks with the crew, but he had a few curiosities he had kept for himself to try that night, including a wandering fern with the sweetest dill-like leaves he'd ever tasted.

They had meandered in circles through the jungle, always within earshot of the shoreline encampment, and Hamfast had let Brogan urge him back several times when the voices grew faint. The escort had not been an imposition after all. It gave him a strong back to carry things, and having a nervous Brogan behind him meant Hamfast could keep his attentions focused on whatever caught his eye.

"Stop a minute and let me piss," Brogan said, his growing annoyance hardly masked. Hamfast looked back over his shoulder, seeing the man was just a few paces behind him. Hamfast stopped as instructed, looking about him from a perch on a set of gnarly roots at the base of a dark and mighty tree. He could throw a tarp on these roots, and it would provide an ample tent for several Lindle, he wondered. It was a permanent twilight under the dense canopy above, the massive trees fighting for every drop of sunlight and the mosses and ferns clinging to them like flowing green dresses. Flowers grew from the crooks formed where the branches met the trunk, life clinging to life everywhere one looked. And the birds were wondrous here, too. Bright pinks and oranges and purples, their songs sweet but completely foreign to his ears.

One landed nearby, and Hamfast walked towards it. The bird was nearly as large as him, black and fiery crimson, with extravagant tufts of plumage protruding from the top of its head. Hamfast approached it cautiously. Its beak was short, and so not a predator, but he didn't want a defensive peck from that large beak either. He eventually got too close and it squawked in alarm, leaping swiftly into the air and flying away. Hamfast followed its flight with a sense of delight. And then, as he turned, he met the gaze of two yellow eyes in the foliage, only a dozen paces from him.

Hamfast's scream was met with a loud, grating screech as a black shadow leapt at him. Hamfast twisted to run, but an explosive impact sent him sprawling. A tearing pain ripped from his shoulder down his back, and he howled in fear and agony as what felt like a dozen knives sank into his shoulder near his neck. The cacophony included a new sound, a great bellow from nearby. The painful daggers let go with another rip of flesh. Brogan's heavy boot kicked the thing, and as Hamfast scampered away he could see the man brandishing his machete at a great snarling cat, black as night, and just as large as the carpenter, if not larger.

Brogan never took his eyes off the beast, wielding his machete like a sword between himself and the snarling maw of the beast, his trousers still untied and his manhood exposed. Hamfast saw that it was no panther, however. Its body was black scales instead of fur, like a snake, and its head was far too wide even for the muscular four-legged body that supported it. It snarled at Brogan, its mouth broad and frog-like and filled with rows upon rows of sharp yellow teeth.

"Run, Hammy!" Brogan shouted, his eyes wide and his knuckles white around the machete.

Hamfast ran. He ran as his shoulder screamed, raw and sticky with his own blood, his satchel flailing wildly behind him and snagging on underbrush in his wake. He flew through the jungle without looking back. He ran until his lungs burned and his side cramped. And still, he ran for his life.

17

# THE QUEEN OF MASKS

The road down from the Upper City was less traveled now that the Skyway was flying around the city, but still bustling with people. Sona rested on a tiered limestone pedestal, a bit like an overly decorated white wedding cake. The upper class could move around the city in skycoaches, and now the Skyway provided similar transport for everyone. But most goods still needed to move by cart the old-fashioned way. Moving from tier to tier was accomplished by four roads, one at each point of the compass, that sloped into great ramps alongside the ring walls.

Aideen walked among the merchants and their carts down the western ramp and into the Inner City, leaving the grand manors of wealth and nobility to descend into the Potter's Quarter, a section of the city filled with artisans of every nature. Their signs were simple, as most here lived on their reputations, and the din of bargaining filled the streets among vendors of every cut and class. Aideen flipped the hood of her cloak over her head. She was grateful that all this skulking around the city incognito had been required during cool weather. She had no idea how she would have done it in the summertime.

From the Potter's Quarter, she turned south and followed the smaller avenues. The crowd thinned into obscurity as she worked her way closer to the small streets near the terrace, and there she walked down the quiet canyon between the backs of buildings and the smooth limestone wall that stretched up above them.

The Red Dress was unremarkable from the outside. It stood half a dozen stories tall, the same brown brick as the rest of the buildings nearby. It had no sign outside, only a wooden door painted dark red and shuttered windows looming down from above. Aideen stood staring at the door for a long time. She had no idea what to expect from this place. She had imagined it would be another tavern, but it did not look like one from the outside. It was too large. Too tall. Too out of the way and nondescript. What was she getting herself into?

"Answers," she told herself, steeling her nerves. With one last look over her shoulder, she pushed on.

Aideen hesitated just inside, easing the door shut behind her. The foyer was small, with doors obscured by fine beaded curtains leading in three directions. The two on the sides were dark, but light and music came from the one before her. She slipped her hands through the beads and peered into the room beyond.

The room was as large as the Lindenhall ballroom, darkly lit by candles ensconced along the walls instead of glowlamps, casting the room in flickering shadows. A large circular stage stood prominently in the center of the room, encircled by many tables. The room was lavish and dark and overwhelmingly red. The seat cushions, the walls, the flowers on the table. It was red upon red upon red, which took on a sickening bloody hue in the dim lights.

If there was any doubt of exactly what sort of place she was in, the three women on the central stage dispelled it. They wore streamers of red silk from their necks and waists that left little to the imagination—and would surely reveal all if their sultry dancing were to speed up in the slightest. A lone cellist provided the music. Only a few men occupied the tables. They were well-dressed and seemed to be paying more attention to their conversations than the women slinking around the stage.

A scatter of deeply cushioned sofas lined the far wall of the room, separated by trellises covered in climbing ivy that created a dozen small nooks for conversation. Or foreplay. Or whatever. The smell of incense hung thick and sweet in the air. Aideen took it all in, her mind whirring. It was a brothel, or something like it. She had never been to such a place except in books, and she had never imagined herself walking into one. She could feel herself blush as she watched the dancers, slack jawed. The unexpectedness of the scene only added to her nervousness. It was morning, which explained its relative emptiness. She could only imagine what it would be like tonight. But how could such a place provide her answers?

"How can I serve you, miss?"

Aideen started at the voice, coming from behind her. A woman, pretty and raven haired, had emerged from one of the side passages in the foyer behind her. She stood with a noble's poise, the feminine features of her body hidden beneath a red silk robe. She smiled at Aideen, bowing her head.

Aideen stiffened, trying to regain her composure. "I'm here to see a woman named Beatrice. Or speak to her, rather."

The woman cocked her head. "Does she expect you?"

"Not at all. Tabitha, of the Dusty Pearl, sent me. But I am quite unexpected, truth be told."

"I see. Wait here, then." The woman walked to the other side of the room, to a corner table hidden from view by one of the ivy trellises. The woman bowed in greeting to someone out of view. Aideen craned her head through the curtain of beads to try to get a better look, but could see nothing through the green foliage crawling up the trellis at the far side of the room. The conversation was short, and the woman returned to where Aideen still stood, trying desperately not to look as nervous or out of place as she felt.

"She will see you," the woman said simply, and then passed back through the foyer's side passage from which she had originally appeared.

Aideen gathered her courage and walked across the room, casting sideways glances at the women dancing on stage. At the corner table, she found a woman sitting alone on a semicircular sofa, piled high with pillows which had been pushed aside. The woman's deep chestnut hair obscured her face as she hunched forward, her attention on the low table in the middle of the half-moon sofa, where she was slowly flipping cards into piles. She wore a sleeveless green dress, a cloak draped carelessly on the sofa beside her. One of her bare arms showed a black tattoo that splayed from the wrist up to her shoulder, a series of branching lines of varying thickness and in no discernible pattern. A wine glass perched near the edge of the table.

"Tabitha doesn't send many people my way," the woman remarked without looking up, flipping a card into one of the many piles. "What makes you so special?"

"My father was murdered," Aideen said, keeping it simple. "My proof is thin, and I'm desperate for answers."

The woman's eyes snapped up from the cards to appraise her. They were a deep brown and piercing from beneath the veil of her dark hair. "Well, that would explain it."

"Explain what?"

"Tabitha sending you here."

"Because you can help me?"

"That's not what I meant. But maybe." The woman shrugged, then leaned back into the deep cushions piled up next to her, pulling her bare feet up onto the sofa and retrieving the wine glass from the table. She studied Aideen over the lipstick-stained rim of the wine glass. "That depends on a great many things."

"I came to you for help. On the advice of a stranger. I've already said I'm desperate because it's true. So whatever I can do to convince you, you need only ask. Beatrice, is it?"

"Yes."

"My name is Aideen Bormia, and if you aid me in any way, I am at your service."

"Oh, I know who you are," Beatrice said, sipping her wine. "You're engaged to Lord Cathal Gwenhert. Have a seat."

Aideen took a seat on the end of the sofa, around the curve of it so that she was roughly facing Beatrice as she lounged. The woman had an exotic beauty, of an origin Aideen could not discern. Her eyes were large and shone with a keen, intelligent light. They had an intensity, an awareness to them, which made Aideen all the more nervous. Her skin was fair, her hair thick and wavy and well managed. Her hands were rough, however. More like that of a servant's hands. And the tattoos on her arm were unusual. Did she work here? Did she oversee it in some manner? Aideen looked back over at the display on the stage. "So is this your place of... business?"

"No," Beatrice said, her eyes still fixated on Aideen. "But I do regularly conduct business here."

"It seems an odd choice of place to conduct business," Aideen remarked.

"And why is that?"

"Oh." Aideen realized that she had spoken without thinking and tried to come up with a way to backpedal. "I just mean..." Her eyes flicked to the spectacle on stage on the edges of her vision.

Beatrice pursed her lips, seeing the direction of Aideen's glance. "Do you think less of them for putting their bodies on display?"

"I didn't mean to imply anything."

"And yet you did." Beatrice shifted on the sofa, crossing her legs and sitting straighter. She gestured at the stage. "Those are good women. There aren't a lot of choices for women without families in Sona. Without skills or connections. Sometimes life deals you a rotten hand, and you have to make the best of it. A woman in a desperate situation might find a job as a scullery maid. Or doing some merchant's laundry. Or she can dance for those same masters here, or sleep with them, and earn enough to change her choices. It isn't how things should be. But it's how things are."

Aideen sighed. "I did not mean to pass judgement. But I'm just a bit out of place here."

"You are," Beatrice agreed.

"Look, I am trying to apologize. I had no idea I was walking into a place like this, and forgive me for finding it shocking. Not abhorrent. Merely something I have never experienced."

Beatrice sipped her wine, squinting at Aideen. "Consider it forgiven. That's a better response than I expected from you."

"From a spoiled Upper City tartlet?"

Beatrice's expression softened, a shadow of a smile finding her lips. She raised her glass. "Exactly."

"It seems to me the assumptions go both ways."

"Maybe so. Maybe so. Just look in the mirror at your privileges before you judge anybody else's choices too harshly."

"You're right," Aideen said. "I am privileged, and I cannot pretend to truly know the lives of others less fortunate. And you're also right about desperation." Aideen leaned forward on the sofa. "Because none of my privilege can do a gods damned thing to bring my father back. I'm just a woman whose father was taken from her. And I'll do anything to discover the truth of it."

"And so Tabitha sent you to me. Fair enough." Beatrice swung her feet back to the floor, smoothing her dress. "I know of your father's death. The whole city knows. I hadn't heard anything about murder, though."

"That's because I'm the only one who suspects it."

"And what exactly are you after, then?"

"My father was poisoned. I need information on what sort of poison it was. It's not the sort of thing one can just ask about freely. Believe me, I've tried and made a right fool of myself."

Beatrice seemed to mull this over. "You know, you're lucky I have a soft spot for broken families. I'll take you to her."

Aideen gave her a puzzled look. "Take me to who?"

Beatrice laughed. "Oh, you're not here to see me. I'm just a gatekeeper in this instance. The one you seek is the Queen of Masks."

AIDEEN FOLLOWED Beatrice up the stairs of the Red Dress, past many landings that branched off into many corridors of deep oaken panels, stained dark and lit only by occasional candlelight. Closed doors lined the halls. They passed a young woman on the stairs, wearing the same silk robe as the woman in the foyer. At the top of the stairs Beatrice led her through a nondescript door, then instructed her to wait there.

Aideen was left alone in the room. It was lavishly decorated, and all in shades of red. The floors were heavily carpeted, with rugs atop rugs, and thick tapestries hung on the walls in exotic patterns. A large desk dominated one corner, and deep sofas and armchairs were arranged much like a drawing room. If there were windows in the room, they were covered by the tapestries. It was a room for secrecy, she noted. The heavy fabrics would muffle any conversation had within. Aideen began to wonder what this place really was, exactly.

Aideen paced the room, unsure how to feel. Her emotions were a muddled mess. She did not know what to expect next, and she had no idea who this Queen of Masks was—and what a ludicrous pseudonym. She felt that answers were closer than she dared hope. But she hoped just the same.

Whatever she had expected, it was not what came through the door. She turned at the sound of it opening to find a woman entering with a slow and regal gait, surveying Aideen where she stood awkwardly in the center of the room. The woman was tall and thin, dressed in a red silk robe the same bloody color as nearly everything else in this place, the hood of the robe covering the top of her head. From beneath the hood, her face was shrouded by a white porcelain mask that covered all her features except her mouth. Beatrice stood behind her.

Aideen could not fathom how she was expected to address this individual. Queen? Your highness? Your strangeness? So she simply stood and waited.

The masked woman walked past her and drew a cigarette from a box that lay on the desk. She inserted it into a long brass holder and lit it, still studying Aideen, leaning against the desk. "Well. You said you wanted information, yes?"

Aideen was at a loss for words. The strangeness of the past hour was just all too much. Her confidence had faltered. She looked back and forth between Beatrice and the robed woman.

"Well?" the woman asked.

"Yes," Aideen said with some hesitation. "I believe my father was poisoned. My father had many rivals, but discovering a specific motive to kill him has been murky at best. If I can discover the poison, I hope to discover who might have acquired it or how."

"I may be able to help you. Tell me of your father's death."

"He died during the Festival of Eridayah, when the city was all out in the park. I found him dead in his study that night, a teacup sitting on his desk. He was not in the habit of drinking tea, and certainly not in the evening. That alone is suspect, I believe. But it was the color of the tea that was damning. I have been unable to find a tea that brews in that color, or with the distinctive ring it left in the cup. And so, I believe he was poisoned. Perhaps by a rival, perhaps by another."

The masked woman pursed her lips. "You remember the exact color of the tea?"

"I have a good memory."

"Ah! Well then, all is well!" The woman laughed. "It's been months since your father's death. The teacup long gone, and your only evidence is your good memory. You remember the exact color of the tea? The exact color? After all this time?"

"I do," Aideen said.

"The exact color?" The eyes behind the mask looked at her with a haughty combination of mirth and pity.

Aideen knew how it sounded. This woman thought she was a fool, or a mad woman, driven to fantasies in her grief. Aideen didn't appreciate being mocked or thought mad. She'd already gotten plenty of that from Riann. Her emotions flared, but she fought to keep her voice calm. "I remember."

The woman flicked ash from her cigarette into a crystal tray on the desk. "Darling. I might be inclined to help you, but surely you must see this is folly. And honestly, Beatrice. I would have expected a little more diligence before bringing a stranger to meet me."

Anger erupted inside Aideen with a sudden fury, and she began to snatch at the ring of hair buns that circled her head. The masked woman and Beatrice exchanged a look, surely wondering exactly how deep Aideen's madness ran. Aideen paid them no heed, pulling at her hair and making a mess of it on one side until she felt the olive leaf curve of her ear pop out from the nest of hair and pins. "Look. Now you're wise to the Bormia family secret. I have elven blood in my veins."

"So I can see," the masked woman said through the smoke of her cigarette, which dangled with a long column of ash.

"The elves observe more than humans do. Or differently,

rather. And those with mixed blood as myself, though it's a messy business, observe differently still. You can ask me about anything in the room downstairs, and I'll recall it to you as though I'd been there a hundred times. I can tell you about the shoes the cellist wears, or how much liquor is in the bottles on the bar. I can tell that you're a Lady for countless reasons, and from Rodomata I'd wager given the cloves in your tobacco and the line where your pinky ring is normally worn. I can tell you that Beatrice was downstairs cheating at her own card game when I walked up. So yes," Aideen sucked in her breath. "On the night of my father's murder, the most traumatic experience of my life, I remember the gods damned tea that killed him. It is burned in my mind, and I will never forget it!"

The cigarette glowed at the end of its brass holder, dropping ash on the floor. The robed woman exhaled the smoke slowly, letting it drift into the air around her. "I like this one," she said to Beatrice.

"I thought you might."

"A bit mad, though."

"Perhaps she has a right to be."

The woman in the mask studied her for a long moment. The light of her cigarette crept down the paper, leaving behind a stinking pile of ash perched precariously at its end. She tamped it out onto the crystal ashtray and leaned against the desk. "Your request is just, and so I shall entertain it. What do you require?"

Aideen pushed down the anger that still roiled in her belly. She took several deep breaths to calm herself. "I have made no progress on finding the truth, and the only shred of evidence I have is my memory of that teacup. I need to know about poisons. I need to know what kinds of poisons could kill a man without a trace, and yet leaves a mark in a teacup as this one did. I need to see them. I need to be sure. I know it's grasping at straws, but all my hope rests upon it."

"This is something I can provide."

"You know I am wealthy. It means nothing to me. I can pay handsomely for this information. My father was my world. Whoever murdered him, I would see brought to justice."

"I deal in information, darling. I care little for money. Secrets are my currency."

"Then what do you need from me?"

"You will bring me information, and I will give you what you seek. Are we in agreement?"

Aideen blinked in confusion. "What information? What can I possibly know that benefits you?" What is it even that you do here, she wondered. The strangeness of it all ran deep.

"Nothing you know interests me, darling. But you can help me gain access to it. You will be assisting Beatrice in a matter."

"Wait, what?" Beatrice interjected. "You cannot honestly expect -"

"You advocated on her behalf, darling."

"It's a simple in and out job." Beatrice retorted. "I don't need help."

"It's the out that concerns me," The Queen of Masks tapped at her cigarette. "Have you found a way to open the door?"

"No," Beatrice said, "Our inside woman has found nothing. But we know where it is, and I can pass through it if I must."

"Oh? So this power is reliable now?"

Beatrice's nose twitched. "It will work if I need it to."

"Perhaps, darling. But that sounds like an unnecessary risk. What she says is true, the elves see as we do not. I know something of the *ke'i gen de'san*, and that stacks the cards in our favor." Aideen blinked in surprise at the elven phrase. She noted that Beatrice did as well, not understanding. "It is decided," the masked woman said to Beatrice, then turned her attention back to Aideen, her eyes narrowed behind the mask. "Are we in agreement?"

"How can I agree when I don't know what you're talking about?"

"You said you would give anything for the information." The mouth beneath the mark pursed into something like a smile. But it was the smile of a snake to a mouse, and it sent a tingling chill through Aideen. "So agree to do anything, or we are done here."

Aideen closed her eyes. She was completely out of her depths. She could not fathom why this woman would agree to help her. And she could not fathom what was being demanded of her. But if her choices were to walk away, or to take a step forward, what choice did she have? She looked to Beatrice, who only shrugged back at her.

"We are in agreement."

## 18

## THE HEIST

It was madness, Aideen thought at her reflection in the mirror. She had no business getting into business with people like this. Kayla stood behind her, running a scented brush through Aideen's hair with practiced strokes. The absolute normalcy of it set Aideen's teeth on edge. She studied her own face. It seemed calm and collected enough while a servant tended to her vanity. Her eyes betrayed her, though. Her eyes glimmered wild with fear and anticipation.

What have you gotten yourself into? These people, this masked woman and Beatrice, were not of her world. They were not of any world that normal people knew. They lived some alternate life in the shadows, dealing in secrets and who knew what else. And now Aideen was beholden to them. For what, she hadn't the faintest idea. And yet, answers were so much closer now. Whatever it was, it didn't matter. Whatever she had to do, she told herself it would be worth it. She hoped she was right.

"I will be out today," she told Kayla.

"Oh, miss? Where to?" Kayla looked up at her with more interest than Aideen had hoped to arouse.

"To call on a friend, that's all." It wasn't exactly a lie, and

Aideen tried to convey it in a voice she thought sounded sufficiently casual.

"I like to see how social you've become lately, miss. It's good for you. I always said your father encouraged you to stay at home more than he ought. Yer hair covers the ears just fine when I do it, and so long as you don't go galloping around on horseback, I says I couldn't see the harm in it. Will you be home for dinner?"

"I don't think so. Tell mother not to expect me, will you?"

"That I'll do, miss."

No galloping on horseback. Aideen smiled at the idea. Who knew what she would be doing by midday? She couldn't deny that there was a sense of excitement in the unknown path that lay ahead of her.

AIDEEN RETURNED to the Red Dress, just as nervous as the last time. She was once again walking through the front door with no idea what would come next. The same woman in the red silk robe emerged from behind the beads. "You are expected. Please follow me."

Aideen followed the woman up a single flight of stairs. At the end of the hallway, the robed woman gestured towards a closed door and bowed. She turned around without another word. Aideen watched her go. She wondered exactly what the woman did here. Was she a prostitute? A spy? Perhaps the women here were all of the above. Aideen turned back to the door and pushed it open.

"Well, just let yourself in," an irritated voice said as she entered. "No need to knock." Beatrice stood in the middle of the room. Clothes were laid out neatly on a bed beside her. Beatrice herself wasn't wearing any. Aideen could see the tattoos on her arm did not stop there, but wrapped around her shoulder and torso and down one muscular thigh. The woman had several scars across her body of the sort Aideen could easily recognize. She might have the same scars if her sparring sessions were not using blunted blades. Beatrice made no attempt to cover herself, only putting her hands on her bare hips and eyeing Aideen with a look of annoyance. "Well, don't just gawk, foolish girl. Shut the door and help me with this."

Aideen closed the door, deciding to skip the apology and questions. Beatrice sighed, retrieving a pile of green fabric from the bed. Aideen helped her into the dress. It was an elegant material, light and airy and decorated with tiny beads of glass that caught the light of the glowlamps. Beatrice didn't wear a corset, and the dress hung from her shoulders in gentle, sweeping lines. It was an unusual design. "I'm not sure I'm dressed for the occasion," Aideen said as she fussed with the clasps of the dress.

"You're not," Beatrice said. "Your dress is hanging over there." Aideen saw a pale blue dress hanging beside the dressing mirror. It was of a similar foreign style.

"Well, I can't say I had any idea what to expect in coming here, but this certainly wasn't it."

"We're after information," Beatrice said as she adjusted the dress. "We'll find it in the house of Duke Brethan Sturlis, who happens to be having a private ball at his manor in the Upper City."

"What sort of information?"

"That isn't important for you to know."

"I see. Then why does the woman in the mask need me here?"

"You aren't needed here," Beatrice snapped. "And her name is the Queen of Masks."

Aideen gave her a look. "And that's a silly name."

"It's an apt name." Beatrice smoothed her dress and checked herself in the mirror. "Undress. Lose the corset and the rest. You and I are posing as women of the Sundrelands. And they do not wear anything beneath their dresses. You'll get used to it."

Aideen did as she was told. She bit back her discomfort in stripping naked in front of a stranger—and in a brothel, no less. There were other things to consume her attention. "And this so-called Queen wants me to help you get some information, but I don't need to know what. And she doesn't really need me to do it, but she's coercing me to be a part of it anyhow?"

"You've got the sense of it."

"I don't mean to sound ungrateful, but that makes no sense at all."

Beatrice sighed. "You aren't needed here, and I'm sorry if I'm cross at your inclusion in this affair. I usually do these things with a different partner. Or alone."

"I understand you don't agree with her, but there is no need to punish me for that. Your Queen seemed to think I can be useful. But I doubt it if I don't know what I'm getting into."

Beatrice studied Aideen through the reflection in the mirror. "Maybe so. I suppose we'll see. Alright, then. We're seeking a ledger that will be hidden in the duke's study."

"Well, that sounds awfully mundane."

"It won't be if it proves the duke is involved in a conspiracy to move illegal cargo around Elora."

"And the door she mentioned?" Aideen asked. "The one I'm supposed to be helpful with?"

"An escape route. Through a secret, hidden door in the cellars. Which we won't need if everything goes according to plan. But if we do, she thinks you'll be able to find a way to open it."

"A secret door? Okay, that's decidedly less mundane." Aideen thought of the many stories she had read, wherein the villain has a secret hideaway for his nefarious business. It seemed to her the evidence should be in the secret rooms, not lying about his study. "Wait, why does Duke Sturlis have secret doors? It's something out of a mystery novel."

"Don't get too excited."

"Oh, I'm not," Aideen said. "A conspiracy to poison my father is also a plot from a mystery novel, and a lot of good those books did me in finding his killer. Questioning doctors and herbalists and tea sellers around the city only got me strange looks. One probably reported me. Maybe more than one."

"Well at least the attempt led you here," Beatrice said. "Now, arms out while I do this."

Aideen stood while the dress was situated on her and the clasps fastened. The dress itself felt wonderful, even if the situation had her nerves prickled. It was many times lighter than the layers of ruffles and lace she normally wore on occasion of a ball. She swished one leg out, and the fabric moved with her like liquid. She appreciated the free feeling of not being stuffed into a corset. It felt more like something to sleep in than to wear to a party. She studied their reflections in the mirror. Their dresses were a far cry from modest, the flowing fabrics clinging here and there to reveal details that were nobody's business.

"Well, that's something," Aideen said. "So what exactly is the plan here?"

"It's simple enough. We attend the ball under assumed personas. We slip away at an opportune moment to go upstairs. I'll get what we need from the duke's study, and we return to the party. At the end of the evening, we leave and your part is done." Beatrice fussed with her hair in the mirror. "See? Simple."

Aideen laughed. "You might be able to dance your way into a party with a made-up name and a silky dress, but I will most certainly be recognized in an Upper City ball."

"No, you won't. You and I will be wearing masks, just like everyone else." Beatrice gestured to two white porcelain masks on the dressing table. "The silliness of your Upper City friends works in our favor."

"Even with a mask, my red hair stands out, and someone is like to recognize my voice. It would be easy to find me out."

"It would. But not if you go with your ears on display.

You're to be my elven lover from the southern continent. Someone might think you resemble Aideen Bormia... but of course, you couldn't be her. Since Aideen is obviously not an elf."

Aideen opened her mouth to protest, and then snapped it shut. She considered, and then nodded. She began removing the pins that kept the hair coiled over her ears. "Alright. Fine, that will work. I suppose you have thought this through. I don't have to pretend to like it."

"Nor do I." Beatrice let a smile slip across her face.

"Then we are united in our mutual distain for the situation?"

"Well, we will need something in common. We're lovers, remember?"

"Right, that's the other thing I don't like," Aideen said. "Why is that bit important to this charade?"

Beatrice shrugged. "I need some reason to bring you along, and it's the simplest cover. No need to overcomplicate things. My Lady Smitherton character is known in a few circles here, and you fit nicely as her accessory. Any other questions?"

"A hundred."

"Look. Just follow my lead and play along. This whole affair will be over before you know it. You wanted information, didn't you? This is honestly a small price to pay for it."

Duke Sturlis of House Gwenhert lived in a manor home on the northern edge of the Upper City, wreathed in gardens that spilled out over the terrace edge in summer. Now they lay dormant in the winter's chill, with peeking color from red dogwood bark, the purple of grapeholly fans, and yellow witch hazel blossoms against a backdrop of evergreen boughs. Aideen walked through the gardens towards the manor with her gloved hand nestled in Beatrice's arm. The paths were strung with tiny glowlamps that crisscrossed overhead. Such things were an extravagance in Sona, and impossible anywhere else. The duke was clearly one to flaunt his wealth, and the expensive lights were only the first hint of it. The manor itself stood four stories tall, but seemed to stretch endlessly in all directions. Lindenhall was large, but this estate made it seem cozy by comparison.

The pair climbed the front steps to the manor, where two men stood on either side of the door. They wore armor more ceremonial than practical, standing at attention with gleaming halberds in hand. Beatrice addressed one of them briefly, who turned and opened the door for them. He entered ahead of them and announced to the room in a loud voice. "May I present— Lady Smitherton of Bryarhart. And esteemed guest, Lilly of Oakshire!"

The door opened into a grand entrance hall. The floors were white marble, polished to an immaculate gloss. The room was as tall as it was wide, with intricately carved panels and columns stretching far above them, ringed with railings where the upper floors looked down upon the room. A massive staircase cut from the same marble as the floor curved up and out from across the room to greet the second-floor mezzanine. The room was already alive with people, dressed in festive costumes and masks. The room turned away from their conversations as they entered.

"Lilly?" Aideen whispered at Beatrice as they walked across the threshold.

"It's an elven name."

"No, it isn't."

"Elves are always named after plants and rivers and such."

"No, they aren't."

"Well," Beatrice smiled as she walked into the room, as eyes descended on them from all directions. "People in Sona fancy that they are, so it will have to do. You're Lilly for the next few hours."

# PART III

*I studied a great many things during my time in the Spire. History, philosophy, politics, and magic. The one topic that received shockingly little emphasis was that of prophecy. I learned of the Talavara Prophecy, to be sure. And others. But I was never taught what to do with that knowledge.*

*Now that I have seen these events come to pass—and moreover, having had visions myself leading up to the events—I now put forth my opinion on the matter. Prophecy is no guide. It gives no direction. It is only a warning, the sounding of an alarm, that when these things are manifested the world must sit up and pay attention. That something is stirring in the waters, and a great tribulation is coming.*

FROM THE FORGING OF THE TALAVARA IN THE SECOND AGE, BY THE SYANI LEANNA

## 19

## THE TEMPLE

Hamfast poured water on his shoulder and down his back from his small canteen. The wound burned anew, and he whimpered as he tried to hold the cleanest piece of shirt he could tear off onto it. He was glad he couldn't see the gashes there. He could only imagine the horror of it just from the way it hurt, from the jagged valleys in the swollen tender flesh beneath his fingertips as he reached back and gingerly pressed the cloth onto them. He hoped he was helping and not making it worse. The jungle's beauty was no longer awe-inspiring. It was terrifying.

He had no idea which way he'd run. And now that he'd stopped and gathered himself, he had no idea which way might lead back. All directions looked the same. The sun was above, somewhere, but with the way the light filtered through the thick canopy it was like trying to find the sun on a grey day. It was all endless green above him, all equally lit by his only compass somewhere behind it all. The shadows played tricks on his eyes. So, he sat for a long time hiding between the roots of a towering tree, fighting against the fear and panic that gripped him, wondering if it was better to start walking or to wait to be found. He tried climbing one of the trees, but his shoulder screamed at him in the effort.

It would be dark eventually. And although the colors of the sunset might give him an idea of direction, they might not. And the night could hold worse things to fear than great snake cats looking for a Lindle snack. He knew that if he picked a direction and kept moving in a straight line, he would eventually find the shore. Seven miles wasn't that far, and then he could follow the beach around to the camp. It would be dangerous. It might take some time. But it would work—eventually. So, after a great deal of internal debate, and an even greater deal of self encouragement, Hamfast pulled himself back to his aching feet. He looked around seeking something, anything, to point him in a logical direction. A breeze blew through the treetops, drawing out a long and billowy shush from the canopy above. With nothing else to direct him, he followed the whispers of the wind.

Walking in a straight line through a jungle was no easy feat, however. He wound around the great trees, over lichen covered rocks and great clawing roots, and all the while glancing in every direction—for a glimmer of true sunlight, for yellow eyes, for evidence of his crew. Hamfast's eyes darted from side to side, certain that beasts lurked in every shadow, that every moving leaf was evidence of a predator hiding just behind it. He felt his heart beating in his chest, heard it pounding in his ears. He began to wonder if the beasts in the shadows could hear it, too.

Perhaps time flowed differently out here on the edges of the world because Hamfast felt like he walked for days with no company but the drumming of his heart and the toothy maws glistening in the shadows. His feet and back ached in protest. He felt tired and weak, and he munched on some of the safer seeming mushrooms he had foraged. Then at last, just as the canopy above him began to dim and the light took a redder color to it, the jungle before him suddenly thinned, the clear dappled light of the western sunset reaching him between the foliage. The beach! At last! Hamfast broke out into a run, breaking through the edge of the jungle. But it was not the beach he'd discovered.

Hamfast found himself in an overgrown clearing, the ground choked with creeping vines. In the middle of this clearing stood the crumbling remains of a building. Carved stone pillars stood side by side along the perimeter of a sun-bleached granite base. These columns had once held a roof, but it had long since collapsed, the remnants now a vine-covered spread of rubble in the midst of the white columns that remained. Fragments of walls still stood, but gave Hamfast little sense of the place. The more pressing piece of information was his sudden realization that the sun told him he'd been walking North all afternoon, in the exact opposite direction of the Dragonfly's camp on the Southern shore of the island. Hamfast fell to his knees and began to weep.

But did this place not look like a temple? A shrine? The kind of ruins one read about in old stories, the sort of place where artifacts of power were discovered by heroes and adventurers? Hamfast didn't necessarily believe these sorts of stories, but the thought triggered something within him. Perhaps this was the wizard's destination! If he had found a building somewhere in the middle of the island, surely the expedition would find it too. Hamfast pulled himself to his feet. Perhaps. Perhaps not. Perhaps they'd already found it and moved on. Perhaps this was just a useless ruin. But at the very least, it was a reasonably safe place to spend the night, and now he knew which way was what. He could shelter here for the night and rest, and in the morning he would decide what to do next.

He climbed the carved stone steps up towards the columns, and began to shiver despite the jungle's heat and humidity. There was something wrong. He stood at the base of one of the columns, looking around at the fallen walls and rubble. He noted that no birds sang here, but then perhaps that was only because...

And then he saw it. Slinking out of the jungle, the great scaly cat made no attempt to conceal itself now. It had been following him after all. The blood in Hamfast's veins turned to ice, and the final strength in his legs fled him. He tried to back away, but fear held him paralyzed. He looked madly around him, terrified to take his eyes off the beast, but desperate for an option. For an escape. For anything. His small legs would never let him outrun the beast, especially here in the open. And the most chilling part was that the beast seemed to know it, too, continuing its pursuit across the clearing at a lazy, sadistic plodding pace. Its wide, grotesque mouth hung open, a long tongue lolling to one side and dripping with what could have been filthy saliva or blood. Brogan's blood.

Hamfast didn't have time or presence of mind to think. He just ran. He slipped and fell several times on the rubble, looking constantly over his shoulder in the fading light. A considerable amount of rubble lay piled next to a lone crumbling wall, and Hamfast desperately clawed his way up the jagged stone. The rough edges cut his hands, his fingers numb and bleeding as he climbed in what he knew was a futile attempt to hold onto life for just a few moments longer. When he reached the top of the pile of rubble, he tried to climb up onto the wall. He threw himself up towards the edge, but could not reach it. "Gods damn it!" The beast was now at the base of the rubble, picking its way with the air of a leisurely stroll, drooling up at him, those yellow eyes and teeth regarding him with a kind of inevitability.

Hamfast swore. He snatched the leather satchel from his shoulder. Holding it by the strap, he jumped again and swung it over his head towards the top of the wall. The bag went over, but bounced right back as Hamfast came back down to his feet. The rubble beneath his feet shifted as he landed, twisting his ankle and dropping him to one knee. He jerked himself upright and tried again, the pain in his shoulder howling protest at the exertion. He tried again, hoping desperately that the bag might catch in a crevice and give him enough to climb up by. It came right back down again, coming open and spilling mushrooms out of its torn belly, and the rubble beneath him shifting with a troubling rumble. The beast was nearly on him now. Hamfast screamed and lunged again, the rubble beneath him complaining with a low groan. But the bag caught, and he tried to pull himself up by it, crying out in clawing fear and despair, feeling the ghost of those yellow teeth at his back.

A loud roar came from below him, something beastly and too loud to be any earthly creature. Hamfast closed his eyes and prepared for the painful end. But the sounds below him were no longer that of a beast. It was something else entirely, and deafening. He hung from the wall by the straining satchel strap for what seemed like forever, but the teeth never came. When the rumbling below him had ceased, Hamfast opened his eyes, terrified of what he might see.

Beneath him was now a yawning hole filled with massive pieces of stone. Half buried in the rocks lay the broken form of the beast, its hindquarters visible, twitching, but its head and body crushed by rocks the size of a carriage. The rubble had been unstable, and the creature's weight had been enough to set a chain reaction into motion, causing it all to shift and fall into whatever hole lay below in a rocky landslide. Relief swept over Hamfast, and he began to laugh—just a nervous titter at first, but soon exploding into a mad cackle. "Not so tough now, are you fucker?!" he called down to the monster. And then his satchel strap broke, and Hamfast fell.

~

HAMFAST PEELED his eyes open a long time later. His head was pounding, his leg throbbed, and he was in darkness. He could see a circle of stars above him. It took him a while to fully comprehend where he was. How he'd gotten there. His head ached so as to make even thinking painful. When he tried to move, a knife of torment shot through his leg and reminded him.

He ran his hands down his leg to his shin and found it to be intact, but moving it hurt like hell. "Broken," he moaned. But no bone protruded from it. That was something. He had broken an arm once, many years ago, after falling down the stairs into the hold of the Dragonfly on a rough sea. But he had no doctor, here. It was almost certainly a few hours since his fall, but for all he knew it could have been a full day. Or more.

Hamfast lay back on his rough, stony bed staring up through the hole above him. He wept, his body ripped and bloody and broken. He was just a cook. Not even a proper sailor. Just a cook from the Lower City, not a hero or an adventurer. He was born to fill tankards with ale in the Dusty Pearl, and now he was dying beneath some ruins on the edge of the world, like a pathetic fool. He had no satchel anymore, no canteen, and his weeping was dry and tearless. Despair and self-pity swept over him.

The wind blew above him, the rustle in the distant tree canopy a calming whisper that seemed to shush him. He listened to it, and his sobs slowed. He couldn't simply give up, he told himself dimly. He couldn't simply lay down and die. The expedition was still out there, and he could still be found. But only if he weren't in a hole. He rolled over onto his side and began to drag himself on his elbows off the pile of rocks. There was no climbing back up the way he had come down, so he would have to find another way up. "I've survived all this," he sniffed to himself. "I won't just die laying down. If I die, at least I'll do it trying to live."

He crawled slowly, carefully, so as not to cut himself further on the rocks. But each jagged bump sent his leg into ecstasies of pain. The movement and agony made his head swim, and he vomited suddenly. He lay down next to the puddle of his own filth, trying to collect himself. Trying not to weep. And when laying made him feel no better, he heaved himself back onto his hands and crept on.

He was in a room, he soon discovered, and not some cavern or a simple hole in the ground. Whatever the building above had once been, it had a basement of some sort. And he was in it. Once he was clear of the rubble, the floor was smooth stone. The moonlight was enough to make out the rough shape of it, and there were definitely passageways that led in three directions. He rested for a few minutes, debating. But he could see no reason to choose one over the other. He settled for the one that was closest. Something felt right about it to him. In his imaginations, he thought he could almost hear something calling him that way. Not a voice, but something anyhow. Perhaps just the wind again. He shook his head, and the motion hurt.

He found that he could crawl on the smooth floor, on hands and one knee, with the broken leg dragging behind him. The pain was familiar after a while, and he suffered it better now that he knew there was no escaping it. The passage seemed to go on forever, but he no longer trusted his senses. Everything was pain and confusion. He felt almost drunk, and he wondered if he was dying. But he was going somewhere. At the very least, he seemed sure this passage wasn't taking him downward. So maybe it was progress. After what seemed like leagues of crawling on his short limbs, the passage turned. And there was light.

Hamfast blinked. How had he not noticed the light before? The room he found himself in was small and round, with a raised dais in the middle and two circular steps leading up to it. But the light! The light came from torches on the wall. The torches did not glow with ordinary flames. They glowed white and purple, and winked without a breeze to disturb them. Hamfast lay down on his belly, staring into the room and wondering if he was succumbing to hallucinations as he died.

The way the torches flickered was strangely familiar. They looked like the glowlamps of Sona, only without the glass shrouds. And in the wrong color. There was no exit to the room that he could see beyond the one he now lay in. And yet, somehow, escape did not seem to be so important anymore. The lights made him feel safe. They beckoned to him, a moth to a flame, and so he dragged himself a little farther.

On the dais was another light, dimmer than the others, coming from a pedestal made of the same carved and polished stone as the floor and walls here. Hamfast felt weak, weaker than before, and yet he crawled on toward it. He pulled himself up the steps onto the dais. Then, getting his good leg under him, he pulled himself onto one foot and strained up at the pedestal.

On it, in a small carved hollow, was a jagged white rock no bigger than a man's thumb. Hamfast blinked. Not a rock, but something like smoked glass. Or crystal. Inside it, the same light that emanated from the torches seemed to live, flickering white and purple. Seemed to breathe. Seemed to speak to him wordlessly.

Without thinking, Hamfast took the stone and clutched it to his chest. Warmth spread through him. A sense of relief—as though it were now all over, and everything would be okay. He collapsed back to the floor, clutching the stone. "This is what they seek," he muttered to himself. "And they'll find it. And they'll find me." Hamfast's mind began to reel, the room fading into a misty haze, a whirling flash of light in his mind, and he welcomed it. He could rest now. It would all be alright. His consciousness faded, and he did not fight it. He faded into mist. Into clouds. Into the sound of distant thunder.

He dimly heard voices. Whitaker. Brogan. Captain Killian. But Hamfast merely slept, secure knowing that all was now as it should be.

## 20

## EXPOSURE

The room was a constant din of conversation layered over the musings of a stringed quartet. Hands held glasses of wine as masked faces danced and mingled around the extravagant gilded rooms, a marble white and silver backdrop that highlighted the brightly colored dresses the women wore like flowers peeking through a Spring snowfall. Aideen sipped her sparkling wine cautiously, careful not to let drink go to her head, yet careful to always have a glass of wine in hand for show.

There was a thrill of exposure—her ears prominently on display, and yet she hid safely behind the white mask and exotic dress and the persona she wore for the evening. Aideen followed Beatrice around the room, mingling with people she recognized that did not recognize her in return. People who would normally be friendly, who would normally show her the respect they held for her family's unusual station. Now, they looked at her only as a curiosity. Elves were never a part of such affairs, and here was an elf who was the exception because she was the guest of a foreign noble. Beatrice—Lady Smitherton—knew many of them as well, apparently. The pair of them lilted from one shallow conversation to the next, all laughter and smiles.

"Yes, but the people there are just so difficult. There is no sense of order amongst them, and our ships are held entirely at their whim." A middle-aged man in an elaborate bird-themed mask, complete with curved beak and bright plumage, had captured Aideen's attention. The group stood off to the side of the room during a dance, the women preening absently while the men made conversation to showcase their wealth and importance. Just the wealthy man's version of preening, Aideen thought. And this man was a direct competitor to her family's business. Being right across from him, anonymously, was absolutely delicious.

"Surely you only need bribe the authorities at port," another man offered.

"Oh, we have. It just buys us nothing. The other ships bribe as well. It matters to none of them that our ships arrived earlier, the importance of the cargo to the city, or even the promise of gold should they tend to us first."

"An unreliable people, I've heard. No offense to you, Lady Smitherton."

"Oh, none taken," Beatrice offered dismissively. She affected an accent of the Sundrelands from the southern extreme of Dahk Ahani. "You speak of Frendar, which I believe may be closer to your Shernah than it is to my lands. I myself have never spent more time there than is necessary for my ship to take on provisions en route to someplace more civilized."

"She makes my point for me," the man said. "An uncivilized people, more interested in making war than in proper commerce."

"They might be forgiven for their obsessions with warfare," Aideen interjected. She found it difficult to keep quietly smiling through all this. "The Frendarians are a kingdom divided, with the cousin Kings of Frendar and Seggrit both claiming the same throne. They have been at war or on the brink of it for a hundred years. Not to mention the constant threat of the roving orcish hordes to the west."

The man peered at her, taking her in. The dress. The hair. The ears. Aideen watched as his eyes traversed her in a lurid way they would never dare if she were Aideen Bormia. He shrugged. "I am disinterested in their history or politics, only in their coin. It is not my problem that they cannot form a stable government or control their borders."

"Perhaps therein lies your problem," Aideen said. Beatrice gave her a cautious look, and Aideen ignored it. "Master..." Aideen hesitated, knowing full well the man's name, but Lilly would not.

"Tonight, I am a peacock," the man grinned.

"Master Peacock," Aideen returned his smile. "Hardly a year goes by where one nation is not at war with another on the southern continent, with boundaries of rulership being redrawn faster than mapmakers can keep pace with. The people there tend not to see themselves as serving their lords as much as being ruled by them. And so the people deal with people, not peoples. Do you understand my meaning?"

"I'm afraid not," the bird-man laughed, and the others in the circle laughed with them. "Though your accent is impressive, my elvish beauty, I fear something is lost in the translation."

"Many of the peoples of the southern continent-"

"Are fickle," Beatrice interrupted. "As are the rabble anywhere, as far as I am concerned." The circle laughed, and Aideen only smiled.

Aideen followed Beatrice to the other side of the room. "He's a fool," she fumed to Beatrice. "I am disinterested in their history or politics, only in their coin." Aideen made a face. "He needs to make friends in port, which is not bought in coin. Not directly. Have his men buy drinks for the dockworkers in the taverns. Have them stay longer than needed, spreading word of their generosity and goodwill around the port. And then send the same ship back to that port next time, bringing gifts of Elorian liquors for those they drank with last time. Do that until the ship's captain and men are known there. The dockworkers will not hurry to bring one ship into port before another for a coin. All the ships offer gold. But a man of Dahk Ahani will hasten to drink with his friends, and will see to their ship first."

Beatrice stared at her. "Are you here to give advice to your brother's competitors?"

"Well, no." Aideen flushed. "But he's still a fool."

"Everyone here is a fool," Beatrice said. "Don't become one of them."

"Right," Aideen said. She sighed into her wine glass. "You're right, of course. But it's maddening when men talk of things I happen to know a great deal about and I'm meant to just stand about and look pretty."

"That is the way of things," Beatrice said. "Your only recourse is to make friends who aren't those kinds of men so you can complain about them together later."

Aideen poured her wine into a potted plant, behind Beatrice's back so that nobody would see. They had both been doing this all evening, per Beatrice's instructions. They needed to be seen getting new glasses of wine throughout the night without actually drinking them. Beatrice poured hers into another plant —both would be wilted in the morning, Aideen was sure. They took new wine glasses from where the servants were pouring. "Now what?"

"You're doing fine, minus the odd rant." Beatrice smiled, and it seemed genuine. "And as I said, nobody suspects a thing. We have no real ties to anybody here, so we are an afterthought. A curiosity at best, just two foreigners. So keep sipping wine and shortly we will head upstairs."

"Under what ruse?"

"Just to be on the walk above, looking down on the festivities and having a private conversation. A group of nobles did so earlier. We'll just slink away and go a bit further up to the study."

Aideen shrugged and sipped her wine. This was even stranger than she had imagined. The room seemed too loud with her ears uncovered, and it gave her the sense of nakedness which she tried to ignore. "I'm going to find something to eat. I've been fake drinking for an hour, and I don't want it going to my head."

"Certainly. Just stay in character."

Aideen ambled back across the room, taking the long way around it since the whole middle of the ballroom was filled with dancers. She smiled as she watched them, the women all twirling dresses and smiling faces. She loved dancing. But she supposed there would be no dancing tonight for her. She had no idea how an elf should dance. It was something that had never come up in her lessons with Lodai.

Aideen was nearly to the table where a lavish spread of foods was on display when her eyes shot wide. Standing there, looking right at her, was Lord Cathal Gwenhert. He looked almost as shocked as she felt. His eyes met hers, and the recognition was plain on his face, even behind the painted mask he wore. Aideen froze in place, unable to decide what to do next. Lord Cathal cocked his head in confusion. Then he walked towards her as Aideen's mind raced, searching for an explanation.

"I had not expected to see you here," he said quietly as he approached. "And I certainly never imagined I would see you, well, on display such as this."

"My name is Lilly, my lord." Aideen tried to keep her voice steady. "Lilly of Oakshire."

"Oh? And where is Oakshire, exactly?"

"I haven't the faintest idea."

"Well, I suppose I knew you were full of surprises."

"As are you, my lord. Here I thought you were engaged, and

yet you did not think to invite your fiancée to this fine ball. It seems quite exclusive."

Lord Cathal blinked, any glimmer of amusement gone from his eyes. "I am here on business."

"Ah, the business of drinking and dancing?"

"The business of House Gwenhert." His voice was flat, and unlike it had ever been with her before.

Aideen had been so caught up with him spotting her here that now it struck her that perhaps she had caught him in something as well. "Is your wife not to be included in that house? It seems to me an odd precedent to set, so early in your engagement, to be attending social gatherings without inviting her. Are you ashamed to be seen with your new fiancée?"

"You have no right to chastise me," Lord Gwenhert snapped, casting a glance over his shoulder. "You have your ears on display for all to see. And here I thought you meant to keep them a secret."

"Mind your voice, my lord. You do not want to draw any attention to us. You do not want anybody to wonder who you are speaking to."

Lord Cathal held his hands up. "Truce," he said, his voice softening. "I do not wish to fight. But truly, what on earth are you doing here?"

Aideen found it hard to be angry with him. And in truth, was she even angry at all, or simply inventing a reason to push him away after being caught in the midst of her charade? She felt conflicted. She felt she had a right to be cross with him, and she wished she did not. She wanted to return to that place of fond feelings for him. But she had no time to consider her feelings now. She needed to get back to Beatrice. She had to lie, of course. She could hardly tell him why she was here. "It was a foolish lark. I thought I would see how it felt. To be an elf in Sona, I mean."

"And how does it suit you?"

"It's different, although certainly not as it would be as

myself. I'm treated with a little respect on the arm of a guest. It isn't the same as being me. So it's hard to know." She sighed. "But it's something."

"Well, I must say, you look radiant in that dress."

"This is not the first time you've caught me strangely dressed."

"There are better words for it, but I'm afraid it would be improper to say them aloud."

Aideen met his eyes, and was suddenly very much aware of how the foreign-styled dress clung to her skin. She felt her cheeks grow hot, and she mentally shook herself. "I'm sorry, my lord, but I really have to be off. Trying this on in secret is one thing, but standing here next to you, people might wonder. They might realize how much I look like Aideen Bormia, only with longer ears."

He considered her. "So then you are not ready for that secret to be out yet."

"Not for some time, perhaps."

"I understand. It's a shame then. I would very much like to dance with you again tonight." He straightened up and nodded. "Well, it was lovely to meet you, Lilly. Your secrets are safe with me. Mind you don't spill them yourself before you are ready."

Aideen bit her lip and smiled at him. "If you only knew." She turned quickly and hurried off before he could ask her any more questions. And without having ever made it to the food, she realized. She doubled back and plucked several prawns wrapped in pastry from a silver tray, eating them quickly as she walked. Elves have terrible manners, for all these people knew. Her eyes darted around the room as she walked, looking for Beatrice. She found her back in the entry hall, chatting merrily with a group of strangers. Aideen quickly sidled up next to her, slipping her hand into Beatrice's elbow, and tried her best not to look as flustered as she felt.

Beatrice smiled over at her, then her brow furrowed. "Oh, darling. You've spilled wine on your dress."

"Have I?" Aideen looked down, and noted that she had, in fact. It wasn't much, only a spot. "I guess I got clumsy when I was looking for you."

"If you'll excuse us," Beatrice said to the conversation group of the moment. She pulled Aideen aside. "What's wrong? You look positively spooked."

"My fiancé is here."

"So?"

"So?" Aideen huffed. "So he's here and knows I'm me. I mean, he recognized me."

"Even with your ears?"

"Especially with the ears! Do you think I would be engaged to a man who didn't know he was marrying an elf?"

"Oh, shit!" Beatrice hissed.

"Yes, shit," Aideen agreed. "Or *fou t'ez*, in this case, if I'm to stay in character."

"I thought nobody knew you were an elf!"

"I said it's a secret, but not from everyone."

"Well, who else knows?"

"Only my family."

Beatrice crinkled her nose. "And your fiancé, apparently."

"Who is soon to be my family, yes. And a few house servants."

"And it never occurred to you to mention this before?"

Aideen huffed. "You didn't ask! This is your plan, not mine."

"You said this would work. I told you the plan, and you agreed it would work."

"Well pardon me, I didn't know he would be here."

Beatrice pointed an accusing finger at her. "But you should have known he might be."

"Indeed I should have," Aideen said. She swatted Beatrice's

finger aside. "But for some reason he did not invite me to this. But I can't exactly have a tiff with him about it right now, can I?"

Beatrice glanced around the room. "This is a mess. We may have to call this off. But I don't know when we'll have another chance like tonight."

"I told him this was a lark, being out in public as an elf, and he believed me. It's fine. You just needed to know. So long as we don't get into any trouble, we're fine. But you cannot keep me in the dark on what else you have planned. If I'm here, and I'm a part of this, I need to know what to expect."

Beatrice thought for a long moment. "Alright. Fine. It's simple enough. We go upstairs. We make our way to the study. I need to open a safe there, study the contents for a few minutes, and we come back downstairs. That's it."

"That's it?"

"Unless something else goes wrong, yes."

"Do things often go wrong on these little heists of yours?"

Beatrice flashed Aideen a smile. "Just follow my lead and be ready to think on your feet. And remember, you're Lilly. Not Aideen."

"I really hate that name, you know."

"You've mentioned that."

## 21

## UP THE STAIRS

Beatrice led Aideen up the wide, curving stairs from the entrance hall to the landing above, arms linked as they had been for much of the night. "Stay calm, and stay in character," Beatrice whispered. "There's no harm in us being on the second floor. Leaving the mezzanine and going higher is where we have to be careful. Just stay calm and everything will be fine."

"As long as nothing goes wrong."

"And if it does, we adapt. Just stay calm."

"You keep saying that. It's not helping."

At the top of the stairs, the mezzanine looked down on the entrance hall. They stood, Aideen doing her best to seem casual, and pretended to be deep in conversation. A large hallway led in either direction. At Beatrice's signal, they ducked down the hallway to the right and quickly out of sight of the guests below. Then they turned immediately left down another passage.

The easygoing attitude of the evening was gone now that they were on the move. Aideen felt herself tensing, her pace involuntarily quickening, and Beatrice kept pulling her back to match her own leisurely pace. Aideen took a deep breath. They were just two tipsy partygoers, and not thieves. Such a mindset clearly took practice, and Aideen had never had a reason to attempt such a thing. They came to another staircase at the end of the hall. "Two flights up, and then..." Beatrice trailed off.

Aideen heard it, too. Footsteps coming down the carpeted stairs. Beatrice pulled Aideen's arm hard—not the calm guidance of before, but an unmistakable silent *this way*. They opened the nearest door and eased it closed as quietly as time would allow. Aideen's eyes darted back and forth. They were in another hallway, a dozen doors lining either side at regular intervals. "Where are we now?" she whispered.

"Servants quarters," Beatrice whispered in return. "Most of the servants will be downstairs."

"Yes, but there's no good reason for us to be in here."

"Agreed. As soon as those footsteps pass, we head upstairs. Two flights straight up to the fourth floor. And when we get there..." The footsteps from the stairwell were now passing in the hall outside. Both of the women held their breath, listening to the slow and rather loud footsteps just outside the door. Beatrice mouthed the word *guard*, and Aideen nodded, her eyes wide. Yes, the footsteps were loud because those were boots, not the shoes of nobility or their servants. The footsteps kept moving, and they both let their breath out in a sigh. "Are you having fun yet?"

"Loads."

Beatrice bit back a laugh. "You get used to it."

"I can't see how."

A doorknob to her left rattled slightly. Aideen and Beatrice both turned to look at it in horror. Someone was coming out of one of the servant's rooms, and they were trapped between whoever it was and the guard walking through the hall just outside. The knob turned. Aideen looked from the door back at Beatrice, panic drawn across her face. She wanted to say something. To ask, now what? Or maybe simply to swear again, but she was cut off. Beatrice yanked open the nearest door and pulled Aideen inside with her so hard she nearly fell.

Aideen found herself in a tiny bedroom, reminiscent of those in Lindenhall only considerably smaller. It was currently unoccupied, thank the gods, although there was no way Beatrice could have known that for certain before barging in here. There were noises beyond the door in the hall, but Aideen could hardly process them over the roaring in her ears. Beatrice's hand was still a vice clamped on her arm. If Aideen had ever thought this whole escapade exciting, it had ceased to be now. Panic and fear griped at her, her heart pounded, and she felt beads of perspiration forming at her temples.

"Shh," Beatrice said from inches away. "You're alright. We're alright."

"Are we?" Aideen hissed between gritted teeth.

"Probably," Beatrice whispered.

The sound of footsteps passed by their door. Aideen held her breath. Her breath came in shallow, shaky rasps as they leaned against the door, as though holding it shut would prevent them being found out. But the footsteps continued on past them, and they heard the door onto the main hall open and then click back into place. Aideen heard Beatrice let out a raspy sigh of relief.

"Probably?" Aideen demanded. "Honestly?"

Beatrice snorted. "I was being honest. I've been caught doing worse."

"That's not as comforting as you think it is." She glared at Beatrice beside her. Beatrice was breathing hard. Their eyes met, and Beatrice's mouth screwed up as she fought back a laugh. "And it's not funny!" Aideen said, finding herself fighting back her own nervous laughter.

"It's a little funny."

"Only because we didn't get caught."

"Obviously. I can tell you, getting caught is definitely not funny." Beatrice seemed to consider this. "Well, sometimes it is after the fact. But only once you've gotten away again."

"Gods, you're enjoying this."

"A bit. This is what I do."

Aideen shook her head, trying to regain her composure and steady her breathing. "So, you were saying? When we get to the fourth floor? Spit it out quickly, please, before another servant shows up and we have to hide under the bed."

"Oh, we probably should have done that, actually. But yes. On the fourth floor, we'll arrive at a landing. There will be a guard up there. We are very drunk, understand? We're oblivious to whatever he tries to tell us."

"We're just happy and drunk. Got it."

"Quite. If there is only one guard, we need to get close to him. You be ready to catch him when he falls."

"Wait, what are you going to do to him?"

"It's just a trick, he'll be fine. Don't worry. Just be sure he doesn't make noise when falling down. If there are two guards for any reason, you're going to get sick. Can you make yourself vomit?"

Aideen recoiled at the bizarre question. "What? No!"

"Okay, then if there are two, follow my lead and play the drunken elf. Then just pretend that you're going to be sick. Gag a little. Make noises. That will have to be enough. We'll convince one of the guards to take you downstairs, and I'll have to deal with the other by myself."

"I..." Aideen was liking this less and less now.

"Look, you said be quick about it. If there's one, you catch him and then you're my lookout. If there are two, you need one of them to take you downstairs and you need to keep him there. Keep him occupied for as long as possible. It would definitely help if you could vomit on him, but if not, just be clingy. You're an elf, so nobody cares if you make a scene."

"My fiancé will."

"Right. Shit. Well, then just be clever about it and don't muck it up. You'll have to read the situation and think on your feet. Got it?"

Aideen shook her head. "I understand, but I am no actress. This is all quite outside of my experience."

Beatrice took Aideen's hands into hers, her voice softening into a kindness Aideen had not heard from her before. "Just remember why you're here. You help me, the Queen of Masks helps you find your father's killer."

Aideen squinted at Beatrice, then nodded. "Okay then. I'm as ready as I can be."

Aideen and Beatrice crept out of the servants' quarters, into the hallway, and up the stairs. Up one flight, and after a look around the corner, up another. Beatrice squeezed Aideen's hand. And at the top of the stairs, Lady Smitherton and Lilly of Oakshire stumbled their way out onto a landing.

Aideen's heart was pounding in her ears. The landing was a room unto itself, the floors thickly carpeted and the walls adorned with dozens of hunting trophies. Three closed doors led further into the top floor of the manor. Standing outside of one of them was a single guard, dressed in chain armor and carrying a sword at his hip. A lot of metal for a house guard, Aideen thought.

"Pardon, m'lady," the man said, holding up one hand. "This floor is off limits. Duke's orders."

"Oh, I know," Beatrice laughed, her gait unsteady. Aideen clung to her arm and began to giggle. "That's what he told us! And that's why we're here."

"Ladies." The man shook his head. "Please."

"Oh shush," Aideen said. She held a finger to her lips. "Shhh. Shhhhh. Shhhhhhshhsh." She let the sound dissipate into giggles.

"We're here to relieve you, solider!" Beatrice saluted, swaying as she did. All the while, the pair of them were getting closer to the guard.

"I canno' let ye stay up 'ere. Don't make me remove you, please. Duke's orders. It'll be a right embarrassment for all of us, yeah? I need ye both to go back down to the party. Enjoy yerselves. Just not 'ere."

Aideen watched the guard carefully as she swayed. He made no hostile moves. Why would he? His best course of action was to get rid of them without making a fuss.

"Isn't he darling?" Beatrice cooed. "A right proper solider, this one."

"I'm not a soldier, mam. I'm..." Beatrice's hand shot out, and then her hand was gone. Her whole arm was gone in fact, the sleeve of her dress empty and fluttering as inky black tendrils of smoke swirled and streaked from the sleeve over towards the guard, wrapping around his neck like a noose. Wisps of smoke snaked into his open mouth and nose. The man's eyes shot wide, a phlegmy clicking sound coming from his throat. Before Aideen could fully comprehend what was happening, she ran and wheeled around behind the man and grabbed him under the arms as he fell.

Beatrice pounced on the guard, pressing a handkerchief against his face. The smoke was gone. Beatrice's arm was whole again as if nothing had happened. The man gasped once, then went limp in Aideen's arms. "Lean him against the wall and let's hurry," Beatrice said.

Aideen swore, leaning the heavy guard roughly against the wall, then spun around to look at Beatrice. "What in the hell was that?"

"Keep your voice down," Beatrice said. "It was magic. Well, and then a kind of poison on the rag. The choking bit was just to make sure he breathed it in. But he'll be fine. He will sleep a few hours and then just have a headache for a bit. And he won't remember the last, oh, hour or so." Beatrice plucked the jeweled hairpin from her hair. She tugged at it, and several small oddly shaped pieces of metal snapped off the back of it into her hand, and she was instantly jamming the small tools into the lock on one of the doors.

"And it didn't occur to you to warn me that you could do magic?"

"It's easier to explain once you've seen it. And I didn't want to scare you off."

"Oh. I see. Well, that's fine then. Because I'm certainly not fretting over it now. And I guess I came to the right people about poison."

"You did. Here," Beatrice tossed something over at her, and Aideen caught it. It was a glass vial. "Splash that on him."

"And what is this? More poison? A magic potion?"

"Gin. It'll make him smell like he's been up here drinking."

"And he won't remember us?"

"Nobody will have any reason to believe anything is amiss except a guard who got drunk while on duty."

"It isn't very kind to the guard."

"No, but it can't be helped. Do you have a better explanation for a passed out guard up here?"

Aideen shook her head, her heart now pounding even harder in her chest. "Fine." She unstoppered the vial and splashed it on the man's face and shirt. Then she tucked the empty vial into a potted plant. May as well stay with the night's theme of hiding drink in pots. "Anything else I should know?"

"Probably not."

"I'm starting to really dislike that word."

There was a click, and Beatrice opened the door. "We're in. Come on."

Aideen followed her into the duke's study. It wasn't much different than Davin's had been. Or Riann's, for that matter. The desk. The shelves of books. The reading chair. Her life had begun to revolve around looking for answers in men's empty studies. Beatrice closed the door behind them and relocked it. Then she hurried over to a carved wooden cabinet and opened it. Aideen could see that the cabinet was merely a facade over a large metal safe. Beatrice set her tools to work on this lock, too.

"Can't you open the lock with that magic of yours? I doubt we have much time."

"I'm not that subtle with it. The magic is a new thing for me, and its more fist than fingers. But this business will be fast once the safe is open. The gemstone set in my hairpin is enchanted. Once I speak the command, it will recall everything it sees for a few minutes. I'll flip through the ledger while holding the stone, then put everything back as we found it."

"So you've got magic hairpins, too."

"The Queen of Masks has magic hairpins. Enchantments are beyond me. I just have a few tricks up my sleeve."

"Quite literally," Aideen said. "Is it the tattoo?"

"It's not a tattoo. More of a marking."

"Of what?"

"It just appeared a while back. And now I can... look, can I concentrate, please?"

"Sorry."

"Just keep your ear to the door and listen for—wait, I've got it." Beatrice grinned over at Aideen. "We're almost done here." Beatrice turned the latch on the safe and opened the door. And from inside the safe, a wail began to sound so loud that it made them both clamp their hands over their ears.

## 22

## THE BACKUP PLAN

"Shit!"

"What is that noise?" Aideen had to yell to be heard.

"A magical alarm." Beatrice snatched a large bound book out of the safe and yelled, "See for me now that I might remember!"

"What?"

"That's the command!" Beatrice started frantically flipping through the pages of the ledger, holding her hairpin over it. Aideen saw the gemstone set in the middle of the hairpin was now glowing with a flickering amber light.

"This wasn't part of the plan, I take it?"

"Nope! There wasn't supposed to be an alarm. So. New plan."

"What?"

"We run like hell."

Aideen fought down the rising panic, looking wildly around the room with no idea what she should be doing. "Right. Good plan."

"Listen at the door. Tell me when they get here. Downstairs will likely be chaos, but we only have a minute." Beatrice continued to turn the pages, swearing under her breath as they sometimes stuck together. "No, wait. Make a mess. Take something that looks valuable. Make it look like we were here for something else."

"Got it." Aideen attacked the room, which felt natural enough in her present frenzied state. She knocked rolls of parchment off the desk, books off shelves. Nothing looked obviously valuable, though. Not the kind of thing a thief would take. Then she wanted to kick herself. The safe, of course. She ran over to where Beatrice was hunched over the book and reached over her into the safe. The wailing sound was unbearable so close. Inside, her hand fell on a leather pouch. She snatched it out and peered inside. Gemstones. Small, but a lot of them. That would certainly do. She dashed back across the room to the door and pressed her ear against it. She could hear a din outside, but it seemed distant still. "Nothing yet."

"Good. We still have the escape route, but it's not a very good one if I'm honest."

"Well by all means, be honest."

"It still amounts to running like hell, and we'll have to figure out how to open the secret door."

"Wouldn't it be better to mingle with the crowd? Lose ourselves back in the party?"

"Maybe, if you weren't here. But that's assuming we could get there unseen. And I can guarantee you, the first thing the guards will do after they check this room is to get everyone together and have them take off their masks."

Aideen's eyes grew wide. "*Ka'sant!*"

"Yes, that. We can go out the window. Are you any good at falling without getting hurt?"

"Gods, not from four stories up."

"No, I mean just one. There's a balcony below this window."

"Oh. Well, in that case yes. That seems doable." Aideen

heard voices growing quickly louder, and heavy footsteps along with them. She rushed over and grabbed Beatrice's shoulder. "They're here."

"Remember all that you have seen," Beatrice said. The gemstone flickered, then went dark. Beatrice closed the ledger. She shoved it back into the safe and stood. "Are you ready?"

"Quite."

Beatrice held up her hand, and this time Aideen saw as the tattoo—or markings, or whatever,—flashed with a dark light. Then her whole arm seemed to turn into thick smoke that shot out at the window. The glass exploded outside into the night. Then, just as quickly, the hand was back to normal and squeezing Aideen's as they stepped up onto the windowsill. There was a rattle at the door as the doorknob jerked against the lock, and then a heavy thump against the door. Aideen didn't hesitate. She looked out the window, saw the balcony below her, and jumped.

Aideen landed on her feet, letting her legs buckle beneath her into an awkward sideways roll. It wasn't graceful, but she was unhurt. Beatrice landed next to her with ease. She helped Aideen to her feet. "You okay?"

"Fine. Now what?"

"Through this door, through another door, left down a hallway to the servant's stairs at the end of the hall. Down into the kitchens. Then through the kitchens and down into the cellars. From there, there's a hidden door that leads into the Under City."

"The Under City? But why would -"

"No time," Beatrice said, yanking Aideen by the hand and opening the door from the balcony back into the manor.

They dashed through a dark room, which must have been a guest room. Aideen snatched two cloaks off hooks on the wall. They launched out into the hallway, and Aideen flung one of them at Beatrice. "Wrap up so nobody knows we're the two foreigners running away."

"Nice. You're learning."

They were not quiet on their way down the hall, and they heard voices and heavy footsteps above them. As they made it to the narrow servant's staircase, they heard hurried feet pounding on the other set of stairs down the hall. They rushed down the narrow servant's stairs, Aideen praying neither of them would trip and fall. One flight. Two flights. They burst through a door into the kitchens, which were full of servants bustling around stoves and washbasins, apparently oblivious to the commotion happening elsewhere in the manor.

Beatrice pushed through the shocked women, who began to scream.

"Think they'll figure out we came through here?"

"The plan was run like hell," Beatrice huffed. "I said nothing about doing it quietly."

Aideen kept the hood of the cloak pulled tight against her head, careful to keep her hair and ears from showing. Pots were dropped. A basin was overturned. A platter of baked fish went flying across the room, and the two women flew as well. They burst through a door on the far wall, which led down into the cellars. They descended yet another flight of stairs and then ran past shelves of jars and boxes and row upon row of wine bottles. They turned between two rows lined with dusty bottles, and a few paces later came to a wall. Aideen nearly bowled Beatrice over at the sudden stop. "Now what?"

"The door is right here!" Beatrice started probing the wall with her hands. Aideen peered back around the corner. There was a lot of noise coming from up in the kitchens. Men yelling, now. Not just women screaming. "There's some kind of latch to open it. Find it!"

Aideen looked around in a panic, seeing nothing but a wall. "Are you sure it's on the wall?"

"Not exactly. I just know it's here. And I've been on the other side of it."

Aideen pushed in beside her and started groping at the wall as well. Her hands found nothing but irregular bricks. "We don't have much time."

"I know that! Do your... whatever it is you do. This is why you're here, remember?"

"Right." Aideen took a step back, taking a deep breath. She closed her eyes and willed her panic down, letting her emotions sink down from tidal waves into ripples. Then she opened her eyes and merely looked around. The cellar peeled back in front of her, the uneven dust on the bottles around her telling her that the air down here moved more than it should in a cellar. The cleanly swept floors, the lack of cobwebs, and the lack of dust on the pantry shelves told her that the dust was left on the bottles on purpose to showcase their age. The wine shelves were very old, too. They had sagged slightly over the years under the weight of their vintage passengers, the bend visible only in the middle of each shelf.

But the one on the left, nearest to the wall, didn't show any signs of sagging at the bottommost shelf. Aideen stooped down to inspect it. The lowest cross piece on this shelf was newer. She let her eyes follow it, peering between and around the bottles. The crosspiece meant something. Aideen pivoted on her hands and knees to look at the crosspiece on the opposite shelf. She saw it was cut flush with the edge of the rest of the shelving. She pivoted back. This one wasn't. This one extended two finger-widths out from the rest of the unit.

Aideen reached her hand around between the wall and the shelves, grabbing the crosspiece. She pushed it. She wiggled it. But it didn't budge. Then her fingers brushed something smooth on the bottom of it. She felt the familiar etched surface of a knob, just like the glowlamps and faucets of Sona. She grabbed it and turned, and the wall made a deep, hollow clunk sound.

Beatrice snapped her head around to look at her. "What'd you do?"

"Turned the doorknob."

Beatrice pushed the wall. A vaguely door-shaped section of bricks receded from her touch, mortar and all, then slid out of the way.

## 23

## THE STORM

Hamfast dreamed of thunderstorms. Not the roiling, rumbling sound of distant echoes in the skies above him. This was different. He was among the clouds. Inside the storm. He could smell the charged, wet air. He could feel energy gathering, could feel it humming in his teeth, could taste the bitter tang of it in his mouth. He felt the energy rattle and build, shifting as it flashed across the dark and drifting mountains that marched with him through the skies. The power of it ached inside him. It itched and burned and made his eyes water. And in the dream, following the hazy logic that dreams tend to follow, he knew the only way to make the aching stop was to let go of it. The ground below was dark and distant, unremarkable. Whether it was dotted with trees or houses or grand cities, he could not tell. And he felt somehow that shouldn't matter. He pointed, almost absently, and felt power drain from the clouds about him and charge through him. It followed his finger and hammered out across the night in a delicious release, lighting the world below in sudden brilliance as the force of it pounded the air like war-drums. The lightning slammed the ground below as the wind and the wet blew hard against his face.

Hamfast became dimly aware that he was cold. He shivered and reached for his blanket. He found it and pulled it up to his chin. The gentle rocking of the hammock beneath him lulled him back towards sleep, and he began to relax once more. As his fingers began to unclench, he felt the hard, jagged surface of what one hand clutched begin to slip. He held it tight in his hand and opened his eyes to see the comforting and familiar view of rough wooden planks above him.

Hamfast was below decks, but not in his room. The three wizards sat around the table in the hold nearby, talking in low whispers, their parchments and odd contraptions a scatter across the table. He watched them, seemingly in quiet debate, and blinked away his nearly forgotten dreams.

"I was thinkin' ye might never open them eyes," a gruff voice said from nearby. Hamfast twisted his head to see Brogan standing in the corner of the room. He was bare-chested, his torso wrapped in clean bandages. "Ye gave me might a scare back there, Hammy."

"You're alive," Hamfast said. His voice came out in a croak, and it set him to coughing.

"Ere, take some water." Brogan lifted a cup to where Hamfast hung in the hammock, and Hamfast drank. The water burned his throat. "Aye, I'm alive. I took a couple o' nasty gashes from that beast, but I gave as good as I got. The bastard ran away."

"And found me, instead."

"Aye. We found it down in the temple just 'fore we found you. How'd you manage to bring down the roof on the bugger's head?"

"I didn't. We both fell down from above. It was dumb luck."

Brogan nodded and took the empty cup from Hamfast. The room had grown silent, and Hamfast noticed the three wizards were watching him intently. Brogan looked back and forth between them. "I think ye've got business with these men. Be careful with 'em. They're a strange bunch. I've got me own business to see to, I s'pose." He shifted the cup from hand to hand awkwardly, hesitating. "Well. There it is, then. I'll be back to check on ya. Get better quick. Grubs been piss poor since Mandle took up yer kitchen." He turned and walked toward the door.

"Brogan?"

The big man looked back at him over his shoulder. "Aye?"

"Thank you."

"Is nuthin. Just a cup 'o water."

"No, I mean for saving my life back there."

Brogan scratched at his unkept beard. "That's what a crew does. We watches out for each other. The big fools 'ave to watch out for the little fools."

Hamfast watched him go, sliding the room's heavy door closed behind him. The wizard Whitaker stood slowly from the table, eyeing Hamfast as he approached the hammock. There was something strange behind the eyes that peered at him from between hood and beard. Gone was the jolly strangeness of their previous meeting. Was this anger? Fear? It was hard to tell, but Hamfast shrunk into the blankets as the man approached.

"Are you feeling alright, my Lindle friend?"

"I think so," Hamfast said. His leg was set with some kind of splint, and he felt the gentle pressure of bandages in several places on his body. He ached all over. "I seem to have been well tended to."

"That is well. That is well." The wizard fussed with his robes and cowl. "It would seem that your accidental expedition was more efficiently wrought than our own. It is peculiar, is it not? That the cook should discover the temple and its bounty before the scholars?"

Hamfast looked down at the crystal he still clutched in his left hand. "I suppose I did. When I found it, I knew you all would find me eventually."

"And so we did."

"And so you did." The wizard continued to study him, and Hamfast grew increasingly uncomfortable under his beady gaze. He lifted his hand towards the wizard, not without hesitation. "I, err, well. So, here it is, I suppose."

The wizard did not reach to take the crystal. Nor did he look upon it. "There are many questions that first must be answered. I ask that you speak truly and plainly, my dear Lindle. Much hangs in the balance."

Hamfast drew the crystal back to him, holding it close to his chest. There was a comfort in it. A tranquility that was hard to describe. Like falling asleep in a thunderstorm, he mused, dimly remembering the dreams. "What is it you wish to know?"

"Everything."

And so Hamfast told him all. Of the trek through the forest in search of forage. Of the beast that attacked him. Of running and getting lost. Of the ruined building. Of the beast's return, and their fall together into the rooms below. Of crawling and dragging himself until he found the room with the glowing lights and the glowing crystal on the dais. Of succumbing to his injuries and exhaustion at last.

The wizard Whitaker said nothing during his tale. He only regarded Hamfast with those half-closed, critical grey eyes that seemed to be set so deeply behind the dip of his blue cowl and the white mound of whiskers on his face. The other wizards listened from across the room, the purple arms of their robes crossed in front of them. When Hamfast was finished, Whitaker turned to his companions, and they began to speak in a language Hamfast did not understand. They talked on and on in serious tones, and Hamfast eventually grew tired of trying to listen to what he could not understand. He settled back into his hammock and rested. He felt sleepy again.

"How did you know which way to go?" one of the wizards

asked from across the room. Hamfast realized the conversation was once more addressed at him.

"When?"

"In the forest. After you fled the monster."

"I didn't. I just picked a direction, knowing I would eventually find the beach and could follow it around until I saw the ship."

"And after you fell into the lower rooms of the temple. You went straight for the altar room. What made you do that?"

"Much the same," Hamfast said. "I was nearly mad with fear and exhaustion. Any direction seemed better than nothing." He thought back to those moments. He thought back to how he imagined he'd heard the wind. But that had just been his muddled mind. "I took a chance."

"One final question, then." Whitaker stepped closed to where he lay on the hammock. "Did the shard speak to you? Did it call you?"

"Speak to me?"

"Yes. Did you hear it call to you?"

"It's a stone," Hamfast said. "Or a piece of crystal, or what have you."

"Even so. This is very important."

"I..." Hamfast thought back to his now hazy memories of the whole ordeal. "I felt drawn to it. I think I knew that it was what you were looking for, somehow. And I knew that if I had it, you would find me."

"And when you took it?"

"I felt safe," Hamfast said.

"Did it let you know you were safe?"

Hamfast shook his head. These questions were strange, and he was tired. "I heard no words from the shard, as you call it. I did not seek it out. I only wanted to be found. To be safe. And when I found this, I knew I would be."

Whitaker looked back to the men in the purple robes. "What is your opinion?"

"I find it unlikely the shard would have chosen a cook when three wizards of Sona were only a mile away," one offered.

"Perhaps it saved him by leading him there," the other said. "But even a feeble mind would sense the power of a shard should it decide to reveal itself to him."

"Perhaps," Whitaker said. He stroked his beard. "The whole of it seems considerably convenient though, does it not?"

"We should not confuse luck with fate, Master."

"Nor fate with luck," Whitaker mused. "The shard does not speak to any of us standing here."

"It is bound for Sona. For the Syani. Why should it speak to scholars when it is being borne to the sorceresses of a Circle? Why would it speak to a Lindle?"

"Why should we not simply allow the Lindle to deliver it to the Syani, then?"

"Because we should lose our chance to study it!" one of the purple robes puffed with annoyance. "The moment the Syani have it, we shall never see it again. We have weeks to observe it here on the ship. Weeks! The Syani should bear it upon our return, yes. I suggest no other end. But in the meantime, why should we not do as we had intended? We did not come as mere errand boys. We could have let anybody retrieve it. Master Whitaker, are we truly forsaking the opportunity of a lifetime because of the cook? The cook?" Hamfast did not appreciate the crooked finger now pointed at where he rocked in the hammock. "This is nonsense. I mean no offense, Master. But the truth seems plain enough to me."

Whitaker turned to face Hamfast once more. "Speak truly, Master Hamfast. You are merely the cook, yes? Nothing else?"

"I've been the cook on this ship for years," Hamfast said with annoyance. "Ask any among the crew."

"I have. But one cannot be too sure. And so, cook. Would you willingly give the shard to me? Without reservation?"

Hamfast looked at the thing he had been clutching since he awoke. Or, rather, since he'd found it, he supposed. How long ago had that been? He'd forgotten to ask. The crystal—or shard, rather—gave him comfort. But there was no reason to believe it was his to keep. He saw the faint motes of light moving in its depths. The swirl of dark mist and twinkling flashes. He wondered at them for a long moment, his mind reaching back to the storm in his dreams. But if this was something of power, he had no business in keeping it. It had brought him back to safety, had given him strange dreams, but nothing more. His hand hesitated for a long moment, but then stretched out towards Whitaker. "I give it to you freely," Hamfast said.

The wizard held out a hand, and Hamfast placed it in the wrinkled old palm. Whitaker smiled. Letting go, Hamfast felt no different. There was a part of him that wished to still be clutching it. To hold it close to him. But he pushed those thoughts down. He was tired and wanted rest. To sleep. To regain his strength and return to his life once more, far from monsters and temples and wizards and magic trinkets. He wanted nothing but the warm hearth of the Dusty Pearl and to hear his family bicker in the kitchen. He closed his eyes and pulled the blanket tight around him.

The storm came an hour later.

Hamfast awoke with a start as the ship lurched beneath him, swinging his hammock wildly. The strong wooden walls of the ship groaned in distress. The wizards were yelling at each other in panicked voices. Hamfast sat up as best he could in the hammock, wincing against the lingering pain in his broken leg as he did. The ship had seen many a storm, and Hamfast was unconcerned. But he also wasn't keen on the idea of being launched from his hammock across the hold by a rogue wave.

"Help me down, please!" Hamfast called to the wizards. They paid him no heed, continuing to yell at each other in that damned foreign language. "Master Whitaker! Help me down, gods damn it!"

The ship made a sudden motion beneath them, a jarring dip followed by the feeling of one's stomach being shoved in on itself. The ship was being launched upward by a massive swell, and Hamfast clambered onto his belly and wrapped his arms around the hammock beneath him as best he could. The sudden motions of the ship sent the wizards' instruments sailing across the room and their owners along with them. The wizards had clearly never been in a ship in a storm before. The ship changed its vertical direction again—an odd sensation, much like a sense of floating. That came to an abrupt end as the ship crashed down into another swell, sending anything in the room not securely anchored flying.

Hamfast was flung from his hammock, although he managed to hang onto it and found himself dangling by both hands. The wizards were sent sprawling. Hamfast tried to keep his wits about him. He wanted down, didn't he? So, he let go of the hammock and did his best to land on his good foot. He landed and rolled with the fall, pain shooting up his leg. He climbed to his feet as quickly as he could manage. The splint was sturdy on his broken leg, and he found it not unbearable to put weight on it. The ship lurched again, and Hamfast lunged for something to hold on to. What he found was the table. But the wizards' table was not fastened to the floor, as Hamfast quickly discovered.

A wracking motion of the ship set the table sliding from one side of the converted hold to the other, with Hamfast clinging to it. The table slammed into the wall, with Hamfast's chest caught between the two. There was a crunch, and sudden agony shot through him. He tried to scream, but he found he couldn't breathe. The heavy table was large enough for a dozen men to dine at. He wedged his hands between the wall and the table and pushed. The table did not budge. The wizards were as helpless as he was, trying to pull themselves up from whatever injuries they had sustained. Hamfast's struggling turned to flailing, and his vision began to grow dark. Then the sea buckled again, and the table slid to the other side of the room, knocking down two of the wizards as it went.

Hamfast gasped for breath, pain wracking his chest as his lungs filled with air. He ran to the door before the ship could lurch again and pushed it open. His chest was ablaze in pain. His head was swimming from lack of air. His feet were clumsy and staggered. And so, he threw himself through the now open door into the lower deck, his hands grasping at anything they could find. There was nowhere to run, but he ran as best as he could anyways. His chest was clutched in a vice, his breath coming in sharp wheezing gasps. He needed to get above deck. He needed to get out to where he could breathe.

The sailors of the Dragonfly were professionals, and Hamfast dimly saw them moving about the ship seeing to their jobs. Hamfast hobbled and crawled past them to the stairs that led above. They paid the cook no heed as he climbed out onto the deck of the ship.

The sky was dark and angry, seething with cold wind and great sheets of rain that tore at Hamfast as he clung to the rails. The sea beneath the ship was inky black and frothing as it churned, a hateful maw that foamed salty spray as it sought to sink its teeth into the hull. This was no ordinary storm. Hamfast thought he saw the captain on the upper deck, pointing and shouting orders. But Hamfast could hear nothing over the sound of the wind ripping around him.

He was useless up here, and his breathing was no less labored. He wheezed and rasped, clinging to the rails. The wind blew with such force that it seemed it would be nothing for it to cast him over the rails and into the angry sea. His duty, if he had been thinking clearly, was to see to the kitchen and larder. Who knew what a mess that would be without him there to properly secure it? Hamfast made his way back down the stairs, a sense of purpose giving him some small amount of clarity in the madness.

Hamfast never made it to the kitchen. The ship shook and groaned, a sound deeper than he had ever heard a ship make before. There was a shudder, a resounding splintering bang, and then a rush of water hit him with a shock. His head slammed into something, and his mind began to swim as he flailed against the water. The sensation of the water disappeared as suddenly as it had come. A cold wind battered him, freezing him in his wet clothes. His vision blurred and his feet sought for a floor that was no longer there. Hamfast tried desperately to shake away the dizziness, and when his vision finally focused, he could barely make sense of what he saw.

The Dragonfly was below him. Far below him. The main mast had broken, and the ship was riding low in the black waters. The ship let out another moan as it surged up over a great wave, crashing back into the black valley beneath. The ship broke. The hull twisted, the aft riding high while the rest settled into the sea. Hamfast could hear the distant cries of the crew, the panicked voices and muddle of desperate orders. Lightning flashed in the surrounding sky, and Hamfast realized suddenly why he had such a vantage point. He was somehow held aloft by the storm winds themselves. Hamfast screamed, flailing his arms in a panic. And then the sea came rushing up towards him.

## 24

## THE UNDER CITY

The door in the cellar wall beneath the duke's manor led to a narrow passage, the walls and floor and ceiling all lined in the same bleak grey stone. Beatrice kicked one stone in the wall, and it moved with an audible click. Aideen could hear the door to the cellar sliding closed behind them as the angry voices of men became rapidly louder. Beatrice turned, and they both ran like hell. All according to plan.

"You're half elf, can you see in the dark?"

"Not well, but better than a man."

"Good enough. Just stay close to me." Beatrice skidded to a stop, snatched a waxed canvas bag from a small recess in the wall. It looked much like Aideen's sword bag.

"What's that?"

"In case the backup plan goes badly."

Aideen swallowed. The pair flew down the tunnel, past several side passages. At a motion from Beatrice, they turned down one passage, then another. Between the curvature of the tunnels and the turns they took along the way, Aideen completely lost her bearings through a maze of identical seeming passages. Then Beatrice held up her hand, and they both stopped to catch their breath.

"We should be safe now," Beatrice huffed, leaning both hands against the tunnel wall. "Safe from the guards at least. There's no way they'll happen to come this way quickly. If they know their way through these tunnels, this would be a foolish way for us to have gone. And if they don't know the tunnels, then they're probably lost."

"So we went the foolish way?"

"Safest bet, I figured." Beatrice blew a loose strand of hair out of her eyes. "The city guard is inevitably involved by now. I'm sure they raised the alarm. They'll start trying to fan out along the tunnels looking for us. But we're a long way from any place to emerge back out. Only way out I know from here is to go down into the Under City itself, and then come up through the sewers. Not a great plan, but I figured it was more important to deal with the problem at our heels."

"Fair enough," Aideen said. She stood looking around, not nearly as winded as Beatrice seemed to be. The tunnel was, well, just that. A tunnel. Bland and boring, something like a drainage shaft. "This isn't how I imagined the Under City."

"We're just about to step out into what you likely pictured. Just around that corner, you'll be in for a treat."

"Oh?"

Beatrice took a deep breath, rubbing at an apparent stitch in her side. "Sarcasm."

"I assumed."

"Keep quiet, and keep your wits about you. It's not safe down here."

Beatrice pushed herself back off the wall, slung the canvas bag over her shoulder, and nodded at Aideen. The pair pressed on through the tunnel and around the corner. Aideen was not prepared for what she saw.

The tunnel looked down into a cylindrical cavern, larger

than any building one could imagine. And still bigger. Dozens of massive stone columns, each the girth of a great house, rose well over a hundred feet from the ground far below them to the ceiling above. At their base, the shattered remnants of a cityscape sat nestled in the lightless gloom, their forms merely shadows below even with Aideen's sensitive eyes. Row after row of buildings, a grid of city streets below them. All of it sitting in shambles in the darkness. "It's quite literally a city," Aideen breathed.

"What's left of one," Beatrice said. "Come on, there's a ladder down."

Beatrice went down first, disappearing over the end of the tunnel's mouth. Aideen took another cautious look, then followed. She did not like exposing her back to all that desolation in the chasm below. They climbed down in silence, down and down on a rope ladder that Aideen wouldn't have trusted if it hadn't been for Beatrice's confidence. Aideen kept her eyes on the wall in front of her, not daring to look down or over her shoulder into the ruins behind them. She only realized she was finally near the bottom when she felt the motion beneath her cease, telling her that Beatrice was off the ladder. Aideen joined her moments later.

The wall beside them curved off into the distance like a dark reflection of the rings of Sona. And Aideen realized now that's exactly what this was. The room—if a space so large could be considered a room—would have been miles in diameter. It was the size of the Upper City itself. All was obscured by darkness and gloom, and the structure of this place was a maze of pillars and columns and arches that supported the city above. Sometimes the arches were connected, forming a massive wall, dividing the space at odd angles. Aideen always assumed the Upper City sat atop the Inner City, like the stacking of a tiered cake. She had never considered the raised portions of Sona might be a singular construction. Her mental image of Sona was shaken, and it only added to her disorientation in this strange place.

From her new vantage point, Aideen had no sense of the space as she would from above. Now she stood on the remnants of an ancient city street. In every direction, the ruins of buildings loomed eerily over her like gargoyles or stone birds of prey. They made her feel watched, like anything could be hiding in them. If the stories were true, something might be.

"Come on," Beatrice said.

"It's so much bleaker than I imagined," Aideen whispered as they walked. "I mean, I've always known the story of it. How the city of Meritil was sacked in the War of the Six Kingdoms. How the siege engines had reduced it to fire and rubble, its citizens long fled. And how the Sorceress Eridayah, after the signing of the Unification, used her magic to build the City of Sona atop those ruins." Aideen shook her head. "I didn't realize how literal that was. It's like a dome. It seems like she could have tidied up a bit first with all that power."

"Keep your voice down," Beatrice said, even though Aideen had been whispering. "The City Guard sweeps Under City occasionally, but it's still a favorite hiding place for unsavories. Brigands. Thieves. Any kind of bad apple, really. And then there's what lies beneath."

"I assumed those were just bedtime stories."

"Do you really care to find out?" Beatrice cast her a look, then led them down what remained of another street. Aideen looked about constantly, her senses on high alert. It was damned creepy down here. And there were distant sounds. The scurrying of feet, though likely rats, made her imagine any number of monsters in the gloom. "Are you alright?"

"You've been asking me that all night," Aideen snapped back.

"Well, I've led you down a rabbit hole. Quite literally now. This evening was supposed to end with us walking out through the front door, and now here we are." Beatrice patted her on the shoulder. "It's okay to feel in over your head."

"Well good, because I do," Aideen admitted. "I'd feel better if I had a damned sword in my hand."

"Oh?" Beatrice shrugged the canvas bag off her shoulder and untied it. Inside, she drew out two swords. She handed one of them to Aideen. "That's simple enough."

Aideen took the sword and removed it from the scabbard. "Elorian short blade. Not my preference, but it will do."

"Feel any better now?"

"Yes. Thank you."

Beatrice smirked at her. "You know how to use that thing?"

"Quite a bit better than most."

Beatrice studied her for a moment, then nodded. "Good. You won't need it, but now we both feel better down here."

The roads were littered with rubble from the decrepit buildings around them. Their stones were grey, the same as the old cobble of the streets, all rendered oily black in the lightless cavern. Aideen's vision was colorless in the dark, a vestige of her elven heritage. Elves apparently saw quite well without light, while humans saw nothing at all. Aideen's sight was somewhere in the middle, seeing everything as degrees of grey and shadow like a charcoal drawing. She wondered how it was that Beatrice could see down here. Something to do with magic, most likely.

They picked their way down what were once small side streets and alleys, the ghostly crumbling brick walls of ancient Meritil looming above them. The main roads they avoided. Too visible, Aideen assumed. They kept their voices in whispers and their footsteps light, careful not to disturb any rubble.

They passed by several of the massive pillars, and the going was more cautious there. The pillars seemed to have sprung from the ground without any heed to what had been there before, laying waste to any buildings in their immediate vicinity. Aideen gazed up from the base of one, at how it towered above her to the ceiling far above them. She wondered at it. These were the very foundations of Sona. How strange that they hid such disaster down here, like sweeping dirt beneath a rug.

After a while, Aideen noticed they were nearing a great circular wall of arches, and that the ceiling was considerably lower just beyond them. The Inner City terrace, perhaps? The pillars and arches gave her little sense of position down here, and she thought of how easy the Spire soaring overhead made traversing the city above them. And that was another wild thought. Above them, atop all those pillars, was most of Sona. Lindenhall. The Spire. Lord Cathal's manor, and also the duke's they had just fled. An entire city above them, oblivious to the mice down here below. And she was now here as well, among the mice.

"Where are we exactly?" Aideen whispered.

"Under the Potter's Quarter, roughly."

That meant the west side of the Inner City, near the western ramps. "How much farther to go?"

"We need to circle back to near the southern ramps. So not terribly far."

They picked their way along city streets yet again, the scene more or less the same as before. At least now Aideen had a sense of where she was and where they were going. "How is it you can see in the dark so well? Is it more of your magic?"

"Probably. I don't know."

"You said before you didn't know where those markings came from."

"They just started to appear," Beatrice said, casting a look over her shoulder. "Not until I entered my twentieth year. The markings came first, and then night sight. And then the magic."

"And no idea what caused it?"

"None. We surmise it is some kind of heredity."

"We?"

"Myself and the Queen of Masks. And to preempt your next question, I have no idea who my parents were."

"I hadn't decided on my next question yet."

"Was that on the list?"

"It was. You were an orphan, then?"

"A street rat. A beggar child. I don't remember anything before that. I got picked up by-"

"Wait."

Beatrice froze at the word. "What is it?" she breathed.

Aideen had frozen, too. "On the right. Movement."

"I see it."

Aideen's eyes played many tricks on her in the darkness, but movement stood out like a beacon, even in this. She had trained in the woods at night with Lodai. To see movement in shadows. To spot game. To sense potential danger—although danger in the woods outside of the family's hunting lodge was of the theoretical sort. But here, beneath the city, anything moving except herself and Beatrice could mean very real danger. It could mean guards seeking them, or something else altogether. Something that was down here, like them, wishing not to be seen. The movement was heading towards them on the street their path was just about to cross.

Aideen's heart pounded in her chest. She tried to push the emotions down, to settle into the cool waters. But she could not find them. The unknown stakes down here were a far cry from getting caught in the wrong room earlier this evening. She was right to be afraid.

"Moving closer." Beatrice's voice was barely audible, even this close.

"What is it?"

"Trouble."

"Guards?"

"No," Beatrice said. "Several armed men. But not guards. Smugglers, probably. There is a way nearby through the sewers that leads to the docks, so one can lie low here as long as needed." Beatrice shifted her feet underneath her. "Things come into Sona, you hide them here, you wait for the buyer or for the ship that will take them onward."

"What do we do? They're stopping." Aideen struggled to make out the details at this distance, but she could see the movement well enough, and now saw it cease. The figures were two blocks away, and she could see them settling down to rest or wait.

"We can go around them. There's no way the guards will find us now, so long as we don't head back. There's just too many places for them to check. The tunnels and sewers go on for ages between the Under City and the surface, and then there's all this."

"I can move quietly enough," Aideen said. "We'll be alright."

"Wait."

Aideen froze, her skin prickling into gooseflesh. Something in Beatrice's voice, even in whispers, made the fear inside Aideen lurch. It wasn't fear she heard in Beatrice's voice. It was a black anger, a burbling fury that dripped from that single, whispered word.

"What is it?"

"They aren't smugglers. They're slavers." Aideen saw Beatrice's body tense. "They have with them two children, both with bound hands. Young elves." Beatrice saw the look on Aideen's face and nodded. "I know. Slavery is illegal in Elora, and yet it is no great secret that indentured servitude and prison labor are alive and well in the nation of Lyramae. The difference between that and slavery is semantics."

Aideen could barely comprehend what she was hearing. "Are you sure they're children? And not Lindle?"

"Oh, I'm sure. Children are much easier to transport."

"I can't believe it," Aideen hissed. "That this sort of thing goes on right under the streets of Sona."

"It's foul business, and just one of many foul enterprises that operates in the shadows. Elves are barely people in Sona, but that's just what happens openly. Elsewhere in Elora, people are bolder in their oppression." Beatrice gave her a look. "News to you, eh? The normal folk know little of the truth in Sona, and the upper class even less. Except for those who are involved, either through participation or with an intentional blind eye."

"Who would involve themselves in such a thing?"

Beatrice gave Aideen a long look.

"What?"

"There are things we should discuss, but it will have to wait. Suffice it to say, I've been trailing those who trade in people. I recently came upon a slaver's trail in Sona, and found imprisoned elves. Much like these children."

"Oh gods," Aideen felt even less calm now. She felt ill. "What happened?"

"We killed the slavers. Freed the children. The same as I'm about to do now."

## 25

## THE SLAVERS

"Stay here, and stay hidden," Beatrice whispered, her grip on the blade in her hand visibly tightening. "I'm not going around, and I'm taking those children with us. If for any reason things go badly for me, you will have to get yourself out. Just follow this street until you find a ditch that smells like filth. Follow it to the sea. You can make your way back into the city from there. And be careful."

Slaves. Children. Elves. Hidden doors. Secrets. The words reverberated in Aideen's mind. If her world had been knocked askew these past weeks, now it crumbled into rubble like the wreckage of the city around her. The final pieces of herself that remained, the sturdy central pillars of who she truly was and what she believed, stood out now above the debris.

"No," Aideen said.

"What?"

"I'm not letting you do this alone."

"You didn't sign up for this," Beatrice said, shaking her head. She put a hand on Aideen's shoulder and squeezed. "This is too far beyond your depths."

"Quite the contrary." Aideen rubbed her fingers into the

leather grip of the sword, getting a feel for it. "Swordplay is the first thing tonight that I'm comfortable with."

"And killing a man? Even an evil man. It's not as easy as you might think."

Aideen considered. Or she tried to consider. Her emotions were a mess, to be sure. She was frightened. She was angry at the very idea that such horrors took place beneath her city. She was worried for Beatrice, a woman she barely knew. And yet she was in awe of her. Here was a woman, born with nothing, who was prepared to risk her life for strangers. Here was a woman who, like Aideen, lived between worlds. Yet who understood the world in a way Aideen only pretended to understand it, and stood in defiance of it. Here was a spy, a thief, and apparently a warrior. There was much Aideen didn't understand about Beatrice and her Queen of Masks. But she knew enough.

Aideen stared at the shadowed stones at her feet, searching her heart for the truth. Looking past the lies she had believed, that she had echoed, that she had told herself to fortify the comfortable walls around her pretty little life. "I've learned a great many disturbing things lately. Nothing in Sona is as I thought it was. My father murdered. Secret societies in brothels. Vigilantes and spies. Slavers skulking about beneath my home. Elves being bought and sold while the Upper City dances. And children? Children?"

"I know," Beatrice whispered. "It's all hard to stomach. But this isn't your fight."

Aideen drew in a breath. She felt unsteady, but she felt it should not matter. "And had my life played out differently? I could have been one of those elven slaves. If I did not have my wealth and privilege, if I did not have my secrets, what would stop such men from taking me? Those children are my people, though I've spent a lifetime hiding from that fact. I cannot simply go back to living with blinders to all this. So no, I'm not willing to leave those children to their fate any more than you are."

Beatrice studied her with pursed lips, her eyes searching Aideen's in the darkness. "Are you certain?"

Aideen settled her fingers into the grip of the blade. Feeling the rightness of it in her hand. "I am at your side."

Beatrice nodded. "Okay, then. Come on. Wait for me to initiate the fight. Capitalize on the confusion. You take the alley there, and I'll take the other. Get close. Then wait, and stay hidden. You'll hear my voice whispering in your ear. Don't let it startle you."

"More magic?"

"Yes. And by the gods, be careful. If things go badly, run. You're fast on your feet and should have no trouble escaping." Beatrice seemed to melt into the shadows. Not figuratively. Like her arm had done twice in the manor, her whole body seemed to be made from smoke. The vague outline of her crossed the street and was gone down the alley. Aideen stared after her for a moment, then slipped off her shoes and cloak. She unsheathed the sword and left the leather scabbard with the rest and turned down the alley nearest her.

The cobblestone was cold against her bare feet, but it was quieter and would give her better traction. She didn't trust unknown shoes in a fight. Her breathing came rapid and shallow as she crept. But she made no noise. Memories of the woods with Lodai flashed through her mind, her fingers clutching a bow in the early morning dew light, her toes testing before committing each step, wary of loose rocks shifting and making noise that might alert her quarry. Creeping down an ancient road was not so different than walking across a dry creek bed. The two city blocks were traversed in little time, and she heard low voices from around the corner.

*Don't try to speak back, I won't be able to hear you,* Beatrice's voice said in her ear. Aideen was glad for the warning ahead of time—it was truly unnerving and sounded entirely unnatural. *There are five of them, two sitting against the wall nearest you. The other three are standing facing them. They seem alert enough. I am going to count from ten, then take one of the ones standing from behind. All bets are off once I do. Be ready for anything, and be careful. Ten.*

Aideen crept along the wall towards the voices, trying again to slide into the cool waters but finding none. *Nine.* The accents were foreign. *Eight.* From the southern continent, Dahk Ahani. *Seven.* There was an irony to that. *Six.* Aideen and Beatrice had been pretending to be from there all this evening. *Five.* Focus, Aideen told herself. She adjusted her grip and tried to concentrate her senses. The drumming of her heart was deafening. *Four.* But she knew how to fight. *Three.* She had studied swordplay her whole life. *Two.* Only that had been swordplay. Fakery. Sparring with blunted blades. And this...

*One.*

From the shadows across the street, an inky tendril lashed out like a whip. Aideen peered around the corner just in time to see it grab one of the men around the throat and yank him back. He made an awful choking sound, clawing at his face in panic. A shout of surprise went up, and Aideen heard the men against the wall leaping to their feet. Aideen hesitated, not giving anything away just yet. Use the confusion, she thought. A man entered into view, swinging his sword down at the black writhing mass that held his companion by the throat. The tendril disappeared, releasing the man. He fell to the ground, clutching at his neck and fumbling for his dropped sword. At the same time, Beatrice materialized from the alley across the street, a sword in one hand. Four men rushed at her, the fifth still on the ground.

Aideen dashed in behind them, ignoring the disoriented one on the ground. She surveyed the situation quickly. All of them wore armor above the waist and carried swords. None of them wore armor below the waist. Something they would regret. The tip of Aideen's blade slashed the closest one on the back of the leg as he rushed towards Beatrice, just behind the knee, sending him sprawling to the ground with a cry of pain. The man to his left turned to face her, his feet digging into a skidding halt. She swatted his sword wide as he turned, and anticipated the clumsy swing that inevitably followed. The fool had barely stopped running the other way, and already he moved to the offense? She moved outside of his strike, letting his own momentum take his sword past her. She stabbed him in the upper thigh, then leapt back before he could scream, much less make another attempt.

One man downed with one functioning leg. One man injured, but still standing. One on the ground behind her, but getting up. Two facing Beatrice. Aideen spun around on the man who was struggling to his feet from Beatrice's choking whip. She brought the pommel of her sword down on the back of his head. She had meant for this to be a mercy, but steel and skull met with a sickening crack. She winced, but had no time to consider this in the panic of the moment. Aideen spun around again. And just in time.

The man she had stabbed in the thigh was upon her, much sooner than she had anticipated. His blade held in both hands, he delivered an overhead blow just as Aideen was turning to face him. She cried out, bringing her sword up to block and twisting out of the way. But he was strong, and the two-handed blow slammed through her hasty defense, driving her sword down with all the momentum of an axe splitting firewood. Her own sword struck her left shoulder with a sickening *thunk* as it knocked into bone.

Aideen screamed. The pain was more than she could have possibly imagined, and she sprang back instinctively, trying to put distance between herself and her assailant. She lost her footing, however, and fell to the cobblestone.

The man was bleeding from his leg, and hobbling slightly. But he was standing above her, only a few paces away, and bringing the sword up to finish the job. Aideen yanked up her sword, and it dislodged from her shoulder with a horrifying sensation. She had the presence of mind to parry properly this time, lurching in one direction while her blade deflected in the other. His sword struck the stone street. And Aideen's foot struck his injured leg.

The man howled and stumbled with the momentum of his swing, and Aideen rolled to her feet and backed away from him.

Across the street, Beatrice was caught between two men. Her ghostly arm shot out, grabbing a man by the sword arm and flinging it wide. Her own sword pierced him through the chest. The sound that erupted from his mouth was gruesome, the horror of it cutting through her mind even in the frenzy. Beatrice spun to face her other attacker.

One man lay on the ground, his head in no condition to fight. Perhaps ever again. One with the tendons behind his knee severed, bleeding and struggling to crawl to where his sword lay nearby. One dead by Beatrice's blade. She was now holding the other at bay, her face stretched taught in grim concentration.

And yet another, angry and bleeding, was snarling his way towards Aideen.

This was not a sparring match.

Aideen was not prepared for this. Terror rose up inside her like a covey of quail taking flight, leaving her dizzy and disoriented.

*This is not the Songs*, Lodai's voice echoed in her mind. She had tried to clear her thoughts, to slip into the cool waters. To calm her emotions, to let the world peel back and draw on her senses as she had countless times in the past weeks. But the fear in her was crippling. She backed away from the approaching slaver, panic clutching at her throat. She held her sword out like a scared child, and felt it trembling in her grip. The slightest mistake, no matter her skill, would mean death. Would mean never finding her father's killer. She was a fool.

Fear turned to anger in her belly. Anger at herself, for rushing into danger so flippantly. Anger that she had been cocky, that she was not as skilled as she thought. Anger that this monster of a man was about to kill her. The heat inside her rose and billowed, and she felt the unfurling of wings. The molten eyes of that beast flared, and Aideen's nostrils flared with them. Something quaked in her belly, a part of herself rupturing like the earth splitting open. Fires belched from beneath, molten rock seeping through the cracks.

The beast did not intend to die.

Aideen heard the beast scream, and she screamed with it. The beast took flight, and so did Aideen. Her sword gripped in both hands, she swung at the slaver's outstretched blade. He parried well, but she closed anyhow, oblivious to the danger. She thundered against his defenses, the squall of pain in her shoulder only fueling the fires that now raged within her. Her blade hammered at him. This was not the Songs, and yet the music of them thrummed through her with each strike, raining down the fury of the conflagration that blazed inside her. She drew on *tanp'et*, the Song of Storms, only now it was hellfire that rained down.

He retreated, and Aideen let him. She watched him with a predator's eyes, seeing him tire. The beast drooled, tasting the imminent end of its hunt. The man feigned, then surged forward, hard and fast, an attempt to use his size and strength against her. *Kouran*, the Song of the Streams. Aideen flowed past him as he came, her blade singing across his as she disappeared from its deadly edge, and she moved behind him with a practiced fluidity. Before he could turn, she slashed the back of his knee like the first man, sending him sprawling into a similar, screaming heap. Then she plunged her sword into his neck, sending up a bloody, gurgling gout of blood that rushed through the space between the cobblestones like black tributaries in the gloom.

The beast screamed in delight.

Beatrice was still fencing with her man. Aideen rushed him from behind. He saw her coming too late as her blade speared him through the ribs, lodging deep in them as he stumbled and fell. He was now a new spring of black blood flowing through the streets. Aideen planted a bare foot on him as he crumbled to the ground, wrenching her sword back out. Her shoulder screamed, and she screamed with it.

Only one man remained. The man with the mangled knee, who lay on the ground. As Aideen approached, he pointed his sword at her in fearful desperation. He was saying something, but Aideen could not hear it over the fires roaring in her ears. She brought up her sword to finish the work.

Something cold grabbed her wrist, and she spun with a snarl to face her new assailant. Inky tendrils were wrapped around her forearm, and Beatrice stood a few paces from her, arm outstretched as the freakish tendril held Aideen's sword hand.

"It's over," Beatrice was repeating. "It's over."

It took a moment for Aideen to comprehend her. When she did, she felt the fires begin to subside, her face relaxing from the grimacing snarl it had been pulled into. She blinked a few times, feeling the beast perch within her, rasping with a reluctant acceptance.

"It's over," Beatrice said again, letting the smoke dissipate and taking Aideen by both arms. "He's beaten. That's enough."

Aideen stared at her. The wings rustled and cooled, shaking ash from them as the beast resigned itself to slumber. Aideen could not speak, and stared dumbly at Beatrice.

"Do you speak elvish?"

"I..." Aideen shook her head, hardly comprehending. "Yes."

"The children. Speak to them. They're terrified."

Aideen then saw the children. Huddled against the wall of a crumbling building, an elven boy and a girl sat with their hands bound staring at the grisly scene. And she saw the horror drawn across their faces. Aideen became suddenly aware of just how much screaming there was, and she winced at it as the gravity of the past few moments set in. Much of the screaming had been hers.

The whole ordeal had been so fast, and yet had seemed to last for ages. Men lay in pools of blood like cattle at the slaughter house. The smell of blood and filth grated inside her nostrils, a foul copper smell that made her nose curl. Aideen gagged, covering her mouth.

Beatrice walked over to the man on the ground. He pointed his sword back up at her. Beatrice ripped the sword from his hand with that disturbing shadow grasp. And once it was in her own hand, she threw it away. "We've freed the children," Beatrice said. Then she gave Aideen a hard look. "I've seen enough death for today." She looked down at the man at her feet. "Get crawling, worm. And bandage your leg before you bleed dry. This mess will attract things you don't want to meet."

Aideen felt a torrent of emotions that overwhelmed her senses. She closed her eyes and fought to push them all aside. She couldn't think about what had just happened. Not yet. There would be time for that later. She let her sword clatter to the ground and walked towards the children, finding some part of her senses as she did. She knelt a few paces away from them. "It's okay. You're safe now. You can come with me."

The two children just blinked at her, their dusty faces understanding nothing but shock and fear.

*"Na'ou pa be'wen pe, jen youn. M'wen sank a'ou. Ga'dei?"* Aideen showed them her ears. *"Don't be afraid, child. I'm like you. My mother was called Saira, and I am called Aideen. You'll come with us, and then you will be safe. We will leave this dark place and find the moon and stars. Alright? Trust us. The violence is done. The evil men are gone. Now you will be free."*

The two children—a brother and sister, Aideen suspected now that she'd had time to study their faces—looked at each other. A moment passed between them, and they nodded. Beatrice untied their bonds and helped them to their feet. They were shaken. She couldn't blame them. She felt blood soaking her dress and noted that her own hands were shaking.

The four of them made their way back to the road they'd been on in silence, and Aideen slipped back into the party shoes and cloak. She could feel the grit on the soles of her feet in them, sweat soaking through her dress mingling with blood. Some of it hers. Beatrice made an awkward bandage for her shoulder without a word, and Aideen held it in place as they walked. Nothing felt real down here. She was floating through a dream. A nightmare. They continued their trek through the darkness.

After a while, Beatrice broke the silence. "Are you okay?"

"No."

"You scared me back there. I know we just met, but you weren't yourself."

Aideen thought back to the fight. She thought of that beastly thing that rose up inside her. And she thought she felt its wings rustling now even as it slumbered. She shuddered. "I almost died." It was truth. But only a partial truth.

"I'm sorry I let you walk into that situation. I shouldn't have."

"You would have died if I hadn't."

"Maybe. I'm good at disappearing."

"What will become of them?" Aideen asked, looking to change the subject.

"Our Lady will take them in."

"The Queen of Masks? You mean they're to be prostitutes?" Aideen balked.

"Of course not. Our Lady sees to more than the Red Dress. If their parents are alive and able to be found, they will be reunited. But likely not. Their parents are almost certainly far away. Or dead. These little ones will learn to sew, to cook, to launder. They'll learn the language and the customs of Elora.

They'll be fed and educated and cared for. When they are old enough, Our Lady will help them find an arrangement of some kind, either in Sona or elsewhere. Or perhaps an apprenticeship if they show an aptitude. These are hardly the first orphans she has taken in." Beatrice patted the girl on her head and smiled at her. "It is not a glamorous life, but it is not a bad one, either. The Masquerade takes in a great many sad souls and cares for them."

"Is that what happened to you?"

"What?"

"She took you in off the streets?"

"No. I should have been so lucky."

Aideen decided not to press the question further. She had enough jumbled thoughts swirling through her mind. She looked down at the two elven children shuffling along beside them, their clothes no more than filthy rags. Sona was nothing like what she had believed. She'd lived here her whole life, and she was just now beginning to see it for what it truly was.

"You said there were things we should discuss," Aideen said, recalling their conversation before the fight. "About who is behind all this."

"I did," Beatrice said. "And we will. But let's focus on putting this place behind us now."

The passage that was their destination was well hidden. Another sliding door in a wall, like the one in the cellar. Aideen wondered how many of these there were in the city. This one was in a huge, curving wall that supported the city itself. Behind it, another ladder. And a sturdy one, this time. At the top, it led to another set of twisting tunnels like the ones beneath the duke's manor, branching off in many directions. Beatrice stopped, turning to the wall. She touched it and whispered something into it, and this too slid aside for them.

The four of them emerged into the light of glowlamps, and Aideen felt herself relax for the first time in hours. She found herself standing in a laundry room. And judging by the garish red paint that lacquered the walls, she surmised they were in the basement of the Red Dress. Aideen blinked at the sudden brightness.

"Wrap up in that cloak." Beatrice said, the weariness in her voice apparent. "Go upstairs to the room where your things are and bathe. I'll send someone up to tend to your injury. I've just stopped the bleeding, but it's like to be a mess. Then go home once you're tended to. Our Lady will send for you when she has the answers you seek."

"You'll see to these two? You don't speak elvish."

"No, but others here do. They won't be the only elves here."

"Alright." Aideen knelt down to face the children. *"I am going to wash, and then I must return home. This woman will take you to wash. She does not speak your tongue, but others here do. Do not fear. There are other elves here, and you will be taken care of. No harm will come to you."*

*"You said we would leave the darkness to find the moon and stars,"* the boy protested. *"These lights are false."*

*"Yes, but in a few moments you must only look out the window. There are many false stars here for light, but the true stars are still visible if you only look."*

*"Will we see you again?"*

*"I will be back tomorrow."*

*"And our mother? Will she find us here?"*

*"I do not know."* Aideen hesitated, looking between the two small faces. Such innocence there, even after all they had seen. After all they had endured. Aideen felt that the world was full of harsh truths. *"But you must be brave in this new life. When you have the years needed, you may seek her. Your fate will be your own to find."*

The boy took this with a stoicism no child should be capable of. Aideen stood and looked down at the blinking children. She could not imagine what horrors they knew. A part of her wanted to never know. And yet another part needed to know. She had much to think about.

Aideen nodded, as much to them as to herself, and flipped the hood of the stolen cloak over her head. Beatrice touched her good shoulder as she turned to leave.

"Hey. You did good tonight."

Aideen cocked an eyebrow at her. "I did well, you mean."

Beatrice nodded. "Yes, but you also did good."

## 26

## THE TAGATA

Hamfast remembered hitting the water. He remembered the cold shock of it. He remembered the confusion. The groaning of the ship as it succumbed to the unrelenting force of wind and water. The realization that he was torn from the chaos in the lower decks and was flung into the angry grey skies above it all. He remembered the terror of the fall back down into the raging waters that tore at the remains of his ship and his crew. The screaming of the men. Of his crew. Of his friends.

He remembered being cold. Shivering, his small arms flailing to keep his head above the waves. His hand found something jagged and splintery in the waters. Hamfast clung to it. The smell of pine tar and creosote, once the comforting smell of home, was now pressed against his face in a mockery that it had ever made him feel safe. Too terrified to weep, he merely held on to this small piece of the Dragonfly and focused on keeping air in his lungs through his chattering teeth.

Things were less clear after that. The cold of the Misty Sea was all consuming, and it drowned out any other thoughts. Hamfast knew he was dying in the dark, cold water without a hope of rescue. He had only that morning awoken in the ship's hold, a broken leg and bruised body. And now he was truly dying. At least this was a sailor's death, he tried to tell himself. At least he was off that island. At least there were no monsters here. But it was a thin solace. He was dying, gods damn it. He wanted to scream but hadn't the strength, and there was not a thing he could do about it but hold on, to try and die of cold rather than drowning. His vision grew dark, and eventually he stopped trying to keep his eyes open in the salty spray.

Dim awareness came drifting back in, and the first coherent thought it brought was that he was no longer cold. His muddled reason told him it was an illusion, and that this must be his body giving up. Or that he was already dead, and he was coming into the afterlife. But that couldn't be because he could still feel horrible pain everywhere. Hamfast groped with feeble hands to tighten his grip on the ship's wreckage that would let him live a while longer. Then he realized it wasn't there, and began to flail about for it. The flailing was what finally brought him back to consciousness.

Hamfast opened his eyes to find himself in a strange place. Any place that wasn't the ocean would be strange, but this place was strange even so. He was laying on the floor of a room, with something soft beneath him. Above, there was a simple thatched roof, and the walls that held it up were made of thick reeds. The air was warm, but not hot. And there was the smell of seaweed and salt in the breeze that came through the gaps in the reeds.

Hamfast tried to sit up, but then fell back onto the mat. He felt weak. His head throbbed. His shoulder burned. Wherever he was, whatever had happened to him, he was alive. Hot tears filled his eyes, and he thanked all the gods he could name in a hoarse whisper. When he was done, he slept. Not unconsciousness brought on by pain and trauma. But the voluntary sleep of someone who knows he is safe in a bed. The details of where he was, how he got here, and what the future held were irrelevant. He slept and did not dream.

When Hamfast woke again, a man was sitting cross-legged beside his cot on the floor. Or, something like a man. Hamfast studied him through bleary eyes. The man's skin was the soft green of sage leaves, his face exaggerated with high, prominent cheekbones and a broad jutting chin framed in the drapery of thick black hair. He wore a robe of some unusual brown material. Hamfast blinked at the strangeness, but lacked the energy to feel any real surprise at the creature.

"Thank you," Hamfast managed to say. His voice was weak, and the effort made him fall into a fit of painful coughing. The man said nothing, but produced a wooden bowl from beside him. He held it to Hamfast's lips, and he drank it. It was a hot broth that smelled like fish, and he drank it gratefully. Hamfast lay his head back down on the cot, and the man put the bowl back down on the ground. "Where am I?"

The man's face was unreadable. He said nothing, and stood. He walked to the door of the little hut, just more reeds lashed together, taking the bowl with him. "What's your name?" Hamfast called after him. But the man seemed not to hear him, pushing the reed door open and leaving him there.

Some hours later—how long, Hamfast could hardly know—the man came back with another bowl of hot broth. The encounter played out much the same. The man helped Hamfast drink, but did not acknowledge attempts at the simplest conversation. "Of course," Hamfast said. "Could I be any more daft? You don't speak Elorian. Here. Let's try this. Hamfast." He pointed at himself. "Hamfast. And you?" He pointed at the man in the robes.

The man hesitated, studying Hamfast. Then shrugged. Funny how body language is mostly universal, Hamfast mused. "Makhal." The man thumbed his chest. "*O as Makhal.*" He jerked a finger at the Lindle. "*Ia asa Hammast.*"

"Hamfast, yes."

The man nodded, then left again without another word.

Some time later, Hamfast awoke with a pain in his abdomen. He needed to urinate, and badly. He dimly wondered how that had been handled while he was unconscious. Maybe he had been so deprived of water out at sea—an old irony overly referenced by sailors—that it hadn't been an issue. But it most certainly was an issue now, and he was not about to do it in his cot. He struggled to his feet, finding that the old leg brace from the Dragonfly had been replaced but was just as sturdy. He hobbled carefully to the door, half hopping on his one good leg, and pushed it open. There was a step down onto the dirt, and he relieved himself in the tall grass at the corner of the hut.

When he had finished, he surveyed his surroundings. There were many small huts, arranged in no particular order, around a larger open space. All was thick and green and lush, shaded by the same kinds of great trees that had been on the island the Dragonfly had visited. High, rocky hills rose on two sides, forming a kind of small valley here, and the other two directions sloped down towards what his senses told him must be the sea. There was a large communal cooking space, which piqued his interest. The remains of several coal fires were ashed over in a semicircle, with a great cast iron pot sitting beside one, and large stones polished to a level on top to serve as working space. This area was swept immaculately clean, which Hamfast could appreciate.

And there were people. All had the same green skin as his friend with the broth, and they bustled around the village. Many carried reed baskets—some laden with fish, some with fruit or fibers or root bulbs. The people cast curious glances at Hamfast, who stood gawking and feeling awkward. The people were of a race Hamfast had never encountered before—nor even heard stories describing. The only green-skinned creatures in the stories were of monsters—goblins, trolls, the roving orcish tribes of the Dahk Ahani plains. These were just people.

A gaggle of children ran up towards Hamfast, seeming to materialize from out of nowhere. He took a step back in surprise, but quickly found himself surrounded. They were just as tall as he was, and bounded around him, speaking in a rapid chittering in words he could not comprehend. Hamfast could only smile and shrug back at them. "Hamfast," he said, pointing to himself, feeling silly.

"Hammast!" they cried, and one took him by the hand.

"Oh gods, no. I can't play. I'm hurt. Hurt. See?" Hamfast pointed to his leg.

*"Pala iatu tetia, lamati,"* came a voice. Makhal sidled up, shooing the children with a gesture. *"Ia liga ma le mau sonay. Aea tu likka loa."*

The children ran along, looking back over their shoulders at the strange newcomer to their village. Hamfast felt dizzy, and groped around for something to steady himself. Makhal grabbed him by the arm, helping him to sit in the grass. "Thank you," Hamfast said.

Makhal hunkered down beside him. *"Ua nasa a tu lou linosa?"*

Hamfast placed his hands on either side of his head, swaying it back and forth. "Dizzy," he said.

Makhal nodded. Another universal gesture. Hamfast wondered at that. Cultures separated by entire oceans, and still people were people. Perhaps there was some truth to the wizard Whitaker's strange ramblings. Maybe we all did come from somewhere. Hamfast put his hand on his chest, patted it. "Hamfast." Then patted the ground. "Here." He repeated the twin gestures, then spread his hands and shrugged. "How? How did I get here?"

Makhal grinned at him. *"Ia aeso lasati. Ioe, oua te palama."*

He held his hand flat in the air, fingers arced back, then gyrated it in a waving motion. *"Iasa".*

"Ocean." Hamfast nodded, and he imitated the waves with his hand.

Makhal's grin broadened. He placed one fist on top of the other. He held them there for a moment, then jerked them back. He pinched thumb and finger together, holding up an imaginary something. He stroked this. *"Kawalasa."*

"Fish. Fishing." Hamfast pointed at a nearby man carrying a basket of fish.

*"Makhal... kawalasa,"* Makhal said, combining gestures. He made the ocean again, and plucked something from it. "Hammast."

"Hah. Simple enough," Hamfast chuckled. It was like a game. "You were fishing and found me." He tried to imitate the words. "*Makhal. Kawalasa* in the *iasa*. Found Hamfast in the *iasa*."

Makhal clapped him on the back. *"O se wahi taoa aloma."*

"I do my best," Hamfast replied. He crossed his hands over his heart and bowed his head, hoping it would translate. "Thank you. Thank you for saving me."

Makhal mimicked the gesture. *"E oleisi masa mea. O le a tatou feiloai lelei. Ae o lea, matou te le iloa lolae mea e fai ia te oe."*

"I have no guesses about what you just said."

Makhal shrugged. *"A'oha ona tatou teloah. Eo i le so ahso. Ae ua tatou malawa i se alataga lelei."*

Hamfast sighed. "I've got a good bit of learning to do if we're to move beyond pantomime."

It was a short walk back to the hut, and Makhal brought him some fruit to eat. He left with a nod, closing the door behind him.

Finding himself alone in the hut again, Hamfast ate. The fruit was something like a banana, only not as sweet. He was tired again, after only being up a short while. He settled onto the cot, and something dug into his hip. He sat back up, fishing his hand for whatever it was. His fingers found something warm and jagged in his pocket. He pulled it out to examine it, but he already knew what it would be despite the impossibility. What he withdrew had a light of its own. It was the familiar smoke colored stone, the familiar jagged edges, and those enticing dancing motes of purple light dancing inside. And there was absolutely no reasonable explanation for how it could be in his pocket.

Hamfast didn't sleep for a long time. He thought of Brogan and Strawn, of Levin, of Captain Killian, of all he had served aboard the Dragonfly. They were dead. Every single one was dead. Some were friends, most were right bastards, and he wept for them all in equal measure. When he could weep no more, the questions began to fill his mind. He turned them over again and again, examining them in bewilderment as he passed the night staring at the floating lights inside the shard.

## 27

## ON LANGUAGE

The morning began as it had for many weeks now. Hamfast awoke when Makhal pulled the blankets off him and began folding them. "That's such a cruel way to wake a man," Hamfast groaned, drawing his knees up against the sudden intrusion of cool morning air. He stretched and got to his feet. "*Ua himae.*"

"*Kume,*" Makhal grunted. Lazy. He grabbed the cot and took it outside, where he hung it over a strung rope to air out in the sunlight. Hamfast took his walking stick and hobbled past him, making his way to the kitchen area.

"Good morning," Hamfast yawned at the young man named Muk, who was stirring the logs in one of the fire pits. Hamfast set to work beside him, unrolling a *tapa* cloth that kept the sand off the knives when not in use. The cloth was a wondrous thing here. The robes Hamfast now wore were of the same material.

The cloth was made from the inner bark of a tree—a laborious process that fascinated him. The making of it was nearly constant, with several men who seemed to be dedicated to no other task than the harvesting, peeling, and processing of bark.

The bark was stripped and beaten with wooden mallets, and the sounds of the beating took on a musical quality. Every day, the rhythm of *tapa* beating rang through the village, drumming out a beat for the dance of daily life.

Hamfast honed the knives carefully. These were metal, a rare thing on the island. He then arranged them on the wooden slab he had perched atop one of the stone work surfaces. Cooking was the one thing he knew. It was his place among sailors, of whose profession he understood poorly even after all these years. And now it was his place among these strangers. It gave him an anchor in this world. A way of belonging, if only a little.

Muk sat a reed basket down beside the knives, and Hamfast studied the morning's bounty. Eggs, as usual. There were birds roaming freely around the island, chickens of a sort although larger and meaner than he'd ever seen before, and someone gathered eggs from their nests every morning. And there was the fibrous root things Hamfast called potatoes, although he knew better. But they fried in palm oil just like potatoes, only sweeter. Hamfast pulled the roots out of the basket to start the process of hacking off their thick skins, and noticed something else in the bottom of the basket. Something wrapped in a waxy cloth. He plucked it out and started to unwrap it. His eyes went wide.

"Bacon?!" Hamfast pointed at the smoked meat accusingly, looking at Muk. "Where in the hell did you get bacon?"

Muk stared straight ahead, busying himself with oiling a large cast iron pan big enough to fry a Lindle in. Muk was a teenager, and there was a glint of amusement in his eyes.

"Honestly! There are no pigs here." Hamfast pinched the bridge of his nose in frustration. He had a very limited vocabulary, but pig was certainly out of the question with none to point at. "*Where? Animal?*" He settled back into Elorian, if only to gripe. "There are no animals at all except the birds and fish. And I was just at the smoke shack yesterday. There was no bacon in there, nothing but schools of drying fish. I'd have smelled it in my sleep if there had been bacon smoking." Muk said nothing, still oiling the pan which was already plenty oiled. Hamfast snatched the rag from him. "Oh, stop it. You're just cooking cloth at this point. Where'd the bacon come from, eh? Elsewhere, that's where. And that explains the metal implements. You bastards don't just use your boats for fishing. There's more of you out there."

Muk said nothing, his face stoic. Oh, but those eyes glittered.

"You think this funny?" Hamfast stomped his good foot. "You know what this means, don't you? It means there's a way off this rock for me, and you know it. Bah!" Hamfast knew there was no point in questioning, and threw up his hands in frustration. He dropped the bacon back into the basket and started back to hacking at the giant potato things with an angry fervor. "You know what? No bacon for you this morning. I'm withholding it, you hear me? No bacon for anybody! And since we don't understand each other, you can't even ask me why I'm not frying it up. So there." He squinted at Muk, then reconsidered. "Bah. I can't deny everyone just because you play games with me. Someone will explain it to me, even if you won't. It's not enough bacon to serve in strips, as much as I'd fancy it. We'll make great, big omelettes. We'll need to fry up some minced coconut, mince some of those onion things with chilis, and fetch some shrimp." Hamfast huffed, trying to find the words for Muk. *"Small small cut coconut and sour root. Hot berry also. Then bring shrimp. I cook the new animal."*

With Hamfast's injuries, he couldn't do much more than hobble from one sitting place to another. And so he'd spent a considerable amount of time with Makhal learning the rudiments of his language through what amounted to pointing, handwaving, and a lot of confusion. But Makhal had been a patient teacher.

Hamfast had spent enough time outside of Elora to have a knack for languages. He spoke nearly fluent Frendarian, or at least the lower dialect used in port. He knew a little Seggrit and understood the flavor of Omaas used in the Dirk Isles, but his responses were always stumbling over their strange rules of verb changes. He had learned Elvish from Davin's wife Saira, on their long journey back from the elven lands. Their marriage had been a secret even to the crew, and Hamfast knew little of the strange circumstances himself. He had made the pregnant woman ginger tea for her constant nausea, both from pregnancy and her first time at sea. A proper linguist he was not, but traveling from port to port for many years had given him plenty of practice in picking up essential phrases, the verbs and nouns, and learning to smash them together enough to be roughly understood. You can skip a lot of words and still make meaning. You may sound like an idiot, but you will be an idiot who can order a hot meal and tell people where to stack things.

These pale green men were the Tagata. They fished. They tended their little village. Whether the Tagata was just this island or a greater culture was now in question. And now it begged a great many other questions. There were many boats secured on the sandy beaches here—small canoe-like contraptions with outrider pontoons that kept them sure in the rough waters, and fishing expeditions were frequent. But he could not imagine daring an ocean voyage in something so small and simple.

Hamfast sat on a rock near the others as they ate their breakfast from wooden plates, sitting in family circles cross-legged. The village came together at mealtimes, a loud and chaotic event where all descended from their various labors across the island to eat, tell stories, and laugh at jokes. The children served the adults —their only real responsibility during a day mostly filled with play and fetching things.

This was the highlight of Hamfast's day. He felt appreciated, having prepared a fine meal. The village was a larger crew than the Dragonfly. But he had the advantage of being on solid ground, of fresh ingredients, and of having the help of Muk and the children to do the fetching and serving. It was still a lot of work to coordinate, but he took great pride in his work.

Hamfast did his best to listen in to the chaotic chatter around him. It was a soft, flowy language. It sounded a bit like Elvish, but he had not discerned many similarities beyond the sound of it. There were words for the way languages could work, Hamfast was certain. Some scholars surely studied language—the way sounds combine and separate, how to count and categorize their usage, how words change one another. And if he ever found a way home, he would find a book on it to make greater sense of how it all worked beyond his fumbling intuitions. For now, he simply let the words wash over him. The language was like the sound of the ocean in the lagoon, rippling gently back and forth, and how well it mixed with the seabirds calling from the rocky outcroppings above. Hamfast was far from home, yet he was at peace here.

As the people finished eating and began the process of cleaning up, Hamfast rose to join them. But a hand on his shoulder pushed him back onto his rock. Makhal and Yakha knelt in front of him. Yakha was the *matai* here. Hamfast knew this meant a leader of some sort, but the specifics escaped him. There was no pantomime for such a thing, and he was left to intuition that he was simply somehow above the others. Wise man, elder, spiritual leader, chief. It was something in that neighborhood, in any case. Yakha was bald with an immense grey bush of eyebrows that sat above his eyes like a sleeping ferret, and had yet to speak to Hamfast after all these weeks.

Yakha ran his hands over Hamfast's splinted leg. Old, gnarled fingers probed at his leg between the hard splints. "It doesn't hurt," Hamfast said. "*None pain.*" The probing continued for a few minutes, and Hamfast let him. Then Yakha stood and took a knife from the kitchen, and began cutting away the cords that held the stiff splint in place. When he had finished, Hamfast stood.

"It feels a bit weak, but I suppose that's from lack of use. It doesn't hurt, at least. Well, the knee hurts. But the leg seems sturdy enough."

Yakha looked Hamfast in the eyes. Then he said something to Makhal and jerked his head towards the sandy slopes that led down to the sea. "I need to walk, is that it? Wonderful." And so Hamfast did, still using the walking stick to steady himself, and taking it easy on his weakened leg. He'd gotten used to hobbling, and it felt nice to walk like a normal person again, even if his knee still ached.

Makhal took Hamfast's walking stick. "*Tau me kai oe keia.*"

"Alright, but it will be a slow hike," Hamfast said. He tested the leg. *"I try."*

The island was not large. The two rocky crags that jutted out on the east and west of the village roughly split the island into thirds. The trees on the island were diverse. There were many variations of palm, their green fronds providing dappled shade in the thicker groves and a constant supply of coconuts. The smaller, bushier specimens created a sparse undergrowth that could be harvested for oil. There were the banana trees—although these were more like large plants than proper trees. Then there were the great trees, like the ones on that dark island, which jutted up higher than all else. These spread their broad shade and created open spaces on the ground where ferns and thick clover flourished, making ample room for huts. The large nuts from these trees were bitter when raw, but toasted up nicely after soaking overnight in water.

Makhal and Hamfast walked a path through a grove on the edge of the village, and once through that, the path sloped quickly uphill as it wound up towards one of the crags. Hamfast breathed hard from the exertion. This trek had been out of the question before today. He had seen nothing of the island but the village and the beach, and his stamina would take time to return. The knee troubled him, and he wondered how long until that would heal. One would expect a sprained knee to mend before a bone. Perhaps it was something else. They walked in silence for most of an hour, Makhal patiently settling into Hamfast's slow pace. Hamfast made no attempt to hurry and listened to the sounds of the waves slushing against the shore below and the seabirds somewhere above it.

The path ended well below the top of the crag. Makhal sat on a rocky outcropping that provided an excellent view of the sea below them. Hamfast joined him, catching his breath. The view was beautiful, and he basked in it. The warm sun on his skin, the calmness of the island below, and the endless expanse of blue-green waters extending out as far as he could see.

"Are there other villages?" Hamfast asked him. *"New animal today. Come from boat? More village? More... village in ocean?"*

Makhal laughed. *"Yes. Many more."*

*"How many? Where?"*

*"We travel the ocean. Find new islands. Build new villages. When a village grows, brave families leave. Choose new leader. The ocean is too vast to ever let an island get crowded."*

*"New animal. Boat come?"*

*"Pig,"* Makhal gave him the word. *"Our pigs had disease. All died. We sent a boat to the island we came from. Just returned last night. You slept. Brought back more pigs. Only a few. It will take time before we raise enough to use for meat. The pig meat this morning was a gift, to raise spirits."*

Hamfast had to ask for repetition, even though Makhal always spoke slowly and simply for him. But Hamfast was amazed. Those tiny boats could indeed dare the open seas. From this new vantage point, Hamfast could see now where the lagoon ended, with some kind of reef that circled the island. The waters of the shallow sheltered lagoon were bright, almost green, compared to the dark waters beyond.

Hamfast realized that the sea was no longer frightening. It beckoned to him as it once had. And now, it seemed, there was a chance. "She's a powerful mistress, there," Hamfast mused. "That's what a friend of mine said once. He's dead now, though. Killed by the storm that stranded me here. And I think it's my fault."

"*I do not understand you.*"

"Right. *Sorry.*" Hamfast sighed. He didn't have a clue how to explain it. Thoughts of the storm had been plaguing him ever since he had arrived here. How long had that even been? A broken leg healed now, and that meant what? Months, surely. It had felt like an eternity. "*My big boat break. Yes?*"

"*Yes, your ship came into a storm. Your friends died.*"

"*Friends die. Yes.*"

"*And you grieve for them.*"

"*Yes. More. More telling. More... do first. Do before.*"

"*Did.*" Makhal corrected. "*Perhaps, more happened before the storm?*"

"*Yes. More happened before the storm.*" Making phrases past tense still eluded him, but he committed the phrase to memory. "*More happened before.*"

Makhal looked over at him with a mild curiosity. "*Take your time and tell me. I can be patient and help you find the words.*"

Hamfast nodded. He could try. "*Boat go to island. Yes? Island has hut. Not hut. Hut made of stones. Old. Old old.*"

Makhal arched an eyebrow. Another universal, Hamfast mused. "*Your ship went to an island that had a building made of stone.*"

"*Yes.*" So there was a word for *building* after all. Here it was all just huts.

"*Where?*"

"*I do not know. Under building. This.* This shard." Hamfast withdrew it, holding it up to the sunlight. It glimmered faintly from within, dancing flecks of otherworldliness that never lost their wonder, no matter how long he studied them. "*I do not have words for this.* It's some kind of magic bauble. A powerful one. Something the wizards of Sona called a shard. They were after it on some island not terribly far from here. I was with them—just as a cook on the ship, mind you. But through a bit of stupidity I got separated from everyone on the island and found it. But now I'm wondering if it was more than dumb luck, and something else entirely. I'm starting to wonder if I was supposed to find it. And then I botched it all somehow."

Makhal looked over at the shard in Hamfast's hand, his face stony. But Hamfast could see as the man's eyes watched the dancing lights inside it.

"The wizards asked me if the thing spoke to me. They were scared to take it from me if so. And, fool that I was, I said no. No, of course not. Because why would it? Why would it speak to me?" Hamfast shook his head. "I think it was a false sense of humility at the time. Because even though I didn't hear a voice, something certainly happened. I was injured and scared, but through the haze of it all I was pulled straight to this stone here. And then, right after I gave it to the wizards, a storm attacked us. That's not an exaggeration, either. I've never seen anything like it. And it killed everyone. My crew—my friends. Everyone except me. And now this stone is right back in my pocket, and I'm here with you lot. It has to mean something, right? It's like I'm being led by the nose, but whatever is doing the leading is being obtuse. Telling me things without telling me. Leaving me to figure it all out."

Makhal looked from the shard to Hamfast. *"I do not understand your words. But I see you are in great conflict. And the thing you hold is strange. You took this thing from a building. From people?"*

"No. No people on island. All old. Broken."

*"And then..."* Makhal puzzled for a moment. *"And then something happened. Something that you regret."*

"Last word. What is meaning of word?"

*"Regret. To do a thing and later wish you did not."*

"Yes! Regret. *Regret.* By the gods, one word helps make sense of things." Hamfast closed his eyes, trying to piece the meaning together. *"I take this from building. My people find me. Give this to man. To leader. Regret give to leader."*

*"Why?"*

*"Think this make storm break boat."* Hamfast pointed at the shard. *"Think... think this alive. Speak."*

*"I think you misuse your words. That cannot be alive. Cannot speak."*

*"Not speak. Not alive. Wrong words. Words hard."* The words were hard to find even in Elorian.

*"But it does move. It is strange."*

*"Yes."*

Makhal stood. *"Come. You have great conflict within you. You should speak to Yakha. He is wise. I will try to help. Maybe then, you can make more meaning of this."*

Hamfast got to his feet. "I'm not sure what Yakha can do, but I'm willing to try. Maybe it doesn't make sense and I'm just rambling. Then again, I do feel better getting it out. I'm certainly grateful for your listening. And for all your people have done for me. You've set me back on my feet. If Yakha is so wise, maybe he can help me figure out what I'm supposed to do next. I could use some wisdom."

*"Will you come?"*

*"I will."*

# PART IV

*The Huntress comes to reclaim us*
  *A ghost in the night*
  *Arrow and sword*
  *Terror and hope*

*Born of two bloods*
  *She is us, yet she is them*
  *She remembers our songs*
  *The men fear her coming*

*Come, oh Huntress*
  *We long for our moon and stars*
  *For the breaking of chains*
  *For the promise of new life*

*Come, oh Huntress*
  *And set our children free*

Translation, Elven slave song in Lyramae

## 28

## POISON

Aideen watched as the children ran and shouted. Lyra and Pomm played with the other children in Salar Park, who seemed not to care that the two newcomers had long ears and colorful hair. It didn't even seem to matter that they only had the barest grasp of the language here. Children have their own language at play, and their laughter didn't need translating. The prejudice would emerge later. The humans would be taught that it was natural for the elves to live in the Fae Quarter, or in the ghettos of Pigtown outside the city walls. That their place was to serve among the lower classes, or be kept out of sight and forgotten. How strange that no child was born knowing how to hate.

Aideen sat on a wooden bench, drinking in the sunlight beneath a bare branched oak. She had been one of these children once. It didn't seem so long ago. She sat where her father would have, watching over the merry chaos and tussle. She tried to keep her thoughts from running away down that particular path, and sought to simply enjoy the unseasonably warm winter day.

Aideen had spent the past week visiting daily to check on

Lyra and Pomm. The children had a tutor, a kind old woman who spoke enough Elvish to instruct them in the Elorian language. It would take time, but both seemed bright enough. In a year or two, they may be able to join a normal schoolhouse in Sona. They had spent no time in the Red Dress itself since that first night. The Masquerade apparently ran an orphanage in the Lower City near this park, and life seemed almost normal there. Aideen wondered exactly what the stories of the people who lived in it were. How many shattered lives were being rebuilt under the care of the very same organization that dealt in secrets and killed in the shadows?

Aideen had given those minutes in the Under City a great deal of thought in the past week. She had killed three men. But she found to her surprise that their deaths did not weigh heavy on her conscience. Perhaps they should have. But there was an issue that overshadowed the death of slavers at her hand. There was the beast that had done the killing. The beast that had saved her life.

She remembered the first time she had felt the rustle of wings inside her. She had thought it merely a personification of her emotions, her anger at Deidre's dismissal of Lodai. It was normal enough to think in metaphor. Lodai had always spoken of the calm, cool waters within. And when she felt them, she felt them as such. It was just that elven part of herself, but his description was apt and she had taken to it. It was a turn of phrase, the manner of thinking a girl does when she spends so much free time cozied into a library filled with good books.

But the beast frightened her. If it was merely a part of herself, no one had told her it was a beast. And if it was her mind's own metaphor for some part of her nature, the wings made little sense. Yet it was there, sleeping inside her. She had felt it. She had heard it, in a way. And it seemed to have a will. It had not wanted to die under the city. It had refused to die, and had launched her to action beyond her fears.

The beast was simply her, of course. It was simply a part of her. It had to be. Metaphor and personification be damned. But she wondered now if it was the very thing Lodai had been worried about. If it was a part of her rending. If this was the madness Lodai had feared, and he had missed it emerging inside of her. Lodai had believed her rending complete, believed her safe from the madness that took his sister, but what if he was wrong? Now Aideen sat, feeling quite herself, in the calm of a park. She was no monster. She was not mad. But a week of consideration and telling herself that her actions in the Under City were merely a natural survival response had done little to ease her mind.

Aideen was running out of plausible excuses for her constant absence in Lindenhall. She was allegedly planning a wedding, but so far she had little to show for her daily disappearances. Deidra and Carolyn were both pestering her for wedding details now. Curiosity was beginning to tilt toward concern on her stepmother's part, while Carolyn was simply growing exasperated with her. Aideen had spent plenty of time pretending to plan the wedding while she sought her father's killer, and now she must make up for lost time. Her solution to this was simple enough— she would give it all over to Deidra. Play the overwhelmed bride. The woman was overflowing with opinions on the matter anyhow, and was certainly more qualified to select cakes and flowers and whatever else they needed to impress their guests. Aideen was preoccupied with other matters. She had a killer to catch, a killer beast inside herself, these two children to check on, and a fiancé who had turned rather stiff since seeing her with her ears out at the ball.

A woman seated herself on the far side of the bench with a sigh. "A fine day," the woman remarked.

"Indeed it is."

"You have taken quite the interest in the lives of those two."

Aideen turned to look at the woman. She did not know her.

She had greying hair that had once been a reddish hue, her face etched in faint lines of age. She dressed as one of the Upper City, in an elegant but functional dress like a Lady out for a picnic.

"You know me, but I do not know you," Aideen said with some suspicion.

"You know another version of me." The woman did not look at Aideen, only watching the game of chase that seemed devoid of any discernible rules. "You will know it in a moment with those special eyes of yours."

Aideen's mind clicked the pieces together. Aideen did know her, she realized. She knew the mouth. She knew the hands. The ring was back in place, where before it had only been the line of its absence.

"Don't say it," the woman said, glancing over at Aideen. "One cannot be too careful."

"I know who you are," Aideen said. "I take it you have something for me? Although I'm surprised you came instead of sending one of your people."

"I'm surprised myself," the Queen of Masks said. "Only my most trusted associates know both faces. Then again, normally the arrangement of favors is merely a transaction. Your part is done, and it is my turn to do mine. But in your case, you seem to have taken what you've found on your little adventure quite personally."

"I came seeking one kind of knowledge, and I found quite another."

"And this disturbs you?"

"Greatly."

"As well it should." The woman scattered a bit of bird seed from a pouch onto the ground before them, drawing the attention of a few warblers that had been bouncing around the grass nearby. Aideen watched them, waiting. This woman, this leader of the Masquerade, was a mystery. But Aideen sensed that her coming here was significant somehow. Aideen held her tongue and waited to see what this all meant. The woman watched the birds hop their way closer, and coaxed them with another sprinkling of seed. "So, why are you here?" the woman asked at last. "These two are cared for, as you can plainly see."

"I don't know."

"Don't you?"

Aideen considered. "Guilt, I suppose."

"Guilt? You rescued them, child. And at great danger to yourself. What have you to feel guilty of?"

"For everything!" Aideen blurted out, a sudden bitter anger flaring up inside of her. Aideen calmed herself, biting back the bitterness. "For a great many things. I've lived a life of wealth, making comments on the city's hypocrisy while remaining a useless example of it. Pretending to be something I am not, standing far above my kin and telling myself their plight is not my trouble. Remaining ignorant of what was really going on all around me. My teacher—my uncle—tried to warn me of it, I think. That there was a darkness behind the facade of it all. But I didn't listen. I believed it had problems, surely. But nothing like this."

"Elora is a wonderful place. We have peace. We have prosperity. But not for all. There is still a bounty of greed and evil. There is still darkness, of which you've now seen a glimmer. There are many who are content with good for themselves. And there are others who believe that is not good enough."

"And so that is what your people are about? Making things better? Saving people from slavery?"

"We do many things," the woman replied. "We are not in the business of saving people, and yet we save people. We are not in the business of ending slavery, though we work to that end as well. We play at a long game. There are many threats to the people of Elora—humans, Lindle, and Elves. But we strive in nudging the whole, while doing what we can for the individuals along the way. We want a better future for all children of Elora. Not just for the fortunate, and not just for those we may save. Occasionally this means violence, as you've seen, but we will not sway the six nations at the edge of a sword. We are too few, and we seek betterment rather than war. With the power concentrated in the House of Lords and the Syani, our primary tools are information and deceit. It means working in shadows, but it also means keeping the company of the very elements we would see gone from this world. The means are not always noble, but the ends most certainly are."

"Why tell me all this?"

"Because I wish you to have context. And perhaps other reasons." The woman paused, seeming to consider something. Aideen felt the silence with a sense of apprehension. The woman nodded to herself and continued. "I have the information you seek. Come tonight after sunset, and you will spend time with an expert in poisons."

"Thank you," Aideen said.

"There is no need to thank me. We struck a bargain. However, I have more to tell you. But this is not part of our previous agreement."

"My last bargain with you nearly got me killed. Do you honestly expect me to make another?"

"You seem well enough to me. And yes, I expect you will. The information concerns your fiancé. You'll not discover it on your own, and I think it pertinent to you in more ways than one."

Aideen blinked. Cathal? What on earth was she talking about? The possibilities ran wild through her mind. "And what do you want for this information?"

"Oh, nothing for now. But a favor, to be called upon at some future date."

"A favor."

"Indeed. Not because you're grateful to me, darling. But because that is how this works."

Aideen slumped back on the bench, exasperated. "I'm not a spy, you know."

"Of course not. You're something else entirely. Do we have an agreement?"

"Fine," Aideen said. "A favor."

"Do we have an agreement?" the woman pressed.

"We have an agreement."

"Good. In that case, I think you should know that your Lord Cathal was also seeking information from me some time ago."

Aideen looked at the woman. The idea of Cathal being somehow involved with the Masquerade came as a shock. "Does he work with your people in some way?"

The woman laughed. "No, darling. Far from it. I mean he came to us seeking information about your family."

"What sort of information?"

"More than three years ago, he sought to know all he could of the Bormia Trading Company—as well as about its ownership. About your father, his investors, and the people he most trusted in the company."

"They were friends. Why would he need to dig when he could merely ask?"

"I have my suspicions, but cannot say for certain. I provided him what I could—for a price. The information seemed harmless to me. A rivalry in commerce, I assumed."

"They deal in very different trades," Aideen said, thinking it through. "And in the past several years, House Gwenhert made no substantial moves in their shipping affairs to rival Bormia."

"It is curious, is it not?"

"So he must not have cared about commerce. It was something else."

"Go on," the woman cooed as she tossed another pinch of seeds to the warblers. "Follow the thread, darling."

"He was friends with my father. I myself did not know him yet, and barely knew of him. What else was happening? Bormia continued in its business, continued growing, but nothing stands out." Aideen puzzled. "Two years ago, Riann began his apprenticeship at the company. The recommendation came from Lord Cathal."

"Which is how your father became acquainted with his mother," the woman agreed. "A coincidence, perhaps. And the young man excelled in this capacity from what I understand."

"Perhaps he had a mentor," Aideen said. Lord Cathal had been helping Riann since Davin's death. Could it be that such assistance had precedent?

"You have a suspicious mind. That will serve you well in this world. Now, leave this aside to consider once you have a fuller picture. Much later, Lord Cathal approached me again. This time, he was looking for information on elven customs. Specifically regarding how wealth is passed down to children upon marriage, upon death, etcetera. That part was simple enough. But he also sought to know the contents of your father's will. I can assure you, that sort of information is not acquired easily."

"Wait." Aideen balked. "Do you mean to tell me one of your people broke into my home and unsealed my father's will?"

"That sort of information is not acquired easily," the woman repeated.

"When?" Aideen demanded.

"Just after your father remarried."

Bile rose in her throat. She felt as though she might vomit. She stared at the birds pecking at her feet, her mind whirling in a foggy mist. The intrusion of her home was repulsive, but the request was worse. Cathal. She could hardly entertain the ideas that sprang into her thoughts. Aideen took a deep breath and ran through everything she knew for certain. Cathal was looking at her father's company years ago, but made no moves against Bormia with the information which must have been costly. Instead, Riann joined the company, then Davin met Deidra. A sympathetic widow with children of a similar age to his daughter.

Elven marriage and inheritance customs were an obscure topic for a noble in Elora. Unless, of course, you wanted to marry a man's daughter who happened to be part elf. A man who bucked convention and might choose to honor Elven traditions instead of Elorian custom and might compose his will to that effect. But Cathal had not even met Aideen when her father remarried. And he had certainly not known about Aideen's heritage. Not yet. He couldn't have. Only the family had known. Aideen saw the pieces plainly before her, even if she did not want to connect them. He could not have known, unless someone revealed it to him in secret.

Aideen searched her memories. She remembered that day with Cathal in the Lindenhall gardens. Her revelation to him. Her emotions were so tangled up in that moment, making it hard to see it clearly. Her nervousness. Her excitement. Her fear of his rejection. Her hope. She could see his face and the surprise on it, and then the way he looked at her when he waved it all away. The warmth in his eyes. And yet, this woman claimed that was all a charade.

How could he have known beforehand? It seemed impossible that her father would have revealed this to him. And Cathal had seemed so sincere! But now she doubted everything. So much she had known was not as it seemed. She'd had no reason for doubting at the time. And yet on second look, he had accepted her secret so easily. She had counted it as an act of love, but what if it were something else? Her stomach twisted at the idea that her fiancé was hiding secrets as well.

"The individual requests seemed mundane at the time, but now? With your father dead?" The woman drew a cigarette from a silver holder and lit it. "And my name is Lady Charlotte Premroe, darling. You were right in your assessment of me, down to where I come from. Who would guess my cigarette choice would give so much away? I've had to switch to Resedian tobacco now when I wear the mark. Disgusting stuff."

"Why reveal your identity to me?"

"Who can say, darling?" Lady Charlotte replied, a serpent's smile on her smoke wreathed lips. "Perhaps because you'd recognize me eventually at some social event or another with those eyes of yours. But I know my secret is safe with you. You're an expert at keeping them, after all. Besides, no one would believe the word of an elf." Her words struck Aideen like a slap across the face, their echo ringing in her ears. She stared at the woman slack jawed. "Ah, I can see I've given you much to consider. And tonight, you shall have even more."

"You've set me spinning, if I'm honest," Aideen muttered.

Lady Charlotte stood, smoothing her dress. "Consider this a lesson. When you seek truth, be sure you are prepared to find it."

THE UPPER ROOM of the Red Dress was all too familiar. Aideen sat on the plush sofa beside Beatrice, not across from her. She found herself on the other side of it all somehow, closer. The Queen of Masks—once again costumed in her robe and mask, sat behind the desk on one side of the room. Aideen and Beatrice wore similar masks, with hooded red robes obscuring their appearances.

The door opened, and a man was ushered in by one of the many nameless women in crimson robes. He was well-dressed, his pants pressed with sharp creases and a lavender vest over a ruffled shirt. He carried with him a leather satchel bag. The man bowed deeply to the masked figures before him.

Beatrice stood. "You have your instructions," Beatrice said

with a professional coolness. She motioned to the low table in front of the couch, where dozens of teacups and teapots were laid out in rows like a formation of soldiers. A coal brazier nearby held a simmering pot of water, and there was a satchel on the floor with a sample of every type of tea in the pantries of Lindenhall, with several others purchased for good measure. The tea in question was likely an evening herbal sort, but Aideen had taken no chances.

"A most unusual request," the man said, his voice tinny with a note of haughtiness that made Aideen instantly dislike him. "But yes, I have my instructions. I suppose let's have some tea, shall we?"

Aideen watched as he set about the task. Hot water and tea leaves were set to steep in the many pots, and as they did the man set small vials along the edge of the table to coincide with a row of teacups. Then he began pouring tea in the teacups down the line with a prim sort of flourish. When he was done, he opened the vials, one by one, and dribbled a small amount of liquid into each cup. Aideen saw before her a kind of grid, each row in one direction a type of tea, and in the other a substance from a vial. Poisons. She shuddered at them. A table brimming with death. A wave of memory came flooding back to her. Of her father laying cold on the floor. Of the teacup on the corner of his desk. She closed her eyes and fought back the sudden need to scream.

"Well, there you have it. As requested. These are all the poisons I know that might kill a man without leaving a trace for a doctor to find, and that kill quickly enough to bring no illness first. There aren't many, and I've taken the liberty of including a few that a skilled doctor should notice tell-tale signs of, under the assumption that not all doctors are as attentive as they should be."

"Remove a small amount from each cup," Aideen said from behind her mask, her voice unsteady from the tightness in her throat. "The poison I seek left a certain ring inside the cup."

"Ah. Then I have my suspicions of which can be excluded."

"Do not tell me," Aideen said quickly. "Let me see them all without prejudice."

"As you wish." He took a spoon and began methodically transferring a portion from each, carefully spooning the poisoned liquids back into tea pots. "I must be cautious not to spill or mix any of these. We will need to take great caution in their disposal. There is much death laid before you now." His hand was steady as it traversed the first column, and he discarded the spoon for another before moving onto the next.

Aideen focused on the slow revelations in each cup. She had the cup in her memories fixed in her mind's eye. Her anxiety mounted as each cup was wrong in one way or another. She had already discounted most of the teas on color alone now. There were subtle differences from the addition of poison as well, she saw. And of all those cups, there were only six that were right. But she waited. She watched as the man worked in silence. She noticed that Beatrice was watching her, dark eyes flicking back and forth from man to teacups to Aideen's masked face.

The spoons made their way down the rows and columns until he arrived at one of the possibilities. As the tea level dropped, it left a slight ring on the cup, and Aideen felt herself tense. But it wasn't quite right. And now she began to doubt herself. Words from the last time in this room echoed in her mind. How sure could she really be? And she began to fear another dead end. The spoons moved steadily, but Aideen felt like it was taking an eternity.

Six possibilities became four. And then two remained. Aideen's eyes flicked from cup to cup, second guessing each one, then returning to those that were closest to right. The two that remained were in the same column, two poisons in the same variation of ginger tea. She held her breath as the spoon approached, terrified of both possibilities. Of the consequences either way. When you seek truth, be sure you are prepared to find it. Aideen tried to quiet her nerves. But then a dizziness washed over her. Her emotions roiled inside her, shock and anger and sorrow all burning in her chest.

There it was. In the second to last cup. The same tea. The same faint ring. She dug her fingers into the cushion beneath her and tried her best not to vomit.

## 29

## HUNTING

"Are you certain?" The man studied her with a doubtful look.

"Completely," Aideen snapped back at him. It took everything in her to keep her rage at bay. She wanted to throw the table over. To rip the room apart. Seeing the cup, the mirror of the one that had haunted her for months, had created a fire inside of her, and she felt desperate to release it somehow. His haughty face looked like a fine outlet.

The beast purred in agreement.

The man spread his hands in apology, and he cleared his throat. "That is Drakewort. Very rare. Very exotic. It only grows on an island far from here. I know only two men in Sona who could procure this. Myself, being one of them, and I can assure you I have sold it to no one in years."

Aideen gawked at the man, feeling her rage begin to take aim at him once more. "You sell poisons? Honestly?"

"Darling," the Queen of Masks cooed. "If you wanted an expert in poisons, who better? You can hardly expect me to find someone wholesome with expertise in these sorts of affairs."

Aideen sneered at the man. "Even so. You disgust me."

The man sniffed. "My dear, I am helping you."

"Only because you're being paid."

The death dealer smiled and gave her a mocking bow. "Indeed, and handsomely. But I am helping you all the same." He looked over at the Queen of Masks. "Will there be anything else? I seem to be less welcome here as the moments pass."

"My friend here will do you no harm," Beatrice said, giving Aideen a look.

"Who is the other man?" Aideen asked, not bothering to keep the contempt from her voice.

"A man named Braebyn."

"And how can I find him?"

"I would advise against it. He is a dangerous man."

"I'm a dangerous woman," Aideen said. And she meant it, with restless wings trembling on their perch. She felt nothing but a frothing rage, and made no attempts to quell it.

"I believe you," the man said. "Very well. I don't know where he lives. Somewhere in Sona, surely. But he frequents a tavern in the Outer City called the Harpy's Nest, on the edges of Dockside. Most evenings he can be found there drinking and gambling."

"And how will I know him?"

"A middle-aged man, most unsavory of character. Dark hair and beard. Poorly dressed and smelling of liquor, usually. He wears a ring on his right hand that is distinct. Gold, with a large brown stone like a tiger's eye."

"Nothing else?"

His face twisted up into a toothy smile. "I'd paint you a picture, but I'm afraid I have no talent for it."

Aideen glanced over to Beatrice, who only shrugged back. "Very well. That will have to do."

"You are dismissed," the Queen of Masks said. The man bowed once more, quickly gathered his little vials of death, and swept out of the room with a satisfied look on his face. Aideen scowled after him.

Lady Charlotte removed her mask and hood. The other two followed her example. The Lady stood. "Well, darling. I have done my part as promised. And do not forget the favor owed. If you seek my aid again, I'll warn you not to do so lightly." She gave Aideen a wry smile. "I now know what you are capable of, after all."

"So what will you do?"

Beatrice sat on the far edge of the sofa, breaking the silence at last. Aideen had been sitting there for a long time now while Beatrice had busied herself disposing of all the teacups and pots, disappearing from the room one tray at a time before eventually returning and joining her in the otherwise empty room.

"I don't know," Aideen said. "I know what I have to do, but I don't like it in the least. On the one hand, I know I must confront my fiancé Cathal on what our Lady told me, but there are too many missing pieces. Like this Braebyn."

"Our Lady?" Beatrice asked. "Are you counting yourself among us now?"

"A slip of the tongue," Aideen said. "But honestly, calling her the Queen of Masks just feels ridiculous."

"You get used to it."

"I know I must confront Lord Cathal. As much as it sickens me to think it. I struggle to imagine him killing my father, although he is certainly suspect now. I just can't wrap my mind around it all. He sought information from spies, to be sure, but that thread doesn't lead him to committing murder. It simply doesn't make any sense. He gained nothing from my father's death before even marrying me. And they were friends, not rivals."

"As far as you know," Beatrice said. "He is a man of secrets, as you now know."

"Yes. But there is a part of me that hopes his actions were harmless, and only appear so suspicious because of a murder he had nothing to do with." Aideen shook her head, scrunching up her face. "Maybe believing that makes me a coward, but I still have too many questions. I think I need to keep digging. And the obvious route is to find the poison seller. Find out who he sold it to." Aideen saw that Beatrice was chewing her lip. Aideen squinted at her. "What is it?"

Beatrice shook her head. "It's circumstantial, but a large circumstance."

"What is, exactly?"

"Lord Cathal." Beatrice sighed, seeming to resign herself to something. "There's something else you should know about him."

Aideen cocked her head at her. "Well? What is it?"

"Nothing concerning your father, I shouldn't think. Our Lady has already given you knowledge on that matter concerning him. It's about what I mentioned in the Under City. About the slave trade."

Whatever Aideen had expected her to say, it was certainly not this. She blinked, shaking her head in confusion. "What are you saying?"

"I told you I've been working to uncover those who enable the slave trade through Sona. And, to be clear, I have nothing damning about your fiancé. But the slave trail to Sona goes through ships belonging to House Gwenhert. And with Lord Cathal as the Master of Ships for that house..."

"You suspect him."

"I do. Him and Duke Sturlis, which is why we were at that ball. The duke's part I can now confirm, thanks to our little heist."

"So you believe my fiancé is trafficking elven slaves into

Elora, like little Pomm, and this whole time you never bothered to tell me?" Aideen's anger no longer knew which way to aim. She glared at Beatrice with gritted teeth. "How could you keep this from me?"

"Look, it's circumstantial," Beatrice said, stiffening. "But I'm telling you now. Because regardless of what else you uncover, you should know Lord Cathal is at the very least enabling it by overseeing the House Gwenhert ships poorly. Or worse, allowing it to happen. Or, gods forbid for your sake, involved in it. In either case, he's a snake. And he's beneath you."

Aideen sank back into the sofa, too overwhelmed to even be angry. She stared at the ceiling, letting visions of everything spin around the room. Her father. The teacup. Lodai. The slavers. Cathal's smile, and the secrets kept behind those kind eyes. Her fiancé knowing she was half-elf long before he should. Before even meeting her at his ball. And now this.

Aideen realized she knew almost nothing of Cathal. Only of his clear interest in her. With his warm smile, his apparent openness, with his playful fencing around controversial conversations, she had never stopped to truly question his sincerity. She had been flattered by the attentions of a charming man. But he spoke little of himself. He spoke of her, and of her interests. Did she really even know him?

She felt like a fool. How could she have been so shallow? So stupid? How could she have agreed to marry a man without knowing him better? Davin had approved the marriage, and that had been enough. But she only knew that because Deidra had told her so. Who could ever really know the truth in a world full of liars?

"So I'm engaged to your enemy," Aideen finally said to the ceiling, her voice sounding small. "I'm supposed to marry him in two weeks. But to hell with Lord Cathal, if any of that is true. Or maybe even if it isn't. I don't know. All I know is I need to find my father's killer. And it very well may be my fiancé, who very well may be the mastermind of the Elorian slave trade. Gods, how did I end up here?" Tears blurred her vision, the tapestries and the carpets smearing into a twisted sea of red upon red upon red.

"So what will you do?" Beatrice asked.

"I fear the road I'm on now," Aideen said. "I'm angry. I'm scared. I'm disgusted. I'm a thousand things at once, and I worry I'm not thinking clearly."

"You killed a man recently," Beatrice said gently. "It doesn't matter if he deserved it. That doesn't weigh easy on a person."

"I suppose not. But what weighs on me is how easily I did it," Aideen said. "I don't regret it. It doesn't torment me like it should. And I'm not sure what that says about me. I'm not sure..." Aideen hunched over her knees, leaving the thought unfinished. Cool waters seeped in, and she felt unbearably calm. Gods, she had become a mad woman. Calm then furious. Clarity, then the murkiness of a thousand feelings surging to the surface. Cool waters and fiery beast, with her somehow caught between them.

Aideen was beginning to understand what Lodai had been supposed to watch for all these years. He had been wrong to think she was through her rending. He had only seen the first snags in the fabric and thought her safe, leaving just before she had begun to tear. This was certainly a kind of madness, this duality inside her, and she wondered where it might lead her. She'd lived an easy life, and had never once struggled so. But stress, it seemed, brought with it a chaos inside of her now. It had awoken the beast. Now that she needed a consistency of mind, now that stress came with the simple act of breathing, every moment seemed like the toss of a coin. Sometimes she could control her natures. Use them, even. Other times she couldn't. And still other times, she knew it was that she simply didn't want to. Like the beast inside of her demanded to be at the forefront. And that scared her, too.

"I'm on a road I can't turn off," Aideen repeated. "I know I can't. And yet I'm afraid of where it might lead me." Aideen cupped her face in her hands as silence hung in the air between them. She hated all this thinking. She needed to be doing something. Hesitation and options, all of them bad ones, tore at her mind. It was all so murky. She knew what she had to do. The next step was right in front of her. She felt foolish for ignoring it, but it was foolish to take it just the same.

"I'm not very good at this kind of thing," Beatrice said after a while. "Sorry."

"Don't be. Thank you for listening."

"You're welcome."

"Do you have a dagger or something I can borrow? I probably shouldn't walk into a tavern looking for this man unarmed."

"Are you up for it?"

Aideen took a deep breath then tore herself from the comfort of the sofa, flexing her fingers. "I have to be."

"Okay then." Beatrice stood up to face her, holding out a long curved knife in a scabbard. A sailor's dirk, Aideen thought as she accepted it. That was at least somehow fitting. "But you won't have to do it alone."

Aideen looked at Beatrice in surprise. "You know you don't have to do that. You have no obligation to me now."

"You'll need someone to watch your back." Beatrice took off the silly red robe, grabbing a pair of simple cloaks that hung on a peg nearby. "You're playing in my world now. You can handle yourself more than most, I'll give you that. But there's no telling what viper's nest you're about to poke. So don't argue with me. I'm at your side."

Aideen stood gaping at her, searching for the right words. Finding none, she walked over and embraced Beatrice instead, burying her face in her shoulder. Hot tears began to well up in her eyes. "Thank you," she whispered. Her words caught in her throat, emotion choking them. Aideen shuddered. "How is it that you're the only person I can trust right now?"

Beatrice, after a moment of hesitation, squeezed her back. "Hey. I just said I wasn't good at this sort of thing."

DOCKSIDE LAY on the east side of the river, well outside the city walls. All but the main road to the city gates were dust and dirt, rutted with the dry tracks of wagon wheels from some distant rainy day that had turned the roads to mud. It was near midnight, and there were no glowlamps here. Only the occasional oil lamp lit their way between the simple buildings that were the workplaces of ropemakers and sailmakers and fishmongers. It was hard not to feel out of place here, even dressed in commoner's clothes and a traveler's cloak that hid her features. The hidden dirk in her belt was a small comfort. But only a small one.

The Harpy's Nest was as dingy as the road it lay on, a small ramshackle building attached to the side of a warehouse. A fitting place for her target. Prey, a voice inside of her corrected. And she shuddered at the thought. But yes. Prey. She was hunting now. Her hesitation had been laid aside when she made the decision, and her senses were focused on the task before her. This feeling was new, and she couldn't exactly attribute it to one part of her nor the other. It was something else entirely. It was the marriage of the two, one taking the lead and the other responding.

The pair of women stopped outside of the building. "I don't exactly have a plan," Aideen admitted.

"Well. You can try to trick him into giving you the information. But we have nothing on him. We know nothing except his name and a description. No leverage, no in. So, I don't see how that can work."

"So I just confront him and hope for the best?"

"It's that, or turn around now. Or follow him. Spend some time learning what you can, try to find a better angle. Some kind of leverage."

Aideen shook her head. It was too late for that. She was on the trail already, her heart was already thrumming for it. Caution be damned. "If it goes badly, I circle back with more information. Some new angle, as you put it. He might not even be here. But I'm here now. I've got gold, and I've got a knife. One or the other will have to do."

Beatrice gave her a long, searching look. Then she nodded. "I'm with you."

They walked into the tavern. It stank of sweat and spilled ale and tobacco. A handful of men sat on stools at the bar. A few more sat playing cards at a scatter of greasy tables in the dim lamp light. Several pairs of eyes followed them through the door. Aideen was very much aware that they were the only women here. And judging from the look of the place, that was likely the norm. She set her jaw and scanned the room. There was no point in making pretenses like ordering a drink at the bar. It would give them no cover here, and would only delay things. Besides, Aideen was on the hunt.

Dark hair. Dark beard. Gold ring set with a brown stone like a tiger's eye. Braebyn wasn't difficult to spot. He sat at one of the tables with three other men, a glass of liquor in one hand and two cards held in the other, the ring plain to see. He had unsavory eyes, and they flicked from his cards to the two women standing by the door. Aideen felt the reassurance of steel on her hip, fighting down a snarl that started to form at the corners of her mouth. Restless wings flickered inside of her, tense with gleeful anticipation. Aideen approached.

"Are you the one called Braebyn?"

The man cocked an eyebrow at her. "Depends on who's askin'. If you're a courier, fuck off. I'm busy. If you've got somethin' else to offer, I've got a few hands left before I take these bastards' silver. But from the looks of you, it won't be enough to afford you lot." Drunken laughter came from the men at the table.

"So, Braebyn then. We have business to discuss."

"Go away, lass." He took a swig of his whiskey. "Whatever it is you think you're after, I've no interest in it. This isn't how I do business."

"And how do you do business, then?"

"Leave us in peace, lass. You'll find nothing but trouble here."

"If you aren't interested in having the conversation in private, I'll assume you have no problem with me discussing business in front of your friends here?" Aideen watched as his head cocked warily at her. To hell with it, she thought. Cards on the table, as it were. She had no real gambit here. On with it already. "You sold an amount of Drakewort to someone in Sona some months ago. I need to know who you sold it to."

Aideen watched as his face twitched, then settled into a calm facade. He looked with apparent thoughtfulness at his cards. "What makes you think that was me?"

"I know it was you. I know there are only two men in Sona who deal in Drakewort, and it isn't the other one."

"You aren't shy, are you?" Anger was welling up on his face now, although he refused to meet her eyes. "Nor are you discrete. I don't deal with people who aren't discrete."

"To hell with discretion. I need to know who you sold it to. I'll pay."

The man slammed his cards down on the table. He stood and sneered at Aideen, his stinking breath now in her face. "Look here, you Inner City tartlet. You're a fool to come in here talking like this. And you're a fool to think that, even if I did sell such a thing, that I would then sell the information. Giving up clients isn't exactly good for business, yeah?" His face twisted as he looked around the room. "Count yourself lucky there are so many people here. Now, if you'll excuse me."

Braebyn made to push past her, his hand thrusting out to shove her shoulder. Instead, it swiped at empty air. Aideen was beside him, her dirk drawn and laid across his belt. "No, I won't."

Braebyn froze, his jaw tensing in anger. The men at the table, seeing the blade through liquor blearied eyes, jerked to their feet. "Stand aside, brat," Braebyn said in an icy voice, the stink of his breath in her face. "Or you won't live to regret it."

Beatrice stepped between Aideen and the men at the table, her own knife in hand. "Sit. Back. Down."

"Well then, have it your way," Braebyn said. Aideen tensed, ready to respond to the slightest muscle twitch the bastard made. But he didn't make a move. Instead, he growled. "Bloody stones."

There was a flash of light from the ring on his hand, and Aideen leapt back, her eyes sweeping wildly around the room, unsure of what was happening. Aideen's footing faltered as the ground moved under her, swelling suddenly, the floorboards shattering and sending splinters exploding throughout the room. The scene before her descended into chaos. Men and tables scattered as what looked like a stone pillar shot up from the ground in a near instant. Then the pillar moved, part of it flying towards her. She brought up the dirk and tried to spin away, but she had no idea what she was defending herself against. Something slammed into her chest. Only much harder than flesh and bone could strike.

Aideen was sent flying, the blow tossing her clear across the room, tumbling through men and furniture until she lay crumbled against the wall. Her vision smeared and spun, her chest afire with pain. In a dim part of her mind, she knew she needed to push all that down. To see past it. But the knowing didn't help her in the doing. She sucked air into her lungs in an agonizing gasp. She'd never been struck like that in her life.

Motion swam before her eyes, anger swelling inside of her. She made out the form of Beatrice dancing around the wild haymaker blows of a dark man. Aideen blinked. It wasn't a man. And yet it was. A man-like figure, some seven feet tall and made entirely of stone, was swinging its massive fists at Beatrice as though they were sledgehammers. Drunken men threw themselves clear and attempted to scatter. Aideen caught the smirk on Braebyn's face among them as he ducked out the door.

"Bloody stones, indeed." Aideen spat blood onto the dirt floor, heaving herself to her feet. "Fucking magic."

## 30

## THE CHASE

Aideen still had the blade in her hand. The thing, whatever it was, seemed to have its back to her. It wasn't smooth stone. It almost resembled a pile of rocks, like a cobblestone street. Well, a moving pile of rocks, clearly intent on smashing Beatrice into a muddy pulp. Aideen expected something from the beast inside of her, but found it slumbered. There was nothing for it. She rushed at the stone monster, aiming her blade for a place where two stones met, hoping that was similar enough to the gap between plates of armor. She gripped the blade in both hands, bracing it against her shoulder as she ran, putting all her speed and weight into the blow.

The dirk struck home and turned in her hand, and Aideen felt the wind gush out of her as though she'd just run straight into a wall. She wheeled around, anticipating a strike from the most likely side of the creature, and danced away. But the blow never came. The creature didn't even seem to have noticed her attack.

Beatrice ducked another fist, which slammed into the bar and sent wood splinters flying as though struck by a battering ram. "You don't have time for this," Beatrice said as she paced backward. "Go!"

Aideen stood caught between the truth in her words and the instinct to help her friend. "It'll kill you!"

"Probably not!" Beatrice yelled, melting into shadowy vapor as the next blow came, passing right through the smoke. She blinked back into existence and leapt back. "Go!"

Aideen obeyed. She dashed out the front door and onto the dusty street, where several wild-eyed onlookers were gawking at the building that seemed to be tearing itself apart from the inside. She saw Braebyn as he looked over his shoulder, spotting her. He started to run. Aideen ran after.

Aideen quickly saw that she was faster, but her quarry had a long head start. She charged after him, her boots pounding the packed dirt of the street. She rounded a corner behind him onto the main road. He was heading toward the sea, not the city. That was fine. She was close enough that he couldn't lose her now. It was over. Braebyn just didn't know it yet. He turned down a side street, and Aideen followed. She was closer now. Closer with every step.

The beast purred.

A pair of Skycoaches sat parked on the road. Aideen had a fleeting thought in the back of her mind—what are Skycoaches doing down here at this time of night? But she had barely entertained this when she saw Braebyn vault up onto the driver's perch of one of them. A man, clad in a driver's tunic, fell into the dirt with a yelp. Aideen's feet pumped faster, panic rising up inside of her. The skycoach flickered to life, a blue glow visible from a dozen points around its edges, and it rose up into the air.

Aideen ran beneath it and leapt, planted her foot on the wall of the building it had been parked beside, then bounding off again even higher. Her hand reached for the wheel as it rose, but she came up just short. She landed in the dirt with a grunt, swearing under her breath. Her head jerked to the other

Skycoach. The driver was still sitting on his perch, staring at her wide-eyed.

"You there! I need a ride!"

"P-please," the man stammered, obviously seeing the blade in her hand.

Aideen jumped up to the driver's perch, eliciting a squeal from the man. She settled into the seat beside him, which was clearly meant for one. "Oh, I'm not going to hurt you." She pointed toward Braebyn with her dirk. "That's a killer getting away right there. But I don't have the faintest idea how to drive these things, and I can't let him get away. So go!"

"B-but I can't just... my masters will-"

Aideen grabbed his face, squishing his cheeks together. "Like hell you can't. Tell your masters I had a knife, because I do. Now follow that skycoach!"

The skycoach swayed into the air like a drunkard. Aideen held on to the seat under her. There was no rope to keep her on the perch. That was fastened across the lap of the driver beside her. Her legs were dangling from the edge of the seat built for one, and in moments they were high enough that a fall would mean her end. Wind whipped at her face as they gained speed. It had never occurred to her what a different experience this was for the driver. Inside the carriage, you were nicely shielded from the elements, sturdy wood all around you and even your view covered in thick panes of glass. For the first time, she had a true sense of the speed of these things. It was like galloping on horseback, only faster. And with very little between you and the world below.

They streaked west through the night sky in a broad sweep around the perimeter of the city. Over the harbor district, and towards Morelle. Braebyn's coach remained steadily ahead of them, the equivalent of a city block between them. "He's wasting time," Aideen said. "Coming up with a plan. We shan't give him the luxury. If this is his game, don't follow him directly.

Take us closer to the city into a tighter circle, and we will circle it faster. Only a little, though. It isn't as though he can fly away. Skycoaches don't work too far away from the Spire."

The driver nodded, edging them into a slightly tighter circle. It was working, Aideen saw after a minute. They were gaining.

"Can I ask what's going on?" The driver dared a glance at Aideen. He seemed to have regained his composure somewhat. He wasn't any older than she was, maybe only eighteen. "I don't want to get into any sort of trouble for this."

"As for what's happening, that man is a killer. Of a sort. And he has information I desperately need. He just tried to kill me and a friend of mine with some kind of magic stone creature. Monster. Thing. Gods, I don't even know. But I need to catch him and find out what he knows."

"Oh."

Aideen saw his hands were shaking. She put a hand on his leg, and he flinched under her touch. "Hey. What's your name?"

"Perry."

"You're doing fine, Perry. You've no need to fear me, alright?"

"Alright."

"I mean it. I'm sorry about this. You don't know me, and I hate that I had to drag you into this. I promise I won't put you in harm's way. Surely your masters won't be too cross with you if you tell them the truth. I had a knife, and I yelled at you."

Perry nodded. "This sort of thing happens sometimes."

"Good. Well, not good, but you know what I mean. Just don't lose him. I'll figure something out."

Braebyn must have realized he couldn't escape like this, looping around the city all night. Or maybe he realized they were gaining on him. Or maybe he had come up with a new plan. Whatever had triggered it, his skycoach turned abruptly toward the city. "There he goes!" Perry cried. "What do I do?"

"Keep trying to get as close as you can."

Braebyn dove his skycoach down just as they passed over the city walls, and Perry followed, two blue dots stitching delirious threads of light across the night sky. In a matter of moments, they were flying right above street level, buildings jutting up on either side of them, the late-night stragglers of Sona crying out in alarm just beneath them as the carriages hurtled violently through the city streets. Braebyn began weaving through the air in front of them, a series of feigns in an attempt to get them turning in the wrong direction before turning down side streets. Any advantage, Aideen supposed. But it hadn't worked. Perry followed each time, and seemed to be reading the lurching movements of the front coach with ease. Aideen didn't understand how Perry controlled the thing. His hands were a blur of subtle twists against rune-carved stones mounted on a wooden shaft in front of him. But the skycoach maneuvered deftly as a bird through the canyon of city buildings.

Braebyn turned sharply left, the momentum scraping the walls of his skycoach against the masonry of a tailor shop. Perry followed, only with less scraping. The street was narrow, and Aideen realized she was close enough to reach out and touch the walls of the buildings as they passed by. A single wrong move of those tiny knobs, and they would be smeared against the stonework. Aideen clenched the seat tighter, trying not to think about it. The carriages jerked up and over strung clotheslines between the buildings, and then turned back onto a main street up from the lower markets. Each hectic turn had brought the carriages closer together as they chased. Braebyn obviously knew how to operate a Skycoach, but Perry knew it better.

Braebyn jerked hard left down another narrow alley. Aideen gasped when she saw that this alley was a dead end, and the buildings that surrounded them rose well above their carriages. The front carriage veered upward without slowing. Perry yanked their carriage higher, giving Aideen a strange feeling in the pit of her stomach as though her innards rose up more slowly than the carriage. She felt dizzy, and when she had her bearings once more, she saw Braebyn skimming over the rooftops below them. Their own carriage was considerably higher up. "They go faster on the way down," Perry said through clenched teeth. "We'll follow from above, and then we can catch him!" Aideen grinned. He might be scared, but a part of him seemed to be enjoying this. She understood the feeling. It was all too exhilarating to have any time for fear.

The carriage pitched to one side in the maneuver that followed, and Aideen gripped the small bit of seat beneath her as tight as she could. Braebyn was heading due east, now. They were close, close enough to see Braebyn turn to look over his shoulder at them. And they were still flying much higher above the city.

"What happens when we get close?"

Aideen hadn't considered that yet. "I suppose I'll jump onto his carriage."

"What? You're crazy!"

"Have you got a better idea?"

"This is your insane adventure, not mine!"

"Fair enough. Just get me close, and get me above him." As they passed over the rise of the Inner City, Perry took the carriage into a descent, and Aideen had to yell to be heard over the wind whipping at them now. "Pass over him on the left, so I have a clear shot."

"You're insane!"

"We've established that!"

They rushed down towards the other carriage, and Aideen pulled her legs under her. She braced them against the carriage wall, her muscles tensioning like a bowstring. She felt calm. Stupidly calm. Stupidly, idiotically calm. Part of her was terrified deep down, but the terror came in ripples now. The other part told her she obviously wouldn't jump unless she was sure she'd make it. But all it took was a slip, or Braebyn deciding to steer his carriage at the wrong moment, and she'd land somewhere in the Inner City for the street sweepers to contend with in the morning.

There was no making sense of the conflict inside her. There was only doing now, only seeing the hunt through to the end. They dove closer and closer, and Braebyn jerked his carriage left under them. Aideen sensed its hesitation, anticipating a lurch back in the opposite direction. And she leapt. Perry must have flinched, because her own carriage moved slightly left as she did.

Braebyn's carriage wasn't where it was supposed to be. Aideen flailed her arms as she fell past the roof of his skycoach. The left rear wheel of the carriage connected with her stomach, knocking the wind from her with a nauseating pain that flooded her senses, and she started to tumble over the wheel. She managed to hook her arm into the wheel spokes, and she was tossed again as the wheel rotated backwards. She found herself disoriented, dangling from the bottom of the wheel, only her bent elbow holding her there. Aideen fought air back into her lungs, at the same time fighting down a sudden need to vomit. Instinctively, she started to climb up to safety, and then swore. You can't climb a wheel like that. It'll just spin again.

Aideen saw that Perry's coach was still behind her, below her now. Good. That meant that Braebyn probably thought he was still being chased. Aideen readjusted her grip, checking to be sure the dirk was still on her hip. It was. Her cloak kept catching the wind, whipping back and pulling at her body awkwardly. She swung her legs, getting the wheel moving back and then forward like a child on a park swing. It took some time. The wheel was big, and her slight weight did not work in her favor. Once she had it swinging back and forth, she managed to hook her foot on the folding step beneath the carriage door. It flipped down, and she hooked her other foot on it. Her arms burned from hanging on to the wheel, and she would still need them. So, she let go.

Aideen hung by her feet, both wedged into the gap between

the step and the lower carriage. She closed her eyes to avoid looking down, shaking her arms to get the blood moving back into them. Then she started climbing, first by getting her hands on her knees and then wrenching herself up to the step, her stomach muscles burning from exertion. She pulled herself up onto the step until she was able to stand on it, feet on the blessedly stable surface and holding on to the rail on the roof usually meant for securing luggage. Braebyn looked over his shoulder, and his eyes went wide when he saw her standing there. Aideen flashed him a wolfish smile. "Are you going to land this thing, Braebyn? Or do I have to come up there and make you?"

"You're insane!"

"People keep saying that, as if it has ever dissuaded anyone from anything at all. Land the damn skycoach!"

The skycoach lurched into a dive of its own. Aideen hung on tightly. Out of the corner of her eye, she caught sight of the great chain of brass cylinders, the Skyway, settling down at the southern ramps below them. "I'll ram us into the ground!" Braebyn yelled.

"No, you won't. You'll be just as dead if you do."

"Not if I have a magic bauble that will protect me."

It was a bluff, she knew. He was desperate now. "You must be a terrible poker player. What would you have me do? Get inside the carriage and promise to stay there? Is that your big escape plan? Yield!"

Aideen saw the Skyway lift into the air, its brassy curves glistening in the moonlight. She also saw Braebyn shifting in his seat as the skycoach began to drift into an intersecting course with the Skyway. She had an inkling of what he was actually planning. He was going to leap off as well, onto the Skyway. If he timed it right it would leave her hurtling off to nowhere, to eventually crash when the skycoach got too far from the Spire. Risky. Desperate. But not entirely stupid.

Aideen weighed her options. She could make her way to the

roof. It would give her better chances. But it might also spook him into changing his mind. Or worse, into missing and killing them both. So she stayed put, watching as the ground came up fast, letting her guess play out. The Skyway began to fly forward. The carriage turned, pulling up and onto the left side of the Skyway.

Braebyn jumped, disappearing from sight. Aideen wrenched herself onto the roof of the carriage. She only had a moment to gauge the distance, and only one step of momentum to achieve it. She leapt from the roof of the carriage for the roof of a Skyway car.

## 31

## REVELATIONS

The relative speed between carriage and Skyway wasn't that far off, but Aideen didn't trust trying to land on her feet. She flung her arms wide and belly flopped onto the curved roof, giving herself as much possible friction to keep from sliding off. She landed with a painful grunt. Looking up, she saw Braebyn was at the front of the same car, clinging to the roof in much the same way she was, craning his neck to see the driverless skycoach flying up and off into the night.

Aideen had to reach him before the Skyway stopped at the next ramp, or this idiotic chase would only continue. She clamored on her hands and knees towards him, taking care not to let the wind rip her off but making haste all the same. The Skyway began to slow as she got closer, and Braebyn tried to sit up. She drew the dirk from its sheath and pounced on him, slamming his back against the Skyway roof. She put the blade against his neck. "That's enough, Braebyn. Now we do business."

Braebyn's whole body tensed beneath her, his voice coming out in shrill little squeal. "How...?"

"Give me the name. Now. Or I spill your insides and soil this pretty new Skyway with them."

The beast inside her bared its fangs in agreement.

"Gods, I yield!" Braebyn shook his head in disbelief. "You're a mad woman."

"Out with it, or I shall be." The Skyway began to descend, gently. Aideen realized this was the first time she'd ridden on it. She smirked at the thought. The smirk coupled with her words seemed to trigger fear in the man beneath her, pinned by a smiling woman with a knife threatening to cut him open. She hadn't intended that, but she would not contradict it now.

"A wealthy woman! I did not ask her name."

"Keep talking."

"She... she had pale skin. A manner of wealth."

Aideen pressed the knife against his jaw, drawing a line of blood. She glowered at him now. "Specifics."

"She wore a necklace! A ruby, a big one. Encircled in diamonds. Not cheap, not cheap."

"That could describe a dozen women, if not a hundred in Sona."

"Of course, of course." His mouth worked open and closed, like a fish laying exposed on the shore. "Ah! But I'll wager there aren't a dozen that wear shoes from Roseglade."

Aideen squinted at him. "Roseglade?"

"In Lyramae." Braebyn's eyes blinked furiously as he tried to crane his neck away from the edge of her dirk. "The open toes with painted nails are fashionable there, where the summers are so much hotter. None wear such shoes in Sona among the upper classes. Hers were blue—the shoes, I mean. Fixed with beige ribbons up the ankle. Her toenails painted to match."

Aideen blinked, trying the pieces and feeling ill as they slowly clicked into place.

A wealthy woman from Roseglade. One who displays wealth and walks in the higher circles, but still does it in the same open-toed shoes she's always worn because Sonarian shoes make her feet feel cramped. A ruby necklace encircled in diamonds. A gift from her new husband. Where does coincidence fit in among conspiracy, she wondered? Was coincidence more or less pertinent when you were already grasping for connections?

Pertinent enough to be tested, she decided. And she hated the ramifications of it. She also hated this man, and was ready to be done with him. "What else?"

"I know nothing else. I swear it!"

Aideen saw a handful of faces gawking up at them from the platform below, late night travelers waiting to take the Skyway. She swore and sheathed the blade. The beast inside her sulked. No, she thought. I'll not take his pathetic life as much as he deserves it. I might need him again if I'm wrong. She stood and untied the pouch of coins she'd brought with her in hopes that the man could have been bribed. She threw it on the brass roof between his legs, making him flinch. "There. Now our business is concluded."

The doors to the Skyway opened, and a few people spilled out of them. Aideen slid down from the top of the Skyway train, joining them and ignoring the curious faces that stared at her. She needed to find Beatrice to be sure she was alright.

A skycoach glided down and settled in the empty market square nearby. Aideen recognized Perry sitting on the driver's perch. She hurried over to him. "Did you catch him?"

"He told me what I needed to know."

"Did you, uh, kill him?"

"No. I paid him."

"Huh." Perry seemed to consider this for a moment. "Well, in that case, do you need a ride?"

Aideen snorted weary laughter, feeling her hands beginning to tremble again as the rush wore off. "That would be wonderful. But if you don't mind, I think I'll ride in the back this time."

"Probably safer," Perry said, hopping off his perch and opening the door with a bow. "Wouldn't want you falling off."

It was quiet inside the skycoach. It was anything but inside Aideen's mind. She knew who poisoned her father now, and the knowledge brought with it new questions. The most important was why. And right behind it, just as pressing, was who else knew? She let all the information she had tumble freely, shaking the pieces and seeing if anything new might fit together. There were some possibilities there, too, but none of them fit neatly enough for her. She would know more soon enough. And then she would have to decide what to do with it.

The thought of justice had never really taken form in all her imaginings. She'd spent so long seeking answers. Now she had the one that mattered most. The motivations were secondary, surely. It didn't matter why her father was murdered. There was no possible justification for it. He was kind. He was honest. He was generous. He was brilliant and noble. Every man has his faults, but who could say that Davin Bormia was not a good man? And since nothing could possibly justify his death, what then did justice look like for the killer?

Aideen was not well-educated in such matters, she realized. She knew a little of trials and judges, but how did such a thing begin? She couldn't imagine simply running up to one of the city guards, waving her arms and crying murder and then needing to explain that it had occurred months ago. That all her proof was in her memories. She'd be the mad woman, yet again. That would take some thinking. Or asking around. Gods, and then she'd be out in streets again, trying to learn how the world truly worked.

If she could fault her father in anything, it would be in this now. He'd failed to teach her the things he surely hoped she would never need to know. How to deal with dishonorable men. How to expose a crime. How to catch a killer. Perhaps he himself had never needed to know. But she had always been able to look to him for answers. Or to Lodai. And now, without them both, she was ignorant and adrift. She wondered how much of the city's darkness her father had known about, and how much he had sheltered her from.

The skycoach settled down in the same alley she had first hijacked it from. She let Perry open the door for her, as much from habit as anything else. "What do you think became of the other skycoach?" she asked.

"It flew on to the east," Perry said. "I guess eventually it will simply fall from the sky when it gets far enough away from the Spire."

Aideen nodded. "At least it didn't crash in the city."

"Some hunter in the woods somewhere between Sona and Aleshah is going to stumble on it and be fairly puzzled, I suppose."

"Look, I'm sorry about stealing you away like that. And, well, for everything after as well. I hope you won't get in any trouble."

"It's okay. I might lose my job, but maybe not. At least it was exciting. In a, uh, terrifying sort of way. It's not every day you meet a crazy flying elf."

Aideen started, reaching a hand up toward her ears. Her hair was a riotous mess, she discovered. It had been up in buns at some point during the day, but now it was wind-blown and tangled and her ears were clearly visible. She remembered Kayla's comment about riding around on horseback, and the memory made her smile. She bid Perry farewell and walked away, pulling out what pins remained in her hair and tried to shake it into some semblance or order with her fingertips. This new life was not well suited to keeping her ears hidden.

∽

AIDEEN FOUND Beatrice sitting outside the Harpy's Nest. Or what was left of it. The slanted roof was caved in, and one wall was mostly missing, nothing but wooden splinters scattered in the street. Beatrice sat making patterns in the dirt with a piece of wood, looking exhausted. She heard Aideen's approach and leaned back against the remaining wall with a relieved smile. "Well? Did you catch him?"

"Of course I did. Are you alright?"

"I'm fine." Beatrice was covered in dirt, which stuck to her like a thin layer of mud where it had mixed with drying sweat. "Just tired."

Aideen sat down beside her. "Me too."

"So?"

"You first. How the hell did you kill that thing?"

"I didn't. I just waited it out. Summoning spells don't last very long. Minutes, usually, unless done by a proper wizard. And he was no wizard, just a smelly snake of a man with a magic ring. So, I only had to keep it busy until it disappeared."

"Ah," Aideen said. "Well, that's anticlimactic."

"It was a damned impressive bit of survival, thank you very much."

"Was it?"

"It was, I can assure you."

"I'd be more impressed if you'd killed it."

"And I'd be less alive if I had tried. Now, are you going to sass me all night, or are you going to tell me what happened?"

Aideen told her. In the retelling of the chase, she felt a strange combination of embarrassment and pride. What she'd managed to accomplish was incredible, she realized. And very, very stupid all the same. Many times over, she could have easily died. She was well-educated in many things, but tonight was something else entirely. She wasn't even terribly practiced in climbing. Certainly not in flying or leaping from carriages. In fact, all her experience in athletics was limited to tennis, hunting, and what was useful in swordplay.

Play, she mused. What a pompous brat she'd been, thinking that all her training with Master Lodai amounted to anything more than play. Yes, she knew how to dance and twirl a sword around. She knew how to strike. But mostly she knew how to strike without killing, how to dodge while never fearing any real harm from her opponent except to her pride. She'd learned nothing of real danger in all these years of training. She had learned nothing of fear, and how it can cripple you. She learned nothing of having a man stare you down, intent on killing you, and the only thing standing between you and your death is your wits and your sword.

Aideen knew real danger now, and the lesson had come hard and fast. She had only survived the Under City because she had let that other part of herself take control. She'd always looked down her nose at those nobles who played at fencing, brandishing skinny play swords and keeping their footwork in nice, tidy lanes. She had just been playing with bigger toys, she realized. The stakes were no different.

Growing up was a curious thing. You could look back on your past and think, "What a child I was. How innocent. How naive. How stupid." And one did it with such a sense of superiority over their former selves. With such pride at how wise, how mature you've become. But you never turned it around, did you? You never looked ahead to acknowledge that one day, you would inevitably look back on that very moment and cringe with embarrassment at your stupid pride. Your ignorance. Your immaturity. Aideen wondered when that ever ended. If adulthood was just a farce, and we were always fools until we were dead. Maybe wisdom was realizing how stupid you are now. Understanding how much you'll never know. It was a depressing thought.

Aideen told what she learned from Braebyn. What it might

mean, how it might all fit together. The implications. The gaps that remained. Then they sat in silence for a long while.

"The truth isn't going anywhere, you know," Beatrice said at last. "You don't have to do anything yet."

"You honestly think I can rest now?"

"I think you should. Sleep on this. Collect yourself. Make a plan."

Aideen traced her fingers in the dirt, making patterns over the ones Beatrice had made while waiting for her. "Maybe."

"You have a temper, you know."

"Do I?" Aideen laughed. "Is that what it is?"

"What else would you call it? Something came over you in the Under City. You were like a woman possessed. Not that I blame you, considering the circumstances. But even still. And you're quick to anger at times. You need to be thinking clearly before you take your next steps. You have had a long day."

Aideen scowled down at the dirt. "You're probably right."

"So," Beatrice prodded. "What will you do?"

"My fiancé can wait. He is not innocent, but I'll deal with him later," Aideen said. "I think it's time I go home."

## 32

## THE POWER WITHIN

Yakha eyed Hamfast, two dark orbs peering out from behind the bushy ledge of grey eyebrows. Hamfast sat cross-legged on the floor of Yakha's hut, with Makhal seated beside him.

*"The stone is alive,"* Yakha said. *"Such a thing can be. But this means faemaneta."*

*"What means faemaneta?"* Hamfast looked to Makhal.

*"It means many things. Power from elsewhere. The power of the gods. Things people cannot do."* Makhal shook his head. *"It is a hard word to define. It is in our stories."*

"Magic," Hamfast said. *"Faemaneta. Magic. Yes. I understand. Yes, leader say this is magic. Leader learn magic. He want this for magic."*

*"Are you one who knows magic?"*

*"No. I cook. But I find this. It speak to me. Not speak. Not know word. Feel speak. Speak not right word."* Hamfast gestured vaguely. *"Speak feel. Not speak hear. I give to leader. Leader fear me give. Leader fear this want me to keep. Give to leader. Then storm come. Break ship. Kill many."*

*"Well, this is horribly frustrating,"* Yakha said to Makhal. *"I commend your patience with him."*

*"He learns well, and you grow accustomed to his broken speech. Speak simply, and he will understand most of what you say."*

*"We have stories of magic,"* Yakha said. *"Some are certainly true. But we know not to believe all stories. Still. If what you hold is magic, then it may be dangerous. Perhaps to you. Perhaps to us all."*

*"Think this killed my people,"* Hamfast agreed.

*"But you believe it killed your people because you gave it to your leader?"*

*"Yes."*

*"Could your leader have used it, made magic, and that was what killed your people?"*

This was a possibility Hamfast had not considered. *"Perhaps."*

*"Then perhaps it is safe so long as you possess it. Or perhaps it, and therefore you, simply being here puts our village in danger."* Yakha scratched his chin and thought for a moment. *"All I know of magic is the stories. In them, the people who had magic held some gift from the gods. Sometimes a blessing. Sometimes a trinket. And in their hands, they could do wonders. Summon fire from nothing. Speak to the birds and fish. Can you do any such thing with this?"*

Hamfast looked to Makhal, who helped him understand. *"No."*

Yakha cocked a large, bushy eyebrow at him. *"Have you tried?"*

"Well, no." Hamfast shook his head.

Yakha chuckled. *"Well?"*

*"You want I try?"*

*"Yes. How can we know otherwise?"*

Hamfast gazed down at the shard. How the hell was he

supposed to just do magic? That was for wizards. Or the Syani. Nobody else in Elora had magic. *"How try?"*

*"How does one try anything? You set your body and will to the task. And you probably fail. And then you try again."*

*"Now?"*

Yakha nodded. *"Perhaps begin by closing your eyes and breathing. Empty yourself of thought. It is something we do when we pray. It will clear your mind and open you to the gods."*

Hamfast had seen them at prayer. Or meditation, he thought. It was something the men and women did separately as the sun set, facing the fading light. He had not questioned it, and had simply lingered on the outskirts until they were finished. He had seen many kinds of prayers in many different lands over the years, and known cultures that practiced forms of meditation in some parts of the world. Prayer was speaking to the gods. Meditation amounted to thinking, or not thinking, depending on who you asked. Funny how that was another custom that crossed the oceans. It didn't make much sense to him, but what the hell? Perhaps there was something to it.

Hamfast closed his eyes and tried not to think. When that didn't work, he just let his mind wander, letting his weary legs rest on the ridges of the reed floor. Images flitted through his mind. Memories and questions. He tried to push them aside, but they would not relent. So many questions, and they all centered around the smoky glass he had in his pocket. He reached for it, and held it in his hands. It felt warm, and there was a comfort to holding it. A rightness.

Again, his thoughts went back to all he didn't warn the wizards about. But how could he have known? He may have killed them all, his whole crew. And if so, he simply hadn't known any better. But it was possible he was innocent. It was possible that the wizards had been the ones to bring the storm.

He felt himself growing angry at himself for not asking the

right questions. Angry at the wizards for not telling him more, angry that they had spoken to him like a child instead of laying out the stakes more plainly. Angry that their questions came when he was barely conscious from his ordeal on the island. Angry that this was all his fault, or that it wasn't, and there was no way of knowing which was true. Angry that the universe had thrust him into the middle of this stupid ordeal and left him to figure it all out on his own. And then the anger inside began to grow. Hamfast's heart began to race, a bizarre fury rising up inside him. He felt it hot in his lungs. And then he realized that, somehow, this anger was not entirely his own.

Hamfast opened his eyes, and between his tiny fingers the smoky glass had come to life. Dark vapors swirled inside, churning and whipping as a tiny storm forming in a glass prison. Purple and blue sparks began to arc deep inside the tumult. Hamfast stared at it, wide-eyed. And still, he felt that anger rising up inside of him. He felt it build, calling to him somehow, and all the while growing stronger and stronger. He felt it swell and was powerless to stop it. It began to boil and froth behind his eyes, a hum of energy inside ready to explode out in a torrent. He felt as he had in the dreams on the ship. Hamfast opened his mouth to cry out. To warn them. And then the little reed hut he sat in was ripped away like the tearing of a cloth.

Hamfast found himself tumbling helpless inside a violent maelstrom. The roar of the gale filled his ears, the blowing rain cutting across his skin like tiny invisible daggers. Up and down were meaningless here as he spun and twisted in an endless grey. He was in a void with no sky above and no earth or sea below. There were only the dark ribbons of the storm, flashing as angry lightning split the air all around him, its crackle humming in the air and through him. The wind screamed, clawing at him, trying to tear the skin from his bones, and Hamfast screamed back.

Hamfast crumbled to the ground with a cry, as though he had fallen from a chair. Makhal stood many paces away from him, his eyes wide and staring, his robes disheveled. Yakha was still seated, but looked at him in fear.

HAMFAST HUNKERED in the corner of his hut, hugging his knees and wishing desperately that he could get proper drunk right about now. The shard lay on his cot across the room. He stared at it. A part of him wanted to pick it up. Needed to. And yet he was terrified of it.

The door swung opened, and Yakha stood looking at him. Hamfast swallowed hard. *"I'm sorry,"* he said weakly. *"I don't understand what happened before."*

*"Come,"* Yakha said. *"You must come before the village."*

*"Bad? Me in danger with village?"*

*"We may all be in danger. We will see."*

Hamfast shuffled across the room and gingerly picked up the shard. He held it out at arm's length, unsure of how to proceed. The shard was quiet again. No swirling storm inside now, just the slow meandering lights and shadows like a dimmed glowlamp. He had carried this thing in his pocket for weeks upon weeks now, and so casually. And now he was overcome with both need and fear for it. He clutched it in both hands, hating how it calmed him. There was such a conflict of feelings around such a tiny, jagged bauble. He pushed down the thought that came next—almost like a storm raging inside of him. Hamfast shook himself and went out the door.

Yakha was walking toward the center of the village where meals were taken. Hamfast reluctantly followed him, leaning on his cane, slow and with all the hesitation of a man walking to his execution. Most of the village was assembled, seated in a wide circle. Yakha stood in center of all. Hamfast stood awkwardly at the edge of the circle, unsure of what to do next.

*"We are here to bear witness,"* Yakha said. *"Our rescued*

*Lindle possesses something of magic. A magic stone. The magic he possesses is what destroyed his great boat, and his people on it. But the circumstances of this are unclear. He found the magic stone, at what I believe was a sacred place. And he believes it called him there when he was in peril. But then he gave it to his leader, and this caused a storm to set upon them all."*

Yakha let the village digest this information for a long moment. The people whispered amongst themselves. *"The decision of what to do with this revelation is not simple. We wish no harm to Hamfast. But we also wish no danger to our village. And so we shall all bear witness to what he possesses, and pass judgement together. We all know the stories, passed down from our ancestors. Magic may be a gift or a curse. Or it may be both. And so we must decide."*

Hamfast was able to make out enough of the speech. He realized he was clutching the shard in his pocket. He swallowed, feeling overwhelmed by everything he was hearing. There was muttering all around the gathering of people. It was not clear if he was on trial. But it certainly felt like it.

*"Come, Hamfast."* Yakha motioned towards the center of the circle.

Hamfast took a cautious step forward, and then another. What else was there to do? He couldn't exactly run away. He saw Makhal seated with the rest of the tribe, his strange green face a tumult of emotions. Hamfast wished Makhal was beside him.

*"Sit down and try,"* Yakha said. *"Simply try the magic again, so that we might see and judge."*

Hamfast nearly fell as he sat. He looked around at all the eyes now intent on him. His heart was drumming in his chest. The questions that had been running through his mind were all muddied. His fumbling hands held the shard in his lap. He closed his eyes and tried to calm his nerves.

Try. What did that even mean? What had he even tried before, except to clear his mind? And when he had, what had even happened? He'd felt himself transported to elsewhere, into a storm. Just like the one that had destroyed the Dragonfly. He wasn't even sure how it had appeared to the others in Yakha's hut. He had been too shocked to ask questions afterwards, too shocked to do anything but run away and hide in the hut. It had felt like it was going to kill him the last time, and now he was supposed to try it again? He would rather give it away, or cast the damned thing into the sea. Yet he knew he could not.

Perhaps he could do better this time. At least he had an inkling of what to expect. Hamfast breathed in deeply through his nose and let the air out slowly through shaky lips. It had felt like anger last time, and then a storm. But surely anger wasn't the secret here. The shard had made him feel safe before, hadn't it? That hadn't been anger.

Hamfast tried to reason through it. What was the nature of this magic in his hands? A storm, but what was a storm? It was wind. It was waves. But weren't those just made by the wind as well? Something felt right about that. And the rightness did not seem to come from his own mind. He ran his thumb across the rough surface of the shard. Wind, then. Wind is just moving air. And again, rightness. Air then. The shard was speaking to him, but not with words. It was an unnerving experience.

Air can mean so many things. It can mean a storm. It can mean the whipping of waves that tears a ship to pieces. But it can also mean the salty hush of an ocean breeze across the bow of a ship. The fluttering billow of sails overhead. It can be a gentle whisper through the trees. Maybe it didn't have to be scary, he thought. Air was life. Hamfast felt the whisper of air at the tip of his nostrils, felt it filling his lungs. He focused on that feeling of it, trying to shut out the obscene pressure of eyes on him. He felt the air going in and out of him as he breathed. The feeling of air all around him, on his skin, in his hair. And he felt a rising inside of him. That presence he'd felt before. He no longer needed to reach out for the air. Now the air was reaching for him.

His vision went wide despite his closed eyes, and Hamfast was once again ripped out of reality and thrown tumbling into a storm that engulfed some far-flung elsewhere. He screamed as the winds tore at him. He tried to right himself, to fight against the chaos and hold himself still inside of it. To shield himself somehow. But there was no way to even try. Nothing to hold on to. Nothing to hide behind. This wasn't working! He felt a scream escape his lips. He had to get out of whatever this was somehow. To get out before this thing killed him.

A thought glimmered, a voice that was not a voice, and it held the rising panic at bay. He wasn't really in this storm, was he? This was all inside of him somehow. In his mind. No, not his mind. Something deeper than that. Something lower down, beneath his mind. Something beneath thought and emotion. He didn't have a word for it in any language. This was all very real, but his physical body wasn't actually a part of it. He was somewhere far away, he was still sitting on the thick clover carpet under the great trees. There was still warm air in his nostrils, still the sounds of the seabirds nearby. In this hallucination, in this other place that was real and yet wasn't, a Lindle could not survive. The Lindle did not belong. Hamfast began to understand in a wordless way. The understanding ran deep beneath his mind and flesh. It was inside him, a truer him. And so in that other place engulfed in storm, Hamfast let himself go. He let himself fall away, and with his will, with that deeper self, he embraced the storm.

Time lost all meaning and there was only the wind. Hamfast was not in it, nor was it inside him. He and the storm were one and the same. But he was not merely a storm. He was the wind and all it moved. He blew through treetops, through the palms of the island, caressing their leaves and shushing them. He filled the sails of ships bound for Sona. He held aloft the birds above them, stroking their feathers and raising them higher in the skies. He rushed into the glistening face of a galloping horse, filling it with strength. He passed the lips of an old man, whispering in his dying breath. He reached out and touched everything over the earth and the waters. He was everywhere, invisible and thoughtless, without kindness or malice. The wind was only the wind, and its purpose was only to be.

After some time, Hamfast opened his eyes. The circle of people was still there, many of them now standing, but they were masked by the grey shadows of slowly churning clouds that hung around him like a shroud. Hamfast unthinkingly brushed at them with a hand, wishing them away. The clouds obeyed, disbursing in a swirling breeze that passed through the village and into the rocky crags out towards the sea. It should have shocked him. And yet it didn't. Hamfast knew they would obey, even if his mind couldn't comprehend it. Even if it made no sense at all. And even knowing, it was still surprising how easy it was. It was effortless in that unthinking moment.

He looked at the faces around him. Wide, black eyes stared at him from the circle of people. Shocked faces, mouths agape or covered with trembling green hands. Hamfast tried to stand, but found that he was no longer sitting on anything solid. He was hovering two feet off the ground, held aloft on an airy pillow that whipped gently around him. The surprise at this realization was greater than the last, and it sent him tumbling back to the ground. His knee buckled and he fell in an awkward heap on the clover.

The Tagata deliberated well into the night, with Hamfast sitting cradled in the roots of a great tree, listening. Many feared him now. Many others believed he was a gift from the gods sent to guide their boats. Some believed they must send him away. None believed they should kill him, so that was something.

There were questions for him. Clarifications on his story. And he struggled to answer them even with Makhal's help. He was exhausted, as though the magic had drained every ounce of energy from him, and he still had his own questions. What even was this shard? Whitaker had said there were others—what were they? And where? And why would this one have called him? But after the events of the day he didn't think he could handle the answers even if anyone here had them. Hamfast fell asleep beneath the great tree, the sound of the Tagata language washing over him like the tranquil waters of their lagoon.

## 33

## THE DRAGONFLY REBORN

Hamfast awoke on his cot in the hut. He must have been carried there last night, like a child. His exhaustion had been complete, and his sleep dreamless. He stretched, breathing in the warm air of the island. It was a long, blissful moment before he remembered. And then as it all flooded back in, he jerked upright.

*"Lazy,"* Makhal said, where he sat leaning against the wall.

"What happened before?"

*"The village has decided."*

"Right, so out with it. *What decide?*"

Makhal sighed heavily. *"There was much disagreement."*

"Yes, and?" Hamfast threw off the blanket, anxiety rising in him. "Don't dance around it, gods damn it."

*"You must leave the island."*

Hamfast nodded. He had feared the verdict, no matter what it might be. The unknown was what frightened him the most in life. A warm bed, a tidy kitchen, things in their proper place—he had come to have all the pieces of home here amongst the Tagata. And now, his future was once again a vast uncertainty. But he took the news on the chin.

*"Wise,"* Hamfast said, swallowing hard. *"I am maybe danger to village. Also, I want to go home.* Not that you all haven't been lovely. I'll never be able to speak your language eloquently enough to give you a proper thanks for all you've done for me. *"I feel two things. Want to go. Want to stay. Many friend here. You... Mikhal big friend. Friend above friend. Not know word."*

Mikhal nodded in acknowledgement. *"A friend is a friend. And you are my friend. But I understand what you are trying to say. You honor me as a true friend, and you will miss me."*

"Yes, well," Hamfast hugged his knees where he sat on his cot. "So how does this work exactly? *How I leave?"*

*"A boat is being prepared. We leave today."*

*"We?"*

*"Do you know how to sail? To navigate?"*

"Well, no. Not exactly. In theory, I suppose." Hamfast shook his head. *"No."*

Makhal smiled. *"I did not think so. And so I will take you."*

Hamfast blinked. *"To where?"*

*"To wherever you come from."* Makhal grinned, bearing his broad set of teeth. *"Did you think we would simply cast you into the ocean? We saved your life. Healed your injuries. We will see you to safety, to where your people may know what to do with what you have found."*

HAMFAST HOBBLED with his cane through the soft clover of the village to a path through the palm groves, which turned to the sands that spilled down to the water's edge. He carried nothing but his cane, the shard, and an extra tapa robe bundled under his arm. The people of the village were gathered on the beach, waiting.

The boat was like a long canoe, rigged with a stabilizing pontoon on either side. A kind of netting connected the pontoons to the canoe in the center. The boat had a single mast sticking up from the middle, set in a simple swivel, and the sail was not tapa cloth as he would have guessed. This was the first time he had seen one up close, having spent so much time stuck in the village in his leg splint. The sail was made from tightly woven leaves set in a reed frame. In the canoe were satchels and baskets, lashed down, and plenty of them such that there was little room for its passengers. It was loaded for a voyage. What would certainly be a long voyage. But at least not a lonely one, Hamfast thought.

Hamfast surveyed the people standing along the shoreline. Not all from the village were present, but many were. He hobbled up to them, one by one, and shook their hands. It was Elorian custom, not theirs, but they accepted it without awkwardness. The village had come to accept all his strangeness. *"Thank you. Thank you for everything."* Some replied kindly. Some with simple nods of the head, gazing at him uneasily. That was alright. He was scared of the magic in the shard, too.

Hamfast bowed to Yakha, who bowed in return and then clasped him by the hand. His old, gnarled fingers were still strong. *"I wish you well, and thank you for understanding our decision."*

*"Wise,"* Hamfast said. *"Maybe danger. Also. I want go home. Thank you."*

*"Makhal will see you to your land, then return to us."*

*"I understand."*

Hamfast mounted the canoe with Makhal's help. As they did, two men pushed it out into the surf. Hamfast settled down amongst the cargo. Makhal set to work with the ropes, bringing up the triangular sail and placing a hand on the wooden paddle that served as rudder. The breeze was light, and the sail filled slowly. The boat settled as it got out past the surf.

*"Give us wind,"* Makhal said. He shot a glance over at Hamfast, raising his eyebrows. *"Use the magic."*

*"What? No. Danger. Maybe big danger."*

*"Then best to try it now while we are still in the lagoon and can swim to shore."* Makhal grinned, bearing his large teeth.

Hamfast stared at him, mouth agape. Then he slumped, accepting the reasoning. *"I try."*

*"I saw you float in the air. Surely you can make enough wind for the sail."*

Hamfast closed his eyes, feeling the shard in his pocket, reaching into the roaring storm he sensed just beyond the doorway inside of himself. He felt the power there, and felt a calm sense that it would obey him if he asked. Alright, then. He held out a hand, pointing it at the sail, and summoned the power in the shard. Like turning one of those wondrous faucets in Sona, he let out only a trickle. The sail sprung to life, and he felt the boat slicing through the water, skimming over the tops of the gentle waves of the lagoon. Makhal let out a whoop. Hamfast grinned. He waved back to the beach with his other hand. The Tagata waved back as the boat crested over the waves that sloshed over the barrier reef at the edge of the lagoon, leaving behind the calm green waters for the dark, open ocean.

*"Which way is your homeland?"*

"East," Hamfast said. *"Point rising sun. No island. Big big land."* We are aiming for a continent, he thought. Surely there's no way we can miss it.

## 34

## CONFRONTATION

Aideen opened the bedroom door. She reached for the nearby glowlamp knob, turning it and letting the room fill with cool light. She had not been in this room in ages. She had barely been in it since Davin remarried. Deidra stirred in the bed, shielding her eyes and screwing up her face. "Pernah? What is it?"

"Wake up," Aideen said. "We need to talk."

Deidra sat up in the bed, her face scrunched in half-waking confusion. "Aideen? What is the matter?" As she squinted at Aideen, she seemed to take in Aideen's bedraggled appearance. It must have been quite something. She'd had one hell of a night. "By the gods, girl. What happened to you?"

"It doesn't matter," Aideen said, closing the door behind her. She turned to face Deidra. "I know you and Lord Cathal have been conspiring. I need you to tell me why."

A great many emotions paraded their way across Deidra's face as Aideen's words struck their target. So many emotions that it was hard to tell one from another. The combined effect was that Deidra sat frozen, her brow furrowed and mouth hanging open for a long moment. "I'm sorry, what?"

"You heard me."

"I know I heard you, but I can't even begin to comprehend your meaning. If this is your idea of a joke-"

"Lord Cathal already knew of my elven heritage long before I revealed it to him. You told him about my mother, then. That was not your secret to share."

Deidra blinked. She had not expected this. "True. It was not." Deidra said, pulling the blankets off her and swinging her feet to the floor, standing to face Aideen with her usual haughty poise, her face was etched in stone. "And I am sorry for that, especially since he could not have cared less in the end."

"But why? I know you wanted me to marry him, but why would you share secrets with him? Why the conspiracy?" Aideen withheld the real question—why did you murder my father? If she threw that at Deidra now, she may never learn the reasons behind it all. She had to tread cautiously, but her rage was difficult to keep bitten back, and she knew it tinged her voice with its venom.

Deidra studied Aideen for a long moment, and then seemed to relax. "I see," she said. She slipped a robe from the bedpost and wrapped it around her shoulders. "Or at least, I think I begin to see. Come, sit with me. Let us speak calmly, child. Perhaps you've uncovered a little hidden truth. But I'm afraid you have conflated it with something far more sinister."

Aideen had entertained the idea that she was wrong many times over the past hour, pacing in the starlit gardens outside. But she continuously came to the same conclusion, despite the gaps in the story. Deidra killed her father, but Cathal was somehow wrapped up in this as well. Deidra might speak truth or lies. She would have to watch her to know the difference.

Aideen followed Deidra to the other side of the room, sitting in a high-backed chair opposite her stepmother. Deidra had regained her composure, the initial shock of Aideen's abrupt confrontation having worn off to some degree. But the tension in the air had not abated in the slightest, even though Deidre seemed to be attempting to disarm the situation.

The beast quivered, trembling amidst the heat of her anger.

"What is it you know about Lord Cathal, exactly?" Deidra asked. "You suspect much, so enlighten me as to why."

"I know he paid for information about Father. About the company. All before you two were wed."

"Is that all?"

"And that later, he similarly paid for information from an expert on Elven customs." And the contents of his will. She bit her tongue.

"And so? What have you concluded in this, exactly?"

"That his interests in this family came long before his apparent intention to marry me. And that he discovered my heritage long before he claims."

Deidra nodded, seeming to relax. And then she smiled. The gods damned woman smiled. Aideen could feel the rage in her redouble, and she glowered at Deidra. "What's so funny?"

"I'm afraid you've caught us, my dear." The woman was smiling, laughing even. And the unexpectedness of her words and her manner made Aideen hesitate for the first time. "I'll admit it. Lord Cathal and I are both guilty." She leaned forward, as one does to speak to a child. "Of playing at matchmaking."

Aideen blinked. "What?"

"Let me tell you all, my dear. There is no harm in it now. Especially since you've discovered a few glimmers of it." Deidra's hands were folded neatly in her lap, her voice taking on that singsong timbre it did when she recounted a story at table. That voice had long annoyed Aideen, and now it set her teeth on edge. "But only a few glimmers, and as a result, you've turned one thing into quite another."

"Then enlighten me," Aideen said. If Deidre heard the venom in her voice, she chose to ignore it.

"Your Lord Cathal is an ambitious man, yes? And despite his

place in House Gwenhert—the second youngest born to the youngest born—he is yet graced with the best his bloodline has to offer. He is charming. Intelligent. Capable. And he aspires to be much more than the House Gwenhert Master of Ships. But his ascent within the House has long been stymied by a single, simple, base thing. Money. Oh, he has wealth, to be sure. But second youngest to the youngest, yes? And so ample wealth to live comfortably, yet not enough to attain real power in Sona. His uncle is among the House of Lords, I'm sure you know. And the man is growing old. Should Lord Cathal wish such a place one day, he would need to rise to prominence in the family rather quickly, lest it pass to another."

Deidra continued. "Lord Cathal knew your father well enough. Their circles crossed in many ways, but most especially because they both oversaw the workings of ships. And so Lord Cathal approached your father concerning an arrangement of marriage some years ago, when you were not much more than a child. Your father rebuffed him immediately, which was quite a shock. To turn down marriage into nobility?" Deidra smiled, a knowing look cast at Aideen. "Davin's reasons at the time seemed baffling, I'm sure. But I'm sure you understand the reasons plainly enough. Your heritage, of course. But Lord Cathal had no way of knowing that at the time."

Aideen said nothing. None of this was known to her, but thus far none of it was shocking. Cathal wanted to marry Aideen for her fortune, and had approached her father to secure an arrangement. If any of this was lies, they were reasonable ones. Yet it felt rehearsed to Aideen's ears already. An explanation too well formed, too much like a story. Still, it did nothing to explain the business of the poison. Aideen listened and watched, studying the woman's bright eyes and the corners of her mouth for any sign of where the falsehoods hid.

"Some years later, I married your father. I have known Cathal since he was a child, as my late husband was well acquainted with Cathal's father. So when he told me of his failed proposition to Davin, I took it to heart. I knew your secret by then, of course. And I saw how your father sheltered you from the world because of it. He proposed I help you and your father see the merit in such a match."

"And so you told him of my mother."

"I felt I must, child."

Aideen suddenly had a foul taste in her mouth. "And so I was meant to merely be a pawn in all this? All because of my father's wealth?"

"Marriages have been forged on far less, child. It is a good match by any sensible reckoning. And it is not as though your father could have ever forced you into such a thing. He only needed to hear some perspective from one he trusted."

*She is telling some truth, but omitting things. I must watch her carefully.* "And you agreed to manipulate me and my father out of your concern for my future," Aideen sneered. "I don't believe that for a moment, stepmother."

"You wound me, my dear." The dainty gesture of Deidra's hand to her breast was far from convincing.

"So what was it you gained by ensuring my marriage to Lord Cathal? You would not have pushed for the match without something in return."

Deidra pursed her lips, studying Aideen. *I've caught her in something,* Aideen thought. Deidra sighed. "I suppose there's no harm in telling. Very well. Should all go well and you agree to marry Cathal in the end, his younger brother would marry Carolyn."

Aideen nodded. Now it made more sense. She took it all in, and the more she considered it the more she hated it. It was simple, really. Deidre's children all taken care of. Riann, inheriting the company. Carolyn marrying into a noble family. Cathal marrying into enormous wealth, and his brother a smaller portion. Everyone wins.

"And my father consented to my marriage to Lord Cathal?"

"I've already told you he did. He was thinking through how to handle it all. With Cathal, with you. You can be quite prickly, my dear, and Davin did not agree to anything without careful consideration. Do not place malice in these things," Deidra said. "You hardly needed convincing of Lord Cathal's proposal, as I recall. Wealth aside, he is quite smitten with you, dear."

And yet, that was full of lies as well. Cathal pretended not to know Aideen's heritage. Perhaps that was not damning on its own. She tried to put herself in his place. Perhaps he was testing her in a way. To see if she would reveal it before the marriage. Or to give the choice of it back to her. Perhaps he sought only to understand her better, and he was innocent in pretending not to know. Perhaps...

No, Aideen thought. That was making excuses for him. That was her getting lost in the soft memories she had of that day in the gardens. That was trying not to taint them with the truth. Honesty was not so difficult. Just telling her the truth would have been the right thing to do. The only honorable thing to do. He hadn't even been honest about why he'd gone alone to that gala, without telling his fiancée. And now that she saw Cathal as a liar, more pieces began to click into place.

"Bullshit," Aideen said. "Cathal sought my wealth before even meeting me, so do not flip it around to dress it up as love."

"Oh, what do you know of love? Of duty?" Deidra huffed with exasperation—the same way she might at one of Aideen's slips in manners at the dinner table. "Your father and I never pretended to be in love. Both of us had already lost our spouses. But we both loved our children. Our marriage was for them. To give you all a family. Look around you and what a lovely household we've built together. What a life we built for you all! How much more could you and Lord Cathal have?"

Aideen eased back into the chair. She added all this new information together to everything she had already gathered. She now had two stories. The first, a conspiracy of matchmaking sprinkled with lies. Distasteful, but relatively harmless if true. The second, Deidra buying poison from Braebyn and killing her own husband.

The two stories needed to meet in the middle, if there was still truth to be found there. And if there was truth, then she needed to understand every scrap of it. Aideen poured over her memories, cool waters quenching the fires inside her. She thought back to the night Davin died. The screaming. The teacup. The first suspicions, and all the roads they'd led her down.

Wait, no. Aideen felt a twinge in the back of her mind. That was skipping a great deal of memories. That was skipping over everything in between Davin's death and her fight with Lodai. She had spent little time thinking of those early days of grief, when the pain was still so fresh, and she'd submerged herself in unfeeling waters. She sifted through them now, letting the memories pass through her like sand between her fingertips, searching for something that didn't belong, examining and reexamining everything she could find. It surprised her just how much her mind had recorded, catalogued, and then simply left to collect dust.

Those first days were cold and unfeeling, bleak and dismal like a winter rain. She had paid attention to so little, she realized now. She had barely noticed how Carolyn had sobbed for hours at a time, while Aideen herself had been numbly staring out the windows of her bed chambers. How the servants had not known what to do with themselves, or with the family they served. Aideen had few memories of Deidre during those days. Not until the reading of the will.

The will.

Aideen nearly choked on the thought. She replayed that day in the drawing room, the droning voice of Mr. Conmera. She had been so caught up in her own misery that she failed to see it.

Or hear it. And that's because it wasn't there. An absence so glaring that it should have stricken her immediately, weeks before her discovery of the teacup. And now, at long last, the shattered pieces of her life were all gathered together again, the broken whole of them clearly visible. The picture of how it all fell apart was now complete in her mind.

"You're a liar."

## 35

## THE CHOICE

"Father didn't approve of the marriage to Cathal. What went wrong?" Aideen stood from the chair, glowering down at her stepmother. The fire of her rage was rekindled again. "What went so wrong, Deidra? What went so damned wrong that you had to kill him?"

"Aideen!" Deidra's eyes went wide, sudden fear on her face. "You wound me! Why would you say such a ghastly thing?"

"I know that you put poison in a teacup the night he died. I know which tea it was. I know what poison you used."

Deidra recoiled from the words like a slap to the face. She stood, moving quickly behind the tall wingback chair so it was between herself and Aideen's mounting anger. "Stop this mad talk at once. Of all people, you accuse me?"

Aideen cut her off. "I even know who you got the poison from," Aideen continued. Her voice was even, but she was far from calm. The anger inside her had simmered down to a thick, syrupy bile in her belly. She could feel it growing heavier and hotter with every word. Her lips were dripping venom. "I know because I just return from chasing him down and forcing it from him at knife point."

"That's-"

Aideen cut her off. "Father must have found you out. He didn't approve of the marriage, and you pressed him too hard. Is that it?"

"You're frightening me. Calm yourself, child! I have no idea what you're talking about!"

"The will," Aideen snapped. "The one read to us all. It wasn't my father's. Those weren't his words. And thus, they must not have been his wishes. You had them changed."

"What are you-"

"My dearest child." Aideen sneered as the words passed her lips. "Those would never have been his last words to me. Did you honestly never listen to how we spoke? Did you never wonder what we said when we spoke in my mother's tongue?" Tears began to well up in Aideen's eyes, and her voice lost its steadiness. "I was his *piti rosandra*. His little flower. He called my mother his water lily, his *t'fle dlo*. And I was his little flower. His reminder of her. I paid it no attention in my grief, but it is plain to me now. His will tells me that I must marry for my own good. That I must not let my nature stand in the way of my happiness." Aideen shook her head. "He would not have spoken so in his final words. Words of instruction, yet nothing of love."

"It is a formal document, and the will bore his signature and seal," Deidra started to protest. "And Mr. Conmera-"

"As if you could not have those forged!" Aideen spat. "You have ready access to his seal. But it all makes sense now."

"You're speaking madness." Deidra's protests had begun to ring hollow. Her alleged confusion and shock wore thin, making a poor mask for the panic that was slowly rising in her voice. She clutched at the back of the tall chair, holding onto it like a shield.

"I knew Cathal had sought information about Father's will. I can't believe it hadn't occurred to me that it needed to be changed for his plans to work out." Aideen snorted a mocking laugh. "Do you know what's funny, stepmother? That you were Cathal's pawn from the beginning. Cathal nosed his way into my father's business long before he had his hooks in you. You were simply an opportunity, a predictable fool he could manipulate. Cathal tutored Riann, didn't he? In maths and accounts, I'd wager. In the business of ships and commerce. A bright boy without a father, I'm sure he took to the attention of a nobleman with all the expected enthusiasm."

Deidra said nothing, her shocked face and lack of protest enough of an admission. Aideen made her way around the chair, stalking towards Deidra. Deidra backed away, her eyes darting around the room.

The beast purred, sensing fear in its prey.

"And so when Riann attained his apprenticeship at the Bormia company, which came at Cathal's own recommendation, he appeared gifted for such a young man. This caught my father's attention, and a little nudging from his dear friend Lord Cathal led to him marrying you. A sympathetic widow with a gifted son already entrenched in the family business, with a daughter close enough in age to be my sister. To give me the family I never had. It was only then that Cathal made you a deal. Cathal already owned Riann, now he would own me and his brother would own Carolyn. All of the Bormia Company would belong to him the moment Davin died. Except the will was a problem, wasn't it? Games of marriage weren't enough. So, you had to kill your husband."

"I would never!" Deidra spat. "You're in-"

"Enough with the lies!" Aideen grabbed her stepmother by the dressing gown. She shoved Deidra against the wall, eliciting a cry of surprise from the woman. "You will tell me the gods damned truth! You have no idea what I've been through to discover your betrayal. My father's life, and for what?" Aideen shoved her against the wall again, harder, pinning her there.

Aideen felt her face growing hotter, tighter, as the fire inside her raged and pulled her lips into a grotesque snarl. "You killed him so you could keep your end of the bargain! Is that it? Father found you out, and so you killed him so Carolyn would marry into a noble house. A life for a title. Do I have it right?" Aideen drew the dirk, holding the blade up so her stepmother could see it. "You will tell me the truth!"

Deidra looked from the knife to the twisted face that was snarling at her. There was no more false confusion on her stepmothers face now. There was fear. And anger. And beneath it all, something else entirely emerged from behind the composed mask she always wore. There was hatred in her eyes. "You wouldn't understand," Deidra said, her voice low and cold. "One day, perhaps you will. There is nothing a mother will not do for her children."

Aideen blinked. "So you confess?"

"If I tell you, will you get that knife away from me, you filthy monster?"

"Perhaps I am a monster." Aideen did not lower the knife. Instead, she inched it closer, laying it on Deidra's shoulder. Not on her neck, but close enough. "Now tell me. What was in Father's will?"

Deidra gasped as the cold steel settled on her skin. Real fear crept in on her countenance, but did nothing to diminish the look of hatred already there. "Fine! Gods, fine!" Deidra licked her lips, then spoke as though the words tasted foul in her mouth. "Davin's fortune would pass to the family of his first wife, citing some Elven law nonsense. You would inherit it without needing to marry—a scandalous proposition. He intended to divide the company among his captains and investors upon his death. To create some kind of counsel to oversee it, with Riann getting little more than a ship's captain. Can you imagine? Common seamen inheriting such instead of his own family?"

"So it comes back to gold," Aideen hissed.

"No. I would not have done it for such-"

"Then tell me!" Aideen pressed the knife against the woman's throat. "Tell me why!"

Deidra flinched away from the cold steel against her. "Cathal forced my hand! If I did not see to your marriage and the will, Cathal had information that would ruin Riann. Disgrace him!"

Aideen hesitated. This much she had not suspected. "Because he is tinged."

Deidra gasped. "You know?" New fears sprung onto the woman's face.

"His secret is safe," Aideen said. As if Deidra deserved the consolation.

"I... I had years to sway your father on the will, but the marriage could not wait. Even with Cathal having captured your attention, it was hopeless with your father's distain for the match."

"So you killed him, replacing the will with a forgery." Aideen shook her head, sadness bubbling up through the anger. "You still had a choice. Nobody forced you to kill him."

Deidra drew in a breath and thrust out her chin, daring the knife to make good on its wicked threat. Some measure of her composure returned. "I will deny it all. You have no proof, and your own household already believes you to be driven mad with grief."

"A closer inspection of the will should provide me with proof."

"Only because you say it should? Honestly, girl. Do you really think anybody will take your word over mine? The word of a filthy elf? Of a half-breed?" Deidra drew the words out, lacing them with all the distain she must have surely held hidden for all this time. "Let me go, before I scream and the whole house finds you like this. You have your truth. And now, my dear, you may choke on it."

Deidra glared at Aideen, the fear gone from her eyes. "Hate me all you want. It is meaningless now. You have no choice but to move forward. Marry Cathal and take a generous inheritance. Or don't, and the wealth remains with Riann in trust until you find someone else to marry. There are no other paths before you. And either way, my family is already seen to well enough. I've done my part. I've already won."

Nobody will believe you. Aideen's mind reeled under the weight of the words. She pictured herself trying to explain it all. To the city guard. To a judge. To anybody who could do something to set it right. Nobody will believe the word of an elf. By all the gods, it was true. And the injustice of it made her stomach churn on itself. The evidence was all in her memory. Her secrets were guarded only by hair pins and the trust she put in her family. Nobody who mattered would listen to her once those were removed. There would be no justice in this world for her father. Or for Deidre.

This horrible, hateful woman who stood there sneering with such distain, such superiority. Aideen wondered how she had never truly seen it all before. Deidra believed she was better than Aideen—she knew it with such complete certainty. And all because she was of pure blood. Pure, human blood. Aideen was the filthy elf, even though this murderer had taken her own husband's life. This woman despised the elves. She had despised Lodai and all he represented. And she had likely despised Aideen from the day the truth was revealed to her. It was all there, hidden beneath that mask of general superiority. Of self-assured propriety. But it was all there all along, while Aideen had done her best to please the woman.

Aideen felt herself letting go of Deidra, but it hardly registered in her mind. She stumbled back as a tumult of emotions went roaring through her, blinding her to all but sorrow and uncertainty. The room ceased to exist around her, and she was tumbling through darkness, her heart burning with a flame that refused to grant any light.

Aideen wondered if she wouldn't have been happier to remain ignorant of it all. How was there no recourse now? With all the privilege, the wealth, the education, and even her newly discovered courage. How could there be nothing she could do but accept this awful truth spewed from wicked lips?

Aideen imagined all the possible roads that lay before her. All the choices she could make, and where they might lead. She could find her own happiness a thousand ways. She could run away from Sona. She could start over somehow, somewhere. But in every possible path she looked down, her father's murderer would still be walking free, living in lavish wealth bought in poison and treachery.

Aideen could not bear to spend her life on any of those paths. The injustice would haunt her every waking moment, and there would be no escaping it. She would spend a lifetime looking for a way to make things right somehow. And she would fail. The truth of it crept into her heart. There would be no justice for her father. Not today, nor on any other. All she had left was to admit defeat. To accept the reality of the world she lived in with all its injustice. Hot tears streamed down her face, and the deepest parts of herself strained against the helplessness she felt as though she were tied and bound to a chair.

The room came back into focus through her tears, and Deidra was backing away from her, her back pressed against the wall as she slinked towards the door. Aideen's blurry eyes watched Deidre sidle away. She would get away with it. She murdered Davin, and she was going to get away with it.

Sorrow and loss and helplessness churned into anger at the thought. The beast inside her let out a rattling hiss, and Aideen's nostrils flared. The spark of anger caught in her belly, and she felt it ignite her very blood. She felt the fires swell inside her, burning hotter and higher with every breath.

And she let them. May the gods forgive her, she let them.

"There's something you failed to consider," Aideen said, fixing her eyes on Deidra. "There's nothing a daughter wouldn't do for her father."

Deidra must have seen something in Aideen's eyes. Aideen the heartbroken. Aideen the wronged. Aideen the desperate, the defiant, blazing against all the injustice in the world. Aideen the vengeful. Aideen the huntress. Perhaps she saw the glowing, molten eyes that looked out at her from behind the green elven emeralds that narrowed at her now. Deidra began to scream. "Riann! Pernah! Come quick! Save me from this monster! Riann! Kayla! Riann!"

Aideen had no more words for this woman. Deidra deserved no more words. Aideen was across the room in half a breath. The dirk plunged into Deidra's breast, the woman's scream curdling into a thing of horror. Aideen held her by the throat, staring into those wide eyes as the woman screamed. The beast writhed in ecstasy as Deidra squirmed in her grip. Aideen withdrew the knife and drove it into the woman's neck. She finished it quickly, as one does with a deer in the woods once felled by an arrow.

The final ghastly burble left Deidra's bloody lips. The room went silent, and Aideen stood above the result of her vengeance. Her mind was still, and she could not bring herself to any further action. She stood staring down at where Deidra lay on the rug. All her searchings had led her to this point, and now it was finished. What could she do now? What should she feel? Satisfaction? Triumph? All Aideen felt was emptiness.

The sound of running feet came from outside in the hall. The door flew open. "Mother! I heard screaming! What on earth is..." Riann stood in the doorway in his night clothes. The color drained from his face as he surveyed the grisly scene. Aideen stood over Deidra's body, the rug beneath her creeping red, the knife in Aideen's hand still wet from the life she had just taken.

"She killed my father," Aideen said in a broken voice. "She confessed it."

Riann was apparently shaken out of his shocked state. He ran over to his mother's body, falling down beside her. The noises he made were horrible, some blubbering combination of sobs and screaming words. Aideen stepped back, her mind blank. Her heart emptied. Unsure of what to do. There was blood on her father's rug. It had been in his bedroom since before moving to Lindenhall.

"The will was forged. The whole engagement to Cathal a conspiracy. She poisoned him... to protect you." Aideen was trembling now. These were the ramblings of a mad woman coming from her mouth. She could hear how they sounded. How this whole scene looked. Aideen knew in that moment that her life was over as she had ever known or imagined it. This was a new path now, and one she had never considered. Now she was the murderer. She owed Riann the truth. But she also knew he would never accept it.

"How could you!" Riann screamed, cradling his mother in his arms. "You monster!"

"Please, just listen for a moment!"

"You sully your father's good name with your wickedness! Conspiracies! Madness!"

Aideen heard movement at the doorway. Kayla was standing there, her dressing gown barely on her shoulders. Aideen looked at her, feeling her throat closing as Kayla's eyes turned from Riann and Deidra to Aideen. Aideen tried to speak, but her voice had escaped her.

Riann stood, stumbling over to the fireplace. He grabbed the iron poker that leaned beside it and brandished it at Aideen. "Drop the knife! Murderer!"

"Please," Aideen said. "Don't do this. I can explain everything. I -"

"Murderer!" Riann screamed, pointing the poker at her in

accusation. Two more servants arrived at the doorway, drawn by all the commotion. "Summon the guards," Riann yelled at them. "Do it quickly!"

Nobody will believe you. Aideen felt the full truth of it now. Her own household was staring at her in shock and horror and fear. Yes, fear. They were all afraid of her. Aideen the killer. There she stood, dirty and bedraggled, holding a dripping knife while her stepmother's body lay on the bloody rug. There was nothing she could say. The truth was harder to believe than the lies. Tears streamed down Kayla's cheeks as she stared at Aideen, the child she had half raised. Aideen the murderer. Aideen, the only Bormia left in Sona, was about to be arrested by the city guard and there would be no convincing anyone of the truth.

Aideen ran. Riann moved to stop her, but it didn't matter. She pushed her way past him and his clumsy poker. Past Kayla and the other servants gathering in a shocked huddle at the bedroom door. She ran down the hall to the staircase. Down the stairs and into the foyer. A vague realization struck her as she ran for the front door, tears streaming down her face. This was the last time she would ever see home. She looked over her shoulder, desperate for one final glance before she reached the door.

Carolyn was standing at the railing above, looking down at Aideen with a sleepy and confused look. A pang struck Aideen in the chest, and she slowed her pace. She wanted to tell the girl not to look in the bedroom. She wanted to tell her that she loved her. That she was sorry. She wanted to plead with her, her above all others, to please believe her story. The front door opened, and Aideen had no time left for words.

Aideen sprinted for the door, leaping into the air and kicking at roughly chest level for whomever might be standing there. She connected with something hard in the dark, and a man toppled down onto the front steps, the soft jangle of chainmail sounding alongside a handful of angry grunts and swears.

The guard grabbed for Aideen. She twisted away from him, but was yanked as the filthy cloak was torn from her back. Aideen vaulted past him. She ran through the shadows of the gardens, past the empty tennis courts, and disappeared into an uncertain darkness.

# EPILOGUE
## AIDEEN THE HUNTED

Lord Cathal Gwenhert gazed out the window of Oleandra, his dark eyes searching the geometry of glittering blue dots below. Those distant glowlamps made a map of the streets of Sona beneath a dark and moonless sky. His betrothed was somewhere out there, lost somewhere in that maze. Was she angry? Afraid? Would she run or hide? And where? The door to his study creaked open behind him. A man's voice followed. "You summoned me, my lord? At this hour it must be pressing."

Cathal turned to face the man. Ralis was dressed in fine pants and a frilly green shirt, the collar askew in his haste to change from his night clothes. His bald head was sweaty, the few wisps of greasy black hair that clung around its perimeter looking like a man who backed into a spiderweb.

"My fiancée has murdered her stepmother," Cathal said. "She is now fled. The city guard seeks her as we speak."

"Oh, hells," Ralis moaned, rubbing his eyes.

"I don't know what she knows, but we must assume the worst. The whole thing is gone to shit."

"She can have nothing that points to you, my lord."

"Of course not!" Cathal snapped. "But that isn't the point. Deidra made a mess of this, and now we must salvage it. The inheritance is in trust, and being a wanted criminal changes none of that. Should she be caught and tried for murder, what then?"

Ralis considered this a moment. "Her estate would remain hers until death. That is the law. It will be held in trust, by her stepbrother I suppose."

"And in death?"

"Then whatever her will states. Or, lacking one, it would pass to her nearest of kin."

"Then she must not be caught," Cathal said. "Not by the authorities."

Ralis nodded with understanding. "What is it you command, my lord?"

Cathal turned back to the window. "This is a proper mess, alright. But I see two options. We can find her first, and then she can marry me. I will get her leniency from the judges."

"It would be a scandal among scandals, my lord."

"Then we are left with the other path. Her inheritance will pass to her new sister, in accordance to a will that we shall place in Lindenhall to be found upon her death. Have some bits of Elvish thrown in for good measure."

Ralis bowed. "I shall see to the will. And so..."

"Put out a contract. No one will mourn the death of a murderer, and her poor lonely sister will make a most sympathetic bride."

BEATRICE FLICKED her cards down on the table, tapping them for emphasis. "Two pairs," she said smugly.

"Oh, well take a look at that. You think you're something fancy, don't you?" Gregory grinned at her and dropped his cards across from hers. "But I think that beats two pairs."

Beatrice scrunched her nose at him. "You're such an ass."

"Come on now. I'm always bluffing. Except when I'm not. You've just gotta figure out my tell."

"You don't have a tell."

"Then does that mean I win?" Gregory asked, leaning back in his chair, winking back at her.

"Hardly." Beatrice poured herself a small amount of liquor from the bottle on the table into her glass and threw it back with a grimace. "Your shuffle."

Gregory plucked up the cards, whistling as he settled them into a pile and then shuffling them with a showman's flourish. He was a handsome young man, with dark hair pulled back to reveal an angular face which always had a sense of mischievousness about it. He was an actor, and a fairly famous one at that in the right kinds of circles. He was also one of Beatrice's oldest friends. The pair of them sat now at the table of Beatrice's apartment above a bakery in the Lower City.

Beatrice's home was a single room, furnished with little more than a small bed, a table with two chairs, and a few cupboards and trunks. But it was tidy and always smelled of bread from the toils of the baker below. She did not require much in the ways of comfort.

It was late, but Beatrice needed to wind down after the wild night she'd just endured. Some late-night conversation with an old friend was good medicine. So was the liquor, for that matter. Aideen's little mystery was all but unraveled, and Beatrice would be happy when she could put it behind her. She had too much other business to see to. But all of that could wait.

There came a knock at the door, and Beatrice jumped.

"You expecting more company?" Gregory asked, one eyebrow raised at the sound.

"No," Beatrice said, tensing as she stood from the table. She drew a dirk from where it hung in its scabbard by the door. Gregory slipped a knife from his boot and stood nearby.

Beatrice unlocked the door, and Lady Charlotte Premroe swept into the room. "Good. You're awake. And not drunk, I hope." The woman cast a glance at the bottle on the table, then at Gregory, then regarded Beatrice. "What is he doing here?"

"Drinking, talking, winning." Gregory shrugged and retook his seat at the table. "Don't worry about me."

"Shouldn't you be practicing lines for a play or some nonsense?" Lady Charlotte asked, pulling the hood of her cloak back and smoothing her grey-streaked hair.

"Oh, probably. But Bea here tells such good stories."

"Gregory is fine," Beatrice said. "What is it?"

"He is not one of us, yet you treat him as such," the Lady said.

"He's useful."

"Oh, is that what I am? Useful?" Gregory asked. "And here I thought I was just good company."

"He's a friend, and you know it," Beatrice said, exhausted by this whole exchange.

"We've all got secrets, Queeny," Gregory said. "Don't you fret about me being here while you two spin your webs. I owe you a favor, after all."

"That you do," Lady Charlotte said. She sighed. "Very well. Aideen has killed her stepmother, and in full view of her house. The city guard seeks her now."

"Oh, gods damn it, that fool of a girl!" Beatrice spat. "I told her to wait. To collect herself. To give herself some damn time to think through it all. I knew she would confront the woman eventually, but I didn't think she would simply rush in there like that. And I didn't think her capable of cold-blooded murder."

"Well, now we know that she is. Take this," Lady Charlotte held out two pinched fingers. "It is a hair she left in the hood of the cloak she wore tonight with the poison dealer. Take it to the Rat Man. Have him make you a blood bead."

"Oh gods, not him. He'll-"

"I know," Lady Charlotte held up her other hand. "I know, he's a repulsive thing. And he will complain that a hair isn't enough, and that whatever we offer isn't enough, but we haven't the time for all that. Tell him I offer a favor."

"That is a high price," Beatrice said, plucking the hair and laying it into the fold of a handkerchief.

"Find the girl. Get her out of the city. Then, send her to Lyramae on horseback. She can mingle freely amongst the elves there."

"Freely?" Beatrice snorted.

"She will not be noticed, in any case."

"Hey, you're sending the crazy elf girl off to my old stomping grounds," Gregory interjected.

"I thought you weren't listening?" Beatrice shot him a look.

"I wasn't."

"Why?" Beatrice asked, looking back to Lady Charlotte. "Why do you care so much about her?"

"I have my reasons." The Queen of Masks placed the hood of her cloak back over her head. "Why do you?"

"I don't," Beatrice protested. "She's just ignorant. And innocent, in a way. She's caught up in things leagues beyond her."

"Oh, please," Gregory said. "It's alright to admit you got emotionally involved. You always do with the sad ones."

Lady Charlotte nodded. "It is your greatest fault, darling. But this one is not so innocent now. Still, innocent or not, she needs our help.

# ABOUT THE AUTHOR

Christopher Nolen is a writer of YA Fantasy. His name is a letter away from a certain famous director, so he publishes under his childhood nickname C.J. to appease the algorithm gods.

C.J. spent nearly two decades working in technology. This included a spy agency, the military, and Apple. It was less interesting than it sounds. In 2024, he left the tech world and moved to the Netherlands to pursue creative work. In addition to writing novels, he is also cofounder of Goo Monster Studio where he directs video game story and art development.

C.J. is a long-time TTRPG fan and is a recovering Forever DM. He is a fan of all games both digital and tabletop, is a mediocre piano player, and loves to cook almost as much as Hamfast does. When not reading or writing, he can be seen biking around The Hague with his wife and son.

*Thanks for reading! Please leave a short review on Amazon or Goodreads and let me know your thoughts.*

Visit CJNolen.com for:

- Downloadable Maps
- Resources for Parents
- Discussion questions and other teacher resources
- The Nolenator Newsletter. Get updates, extras, and sneak peaks into what's next in The Talavara Prophecy

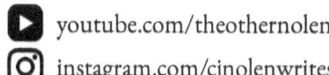

youtube.com/theothernolen
instagram.com/cjnolenwrites

www.ingramcontent.com/pod-product-compliance
Lightning Source LLC
LaVergne TN
LVHW091702070526
838199LV00050B/2255